FAR FROM HOME

"I've never seen a bedroom quite like this one."
Shane stepped toward her, his gaze multifaceted in the light. Her pulse quickened.

"And I'll wager you've never met a man like this one, either," he whispered, and stepped so near to her that the heat from their bodies mingled between them. "Have you, my girl?"

"Oh, many . . ." Nina started to scoff, but her voice caught in her throat when he reached for her. His hand was strong and warm, and her own was completely engulfed by it.

"There is one thing you haven't seen yet," he said, drawing her slowly and deliberately toward the bed.

"I . . . I've seen enough for now, I think," Nina breathed, resisting his pull.

"You'll enjoy this," he said, not giving in to her resistance. "I promise . . ."

GARDA PARKER

TEMPTATION'S FLAME

ZEBRA BOOKS
KENSINGTON PUBLISHING CORP.

TO

Elizabeth & Beth
Meredith & Carin
with appreciation

ZEBRA BOOKS

are published by

Kensington Publishing Corp.
475 Park Avenue South
New York, NY 10016

First Printing: January, 1993

Printed in the United States of America

Chapter 1

Nina Cole stepped into the Sydney Customhouse, but her head and stomach felt as if she were still on the *Sea Eagle,* rolling and churning with every swell of the ocean. Her queasiness increased as the building vibrated to the rush of arriving passengers and greeters, and a mixture of sea smells and foreign dialects assaulted her senses. A hesitant step forward into the crowd sent a shiver of apprehension skittering through her. God in heaven; she thought, I couldn't be farther from home if I were on the moon.

If only her head would stop spinning, perhaps she could get her bearings and figure out what to do next. Nina dragged her plump traveling case to the end of a long bench and sat down with several other passengers. Her arms felt almost too heavy to lift, but she managed to pull off her brown bonnet and secure it to the case, then move it behind the bench. She opened her brown wool cloak and smoothed both sides of her coiled coppery hair as she let her gaze wander around the room.

Nina had never been outside New York City in all her life. Now it seemed as if she'd gone to sleep there and, after a long bout of upset stomach, awakened here. Here, in Sydney, Australia. Her mind whirled at the thought.

She lifted her chin. It was no good looking green about the gills when she was soon to meet her new employer, Amy Winslow. Best to focus on the line of livery drivers and look for her name among the signs they waved.

Butterflies of excitement competed with the remnants of seasickness inside her. Nina moistened her dry lips, put on a smile, and read the signs. No Cole. She must have missed the one with her name on it. She read them again, this time more carefully. Her smile faded as each sign was dropped when a passenger identified himself to the drivers. Excitement gave way to returning apprehension. If Mrs. Winslow had sent someone to meet her, she couldn't tell how she was to recognize him.

Nina twisted her fingers through the strings of her reticule. Don't panic, think clearly, she instructed herself. Halfway across the room she spied a bored-looking man in uniform behind a counter, and she gathered the courage to try to step into the line in front of him. By the time she reached him, perhaps she'd feel calm enough to ask for assistance.

Very tentatively she stood up. Her head reeled with a new wave of dizziness, and she felt her body crumple in the middle and sway backward.

A pair of strong arms from somewhere behind caught her and set her down gently on the bench. "Here now, my girl," a rich baritone voice said in her ear, "are you all right?"

Nina lifted her heavy lids to a pair of sky-blue eyes set into a suntanned face. She blinked as his gaze seared to her already fluttering heart, and she could barely find voice enough to answer him.

"Yes, I . . . I think so. I felt faint for a moment. The ship, I guess."

He gave her a smile, and its brilliant warmth did something to her knees. What was this strange new weakness that now threatened to engulf her?

"Aye, t'was a difficult crossing for many. Got the collywobbles, have you?"

"What?"

"Going to chunder your breakfast?"

Nina closed her eyes and held her head. "Don't mention food."

"Sorry. Will you be all right now, my girl?"

She swallowed a shaky breath and sat up straight. "Yes, of course. Thank you for your trouble."

"No trouble atall."

He bent down, and the scent of fresh air and sun drifted from him and washed over her. How could he smell so wonderful after that devastating sea voyage? Nina felt perfectly wretched—and oh, dear God, looking at him made her painfully aware she must look just as rumpled and unkempt as she felt.

Nina could not draw the strength to avert her eyes as a lady ought to. She appraised him fully, and enjoyed the unaccustomed feeling of boldness in the act. His lean body moved sensually, reminding her of a cat reveling in a patch of sun on the parlor floor. A fleece-lined buttery tan leather vest floated over his open-necked blue shirt, exposing a vee of tanned skin

7

and a light thatch of sandy curls on his chest. Pushed to the back of his head was a dark brown leather hat, its flat crown encircled by an uneven row of what Nina considered could be large pointed teeth. Wondering from what animal teeth that size might be extracted, and how they ended up in a hatband, unsettled her further.

Nina's eyes followed the seam of his softly faded denim pants from where they strained over his muscular thighs down to worn shin-high brown leather boots, then traveled back up his full length. She blushed at her own audacity in looking at him in such a manner, and her eyes flew to his face to see if he had noticed. Thank fortune, he seemed occupied with a collection of paraphernalia behind the bench.

An unruly shock of cornsilk-colored hair fluttered over his forehead. He was so near it brushed along Nina's cheek, and she felt the whisper of its trail long after he'd lifted his head. Her gaze was riveted to his face now, and the throng of people around them ebbed into the background. He looked up then and winked at her, making her already feverish skin catch fire. He'd caught her blatantly staring at him, Nina realized, and no doubt she'd had an awestruck look on her face.

"Sorry." His rich voice and clear gaze penetrated Nina's entranced mind and sent a shiver over the back of her neck. His eyes glittered with diamond facets.

"It's not your fault." Her voice was soft. She'd never been near a man so decidedly appealing as this one, and it was perfectly fine with her if his hair brushed her cheek.

"Aye, but I fear it is. Seems I've crushed your bonnet with my saddle."

She caught herself and squared her shoulders as he spoke again. "Your what?"

"My saddle." He picked up her flattened hat and handed it to her. "Your bonnet."

"Oh no," she breathed, horror transforming her features.

"What's this? It's not all that bad, is it now?"

"I'm afraid it is. I'm going to meet my new employer, and I wanted to look neat and proper. How can I possibly now with . . . *this?*" She raised her eyes and saw a playful smile tip the corner of his mouth.

He cocked his head. "American, are you?"

She nodded, willing back insistent tears. Being in the presence of this man had somehow caused unusual helplessness to overtake her, and she deplored the feeling.

"Didn't see you on the crossing," he pressed.

Nina dropped her head and studiously tried to smooth her bonnet. "I didn't do much socializing."

He nodded understanding and gently took the bonnet from her. With long, tanned fingers he quickly reshaped it.

"Here now, my girl, don't fret. Your bonnet's good as new." He handed the bent thing to her.

Nina barely recognized it as a hat. She stared at it as if it were an unconscious squirrel. She felt awful, she looked awful, and now she'd have to wear an awful hat that resembled a stunned rodent. Hardly a fitting first impression for a new employer. Unable to understand why and powerless to control it, she

9

started to laugh, low, from somewhere deep, below the fiery flutters in the pit of her stomach, a laugh that toppled off the edge of her nervousness.

"That's the ticket. It's not so bad," his warm voice soothed. "I'll square off with you and pay for the damages. You can pop off and buy a new one."

Her laugh bubbled a trifle more.

He reached into his back pocket and extracted a flat purse, flipping it open in one smooth movement. Incredulity swept over his face as he felt inside it. He tipped the open purse upside down, shaking it roughly. Nothing fell out.

"Well, now, would you look at this? Seems somebody's pinched me funds." He chuckled in amusement. "Looks like you'll have to wait on that new bonnet, my girl."

Nina's laughter erupted then, almost hysterically, and soon they were laughing together. Abruptly she stopped, eyeing him skeptically. He didn't seem very upset about having been robbed. He might have been the most handsome man she'd ever laid eyes on, but she couldn't bring herself to believe a word he was saying now. No doubt he was just a stowaway. Not a penny to his name. And what was she doing, talking to him, laughing with him, for heaven's sake, as if he were her neighbor or something? She could almost hear Aunt Sadie clucking over such shameless behavior.

She watched him sling the huge black saddle over his shoulder, noting its elaborate silver ornamentation. It looked very expensive. Why would anyone traveling by ship be carrying a saddle? Probably pinched it himself, she mused, unless, of course, a horse had traveled with him. Somehow Nina knew if she caught a glimpse of one loping through Customs, she wouldn't be surprised.

Moistness formed at her temples. The room was stuffy and warm, but the nearness of this charming man—though he was likely a thief—kept her pulse racing. She reached into her reticule for a handkerchief. In her nervousness she could not put her hand immediately on the lace square. Perhaps she'd put it somewhere else . . . Her breath caught in her throat. With mounting fear she searched frantically through the contents of the bag. Then her hands fell limp over it, and she closed her eyes.

"My money purse," she choked. "It's gone!"

The blond head bent forward and peered into her bag as if to verify her findings, or lack of them.

"Well, now, it seems we've both been pinched." He chuckled again. "Come, my girl, we'll report the thievery to Customs. I'll help you. It's the least I can do. I mean, your bonnet and all."

Nina's eyes began to fill with tears, but she checked the urge to weep. Reluctantly at first, then in complete surrender to her situation, she allowed him to carry her traveling case and lead her to the Customs office. Perhaps she should be less eager to let a stranger take over her affairs, she cautioned herself. After all, a charming, handsome man could be just as criminal as a crude, sinister-looking one. Yet, strangely, she didn't feel threatened by him. What else could she do? She had no choice in the matter, she reasoned. Ignoring her own counsel, she followed him, marveling at the ease with which he seemed to glide through the crowded room in spite of

11

his unwieldy burden.

The Customs agent looked at Nina's name on the theft report, scratched his dark head, and turned to several boxes mounted on the wall behind his desk. "Nina Cole . . . Nina Cole. I believe I saw a letter for you." He reached for a stack of packets and flipped through them. "Aye, here it is." He handed an envelope to her.

Nina briefly wondered who could have written to her, then realized it could be instructions from Mrs. Winslow. The thought pleased her. Without looking at it, she hastily placed the letter in her reticule and followed the tall man and his saddle out of the office, back into the crowded room. He escorted her to a bench, set down her bag, then turned to her. He stood still, holding her gaze. For a moment Nina thought he meant to stay with her, and the idea quickened her pulse. But the thought soon vanished when he touched the brim of his hat with two fingers in farewell.

"G'day, my girl. You'll be met soon, I'm sure. I hope you get your money back, though I don't hold out a Buckley's chance for either of us. Have a pleasant go in Sydney, and no worries, now." He turned and walked away, soon swallowed by the crowd

Nina watched him inch his way out of her sight. As the last glimpse of his hat disappeared, her spirits sank lower. Perhaps they'd never meet again. The thought saddened her, and she felt more alone than ever. She didn't even know his name, but somehow she'd felt a sense of attachment to him.

But then her spirits lifted. At last she was about to

begin the adventure she'd dreamed about for as long as she could remember. This mounting feeling of freedom was quelled only momentarily by the thought of how she'd left New York and Aunt Sadie. Don't think about that now, she commanded herself. Don't think about seasickness, or a crushed bonnet, and don't even think about being robbed. She sensed it would all fade in the light of her new life, and she smiled to herself. Not think about the handsome stranger? No matter how exciting her adventure, she knew that would be next to impossible.

Nina took in a deep breath that strengthened her self-possession. Her stomach growled, reminding her she hadn't eaten anything in recent memory. She could almost taste and smell a delicious meal, and savored the sensation. Regardless of the kind of house Amy Winslow lived in, Nina felt confident the dining room would not pitch and roll as the one on the *Sea Eagle*, and she'd be able to keep food in her stomach.

Remembering she hadn't yet read her letter, Nina retrieved it from her bag, excitedly tore it open, and read the message. No, this couldn't be possible! Her stomach churned anew.

. . . and sorry to say that Mrs. Winslow expired soon after you sailed. No means to contact you. Under the circumstances, your services will not be needed. You understand. Most sorry. Most sincerely . . .

Numbed, Nina sat clutching the letter, vaguely aware of people rushing past her. She heard their laughter, saw them embrace each other. And then the full realization struck her—she was half a world away from home, with no work and no friends. Completely alone. She pulled her cloak snugly close, and shrugged the deep collar high around her face, needing to surround herself with something familiar. She felt desolate, cast amid a sea of nameless people. If she faded into the steamy mist around her, who would notice? And worse, who would care?

Shane Merritt checked the clock on the bureau in his second-floor room in the MacQuarie Place Hotel. Tomorrow at this time he'd be on his way to Flame Tree. Flame Tree. He could breathe there, and move, and feel free again. He stretched his long frame on the lumpy iron bed and plumped the flat pillow under his head. The threadbare quilt thrown over him slid away from his naked torso as a tangled mass of white-blond hair emerged from under it.

"What's the matter, honey?" came a husky voice. "Ain't I doin' it right?"

Shane shifted his weight under the full bosom and looked down at pouty red lips. "Ah, Denise, you always do it right." She grinned and disappeared under the quilt again. Denise was ardent about pleasuring him, but Christ, why couldn't he concentrate and enjoy it? God and everyman knew Denise was the best at her particular talent, and he'd reveled in it on more than one occasion. But today, today he was distracted and couldn't figure why.

This room looked seedier than usual to him. He closed his eyes to it and let Denise work her magic.

14

The American girl's aquamarine eyes and coil of copper hair drifted in front of his mind. What kind of a muddled galah was he now? He snapped his eyes open.

This place wasn't really any worse than the ones he'd been in the last few months in America. What made it seem so bad now? Perhaps it was the thought of Flame Tree. Or perhaps it was the still fresh memory of the unspoiled look of that girl that set his new vision.

Denise moaned. Relax, he instructed himself, relax and enjoy this. Denise does. Denise always did. She enjoyed giving pleasure with as much gusto as did the scores of sailors she'd been with, and she didn't play coy about it. He'd wager a whack that the little American waif wouldn't be so fair dinkum.

It had been a long and uneventful crossing, without so much as a light romp with any of the lovelies who'd flirted outrageously with him. What was wrong with him? Was he getting old or something? Nay! But of late he had been sensing an odd mix of stirrings somewhere inside him, the reason for them still unclear. He was tired of all the women he'd trifled with, yet tired of being alone.

Well, bloody hell, there was only one reason why he was here, why he was with Denise. So just let go and get on with it, and forget about this confounding agitation. And forget about—what was the name the Customs agent used? Nina Cole. He'd never see her again anyway. Her with those aquamarine eyes that drew him in almost against his will. And that hair. He fantasized slowly uncoiling it, letting its silken lushness slip through his fingers to fall free in a

15

copper cloud around her shoulders.

Denise's provocatively massaging hands reminded him she was still there, and brought him back to reality. Deftly Shane slid under the quilt, reversing his position. Denise moaned in pleasure. Then he slid over her, pushed into her, and let his power thrust hotly and lustily until he was spent. Denise continued to move under him, but he did not respond as he usually did. He sensed when she realized her efforts were good as a silk shirt on a pig. She gave up and fell asleep.

Denise lightly snoring against his chest, Shane lay still and stared up at the cracked ceiling. His thoughts tumbled together. Why did he feel so restless? He was worried about the Mum, no doubt about that. She'd been failing the last few years since Daniel's death, he thought, become frail, distracted. He wanted a well-bred female companion for her, especially now when he was so involved with the flocks and the wool business he'd been building. And a new person around the place might pick up the Mum's spirits.

He flung his arm up over his head. Denise grunted in protest in her sleep. He looked down at her white-blond head. He certainly couldn't take this fluff home with him. She'd hardly be a fitting companion for the Mum. He chuckled silently, picturing himself presenting Denise to the Mum in the front parlor.

Well, damn. His endeavors to find a suitable lady's companion had come a guster, although he had to admit to himself that he hadn't tried very hard to secure one. But, no worries. The Mum was still capable, no doubt, of shearing his hide as deftly as

16

she'd once sheared a lamb if he were to bring such a creature home with him, anyway. She was too independent, too proud to admit she needed anyone else around except the housekeeper. Just as well no one had answered the notice he'd placed in the newspaper before he'd left for America.

He gave Denise a friendly swat on her bare backside.

"Come now, m'love, and I'll buy you a schooner or two. No point in wasting a perfectly good day rolling about in bed, now, is there?"

With an unceremonious flick of an arm, Shane threw the quilt off them both, and leapt out of bed to a chorus of creaks from the springs and squeals from Denise. He meant to alter his mood, and do it immediately.

Denise rolled over and held out her arms invitingly, licking her lips, and regarding him below the waist. "*That* should not ever be wasted, dear boy. Come back here and let me show you how to make best use of it."

"No, you don't, you wanton thing. Come along, now. I've a thirst that needs quenching, and a spirit that needs wenching! Would you just listen to that now? I'm a bleedin' poet!"

Chapter 2

With trepidation, Nina opened the door of the MacQuarie Place Hotel and stepped inside. Gaslight flickered in the bustling lobby, lending a softer atmosphere than the building's reputation allowed, if the man at the dock had been speaking the truth. Eyes darting around warily, she closed the door quietly so as not to call attention to herself and walked toward a high-backed oak bench on the far side of the room.

Nina dropped down on the bench, opened her cloak, and took off her misshapen bonnet. Lifting her heavy hair, she drew her palm over the moistness at the back of her neck. March was the beginning of autumn in Australia, but the air still carried the heat of summer. Her usual clothing, worn to ward off the chill of a late New York winter, was clearly the wrong choice here. The sheer effort of carrying it around on her body, in addition to the heavy traveling bag, tired her quickly.

She rested her throbbing head against the bench in

weariness and disbelief. What had started out as the dream adventure of her life had turned into a nightmare. And she'd just now been at the docks, where her inquiries netted even more distressing news—the next ship to America would not sail for at least two months, and it was bound for San Francisco. She'd need money to book passage, and she'd need more money for the cost of overland travel to New York. She closed her eyes and swallowed over a tight knot in her throat. The last thing she wanted to do was go back to New York, to Aunt Sadie, to life as a seamstress in a dark, deafening shirtwaist factory.

Nina reread the letter, then stuffed it into her reticule, sighing in desperation. Never in her life had she felt so unconnected to anything or anyone as she did at this moment.

The pungent odor of long overdone coffee wafted around her from somewhere. Nina longed for a cup. Now that the nausea had subsided, she realized she was very hungry. She also needed a ladies' comfort station. Shooing pesky flies away from her face, she sat up straight and scanned the lobby. There were many doors, all paneled in the same dark wood as the walls, all unlabeled. The only sign in the room hung above the front door. Dirty and chipped, it bore gilt letters proclaiming the hotel's established year as 1835.

When she'd inquired at the docks about lodging, the ticket agent had mentioned the MacQuarie, but commented as he noted her prim appearance that it was no place for a lady. He told her it was a notorious watering hole for seamen and fishermen and less

20

than honest ship owners, making it attractive to gamblers, sporting women, and every kind of lowlife. Observing exposed lath where plaster chunks had fallen from the ceiling, the filthy threadbare Oriental carpet, and the well-worn sparse furnishings, Nina decided that the last twenty-five years hadn't been kind to the place. And the prevailing stale odor of dead fish threatened to upset her stomach once again.

Well, it was too late now. She'd dragged her traveling case for what seemed like miles, and hadn't the strength to look further for a place to rest and think. Besides, there was the matter of money. Without funds, how was she going to pay for a room and food wherever she went?

Chatter around her blended into cacophonous singsong tones and raucous laughter. The clipped words and curious, sometimes rhyming expressions seemed to carry meanings unrelated to the words themselves. How they understood each other was a mystery to her. Nina listened intently, trying to comprehend, feeling she'd lost even the ability to understand her own language.

A portly man swung through the door, stomping his heavy booted feet on the faded carpet. He tipped his cap and flashed a yellow-toothed grin at Nina as he made his way to a knot of people in front of the high registration desk. The line had grown longer since she'd come in, but the little man behind it gave no notice. He kept his back turned, studiously directing pieces of mail into numbered slots.

Nina anxiously searched the room for a woman she could ask about the comfort station. Fear gripped her stomach—she was the only woman in the lobby. Several men were eyeing her, and she moved uncomfortably under the heat of their suggestive glances. I should get out of here, she thought in a wave of panic.

Her eyes fell to a wrinkled newspaper on the bench. Quickly she opened it and put it up as a shield against the rude stares. And then she spotted it, a boxed notice in the lower corner of the page.

Wanted, lady's companion. Applicant must be well mannered, educated, able to concentrate fully on duties. Vigorous health a necessity, experience not. Apply Shane Merritt, care of MacQuarie Place Hotel, before March ten.

An idea took fuzzy shape in Nina's weary mind. Perhaps she could find other employment in Sydney, and earn enough money for passage on that ship back to America. Excitement began to eclipse her apprehension. Or . . . maybe something else just might work out, and she wouldn't have to go back.

Nina read the notice again. Why not inquire about the position? She was right for it. After all, hadn't she come to Australia to be a lady's companion? And if Amy Winslow hadn't died, that's exactly what she'd be doing right now.

What day was it? Her eyes flew to the calendar behind the desk. March nine. Perhaps the position was still open. It was worth a try to find out.

Determined now, Nina stood up too quickly and another wave of dizziness seized her. She clutched the arm of the bench for a moment to steady herself, then moved to the end of the ragged line of men. Again she was conscious of many pairs of eyes roaming over her. Insecurity flared inside her. Vowing not to show it, she pulled herself up as straight as possible, squared her shoulders, and fastened her gaze on the clerk's back.

Then, to her astonishment, the men moved out of her way, smiling, some pulling off their caps, making a path directly to the desk. Nina could not grasp the meaning in their sudden gallantry, but she nodded her thanks, advanced to the head of the line, and smartly rang the desk bell.

"Excuse me," she said firmly to the clerk's back.

"Aye, what is it?" He didn't turn around.

"Could you tell me where I might find Mister Shane Merritt?"

"Nup."

With obvious amusement, the men watched for her next move. Undaunted, Nina drew herself up on tiptoe and leaned both elbows on the desk. She was not about to let the clerk's rudeness weaken her now.

She rang the bell again. "Excuse me, do you mean no, you don't know where he is, or no, you won't *tell* me where he is?"

Still he did not turn around. "Aye, and stop ringing that bloody bell."

"Outta me way, miss," a surly sailor pushed her aside. "Terwilliger, toss the key!"

The clerk snapped around to attend the sailor, briskly handing a key to him, and then speaking to another who approached. Jabs of sharp elbows jostled and pushed Nina away from the desk, and large men smelling of fish and sweat surrounded her.

Apparently the moment of gallantry had ended. Hands at her temples, she ducked and bobbed out of the knot of bodies. Her head pounded. She needed air desperately. And she was growing more agitated by the minute.

The front door opened wide to a group of fishermen pushing in with jubilant shouts of a successful catch, their entrance accompanied by a whoosh of air, pungent with odors from the quay. Nina wrinkled her nose. There didn't seem to be an abundance of fresh air in this part of Sydney, she thought. But there were flies, increasing numbers of flies with every opening of the door. She brushed a lethargic one from her face. For a fleeting moment she considered bolting out of there, but stopped herself. Just where did she think she would go?

"Say, Sheila," the pinch-faced clerk called over the crowd. Nina did not turn around. "You there, girlie, you asked of Shane Merritt?"

Nina arranged the calmest smile she could muster, squared her shoulders, and turned around slowly, flashing dark aquamarine eyes.

"Were you speaking to me?" she asked, forcing sweetness and wondering what had made him change his mind and offer assistance. "Yes, I did ask about Mister Merritt," she said firmly, "but my name isn't Sheila, it's . . ." She looked around at the still gaping men, and decided not to offer her name.

"Figured *you'd* be looking for him," Terwilliger continued, and Nina felt the sting of his sarcastic tongue.

A collective low laugh traveled around her as she walked back through the crowd toward the desk.

Above his wire-rimmed half-spectacles Terwilliger's squinty eyes assessed her, from the top of her hair to the hem of her skirt.

Nina moved uncomfortably under his scrutiny, but held her reserve. "Pardon?"

"Never mind. You don't look like any of the usual fluff, but I suppose you're just like the rest."

"The rest?" Nina tilted her head.

"The rest?" the clerk mimicked her in a high voice. He snapped off his glasses and leaned toward her. "Don't play so innocent, girlie. You're all after the same thing."

"Oh dear, I was afraid of that. I'm too late—he won't take me now."

Terwilliger clucked disdainfully, and leaned his small chest over the desk to peer down at her with an air of superiority. "No worries there, girlie, Shane Merritt takes 'em all!"

Nina was openly surprised. "You mean he's able to take more than one?"

"How many *are* there in the bleedin' world?"

A chorus of rough guffaws bounced off the wood panels and crashed around Nina. Smiling with smug victory, Terwilliger made a broad ceremony of replacing his glasses. Then, picking up a stack of envelopes, he fanned them and presented his back to her once again.

Nina frowned. Her clothes clinging to her moist skin and the closeness of the room and oppressive odors made her stomach churn anew. She felt she might suffocate. Drawing another ounce of courage from somewhere, she rang the bell again. Terwilliger continued to ignore her.

She dropped her hands to her sides. Forget it, she thought, I don't feel like playing a game of wills with him. Anyway, what kind of man could Shane Merritt possibly be if he requests a lady's companion to meet him in a place like this? She shook her head, guessing if anybody wanted to meet anybody for almost anything, this was the place. Deciding it was best she hold onto her courage and search for employment elsewhere, she started toward the door.

With a sneer in his voice, Terwilliger called to her, "Afraid of the competition, eh, girlie?"

Nina stopped, gripping the strings of her reticule tightly, and setting her jaw. She turned around and glared at him with eyes of fire.

"Of course not. I was just going to wait until he . . . weeded the others out."

The clerk's pointed face shattered into a grin. He peered over his glasses with a smug look that set Nina's teeth on edge.

"Hah! That's a good one, that is! Well, girlie, if you decide to wade into the weeds, Merritt's in the tavern."

"And would you mind telling me where the tavern is?" Nina shot back.

Terwilliger nodded in a vague direction toward the front of the lobby, laughed, then turned back to the mail slots. Annoyed, Nina rapidly slammed the desk bell numerous times and watched his shoulders twitch in irritation. She stormed away to a burst of applause from the roomful of men.

Terwilliger glanced over his shoulder in time to see her, traveling case and cloak dragging behind her, bonnet bouncing over her hip, stride resolutely to a door—and walk directly into the ladies' comfort station.

Inside the dark taproom, apprehension returned and overtook Nina. Shouts of rowdy men much the worse for the brew, heavy glasses thudding against wood tables, and a tinny piano pounded by a bearded fat man mingled with the odors of damp wool and oilskin and fish and smoke, assaulted her senses, and disoriented her.

"What'll ya' have, lady?" a barrel-chested bartender barked from the end of the long wood bar, eyeing her with obvious curiosity.

Nina moved hesitantly toward him. He watched her with an impatient expression on his shadowed features.

"Come on, lady, I don't have all day, even if you have."

"Sorry." Nina walked closer, letting her gaze glance off him.

In his stained white jumper with exposed hairy forearms and tattooed muscles bulging below massive shoulders, he was an unpleasant reminder of the sailors around the wharves near the fish markets in New York. She'd never made eye contact with them, let alone converse with them. Here she felt as if everywhere she turned a new experience challenged her. It was at once frightening and thrilling.

She pushed her voice to as much timbre as she was capable, given the state she was in, to speak to him. "I'm looking for Shane Merritt. The desk clerk said I could find him . . ." she peered around the room

". . . in here."

"Merritt!" The burly man boomed so loudly Nina's ears started ringing. "Bit of Sheila to see you!" He pointed toward the back of the room.

Nina twisted in the direction he indicated, then turned back. "Sheila? That's the third or fourth time today . . ."

The bartender paid no attention to her. He was wiping glasses, and Nina understood he'd done all he was going to do to help her. She strained her eyes through the smoke and dim light around several hat-covered heads. Picking her way across the sawdust-strewn plank floor, through the crowd, she smiled nervously, weaving out of the reach of grasping hands. Several provocatively dressed women with large bosoms lounged around a table in the back. Through the haze Nina could make out a man seated there. He stood up.

"Mr. Merritt?"

"Can't hear ya', lass."

The deep voice sent a shiver of recognition down her spine. How could that be?

"Are you Mr. Merritt?" she repeated, louder this time.

"Who wants to know?"

Nina was almost tempted to say "No one" and bolt for the door, but something about his voice kept her rooted there. The man advanced and stopped a few feet from her, standing under a crude chandelier that cast a flickering light over him. She tilted her head back to see into his face.

"Well, you wanted Shane Merritt, my girl, and you got him. Speak your mind."

Her rescuer from the Customhouse! Nina's heart slammed wildly against the wall of her chest.

He stood with long tanned fingers fanned over his slim hips, one leg a bit forward and slightly bent at the knee, an insouciant pose that almost unnerved her. The magnetic sky-blue force of his eyes penetrated the thick smoke and took her breath away. Never before had she experienced such a sensation when a man looked into her eyes. Her hands felt as if she were holding countless pins and needles, all stabbing her at once. No matter how she struggled, her quick breaths would go no deeper than her throat, and she knew she was not covering her unsettled feelings very well.

A lazy smile crept enticingly across his lips, then broke into a brilliance so dazzling Nina stepped back from it.

"Well, now, if it isn't my fellow pinch victim. How goes it, my girl? Could it be? Nay! It's not here at Old Mac you've taken work now, is it?" He looked her up and down, thumbed his hat to the back of his head, and gave a low whistle. "I'd never have guessed. I'll say the bonnet made a proper entrance, then, despite its near demise, so?"

Nina's face burned with his mistaken idea of her employment. Or was he just playing with her? In either case, she was glad they were standing in darkness and he couldn't see her face clearly.

She composed herself into a demeanor of business. "If you are Shane Merritt, I've come about your notice in the Sydney *Herald*. Has the position been filled . . . ?" She peered around his bent elbow, a bit of playfulness emerging through her apprehension. "Or are you still . . . interviewing?"

Shane Merritt turned in the direction of her gaze. When he turned back to her, his smile flashed brightly.

"You mean the ladies? Hell no, lass, they're just some cobbers to fill the waiting time." He cocked his head and looked her over, making a long process of it. His eyes snapped with amused golden glints. "Jealous, are you? No need to be. You're a neat bit of sheila, yourself."

"Sheila? Why is it people keep calling me that? My name is Nina Cole." The full realization of what he'd just implied struck her. "And . . . and why should I be jealous?"

Merritt laughed again, warm and friendly, and Nina was beginning to like it. "I would have no notion of why you're jealous, lass. And sheila isn't a name. What it means is, you're comely yourself."

He motioned toward a table near the door, then called to the bartender, "Schooner for me, mate, and a lady's waist!"

His hand felt comforting on Nina's elbow as he guided her toward the table. Shane Merritt had complimented her, she guessed, but how utterly presumptuous of him to accuse her of being jealous. He hardly knew her; she hardly knew him. Why should she care about those, what did he call them? Cobbers?

Nina's mind whirled in a jumble of confusing thought. Why on earth would he ask for a lady's waist? She was wearing her best shirt, and he certainly couldn't get one to fit over his muscular shoulders. And why would he want to? How peculiar. What was he talking about? The hint of a questioning frown flickered between her brows.

Shane nodded. "Americans always get confused with our Australian language."

Nina's eyes flew to his face. Could he read her mind? If so, she'd certainly have to be careful, she cautioned herself.

"Makes perfect sense to us. You've a few words we wonder about, you know. You'd never know we spoke the same language." He watched her big eyes staring at him through the smoke. He could tell she'd hardly heard what he said. "Isn't that right, my girl?" he whispered.

"What? I'm sorry?" Nina shook her head slightly, and a wayward curl flopped over her forehead.

"I was just saying we speak the same language."

"Yes."

"Aye."

Shane cocked one sandy eyebrow, surprised to feel that he was glad to see her. He was glad he'd placed that notice in the *Herald*, glad she'd sought him out. Bloody hell! What did that mean? She wasn't the kind to spend the night with a man, then move on to the next, was she? She said she'd come about the position he'd offered. Was she sincere about that, or . . . ?

The bartender lumbered over, interrupting Shane's thoughts. He plunked down an enormous glass of foamy brew so hard some of it sloshed onto the table. With a display of mock daintiness, he set a small tapered glass of the same in front of Nina.

"Oh, I didn't want any . . ." she started to protest.

"Take it, lady," the bartender ordered gruffly. "I

31

just learnt how to understand this bloke, and I ain't pourin' it back in the cask fer you or nobody." He scuffed back to the bar.

"What . . . ?" Nina's eyes followed him with unmasked confusion, then slid back to the glass.

"Transported American," Shane laughed. "Don't fret. Takes a bit of getting used to." He pointed at his glass. "The schooner's the big amber." He took hold of her glass, "and this is a lady's waist, a little amb . . . beer." He lifted it toward her. "Drink up, my girl!"

"Mr. Merritt, really, I don't . . ."

She coiled her fingers around the glass to take it from him and her gaze settled on their hands where the warmth from his fingers melded against hers. He slipped his hand away from hers, almost reluctantly, she thought briefly, and drained half the schooner in one drink. Nina marveled as she watched the knot in his throat bounce to the rhythm of his swallows.

Regaining her composure, she said, "I wasn't certain what to expect when I came looking for you, Mr. Merritt. I mean, here, in this . . . this place." She looked around the room, then back to him. "And then I recognized you from the Customhouse." That's putting it mildly, she thought. Recognized him? She was struck almost senseless by him!

"You were carrying a saddle then. Are you a cowboy? Or . . . you're not a gold miner, are you?" Nina's eyes narrowed as she studied his face as closely as she could through the smoke, waiting for his answer.

Her guard went up. At home she'd heard about many a young woman who'd answered a newspaper advertisement for a teacher, and found herself in the hands of an unscrupulous man who took her west and sold her as a bride to a miner. Rumor whispered about the unspeakable fate of such women.

Nina vowed she would never allow any man to be in a position to do that to her. She'd never be so desperate as that for adventure—or marriage, for that matter. Yet here she was, she reminded herself, in Australia, for heaven's sake, and in a very compromising predicament.

Shane's rich laugh brought her back to the present, and the sound of it went around her like her cloak, warming her and making her feel oddly safe.

"Gold miner? Nay. But cowboy? Aye, that I am, my girl, that I am. Of a sort. Not cattle, mind you, but sheep, on a station in N.S.W."

"Station? N.S.W.?"

"Aye, a ranch. In New South Wales."

"There are ranches in Australia?"

"Aye." He turned his head slightly. "Where'd you live in America, my girl?"

"New York. You live on a ranch, not in Sydney?" Nina could not conceal her obvious disappointment.

"That's what I said."

"The position you offer is on this ranch?"

"That it is. Beautiful land," he said proudly, "far as the eye can see. Not all squeezed in, like New York. Just got back from there myself. Stayed much longer than I ever wanted to. So, now tell me your qualifications and we'll see if you're suitable. I was beginning to think I'd never find anyone . . ."

"Oh, Mr. Merritt, I'm afraid I . . ."

Nina was immediately stopped by the steel-blue

33

intensity of his eyes on her. Gaslight reflecting from the bar flickered over his face and tipped the ends of his hair with an amber glow almost as deep as the brew. Nina felt she was looking at a life-sized cameo. She froze, her heart pounding wildly and so loudly her own voice was almost inaudible to her.

"I don't think I could possibly go to a . . . a ranch."

"Why not?" Shane's voice reflected his shock at the ridiculousness of such a statement.

"It would be so far away from anything civilized. This country is hardly settled yet. I mean, convicts, and . . . and Aborigines . . . I don't see how I could . . ." Nina knew she was struggling for the right thing to say, but she didn't seem to know what exactly that would be.

"I don't bloody believe this!" Shane's exasperation flared. "What do you think we've been doing for the last forty or fifty years? Watching eucalyptus grow? Your education is sadly lacking, my girl."

He stood up quickly, scraping his chair across the wood floor. He drained his schooner, then leaned over so close to her she could feel his breath on her face.

"You wouldn't last a day out of Sydney, I can see that. Some wild roo might pack you off in her pouch to the Never-Never, and you'd not be heard from again. Why don't you go home and stay nice and safe in your New York America? G'day, miss."

Shane pulled his hat down hard over his forehead and elbowed his way out of the tavern. The double doors swung in the air of his departure, and Nina felt a cold wind blow over her heart.

Chapter 3

Nina walked along the Circular Quay drawn by the activity at the wharves, the throng of people, the sharp breeze. Sydney was a lot like New York, she decided, surprising herself with the comparison.

Her thoughts tumbled back to her last night at home. Home. She hardly thought of the apartment she'd shared with elderly Aunt Sadie as home, even though she'd lived there ever since her parents had died, when she was six. Nina recalled pouring their usual evening cups of tea, then sitting silently on the horsehair sofa drinking hers. The shelf clock ticked methodically over the cold fireplace, its monotonous tones cutting dully through the heavy silence that hung between the two women.

Aunt Sadie spoke at last. "Well, the least you could have done was to ask about the terms at the factory," she harped on a favorite topic.

Her father's only relative, Aunt Sadie was a spinster. Nina knew she'd been a bother to the woman since she'd moved in.

"Honestly, Nina, where is your head? You've never been able to think rationally. Got that from your mother, I daresay. If she hadn't married my nephew . . . well, it's difficult to say just *what* would have happened to her."

"Aunt Sadie, if you'd seen the place, you'd understand why I could never work there," Nina countered. She had considered the opening at the shirtwaist factory for a seamstress. After all, it was very difficult for women to find employment that paid any kind of decent wage. But once she saw the disgusting working conditions, and the sad, perspiring faces, she knew she could not spend her days there. "No woman should have to work in a place like that. And there were children working there, too, poor things."

Ignoring her remarks, Aunt Sadie went on, "Who do you think you are, anyway, some uppity miss from the other side? You're selfish, just plain selfish, to turn down that job. Have you ever *once* given any thought to me? After all, I've supported you, seen to your needs. Time you started paying back. You'll never amount to anything. Twenty years old and no marriage prospects in sight. Easy to see why. Nose in a book all the while, dreamy eyed about some wild adventure. No self-respecting gentleman would want to waste time on such as you."

Nina shut out the voice as the prunish woman droned on. Listening to Aunt Sadie tonight disheartened her more than usual. She knew her contributions to the household hadn't been much, but she'd worked hard from the moment she'd moved in, cleaning, cooking, doing laundry, running errands, taking care of Aunt Sadie. All of that, along with her schoolwork, was time-consuming, and it left her little time for herself.

Not that she'd lacked for possibilities, but Nina deliberately had no marriage prospects. None of the young men who'd come to call were very exciting to her. And deep in her heart Nina knew she wanted excitement, wanted to experience as much as she could. She felt her life had no texture in or out of the third-floor brownstone apartment. But no matter how hard she tried, she did not find any of the men acceptable, and she could not find suitable work— suitable to Nina. Anyone and anything would have been deemed suitable by Aunt Sadie.

"More than likely you'll end up a spinster cooking in a convent kitchen somewhere," the old woman harped on.

Nina checked the impulse to comment about her aunt's own spinsterhood. Somehow Sadie's definition of it never applied to herself.

"Mark my words, I know these things. You should take the position in Australia. You could be sailing on the *Sea Eagle* at midnight tonight."

Amy Winslow, a friend of Aunt Sadie's, had moved away from New York during the heat of the Australian gold rush. After her husband died, she'd written Sadie and complained about the difficulty of engaging the right kind of young woman to live in as a companion. Aunt Sadie had dispatched a letter to Mrs. Winslow saying that her grandniece was perfect for the position, and would sail on the next ship.

When Nina learned of the letter, she protested vehemently. Becoming a lady's companion was not

37

the kind of work she wanted. And Australia? Why, it was hardly more than a crude outpost somewhere in the middle of the ocean at the bottom of the globe! And besides, she thought, why trade one Aunt Sadie for another just like her?

"Since you won't go to Australia, you'll go to the factory. I've already talked to someone there about you. They'll take you tomorrow."

"You had no right to—"

"Right? Don't talk to me about rights, young lady. You have none, remember? I'm your guardian for another year. Your inheritance, pittance that it was, is all but exhausted, and I have neither the desire nor the means to support you."

Shocked, Nina fought back tears. She'd had no idea there had been money from her parents—her money. And now there wasn't any. Perhaps if she'd known about it sooner, she'd have found a way to get it and run off to England with it. That was the adventure she'd dreamed of—England, castles, noblemen, grand balls, and sumptuous feasts, light and laughter everywhere. And a life far, far away from New York and Aunt Sadie.

The old woman set down her cup. Muttering something about crosses to bear, she laboriously stood up with the aid of a cane and walked slowly to her bedroom. Nina watched the black-clothed figure retreat, and felt more heavy of heart than ever.

She gathered up the tea things and dutifully washed them, then went to prepare for bed. She sank down onto the narrow bed in her cold bedroom, where it was always dark because of the heavy drapes covering the single window's drab view of the stone building next door. Absently she smoothed the sides of her hair, still neatly coiled to the top of her head as it was from the minute she arose in the morning. Her eyes filled with hot tears, then spilled over.

"I wish I could just run as far away from here as humanly possible!" she wailed.

She threw her head back on the pillow. No, I could never do that, she admonished herself. And besides, where would I go? To some wild place like . . . like Australia? She turned over and cried harder into her pillow.

And then the crying subsided. She lifted her head and sat up, wiping the tears from her face with the back of her hand.

Australia . . . why not? Why not Australia? It was certainly far away, probably not near anything civilized people ever even heard about. Perhaps for the first time Aunt Sadie had the right idea: there was nothing to keep her here, nothing she would ever feel sorry to leave. Nina smiled. Perhaps this was the adventure for her!

With pounding excitement she ran to the clothespress, pulled her mother's old traveling case from the back, and stuffed clothes into it. Then she threw them out again and started over, becoming more selective, filling the bag and her reticule with only her best things, pictures of her parents, and a money purse containing a small cache she'd managed to tuck away. She glanced at the clock. Barely time to make it to the pier before the *Sea Eagle* sailed for Australia.

No point in waking Aunt Sadie. Nina left a quick note on the bureau for her. Wrapping the strings of the reticule tightly around her waist, she dropped her traveling bag out the window onto the fire escape, slipped out after it, and eased carefully down the iron steps to the alley below. The feat was delicious and gave Nina a heightened sense of adventure and freedom. Who would have thought that sneaking out of the house by window could bring so much excitement?

Now in Sydney, walking along the quay, Nina felt that sense of adventure begin to return to her. She stopped still, her thoughts a jumble.

She thought, how bad could a sheep station be? All those cuddly little lambs. Maybe I could be hired to feed animals or something. What am I saying? I've had experience with a crotchety old woman in a dark apartment for most of my life. I know I could tolerate anything this woman, and even this disturbing man, could hand out, and I can do it on a ranch, at a sheep station, wherever.

Turning around, she quickened her pace back toward the MacQuarie. Her resolve spurred her into a run with a fervent hope that during her momentary loss of courage Shane Merritt hadn't hired someone else. She burst into the lobby, stopping, breathless, in front of the registration desk.

"Still looking for Shane Merritt, girlie?" Terwilliger was still on duty, and he peered at her with annoying superiority. "Didn't get enough earlier, eh? Doesn't surprise me."

She didn't take his bait. What was the use of reasoning with this little worm? "Do you know where he might be right now?" she breathed.

"Aye." He dusted the desk top.

Nina sighed. "Would you mind telling me?"

"Aye, that I would," the clerk replied in his snootiest tone. When he saw her hand poised resolutely over the desk bell he added quickly, "But I'll tell you anyway. He's in the tavern."

"Still?" Nina was genuinely surprised.

"You'd better hurry. Won't have much time to, ah, accomplish what you've set your mind on before he leaves." He winked at her.

Nina pushed her small chin into the air, gave the bell a final slap, and turned quickly toward the tavern doors.

She marched into the smoky darkness and went directly to Shane's table. He was still there, and she was disturbed to see that once again there were several women around him. Didn't he ever get tired of interviewing?

"Mister Merritt," she pushed her voice over the noise, "if you haven't found someone to take the position at your . . . station, I want it. I'm ready to leave immediately."

"Oooo, Shane, she wants a position at your station," a blond woman teased. "What about the positions right here in Sydney, eh, love?"

Another woman laughed. "Really, Denise, we've filled all those positions! I don't believe there's one available for a baby like her, unless it's in the nursery!"

Their laughter surrounded Nina. Two sailors clapped Shane on the back, grinning and urging him on. She felt her face burn with embarrassment and anger. Shane Merritt was smiling, having as much fun at her expense as everyone else, she thought.

41

Whatever made her think she could just waltz right into this seedy place and demand a respectable job from such a questionable man, anyway? She began to wonder if there were convents in Australia. Red-faced, she turned to quit the tavern. The teasing followed her.

Shane's eyes twinkled with amusement. Nina Cole had returned with a determination to take the work he offered, and he was thrilled thinking she possessed a courage that might never have been fully tested. And he knew he was becoming more fascinated with her big aquamarine eyes and that mane of copper hair which even now was beginning to tumble from its pins in lovely disarray. He wondered what that hair would feel like, look like, loose and flowing over her shoulders. She still clutched her reticule and dilly bag. He surmised they probably held everything she owned in the world. His musings made him smile, and a curious warmth spread through him.

Shane watched her turn, and knew he couldn't let her leave. "Wait a minute, little baggage. You didn't wait for my answer," he called to her.

He saw her stop and square her shoulders. Now what was he to do? Stalling for time to think, he stood up and drained his schooner. He wanted to say the right thing to Nina, but for the life of him the words would not come. Bloody hell! How had he become so muddled in so short a time? If he wasn't careful, he could lose his reputation with the ladies, mostly fabricated by their talk, but widespread.

"You're hired, my girl," Shane said calmly, setting the schooner on the table.

He found it curious, but he couldn't think of

anything more clever to say. His cronies fell back, shaking their heads and grinning wryly. He knew they figured he'd been bested by a plain fluff of a girl. But . . . so be it.

"Meet me at Pier 17 at dawn tomorrow. Don't be late." He said the last firmly, believing he should sound like a stern employer at the outset. Mostly, he knew, he was doing it for the benefit of the others.

"I'll be there," Nina said breathlessly. "Thank you." She turned to leave.

A drunk seaman who'd been watching their exchange reached out and grabbed Nina's arm. "Well, now, that leaves some time for you and me to get to know each other, sweetface," he grunted.

Nina grimaced and turned her face. "No, thank you," she said firmly.

"That's what they all say, and they never mean it." The drunk took a firmer hold of her arm.

"Well, I do!"

Nina slammed him in the chest with her small fist. He grabbed hold of her wrists and started to drag her to a corner. She struggled against him, and in the confusion her reticule fell to the floor, its contents spilling out.

Shane lunged forward and pried the drunk's fingers from Nina's arm. "Shove off, screamer," he said gruffly.

Cheers and laughter swelled around the room, and the fat piano player pounded the keys faster and louder. This crowd loved a fight, and they rallied to the spirit of one in which a lady's honor was championed.

The seaman ignored Shane and yanked hard on

43

Nina's arm. Shane let fly with a doubled fist that landed directly on the man's chin and sent him reeling backward into several chairs, out cold. The music came faster. More cheers. Nina's knees buckled when she realized what could have happened if Shane hadn't been there to rescue her—again. She knelt down as much to cover her apprehension as to gather her belongings. Shane knelt to assist her. His hand brushed against hers several times, and he was struck by the way its softness cooled his bruised hand. He saw how quickly she pulled back when they touched, as if she'd been brushed by flame.

Holding her reticule between them, they stood up together. Shane suddenly remembered the robbery on the ship. He was certain she had no money.

"Where are you staying, my . . . Miss Cole, is it?"

She nodded. "I don't . . . have a room. Perhaps I'll just stay in the lobby . . ."

"Come with me, my girl." Shane took her arm and steered her out of the tavern and up to the registration desk.

"Terwilliger, put Miss Cole's things in my room for tonight, and send up a supper tray."

"Naturally, Mr. Merritt." Terwilliger winked at him and cast a knowing look at Nina.

"Oh, no!" Nina protested, "I couldn't . . ."

"It's part of the arrangement," Shane interrupted.

"It always is," Terwilliger put in.

Shane's steady gaze held Nina motionless. "No worries. Your virtue will remain intact. I'm bunking on the boat tonight."

"Oh, what a shame," Terwilliger clucked.

Shane gave him a stern look. "Terwilliger, you'll

see to Miss Cole's comfort, I'm sure. That means she's not to be bothered this evening. Do we understand each other?"

"Oh, perfectly, Mr. Merritt, perfectly." He turned toward Nina and said politely, "I know you'll be very happy here, Miss Cole. Rest assured."

Nina was most uncomfortable with what seemed to be an improper transaction, but she accepted Shane's offer without further protest. It would never do for her to sit up all night anywhere, especially in the MacQuarie lobby. And something in Shane's eyes made her powerless to resist him.

Shane settled the bill, then turned to her, took her arm, and edged her toward the stairwell on the other side of the lobby.

Nina stopped a moment, turned back, and gave the desk bell a final ring. Over her shoulder she tossed a satisfied smile at Terwilliger, and ascended the stairs on Shane Merritt's arm.

Chapter 4

Precisely at dawn, Nina waited at the end of Pier 17. Warm and misty, the morning boasted golden rose colors that promised a fitting beginning to a new day and a new life. She almost didn't care that the harbor breeze whipped around and loosened her freshly brushed and pinned hair. It was a freeing wind, blowing away the old, leaving her vulnerable to the new. She felt unafraid, almost daring.

Nina joined a crowd watching the mooring of a great clipper ship. Shouting orders to each other, the men of the tug crews caught long towlines and smoothly guided the incoming ship to dock where her tall masts blended into the forest of others bobbing in the swells along the wharf. Nina breathed in the scent of salt air and sense of adventure the ships exuded. Would she fit into her new port as easily as this ship? Not without a tug crew, she answered herself.

She smoothed her skirt, pulling it away from her legs where the wind pressed it, and opened her short

47

jacket and brocade waistcoat. The high neck of her ivory lace blouse set off her flushed face and sun-flame hair perfectly. If Nina possessed any vanity, it was about this suit. The deep forest green made her eyes glow like emeralds. The peaked belt above the generous skirt over many petticoats accentuated her slim waist, making it appear as tiny as those of the ladies in the French costume books she loved to pore over in the library.

The morning grew warmer, and so did Nina, beneath all the layers of clothing. She tried to ignore a fact that unnerved her—Shane Merritt was nowhere in sight, and she was growing increasingly uncomfortable standing there alone. She decided if she concentrated on familiarizing herself with her new surroundings, she would feel calmer.

She set about the task, and discovered it to be an absorbing exercise. Sydney appeared larger than New York, spread out as it was beyond the wharves in a jagged half circle, a range of hazy blue mountains shimmering beyond. Nina marveled at the throngs of people in colorful civilized suits and dresses amid the bustle of activity at the pier so early in the morning. The realization came to her that she'd expected to see drab, ragged garb on convicts, and loincloths on half-naked spear-carrying black men with wild hair.

Two muscular young wharfies, naked from the waist up, loaded innumerable boxes and bags bearing Merritt labels onto a long cart. Avoiding their eyes and low comments, Nina waited for Shane a safe distance from the cart. Seamen in caps and dirty pants boisterously shouted and slapped each other on the back as they passed her. Down the pier, raucous laughter rose in swells from a small tavern already filling with early-day revelers. She could hear the clink-clunk of beer schooners coming together and slamming down on the wooden bar.

Ladies passed her looking cool and fresh in long, crisp linen dresses and wide-brimmed hats. They carried lacy parasols, and their soft perfumes drifted over her, making her even more painfully aware she'd been forced to dress this morning without a bath. The hotel had been too full to allow for many before the water supply was exhausted.

Her skirt, wrinkled from traveling, together with many undergarments, clung to her in the mounting heat. She hoped no one would notice. But it was all too clear to her that no one did notice her except the wharfies. At any moment she half expected them to hoist her up on the cart with the rest of the Merritt baggage.

Shane Merritt certainly seemed to be taking his own sweet time to meet her. He'd insisted she be on time, but that did not seem to be a rule to which he himself adhered. Nina felt she'd been waiting for hours. As the crowds began to thin out, a wave of panic threatened to sweep over her.

She turned right and left, her eyes rapidly scanning up and down the pier. Where was he? Had he simply left her there to fend for herself? Was last night only a dream, or had he truly promised her employment? Whatever had possessed her to make such a rash decision and run away to a strange land and take up with a strange man?

Her pulse quickened and she was conscious of

wringing her hands through the strings on her reticule. Perhaps he'd abandoned her. He seemed to enjoy playing games with women. She started to fume. This was one woman he'd discover he couldn't toy with. It wasn't too late. She could go into Sydney and look for other work. Just as she picked up her bag and started off the pier, she saw his tall, lean form advancing toward her from a long way down the wharf. Over his shoulder was slung the saddle, the morning light catching the silver studs and flashing over them like sun dancing on water. Nina saw his body shift to one side to balance its weight.

His shock of sunny hair blew up against his hat, which was pushed to the back of his head, and she could see his gleaming white smile even from the length of distance between them. His vest blew open, creating a bright contrast against his dusky blue shirt, sleeves rolled to expose tanned forearms.

His leather boots made no noise on the stone pier as he drew near, but Nina's heart beat to the rhythm of his long strides. Her earlier apprehension had turned to anger directed at Shane, but now she seemed to have no control over the peculiar way her emotions were reacting to the dashing figure gliding toward her.

From the moment Shane rounded the corner past the cargo office, he could see Nina Cole waiting for him halfway down the wharf. She turned around several times, peering up and down its length, searching for him. He started toward her, shutting his eyes for a moment, hoping his quickly made decision to take her to Flame Tree would not come the guster of his life.

If the Mum disapproved of her, what was he going to do about her then? He opened his eyes. Rosegold sun rays bathed her face and glinted off her copper hair like precious metal in the hills along the Hunter River. He was positive he saw a burnished copper halo above her head. A thought jumped into his head. If the Mum did disapprove of her, he'd simply have to figure out another way to keep her.

He frowned. What was he thinking? He wasn't supposed to admire Nina Cole's beauty. That wasn't in the plan. She was the girl he'd hired to be the Mum's companion, that was all, and he'd best remember it.

Suddenly it looked to him as if she were leaving. Bloody hell! He couldn't lose her now! Wait: what he meant was, he couldn't lose the only woman who'd responded to his notice, he corrected himself quickly. He quickened his pace.

"Well, we're ready," he called as he drew closer to her. "Took longer than I thought to clear the goods."

She fell into step beside him and they walked toward the end of the pier. Noisily the wharfies pushed the cargo cart ahead of them and rounded a corner.

Shane slowed as they came upon a painted door at the end of the pier. "Facilities in here for ladies."

"No, thank you," Nina said, attempting to hide her nervousness. She would not be a bother to Shane Merritt. She would simply wait until they got to the house, and take care of her needs in private.

"You're sure?"

"I'm sure."

"It's a bit of a jaunt to the house . . ."

"I'll be fine."

"Suit yourself."

He directed her toward an open wagon, long and painted yellow. A wiry-looking older man had been watching them from atop the high bench seat. Leather reins looped over his hands and snaked down to a harness hung over the necks of a pair of matched bay horses. They stood impatiently flicking flies with shakes of their big heads and switches of their tails.

"Aye, Derrick!" Shane called with a wave.

The older man waved silently with a big grin. Nina caught his cocked eyebrow as he assessed her, and felt the heat of blush rise up her throat. Shane gave her a boost up to the seat as the men loaded the cargo onto the wagon.

"Derrick, meet Miss Nina Cole."

"How do, missy."

Nina smiled, and Derrick gave her a tip of his battered brown hat as she sat down next to him. Shane pulled his long frame up, the weight of him compressing the seat with a crackle of springs. The horses jerked away almost before he was seated, and the wagon's lurch brought the small of Nina's back hard up against the wood seat. She winced slightly in pain.

The bays worked their way out of the wharf area and down a narrow, winding road behind the outskirts of Sydney. Nina strained to catch better sight of the city, but the buildings were settled so close together she could not get a clear view. Surely this elderly woman would frequent the shops and perhaps the theater now and again, she decided, and there would be plenty of time to do and see everything.

A surge of excitement welled up from the bottom of her stomach. This might turn out to be a pleasant experience after all. From where she was perched on the high wagon, Australia looked civilized, habitable, brighter than New York

"How's the go, Derrick?" Shane leaned around Nina to speak to his friend.

Derrick nodded questioningly toward Nina, and Shane nodded back, indicating that it was all right to speak in front of her.

"Fair, mate. Weather's cooperated, plenty of range grass, wool's good. Bushrangers have been a bit of a bother. And Colin's caught the gold fever. Got a few unsavory mates with the same sickness. Young twit . . ."

Shane nodded thoughtfully. "Colin has always been easily led. I'll have a go at him when I get there. What about the jackaroos?"

"They'll be glad you're back."

"And the Mum?"

"No change there."

Derrick uttered a low laugh and sent a cryptic glance toward Shane. Nina caught it, and it gave her an unsettled feeling. They talked as if she weren't there, and she was beginning to feel like part of the cargo once again. She thought they needed reminding of the reason she was there. She turned to Shane.

"Is 'the Mum' the lady I'm to be companion to? What is she like? Is she bedridden?"

"Aye, she's the one, but bedridden she's not!" he laughed. "She's a tough old bird, but then, she's had

53

to be. Had a hard life. Started out in a humpy with nothing, but she and her husband built one of the largest sheep stations in Australia. She knows every inch of it, and every jumbuck by the wrinkle of its nose."

His sky-blue eyes crinkled with genuine warmth into fan-folded creases at the edges. Nina liked the golden tan of his skin, and the way those creases showed white when he wasn't smiling. Caught up with the thought in combination with her discomfort, she found it difficult to concentrate on what he was saying.

"Started out in . . . what did you say?"

"A humpy, a little cabin."

"Knows every what?"

"Jumbuck . . . sheep. She used to be so attached to each one of them that she couldn't bear to watch the ringers shear 'em." He laughed. "Grew out of that fast, once the station got so big and her husband was gone. It was all up to her to keep the place going and raise two little boys. 'Twas a hard go, but she's done it. Now she's getting frail, and I fear a mite lonely. Doesn't want to admit it, tough as that, she is."

"What about the little boys?"

"They grew up," he answered with a wry smile.

"And you work on this ranch?"

"Aye, that I do."

"Are there . . . other women . . . nearby?" she ventured, visualizing being cast into a wilderness in a cabin with just the old woman to care for.

"Two." He frowned. "What is it you truly think, Miss Cole, about Australia?"

54

Nina swallowed hard. No point in holding anything back. "That it's hard, hot, and full of strange, wild animals and savage people who live in bushes."

Shane relaxed his frown. "That's true. Except I think you mean the bush, the outback."

"Outback? You mean you have no, ah, indoor facilities?" Now she was truly concerned.

At this, Shane threw back his head and roared with laughter. Nina's face deepened to crimson.

"The outback, my girl, has nothing to do with 'facilities.' Well, I take that back. Maybe it does, depending how far back you trek. The outback is . . . the bush, uninhabited country, or uncivilized, if that's more to your liking."

"No, it is not more to my . . . are we almost there?" she asked with some urgency.

"Where?"

"To . . . the house."

"Oh no. We're tracking toward Devil's Backbone right now, up the Great North Road toward the Hunter River Valley. Then we'll begin to draw near Flame Tree."

"Flame Tree? Is that a town?"

"Nup, missy," Derrick cut in, "that's the name of the station."

"Flame Tree," Nina pondered the words. They sounded rather nice. "Devil's Backbone?" That didn't sound so nice.

"Aye. Named by the iron gangs when they built the road."

"Iron gangs?"

"Convicts. No doubt you know about them. All

the foreigners do."

"How'd you know I'm a foreigner?" Nina asked lightly. "Oh, I suppose it's the way I speak."

"Aye and nup," Derrick replied, giving a clucking noise to the horses.

"Excuse me?"

"Knew it 'fore I seen ya'. Heard on the pier this morning that Shane had plucked himself a Kiwi this time."

"A what?" She turned toward Shane, who kept his eyes straight ahead. Nina sensed she'd get no more detail, and went back to the original subject.

"Are there likely to be any convicts along here now?" Her voice held a tremulous note.

"Nup, just bushrangers." Derrick slapped the long reins along the wide flanks of the horses.

A pair of colorful lyrebirds minced across the road in front of them and disappeared into dense brush. Nina watched them with fascination.

"Bushrangers? You mean highwaymen?" she urged.

"Aye, you've heard of 'em." Derrick cleared his throat. "Then you know about Mad Dog Morgan."

"Why was he called Mad Dog?" Nina was afraid to know, yet was very curious about such a descriptive name.

"I couldn't truly say, missy. You wouldn't want to hear it. But I heard once he bit off a bullock's ear when it wouldn't hold still for him. He was a mean one, that one."

Nina shuddered at the image and asked no more questions. The sun rose higher and warmer and she removed her jacket. The wagon seat was growing harder under her skirt, which clung damply to her legs. With each bump in the road she could feel even more acutely the hard length of Shane's thigh as it pressed alongside her own, and its intense heat penetrated the folds of her skirt. She shifted uneasily on the seat. Surely the river Shane mentioned would appear on the horizon soon. How much farther away could Flame Tree lie?

"Parramatta next," Derrick announced into the air. "Need anything?"

"Nay. You, Miss Cole?" Shane looked toward her. "Now's the time to speak up. I'm sure we can find some facilities there for you as well."

"No, thank you, Mister Merritt. I'll be just fine."

Derrick shot a glance toward Shane. "I'll say one thing for her, she's got a strong constitution, she has. Not one stop at a loo yet!" He clucked the horses into a quicker gait.

"Well, she ought to know herself," Shane laughed.

Nina tilted her head questioningly. Perhaps she should allow them to stop so that she could use the facilities, but she was too embarrassed. And she was certain she would soon be at the house and would find privacy.

"Ah, there are the Blue Mountains, and see, way off there in the distance?" Shane pointed straight ahead. "That's the Great Dividing Range. I'm always glad to see that after a trip like this last one. Makes me know I'm home."

Shane's comment reinforced Nina's belief that they would soon arrive at Flame Tree.

In Parramatta the horses plodded with quick familiarity toward a large watering trough at the end

57

of the main street. With excited interest Nina watched the people and buildings on both sides of the street as they passed. It looked almost like the American western towns she'd read about, except that it appeared to be more civilized. There was a bakery next to a small tearoom, a barber shop, a stationer, a tobacco and candy shop, a newspaper office, and a large clothing emporium with ornate white latticework decorating the facade. Neatly dressed people strolled the boardwalks and went in and out of the various shops.

Nina thought Parramatta would be a nice place to live, even better than New York. She smiled happily. She was going to be fine, just fine.

The horses drank deeply from the watering trough, and then seemed in a big hurry to leave. Derrick hauled them out onto the road and headed them north. Nina turned around and wistfully watched the town disappear behind her. Well, of course, she reasoned, the ranch would be outside of town. After all, there were animals to be tended. It couldn't be too long before they'd reach Flame Tree.

Shane leaned his back into the hard seat, threw one leg up over the front of the wagon, and drew his hat down over his eyes. As he dozed, his thoughts filled with his return to Flame Tree, the long shearing period ahead, the sorting, and readying the fleece for shipment. And other things. At twenty, Colin was having a difficult time growing up. Shane would have to think of something to help him, although their seven-year age difference had always been an obstacle to mutual understanding.

And the Mum. Shane fervently hoped she would

like Nina Cole, and he hoped Nina Cole would adjust to the Mum and to Flame Tree. He had nagging doubts about it, now that they were on their way. She seemed so innocent, untouched, untested. Could she endure this life? And for how long?

He pulled his hat down harder over his face. Nina's closeness to him in the wagon seat disturbed him. He opened one eye and stole a glance at her. Her profile was high and delicate, and again there was that golden glow hovering over her hair like a halo. She looked like an angel. He shut his eyes. How would he know what an angel looked like? When he wasn't in the outback he was in the rooms of hell in Sydney or somewhere.

"Aren't we nearing Flame Tree yet?" The rising concern in Nina's voice roused him from his half-sleep.

"We've a lot of track before the river yet, missy," Derrick answered.

"But, I thought . . . Mister Merritt said it wasn't far from Sydney." There was the hint of worry behind her words.

"Strewth! Just shy of a hundred fifty kilometers."

"A hundred fifty? But . . ."

"Once we get on the boat it's only about sixty kilometers up west." Derrick looked her full in the face. "That's not far atall, missy, now don't you fret."

Too late. Nina was fretting a great deal. She desperately had to relieve herself and she fully realized that she was something of a . . . what was it Derrick had called the one named Colin? A twit? Yes, she was a twit for not swallowing her pride and using the facilities at the pier or back in Parramatta. Now

59

what could she do? She would simply have to request that they stop in the next town.

"Next town!" Derrick boomed. "Missy, there's no next town. Parramatta was it between here and Flame Tree."

"I see. Are there, uh, facilities on the boat?"

"Nup." Derrick snapped the reins and the horses took a hard left. The resulting jolt was an even sharper reminder of Nina's need.

Shane listened to the exchange and caught Nina's inference.

"Are you saying that *now* you need the loo?" When she looked at him blankly, he added, "The, ah . . . facilities?"

She nodded silently, her eyes wide, the corners starting to fill.

"Hells bells," Derrick muttered. He pulled the wagon over to the side of the road and reined in the horses.

"Wha . . . why are we stopping?" Nina twisted around in the hard seat to see whatever Derrick and Shane were looking at. "Is there a place around here?"

Shane silently unfolded his length and dropped down to the ground. He reached under the seat and withdrew a small shovel and propped it against the wheel, then held up a hand to Nina. When she looked at him questioningly, he reached farther and took her hand.

"Come on, my girl, I'll help you down."

"Please stop calling me that. Why would you want me to get down?"

Shane shoved his hat farther back on his head.

"Well, Miss Cole, I think it's pretty obvious that there are no 'facilities' on this wagon, or anywhere near here for that matter. Your duty to nature will have to be met out there." He motioned toward clumps of spinifex, rocks, and gnarled, bleached trees in the distance.

Nina's mouth flew open and she snatched her hand away from his. "Out there? You can't be serious!"

"Couldn't be more serious in my life, my . . . *Miss* Cole. Now the sooner you get down here and get to it, the sooner we'll reach Flame Tree."

"But I . . ." She looked doubtfully around her.

Derrick had walked to the back of the wagon and was rolling a smoke.

"Well, I can't go back there if he . . . couldn't I just wait till we get to Flame Tree?"

"I think you could answer that better than I. Come."

Shane took her hand and yanked hard. She tumbled down off the wagon seat and into his arms with a rather ungainly thud. He looked her full in the eyes for a moment, then stood her upright. He picked up the shovel and handed it to her. She looked at it as if she'd never seen one in her life.

"Now, you just walk up there and take care of things." He motioned ahead of the wagon.

"Ahead of you? Surely it would be more discreet if I went behind the wagon. If Mister Derrick might be so kind as to . . ."

"Look, my girl, we don't have time for this. The boat has most likely been waiting a good bit for us. As you might have noticed, you will have to walk quite a distance to get out of range of our vision so that you can feel more comfortable. It wastes time and energy in this heat for you to walk far enough behind the wagon and then back."

Nina finally understood his reasoning. She handed the shovel back to him. "All right. I will let you know when I'm ready to be picked up."

"I can see you haven't figured out the system. You will need this." He handed the shovel back. At her questioning frown he answered with an uncomfortable edge in his voice, "You will have to, uh, create a spot. Then . . . well you get the idea. Then you can use the shovel to wave to us so we'll know you're ready. Do you understand now?"

Her face reddened, and she nodded woodenly. Turning quickly she walked briskly ahead and disappeared behind the largest rock formation she could find.

"Go ahead, call me forty kinds of fool for bringing her, I deserve it." As Shane spoke, Derrick stood stoically smoking. "I just couldn't find anyone suitable for the Mum. It seemed like a reasonable solution at the time." Derrick let out great puffs of blue smoke. "Bloody hell, Derrick, say something!"

"What can I say, mate? Seems like you're saying it all. You did what you had to do."

"That's right, I did what I had to do. That's right." Shane nodded in vigorous agreement. "Aw, Derrick, she'll be right, so?"

Derrick crushed his smoke under his worn brown boot. "Well, now, looky here. Can't recollect ever seeing Shane Merritt all at sixes and sevens over any decision he made! I hafta watch this some more!" He stood back in mock rapt attention.

"Come on, mate, I need your help with this one. What do you honestly think?"

"Strewth to tell, mate, you'll just have to give it a go. No tellin' how the Mum will take your bringin' her a companion. Things are far worse than I wanted to say earlier. She's taken sick again."

Shane looked down and rubbed the toe of his boot back and forth in the dirt. "How bad is it this time?"

"Bad enough, but she'll hold on a long time. Made of strong fiber, she is. The young miss might just be good for her. But whether *she'll* be good for the *miss* . . ." Derrick scratched his head.

Shane grinned and clapped a hand on his old friend's shoulder, then started back to the front of the wagon.

Derrick's hand shot out to grab Shane's arm. "Wait, there's more." He looked down at the ground for a moment, then back up full into Shane's face. "You been away a long time, mate. Flame Tree's in a bit more trouble."

"What? Bushrangers? We can handle that . . ."

"Nup, it's more than that. Colin's been kinda . . . unruly. Partly it's those blokes he runs with, but partly it's . . . well, let's just say the Mum's been saving his hide, paying off his debts. And since he doesn't really do any work, she supports his high livin' life. It's been cuttin' into the funds."

"Well, I'll talk to her about it when I get there. Fault's partly mine, anyway. I should have taken a stronger hand in his upbringing. Spoiled, he is. That's what comes with going without a father."

"Not me place to point out you went without a

63

father, too."

"But I was older. I understood more, or thought I did. Thanks for telling me, Derrick. Has the doctor seen her?"

"Aye. Now listen, you can't let on you know all this. Maudie'll skin me alive if she knows I told you. She overheard most of this when the doctor visited. Bit of a quack, he is, if you ask me."

"You think all of them are quacks."

"Only met but two in me life, and I wouldn't give a tuppenny bumper for the lot." He slapped his hat against his leg to loosen the dirt. "Young miss must be ready by now, you think?" He started around to check the harness.

"If she's not, she's sure going to be!" Shane looked in the direction Nina had taken. Then he saw her with the shovel hoisted over her head in a frantic two-armed wave. He grinned. She was ready all right, but probably not quite for everything.

The three rode in silence for a good bit. Now and again a mob of kangaroos loped past them, their long leaps consuming the distance. Shane was taken with Nina's wide-eyed enchantment at their prowess, and how she twisted in the seat to catch the last glimpse of them. He was accustomed to living with the roos, but Nina's fascination with them warmly amused him. An overwhelming desire to show her everything there was to see in his beloved country filled and surprised him. Would she come to care about it as he did? Suddenly it was very important to him that she did, and he wondered why.

When the river appeared winding like a silver ribbon across the far horizon, Nina let out a relieved sigh. Although she wasn't looking forward to more water travel, the boat would be a welcome respite from the wagon. The backs of her thighs were cramped and her back ached.

"My, it is lovely around here." She tried to sound convincing in her appraisal, but as she surveyed the uncompromising landscape with its long stretches of scrub trees and rocks, she knew she should keep silent.

"And you don't mean that one neither, missy," Derrick said with his usual bluntness. "Not lovely out here atall till we get nearer to the river."

Nina tried not to appear too taken aback by Derrick's directness. A flock of huge flightless emus ran alongside them for a few moments, and she was thrilled by their height and long strides.

"Are there many wild animals around here? And near Flame Tree?"

Shane knew what was coming. He cleared his throat and hunched down into the wagon seat as Derrick seized an opportunity to throw a scare into the newcomer.

"I suppose you're referring to the hairy laughing jackass bird. That's the one you've probably heard the most about, what with the sheep rampages and all."

Nina snapped her head around to face him wide-eyed.

"And o'course there's the Tasmanian devil. Whirling dervish of just plain meanness, he is. Nobody's ever caught one, they're that fast. 'Cept once I heard of a backward flyin' crow that tried to pass one. The devil just made the wrong turn and got

65

hung up on the crow's long bill, and there they were, hoverin' over the ground together, goin' nowhere. 'Twasn't a pretty sight.''

He shook his head and stole a glance toward Nina, who was now struck dumb by incomprehension. Derrick enjoyed his tales far more than anyone else ever did.

"Now, there's the giant boomer roo, o'course," he went on, seeing that he held her captive in his weaving yarn. "They won't hurt ya' none if ya' treat 'em with respect. But don't rile 'em. Nup, nup. They're a moody lot. Got one takes the mail run in his pouch along here. He's faster'n any of our wagons. We give him our most important packets whenever we see him."

Shane's shoulders vibrated with the laughter he was holding in. He felt Nina frozen in her seat, taking in every word. He supposed he should put a cork in Derrick's mouth, but at the moment it had carried so far there was no turning back.

The horses rounded a bend, then grew skittish and stopped, their front legs prancing. There, in the middle of the road, stood the biggest animal Nina had ever laid eyes on. A dark red-brown kangaroo, sporting a hairy underchin that gave him the look of an old man, stood up on his enormous tail and long back feet. Nina was so shocked she could not open her throat enough to let out the shriek that was locked there. Derrick calmed the horses. The kangaroo stood watching them in his curious way, his glassy brown eyes scrutinizing the wagon and its occupants.

Derrick tipped his hat. "Nothing today, Big Red.

Thanks anyway."

As if that were his cue, the kangaroo turned, and with widespread leaps disappeared over the flat terrain and out of sight.

Shane could hold it no more. His husky broad laugh exploded out of him and echoed off the surrounding rocks. Observing the lack of a similar response from Nina, he pulled his hat down over his forehead and focused on the scenery passing beside the wagon. Derrick geehawed the horses into a fast clip. He set his mouth in a quivering straight line and concentrated on driving. Nina slumped back against the seat and stared straight ahead.

Closer to the Great Dividing Range the road pulled away from the rough sterile gorges and sandstone that had made up most of the scenery on the journey, and climbed and wound past misty eucalyptus woods, dripping with the rains that kept the eastern flanks of the mountains lush and green. Streams tumbled over mossy boulders on their way to the great meeting place in the sea. Overhead, shrieking white cockatoos swooped against an all-blue sky.

"Beautiful," Nina breathed, and Shane enjoyed the sound .

"Aye," Derrick responded. "Didn't I tell it so? Green as it is on this side of the mountains, it's as brown and dry on the other side. The range cuts off the moisture. Outback's as dry as a bone. Sometimes it rains too much in the valley, and sometimes it's a drought. Can't count on much here."

"Not altogether true," Shane said from under his hat, gazing straight ahead.

Nina gave him a sidelong glance full of unasked questions. Derrick was wrong. She sensed she could count on at least one thing here—uncertainty. It was at once an exciting and terrifying realization. There was no turning back now. But that was all right with her.

Chapter 5

Led by Shane hefting the ornate saddle and settling it carefully in the cargo hold, the dock boys, in a hurry to get moving, smoothly unloaded the cargo from the wagon and onto the riverboat moored along a wood dock. As eager as the dock boys were, a large flock of sheep that had been loaded earlier seemed even more impatient to get moving toward grazing lands. The animals bleated incessantly in what sounded to Nina like a mournful plea to be released.

Aboard the boat at last, Nina sat rather uncomfortably on a wooden seat next to an open window and looked around. The boat swayed from side to side, and for a fleeting moment a wave of queasiness washed over her, a sense memory from the ship voyage. She tried to set her mind against it, but every now and then a warm breeze sent forward the pungent odor of sheep manure and damp wool, triggering yet another wave of nausea in her stomach.

It seemed as if something new assaulted her senses

every other moment; there were so many new experiences to grasp. The most difficult might be in understanding the people. She shook her head. How was it that she and they supposedly spoke the same language, but at times they didn't seem to at all? Ordinary English words simply did not come out that way, especially from Derrick. She had difficulty catching some of the things he said, and half the time he seemed to be rhyming everything. When he and Shane spoke to the dock boys, she had no idea what they were saying, even though some of it appeared to be directed toward her and was followed by raucous laughter.

The boat pulled away from the dock, and Nina concentrated on the slowly passing landscape. The river valley was green and fertile, and the excursion on one of the Hunter River New Steam Navigation Company's iron paddlewheel vessels promised to be more pleasant than the wagon ride, at the very least.

Nina relaxed and let the cool breeze fan her moist brow and throat. Upon inspection, she discovered how truly dirty and wrinkled her skirt had become. Lifting the folds, she found the hem ragged and stained from the ground where she'd been forced to stop and go to the . . . loo. There was a long slit on one side; it was a mystery how it got there, and her shirtwaist was grimy and wrinkled. Apprehension filled her mind—this was no way to meet a new employer!

She reached into her bag and took out a mirror for the first time since preparing to leave Sydney, and the act further disheartened her. Her hair tumbled from its pins, and her cheeks, covered with tiny dirt particles, stung with unaccustomed dryness from sun and wind.

She took out a white handkerchief and tried to wipe the dirt away as best she could without water and soap. Her hair was almost impossible to control, what with the wind and dry air moving it about, causing flyaway strands to go their own way. Frustration welled up inside her. She was just plain miserable. A visual search around the boat told her there was no place available that offered enough privacy where she could rectify her state.

"Now here's the spot where we've seen the great white platypus. Seen him only twice on these trips," Derrick was saying as he passed by her seat.

"I've read about them," Nina replied in a friendly tone, even though she seriously doubted they were white.

"Oh, not this one," Derrick countered, scratching the back of his head.

"Aren't they all alike?"

"Nup, missy. This one's p'tiklar fond of ladies' hair. Been known to come right up out of the water, balance on his enormous tail, and with his great gaping bill, reach over the side of the boat and grab a snootful." He nodded his head knowingly.

"No!"

"Aye! From what I hear, he takes it back to his cave and makes a nest out of it for his young. Doesn't seem to be attracted to dark hair, though. Seems more interested in the brighter hair, the type the sun shines off."

Instinctively Nina's hand flew to the side of her loosening coiffure. She slid down the seat toward the center aisle while Derrick nodded approvingly, as if she'd made the right move.

Shane caught the tail end of the conversation as he strode down the deck, and supposed he should begin to rein in Derrick and his teasing. Nina wouldn't survive the first day if she was petrified all the time.

He slid in next to her, dropping a small dilly bag next to his feet. "Derrick does exaggerate some. It's best not to take everything he says as the gods' honest truth."

"Maybe," Derrick said out of the side of his mouth. "Maybe." Then he winked at Nina and strode away, scuffing his boot heels on the wood floor.

Nina looked out the open side window with some trepidation. Then Shane's logic took over in her mind. She'd succumbed to Derrick's teasing on the riverboat, and now she began to realize that he'd probably been spinning his tales about ferocious animals while they were on the wagon as well. However, there *had* been that kangaroo . . .

"Will you tell me more about Australia, and where I'll be working, please, Mr. Merritt?" Nina hoped she would receive some straightforward answers this time.

"Yes, my girl, if you will call me Shane."

"All right . . . Shane . . . if you will stop calling me 'my girl.'"

"Oh, now, I don't mean anything by that. Just a friendly something we say. You'll get used to it."

Nina looked doubtful. She had a strong feeling there would be things in Australia that she would have to try mightily to get used to.

Shane launched into a description of his country,

72

and the warmth and excitement in his voice told her that he held a deep love for it and Flame Tree, adding with a gleam in his eye, "but you'll see what I mean when you get there."

He told her about the lush green foliage near the mountains, and the tawny flatlands of the bush, baked dry by summer heat and long droughts. Tales of a wild, rugged country with boatloads of convicts still arriving from other lands to the outlying districts caused Nina to frown. When he added that there were probably more sheep than people before they stopped counting, she wondered if she herself would feel like a prisoner, or just part of a flock.

He described plants and animals with names so foreign to her she could not picture them in her mind in any kind of rational form—coolabah, eucalyptus, and other timber gum trees, and banksia, and animals and birds like emu, koala, and the platypus Derrick had spoken of, except that Shane's description was slightly different.

Tentatively she asked about Aborigines.

Shane frowned. "Being pushed farther and farther off their sacred lands by insensitive foreigners." That was all he would say.

"I'm sorry." Nina was deeply touched by the thought that people, no matter how "savage," were forced to leave their native lands through no fault of their own. There was a twinge of kinship with them in her heart. "No one should be made to live where they don't want to."

For a moment she drifted back home. A breeze caught a stray lock of her hair and blew it across her face. Wearily she lifted her hand to move it and to shoo away a fly at the same time, but Shane's hand was there first. He flicked lightly at the fly, then lifted the lock of hair and looped it around a tortoiseshell pin behind her ear.

Nina's soft gaze was fixed upon his face. His hand brushed her ear, and a tingle slithered down the back of her neck.

"I'm . . . a sight, I know," she said quietly. The sun felt warm on the back of her neck where the tingle had been.

"Aye, that you are, my girl," he responded as quietly.

Shane was so near that Nina could smell the unique air about him, a heady blend of outdoors and sky and soap and rain and an unnamed spice that stirred her blood. In the open neck of his shirt a thatch of sand-colored hair curled above the vee. Suddenly Nina felt the urge to find out if it felt as soft as it looked. If she could just nestle her head against his chest, close her eyes, breathe in the freshness of him . . .

Abruptly she drew her eyes away from his chest. Her cheeks burned with embarrassment, intensifying the heat already in them from the weather. Instinctively her hand flew to her face.

Shane sat motionless. For a moment he felt locked inside her faraway gaze, now fastened on him, and he wanted never to find the key. Then he noticed how she was gingerly pressing her fingertips against her reddened cheeks.

"Here, my girl," he said, reaching into his bag and producing a container of white cream. "Looks like our sun and dry wind have done some mean work on your skin."

"What's that?" she asked timidly, holding out her hand.

"Doctor Merritt's cure-all for foreign visitors' malady," he replied, ignoring her outstretched hand.

He scooped up a fingerful and gently patted it over her flushed face. She winced, whether at the sting or his touch he couldn't be sure, and pulled back.

"Now, now, hold still. It only hurts for a bit." He patted her skin tenderly, holding the back of her head with the other hand. "Very healing, very soothing," he murmured, caught up in the depths of her liquid eyes. He spread a thin layer lightly over her forehead and chin, and left a tiny dollop on the end of her pert nose. Then he spread the cream along her throat and lower, toward her collarbone. His eyes dropped toward the opening at the front of her blouse, and for a hazy moment he visualized his hands disappearing inside it, slipping lower, lower . . .

He shook his head, covered the container quickly, and handed it to her. "Here," he said hoarsely, "keep this. I'm sure you'll be needing it again."

She put her hand around the container and her fingers entwined with his briefly.

"Well, my girl, work to do." He slid his long frame out of the seat and stood up.

Her eyes still on his face, Nina tilted her head back to hold his vision. "When . . . once we're at Flame Tree, will we, will you be around the house often?" She remembered how he told her in Sydney that he didn't like being inside much, and her heart sank.

Shane took a deep breath. His eyes sparkled as he let it out. "More than you'll probably want me to, my girl. That is, if they'll let me inside the place at all!"

He turned then, and she watched his broad back and slim hips sway down the aisle and disappear around the deck.

Bone weary, she gave in to the heaviness in her eyelids and dozed for a while. Her nap was plagued by half-awake dreams of wild white animals, people speaking in rhymes, and Shane Merritt's inviting chest and teasing grin. The last dream was of herself bleating like a lost lamb somewhere from behind a huge rock where her only weapon for self-defense was a small shovel.

She awakened with a start at the sound of shouts and the jolt of the boat hitting the side of a long wooden dock. The dock was lined with men in brown or green hats, the brims of which were fastened up on one side; bright-colored loose shirts; lean-fitting pants; and slouchy leather boots. They reached for the hawsers thrown by the hands on the boat and tied them down quickly to stout wood pilings pointing up in threes every few feet along the dock. Nina smiled. The New York waterfront paled to dull gray in her memory as the action in front of her waved like a colorful flag over the water.

Sensing land and grass, the sheep set up a din of excited bleating and pawing of their small hooves. Their noise was almost deafening, and Nina watched as the men ignored them and shouted to hear each other over it.

She stood up quickly in her eagerness to get off, and was immediately rocked by vertigo as the boat moved in and out against the dock. The inside wall had a rope strung along it to hold life preservers, and grasping it she made her way to the foredeck while the dizziness in her head and the moistness forming over her stomach grew stronger.

By the time she reached the dock and was helped up onto it, she was shaking visibly. Shane watched her and fervently hoped the Mum wouldn't catch sight of her until she'd had a chance to pull herself together, for her own sake as well as his. He felt the urge to comfort her, assure her everything would be all right, but now one of the dock boys was calling him over.

Nina looked up wanly in Shane's direction and saw him turn away and go off to speak with the boys. She took a deep breath and pulled herself up to her full five feet three inches and started after him. A loose board in the dock caught the heel of her shoe and she tripped over her skirt and fell headlong toward Derrick's feet. Even as she felt herself falling, she heard a sickening rip and felt the heel tear away from the rest of her shoe.

Derrick grabbed her just before she hit the dock boards and pulled her upright. The last of the pins holding her hair fell out and the copper locks tumbled over her face. That was the last straw. She was so tired and frustrated, and felt so sick, she could not speak. All she could feel were hot tears pushing against the back of her eyes, and an intensified ringing in her ears that signaled she was about to faint.

Holding her up under her arms as if she were a rag doll, Derrick looked helplessly over his shoulder toward Shane, back at Nina, then back at Shane. Sensing her knees were about to buckle under her, and seeing Shane's back as he bent into conversation with one of the boys, Derrick did the only thing he could think of at the moment: he scooped Nina up in his arms, and with her bag dangling against his leg, carried her in a half-run toward Shane. Shane turned around just as he reached him with his disheveled burden, and Derrick dropped her directly into his outstretched arms.

"I think this belongs to you, mate," Derrick muttered. Then he was off at a run up the hill toward the house.

"Welcome to Flame Tree, Nina Cole." Shane turned around and shifted her weight in his arms.

Through heavy-lidded eyes Nina saw the roof of a low sprawling house beyond several thick stands of cedar. She stared up at it, then at Shane, then back at the house. She stiffened in his arms, blinked back her tears, and gritted her teeth as he carried her up the hill.

"If you don't mind, I believe I'm capable of walking," she asserted.

"Oh, I wouldn't hear of it, my girl," Shane replied, a taunting twinkle in his eyes as he bounced her along. "A lady of your stature should arrive at her new place of employment riding in style."

He pulled her closer, and the female warmth emanating from her open blouse filled his senses and unnerved him for a moment. He felt stronger than ever, her body an easy burden, and it wouldn't have mattered if the house were a million kilometers away.

Nina could tell Shane had no intention of putting her down, and while propriety commanded she insist he do it, in her heart she knew she wouldn't. She could feel the hard muscles in his arms along her body, and she wanted to be carried into eternity by them. Her energy left her, and she relaxed, letting her head bob against his broad shoulder. Vaguely she knew she'd better snap out of the fantasy and wake up. She'd need a great burst of energy once she was inside the house. And he was already at the back door, knocking on it with his foot.

"'Sakes alive, Shane Merritt! Welcome home, love!" Maude Whittaker exclaimed as she opened the door. "Lord love a duck, was there an accident?"

Shane dropped Nina unceremoniously in the middle of the huge kitchen, shaking his head and laughing while she stared at him. Maude gave Nina a once-over look, and then the dawn of recognition broke over her round face.

"Ah, Derrick said you brought someone for the Mum. What happened to her?"

Shane nodded, stifling a laugh, then kissed Maude's ruddy cheek. "I couldn't begin to tell you . . ."

"Maude?" The sound of a woman's voice echoed down the back hallway to the kitchen.

"Uh-oh. You haven't seen me, Maudie!" Shane whispered, a hasty finger planted across his lips. He disappeared out the back door.

The kitchen door flew open, and a perfectly coiffed, frail but imposing-looking woman came into the room. Impeccably dressed in a dark silk print, she seemed to Nina to be very out of place there.

"Maude, I've just seen your husband," her thin voice carried a tone of authority, "and that must mean Shane has returned—who is this?" She stopped

79

with one hand on the door the moment she caught sight of Nina.

"Aye, Derrick's back. Shane's probably unloading cargo." Maude wiped her hands over and over on the large print pinny that covered her long green dress.

"I do not enjoy repeating myself, Maude. Who is this woeful creature?"

Maude looked at Nina, then back at the woman standing in the doorway. "Her, ma'am?"

"Yes, her. *Maude . . .*" she urged in a calm voice.

Nina's insides were quaking. For some unexplained reason she felt herself curtsy, and in as even a voice as she could muster, said, "Nina Cole, ma'am. I'm your new . . . companion."

The woman's expression did not change. Her composure remained well under control. She inhaled deeply.

"Dinner is served promptly at eight. I shall expect you in the dining room at seven forty-five."

With a swish of silk petticoats she turned and swept out of the room, leaving the kitchen door swinging behind her. Maude let out a long, low sigh.

Nina's stomach relaxed. "Yes, welcome to Flame Tree, Nina Cole," she repeated Shane's words under her breath.

Chapter 6

Freshly bathed, her hair washed and pinned up in loose coils, Nina sat on the high bed in a guest room. Maude's daughter, a thin, open-faced girl named Anthia, had drawn the bath in a handsome oval copper tub, and brought towels and soap. She had helped her unpack, hung the few things Nina had brought with her in the cedar-lined clothespress, and taken away Nina's ruined clothes.

Nina looked around the room. It was more luxurious than any she'd ever been in. She ran her hand over the white candlewick bedspread covering the four-poster. Overhead was an intricately laced canopy. The wallcovering was pale blue and made of a fabric that felt so lustrous it might have been silk.

Spread over the shining wood floor was a wool rug dyed a deep blue. A comfortable blue print upholstered wing chair sat next to a white stone fireplace with an oak mantel. An oak commode with a mirror and towel rack stood against one wall, and next to that was a low oak stand with an ironstone pitcher and bowl. A pastoral oil painting framed in dark red wood hung above the fireplace. There were lovely handpainted glass oil lamps in every corner, and extra candleholders and candles.

Imagine this! She, a servant on an Australian sheep station, but living in a room fit for a princess. Aunt Sadie would never believe it!

A light rap came at the door, and Nina rose out of her happy trance to open it. Anthia stood with her hands behind her back. Standing next to her, bearing a curious expression on its wide face, stood a large, heavily furred dog. He looked up at her with what appeared to be a question in his eyes. One eye was brown and the other blue.

"It's almost seven forty-five," Anthia spoke in her breathy small voice. "My, you look nice, Miss Nina."

"Thank you, Anthia."

Nina spread her hands over the skirt of her best cotton frock. Cream-colored, with a high neck, pleated yoke, and long sleeves, it was nipped in at the waist above the full skirt, which fell softly over her hips. Added touches of cream tatted lace at the neck and sleeve edges gave it a soft, feminine look. She had spent a long and careful time washing and pressing the folds and pleats some weeks ago, never dreaming that when she wore it next she would be in such an incredible place.

"Who is your lovely friend?" Nina bent down and patted the dog's head.

Anthia smiled down at him and ran her hand along the dog's back, an easy thing for her to do, since his back came up as high as her hip.

"This is Mate. He's my best friend. He works at the

out station with all the other dogs. 'Ceptin' he's the head dog of all," she said, great pride evident in her voice.

Mate's voluminous fur was a combination of several shades of black and white, tipped with a shade of charcoal so deep it almost looked blue. A copper mask surrounded his eyes. His bobbed-tailed back quarters wagged vigorously, and his ears atop a bearlike face flopped, then perked, then flopped again, adding to the animated expression in his bicolor eyes.

"Well, how do you do, Mate?" Nina bent down to scratch behind his ear. "I hope you'll let me be your friend, too."

In friendly response, Mate sprang up on his hind legs to deliver his greeting, furry face to Nina's astonished one. Before she knew what was happening, he'd placed two large paws on the bodice of her dress just above her breasts.

Anthia yelled and pulled Mate back, but not before he'd left two distinctly dark imprints on the pleated yoke. The two young women stood like statues, their faces stricken.

"An-thee-ya!" Maude called up the stairs to her daughter. "What's keeping you? Miss Cole is to be in the dining room promptly—now!"

For a moment Nina stood stockstill. Then she turned and ran frantically toward the clothespress.

"Oh," she wailed, "what will I wear now?"

Anthia ran after her, pulling up the end of her white pinny and dabbing at the two dirty pawprints on Nina's chest. "No time for that, Miss," she said in a worried voice. "You'd best hie yourself to the dining room right away!"

She grabbed Nina's arm and fairly lifted her off her feet, dragging her down the stairway. Mate, the culprit, followed close behind, his offending paws making padded clumps on each carpeted stair.

Anthia pushed Nina through the dark wood double doors of the richly paneled dining room, letting them come quietly together behind her. The doors tapped her lightly on the behind as they closed, forcing her to take one quick step into the room.

Stretched before her, dressed in white linen, was an elegant dining table aglow with white candles in etched crystal globes, and adorned with crystal bowls of fresh orchids, purple lilies, and other flowers in shades of crimson, purple, and white, set off by deep-green waxy leaves. A delicate scent of what she could only describe as expensive chocolate drifted out of them and floated in the air. The table was set for four, though it could easily have accommodated twenty.

The clearing of a throat startled her and she tore her gaze away from the beautifully appointed table. A sharp-featured young man in a dark formal suit with a stiff white high-collared shirt sat lounging at the side of the far end.

"So, you're what Shane dragged back on the boat with the rest of the cargo." He tipped the chair back further, and chewed on an unlit cheroot. "And we all thought he had a sharp eye for good breeding. Must be it only runs to sheep."

"I beg your pardon?" Nina asked shyly. "We haven't met, I'm Nina Cole." She held out her hand in friendly greeting.

The young man ignored her gesture and laughed

in a high-pitched laugh. "That's not all you've begged for, I'll wager!" He spat out a piece of tobacco. "It appears the lower classes are the same everywhere."

Nina was considering backing out of the dining room when the doors opened silently and the matriarch of the house stepped in.

"That will be quite enough," she spoke with a superior strength in her voice that belied her frail exterior. However, it did not provoke the young man to have the courtesy to stand when she entered the room.

The woman walked with regal posture toward the end of the table, her long, flowing emerald-green gown making an elegant swishing sound along the richly patterned Oriental carpet. Ramrod straight, she glided along the floor with the use of an intricately carved ivory cane. Her sungold hair, only lightly brushed with gray, was still coiffed with every strand in place, and from her ears swung emerald drops which picked up and reflected the candlelight. Behind her, head up and just as ramrod straight, strode a white Persian cat with a heavily bejeweled collar around its thickly maned neck.

Passing Nina without a word, the woman turned and stood at the head of the table. The cat nestled at her feet with a small sigh of familiarity. Taking first a long, hard-edged, sweeping gaze over Nina, the woman then made a circular motion with her thin, long-fingered hand indicating that she was to turn full around. Nina complied, her toes pinching in the ends of her best shoes, causing the turn to be a little faltering.

Producing a thin volume of poetry from the pocket of her dress, the woman opened it, and handed it to the young man. He handed the book to Nina without looking at her.

"You're to read this—if you think you've mind enough to," he said.

Several verses of Robert Browning's "Love Among the Ruins," printed in the smallest script she'd ever seen, lay on the goldleafed page. Nina looked up at the commanding figure at the other end of the table. The graceful hand waved toward her to read it.

"Where the quiet-coloured end of evening smiles . . ." Nina began quietly. In spite of the presence of three people at the table, she felt as if her voice echoed around an empty and cavernous room.

The young man chuckled and shifted in his chair. Nina took a deep breath and began again, stumbling over the words *". . . thro' the twilight, stray or stop . . . As they crop—"*

She began again, and managed to get through the first three verses without stumbling more than two or three times. Her mouth was dry and her throat seemed to be closing behind every word she uttered.

The older woman waved a hand to stop her. She fastened a long, hard stare at Nina, silently appraising her performance. "Adequate," she pronounced. "You may be seated." Nina started to pull out a chair. "But . . ." came the strong voice again, "the next time you appear at table, you will please be good enough to wear a clean frock." She seated herself regally straight in the high-backed chair.

Nina's face colored, and she sat down to yet another chuckle and snort about the lower classes from the young man.

"Enough!" boomed the voice from the frail body.

"Yes, Mother," came the meek reply.

Maude pushed through the double doors hip first, carrying a silver tray bearing stemmed crystal glasses filled with fruit.

"Ah, kiwi for the Kiwi, I see," the young man chided, using the Australian tag for foreigners. "How appropriate, Maude."

His mother glared at him, then spoke in a weary voice. "Maude, why is my elder son not at dinner?"

Maude shrugged silently and served the exotic fruit cup.

"Late, as ever my dear big brother can be," the young man put in, ignoring the frown that passed over his mother's face. "And no doubt improperly dressed, he'll be. Fancies himself a ringer instead of . . ." He made a wide, sweeping gesture with his arm, and finished in exaggerated court announcement, ". . . Lord of the manor."

Nina was only half-aware of the conversation between mother and son. With honest curiosity she inspected the fruit, pale green wedges with dark specks at their centers, a slice of lemon perched at the lip of the glass. Her first taste of the fruit reminded her of a combination of strawberry and banana.

Maude was about to take hurried leave from the room when the double doors burst open. Nina's face dropped in shock. Shane Merritt entered the room.

He looked nothing like the sheep herder she'd met in Sydney. Now he was dressed in an expensive dark blue suit, the jacket cut wide in the shoulder and narrow in the waist. His trousers were creased to perfection, and below them a pair of black boots shone brilliantly in the faint light. But there was no mistaking the crop of sandy hair and the clear blue eyes.

The sight of Shane Merritt took Nina's breath away.

He made a dashing figure as he swept along the table to the woman seated at the end. "Forgive me, Beautiful," he bade her as he heartily kissed her cheek.

The woman smiled warmly for the first time since Nina had laid eyes on her, and patted his cheek. "Of course you are forgiven, my son. I am so pleased that you have returned to Flame Tree," she said crisply, "and I do appreciate your thoughtfulness in providing a companion for me. I wish you'd discussed it with me first. But your choice is acceptable."

"I knew it the moment I saw her, Mum." Shane looked over at Nina's astonished face with an almost audacious wink. Undaunted by his mother's admonition, he went on brightly, "You've been introduced, then—or haven't you? Miss Nina Cole, may I present my beautiful mother, Vanessa Windsor Merritt . . ." He made a sweeping gesture and bow toward his mother. His other hand swept in the young man's direction. ". . . and my irrepressible brother, Colin."

Nina sat speechless, still shocked at Shane's entrance and even more shocked to discover his identity. Vanessa Windsor Merritt smiled faintly toward her.

Colin sipped a glass of water, and without looking at her, muttered, "Charmed, I'm sure."

Shane seated himself across from Colin and Nina, his chair strategically placed at his mother's right hand. He smiled broadly at Nina, and suddenly the room didn't feel as empty as it had to her, as if it had been filled with heated excitement by his presence.

"So, my girl," he said, looking directly at Nina. "Have you settled into this old barn yet?"

Nina's jaw froze shut. Shane Merritt was the biggest liar she'd ever met! He didn't just work on this estate, as he'd led her to believe; he owned it, and the woman for whom she was to work was his *mother!*

He read the look in her eyes and spoke for her, covering her agitation and protecting himself from the barrage of words that threatened to erupt from her. "No need to answer. Flame Tree is a bit overwhelming at first, I admit. Say . . . what a pretty frock. But what's that dark stain on the bodice?"

He stood up and leaned across the table, napkin in hand, as if about to wipe away the spots. She pulled away from him, a look of horror on her face, and he sat back down with a mock dramatic hands-off gesture.

"Ah, I see now—Mate's left his usual mark of greeting on a stranger. Not to worry, my girl, it's just his way. Friendly sort, he is, just like the rest of us." He smiled and winked at her.

Nina colored more deeply with every "my girl" Shane uttered. He was doing it on purpose when he knew she could not respond in kind without appearing rude in front of his family. Both Vanessa and Colin Merritt seemed to be waiting for her to react.

She took a sip of water to give herself time to regain some composure, and glared at Shane over the rim of the glass. He was still smiling, an engaging tease playing about his eyes. She swallowed, set the glass down slowly and carefully, then leveled her gaze on him.

"Mate is indeed friendly," she said sweetly, "almost as friendly as the other ... ah ... pets you were playing with in Sydney." She held her eyes steady on him. "It's a shame you couldn't have brought them home with you, too. They seemed very ... companionable."

Shane's eyes crinkled in enjoyment of the verbal sparring. Nina Cole surprised him, and he liked it. He lifted a wineglass to his lips, holding her eyes with his own, and offered the merest hint of a toast to her.

"Touché," he said, and swallowed the contents.

Chapter 7

Over dinner Nina thoughtfully observed the three Merritts as they interacted with each other, or didn't, as was the case with Colin most of the time. She loved listening to Shane talk and grew more intrigued with the lilt of his voice as he related to his mother the events of his latest journey to America. His voice mounted in enthusiasm as he told her about his success with American wool importers, but added how eager he was to get out to the flocks and jackaroos.

"But perhaps Colin's already been out." Shane sent an intentionally hopeful glance toward his brother, knowing full well that Colin rarely went near the flocks and herders.

"I wouldn't want to take that distinct pleasure away from you, dear brother," Colin replied disagreeably. "Mother, is there other wine than this in the cellar? It's quite unacceptable." He sipped, then grimaced.

Vanessa swirled the wine in her crystal goblet, and

slowly set it down on the table. "This is a fine wine from one of our best valley vintners. I chose it especially for Shane's homecoming dinner."

"I've developed a taste for French wines of late," Colin sniffed, "but I'm sure their delicate bouquet would be lost on the less cultured of my dinner partners." He sent an altogether disdainful glance at Nina.

Vanessa was silent, her mouth set in a firm line. She picked up her goblet and stared thoughtfully into its contents.

"It's a lovely wine, Mum." Shane drained his glass. "But I'm afraid my taste has become a bit jaded. In New York I found more ambers and ales than wine. Or perhaps they found me!"

Remembering her meeting with Shane in the MacQuarie tavern, Nina thought his last remark completely appropriate, and would have altered it only by adding that other things had found him as well.

She worked hard to avoid looking at him throughout dinner, but at times found the task quite impossible. The candlelight caught thick strands of his hair and sent off rays of gold and silver. When he talked of how glad he was to be back home, his eyes sparkled with sapphire facets. His laugh was warm, and his voice cut through Colin's continual barrage of icy remarks to melt the strength of their impact on her. Too often her gaze was inextricably drawn to Shane's face—to his eyes when he wasn't looking at her, and to his full mouth when he was.

He chided her about their wagon trip and river voyage, making her face turn a deep crimson as he described her experience with the lack of facilities in the bush, and Derrick's preposterous stories. With every injection of "my girl" Nina shot him a look that would have withered a lesser man.

Colin saw that this exchange was not lost on his mother. He knew she felt the spark of electricity between Shane and the American woman, and was not pleased. He, on the other hand, sensed Nina's presence and Shane's reaction to her as a way of bolstering his own flagging ego. Perhaps he could beat his brother just once, and in the process could use that to endear himself more to the mother he had grown to resent.

"My dear Miss Cole," Colin sat up straight for the first time since Nina had entered the room, "you mustn't let my brother's crude sense of humor make your stay here unpleasant. I do hope you will allow me to escort you on a tour of Flame Tree and the out stations. I'd be most happy to answer your questions and afford you the possibility of the company of another, more genteel, Merritt. Will you do me the honor?"

Surprised at Colin's sudden change of attitude toward her, Nina looked first at Mrs. Merritt and then at Shane, unsure of how to answer. Colin had made her feel uncomfortable with his earlier remarks, yet she knew she must be polite to him now. She certainly didn't want to offend Mrs. Merritt. And she supposed it was quite possible that Shane was relieved to be rid of his responsibility toward her and would welcome his brother's willingness to be helpful.

The air hung heavy with curious anticipation of

her answer. Nina felt uncomfortable searching for something appropriate to say. At last she felt confident enough to speak.

"That's very kind of you, Mr. Merritt," she said quietly. "However, I've not been apprised of my duties yet, and so I cannot say that I will have the time . . ."

"This sort of thing does not have to be discussed now," Vanessa interrupted. "Shane, I will meet you in the study in fifteen minutes. I would like to have a private word with Miss Cole. Colin, you are excused."

With a few clipped words, Vanessa Merritt had ended the dinner hour and succinctly arranged the time of everyone else in the room. Colin threw down his napkin and stalked out of the room, letting the heavy doors swing widely as he left.

Shane excused himself and stood away from the table. "I hope you will be happy at Flame Tree, my . . . Nina. I'll see you now and again. G'devo." He looked directly into her eyes for a moment, then walked quietly from the room.

Nina watched his broad back and the wheat-colored hair that curled over his collar in bright contrast as he smoothly pushed his shoulders through the dining room doors. All warmth left the room, and Nina felt the kind of loneliness she had during her last conversation with her aunt.

"Miss Cole," Vanessa Merritt began, a distinct iciness in her voice that added to the chill of the room, "I think it is imperative that we set down a few things, some guidelines for you concerning your employment at Flame Tree."

"Yes, ma'am." Nina sat attentively straight.

"First, you are privileged to take all of your meals in the dining room with us. Breakfast at eight, luncheon at one, dinner at eight. You are obliged to be prompt . . . and neatly dressed. Tea is served at four in the second parlor. At that time you will read aloud whatever I have selected for that day.

"You will not accompany me to my social engagements. However, from time to time I may take you to Parramatta for shopping, but that will be the least of your duties and privileges. You will find Flame Tree to be equipped to meet your few needs.

"Your evenings will be free after dinner unless I request your presence, but you would be wise to retire by ten. You may have every other Sunday off to do as you wish, but permission must be granted for use of any servant or conveyance. Is all of this understood?"

Nina nodded woodenly. "Yes, ma'am."

"And one more thing, Miss Cole," Vanessa stood up with the use of her cane, pulling herself up straight with some discomfort. "My sons have separate lives, apart from yours. Colin is young and impressionable, with much to learn. And Shane has full responsibility for Flame Tree and all its inhabitants—except you. The day will come when he will marry an acceptable young woman from one of the valley families. Strength lies in the acquisition of land, and his suitable marriage will ensure Merritt bloodlines and property holdings for generations. It was the dream of his father, and now the will of his mother. Do we understand each other?"

"Yes, ma'am." Nina's response was automatic, even as she swallowed over the hard knot in her throat. She started to rise, but was stopped abruptly as Vanessa Merritt spoke again.

"Something else you should know, Miss Cole. I did *not* ask for a companion; I have neither the need nor the desire for one. All my needs are met by my son and Flame Tree. It was Shane's concern for my welfare that prompted him to make these arrangements, and I will not disappoint him by being less than gracious in my gratitude. But neither will I tolerate anything less than a peaceful coexistence while you are here.

"In a respectable amount of time you will find that you cannot acclimate yourself to the life on a sheep station in a foreign land, and will wish to return to America and the familiarity of your home. I trust we understand each other, and that it will be unnecessary to discuss this any further."

The two women stood, locked in a gaze of conflict. Vanessa glided along the opposite side of the table, the imperious Persian cat following haughtily behind. She paused at the doors and turned back to Nina.

"You will speak to no one of our conversation. You are dismissed for the evening. Do sleep well." Then she turned and was gone, the doors barely moving from her exit.

Nina was stunned. Vanessa Merritt was not at all the frail old lady she'd seemed. Nina had not been prepared for a speech so precisely and eloquently delivered from such a strong-minded, purposeful woman. She was beginning to suspect that she had been dropped into the middle of a complex family situation even more uncomfortable than the one she had shared with her aunt.

Escaping out a window and running away was going to be nigh onto impossible here. She'd never made a rash move in her life, and the one time she had had turned into a full-scale disaster before it even got started, it seemed.

And Shane Merritt was at the heart of it. But . . . was it possible Shane might be an unwitting victim in this as well? Perhaps in his misguided notion that his mother needed a companion . . . No, he certainly could not be unaware of his mother's desire to ensure the correct propagation of future Merritt generations and wealth. That was not something a mother could withhold from a son . . . or was it?

She felt the fool, a naive, unsuspecting fool. She was positive that at this very moment Shane was laughing over her utter gullibility at believing she was going to serve as companion to a sweet old lady. Certainly he knew his own mother! Was everything in life just one big joke to him?

Maude entered the dining room quietly, apologizing for disturbing Nina.

"Oh, Mrs. Whittaker, you are not disturbing me. I was dismissed, and I'm afraid I've been lingering when I shouldn't have. Here, let me help you clear the dishes." Nina picked up a couple of the plates and began to stack them as she had at home.

"Oh, no, no, Miss Cole—Anthia will help me as soon as she has finished ironing tomorrow's linens. It's not your place to do scullery work." Maude gathered as many dishes as she could on a long oval tray.

Nina's eyes began to glisten with the first flush of

97

tears. Maude set the tray down and hustled around the table to her side.

"Now, now, no need for that. You're just homesick, is all. You'll get used to our ways here, you'll see." She placed a strong arm around Nina's slim shoulders and patted her arm.

"I'm not so sure I will. And even if I could, there won't be time . . ."

Nina caught herself before she said more. During the moments with Vanessa Merritt she'd forgotten her plan to work until the next ship sailed for America, or at least the one following it. Now she realized Vanessa Merritt had underscored that decision with a command of her own: in an odd turn of events, she was making Nina's eventual departure that much easier to achieve. At least Nina would not feel she'd done someone a disservice by accepting a position she knew she'd keep for only a short while. Yet something had occurred along the way, and she'd not become aware of it until this moment—somehow she'd come to think of not leaving Flame Tree at all.

"All right, come to the kitchen," Maude was saying. "You can't help, mind you, but you can sit and keep us company while we work. But don't breathe a word of this to the Mum—she'd have my hide!"

Nina followed Maude's ample figure to the kitchen and spent the next hour in the relaxed company of her daughter and Derrick as they ate their supper. And she felt at home.

98

Chapter 8

Shane waited for his mother in the study. As he always did after a long trip, he gazed at the image of his father in an oil painting which hung over the ornate mahogany mantel. In it Daniel Merritt seemed oddly out of place in his own home, dressed as he was in the garb of a sheep herder, his bushman's hat perched on a bent knee above a black leather boot that rested on a wool bale.

Shane was so engrossed in the painting, and in the stirring in the back of his mind of the wonderful times past that it recalled, that he did not hear his mother enter the room behind him. She closed the heavy door noiselessly and stood gazing at her son's back for a long time before she broke the silence.

"You are discovering how very much you are like him, aren't you, my son?" Vanessa asked softly. Her eyes traced Shane's sharp jawline, identical to that of her beloved husband.

"No, not discovering. I've always known that we're still joined at the heart, Mum. I was just thinking how different it all is since he's been gone. But then . . . I always think that." He turned to face her. "Don't you ever long for the way it was? The old days, when we worked side-by-side at lambing time, or in the shearing pens?"

"No, I'm afraid I don't, Shane. The only times I would want to recapture are when your father commanded Flame Tree at the height of its glory."

"I've never thought of him as commanding, I guess. He had such a gentle hand with everything he touched."

"Yes. Well, times have changed. Greed has changed them. With the outrageous open stealing of animals, and the conflicts between stockmen over grazing lands, a gentle hand only brings loss. And now, with the discovery of gold . . . it turns heads. One must be strong, single-minded in defense of home and property. We must hold onto the land forever—at any cost."

"Now, Mum, I'm not so sure everyone has to live that way. He wouldn't have handled things with an iron fist, I'm sure." He gazed lovingly up at the strong, kind face of his father.

"Don't be so quick to judge what might have been Daniel's actions. You did not know him as I did." His mother moved to a settee near a wall of books. "Shane, there are more pressing matters that we must discuss, and you must think about them in the new ways of today."

Shane sat in a dark red leather wing chair opposite her. He had never known his mother to speak so harshly and in such dire tones.

"I fear we shall lose Flame Tree if we do not take

drastic measures to ensure otherwise." At her son's astonished look, she added quickly, "It won't happen tomorrow, but the possibility exists. And you may not know this, but, Colin . . ." she sighed wearily, "Colin has not been . . . the contributing partner I thought he would. I know, I've had a hand in it. Spoiled him as a child, gave him too much. And now . . ."

"He doesn't do a lick of work. Never has."

Vanessa searched Shane's face for signs of bitterness in his response. Detecting none, she continued, "He wasn't born to it, as you were, and he didn't possess the robust health you enjoyed."

Shane harkened back in his mind to his childhood. His father had him working by his side from the time he could walk, and he had loved it. But Colin always clung to his mother, who alternated between coddling him and almost ignoring him once her new social standing was established with their growing wealth and their increased influence on the inhabitants of the valley. As a result, Colin was weak, given to bouts of stomach ailments which Shane supposed were nothing more than bids for attention.

". . . And now I'm afraid he is involved with some rather unsavory characters who expect to get rich overnight with gold," Vanessa's voice penetrated his thoughts. "He spends far too much of his time away from Flame Tree, gambling and carousing, and who knows what all, and returns only long enough to obtain more money to pay off his debts and start all over again. He . . . what is it they call it? Grubstakes, I think. He gives money to subsidize illiterate miners, and in most cases they are foreigners, Americans. He

101

thinks they'll strike it big—bigger and much faster than anyone else, because they work like bulls with bull intelligence—and he'll become rich because they won't be smart enough to claim it for themselves."

"Why do you help him, Mum?"

"Because . . . he seems unable to help himself, and because perhaps I've contributed to his lack of determination and ability. But now that you're back, Shane, perhaps, you can find a way to direct him."

Shane let out a long sigh and spent the next few moments in silent, hard thought. He realized how much he'd romanticized the past and had chosen not to see how much the present was changing. All he'd ever longed for was a simple life, doing what he loved to do most of all, raising sheep and selling wool, and living free. The growth of Merritt wealth had certainly afforded him much more than he'd ever dreamed, but with it and his father's death came complications of the kind he'd never wanted. And loss of real freedom.

Nina Cole did not know how lucky she'd been living in New York, as far as he was concerned. Nina Cole: her face flashed across his mind without warning, those aquamarine eyes wide, framed by that mass of copper hair. He supposed this might be a good time to speak to the Mum about her.

"Ah, about Nina Cole, Mum . . ."

"Yes?" Vanessa set her jaw.

"I hired her without thinking things through completely. I didn't prepare her for . . . for anything. She has no money. She's in need of clothes and things, and, well, all I was thinking about was

102

making life more pleasant for you. I should probably admit that I made a mistake bringing her here, but . . ."

"Thank you, my son, for your consideration," Vanessa said quickly. "I think we can help poor Miss Cole rather nicely. She can stay for a while, three, perhaps four months. Then you can tell her that . . ." She looked as if a plan was forming in her mind. ". . . That Colin is taking a more active interest in being my companion. You can save face that way, keep it in the family. You can book passage for her on the ship to America when you send the wool. She will have had an adventure to share with all of her friends, and . . . it will be done with."

Shane listened intently to his mother, and winced when she referred to Nina as "poor Miss Cole." The idea of sending her back to America along with the shipment of wool made him uncomfortable. It was certainly a practical idea, but it made him feel as if Nina were nothing more than another Merritt commodity. He didn't like that at all. The idea of sending Nina back to America in the first place was a notion he was beginning to feel unwilling to accept.

Shane spoke with authority. "I believe Nina has the strength and the backbone to survive here. But if you really think you don't need anyone, perhaps there's something else she could do."

"I do not need anyone, Shane, but you. In the meantime, take care she does not develop an infatuation for you. That would never do. You're quite handsome, you know, and a poor child like that, unused to the ways of a sophisticated man . . .

well, she could have a bad time of it. You understand."

"Nina's hardly a child, Mum," he said, and he
knew he was defending her to his mother.

"Oh, but my dear, she certainly is. And much in
need of refinement. I'm sure she'll be much happier
in her own element. You see that I'm right about this,
don't you?"

"Well, I can see that you're certainly adamant
about it, dear Mum," he teased her, and bent over to
kiss her cheek. "Now, what of your health? We
haven't spoken about it. Have you been feeling
well?" He was careful not to give away Derrick's
confidence, and he hoped his mother would be
honest with him.

"My health is just fine, Shane," she replied evenly.
"Oh, I have the old problem with my heart, but if I
keep my life calm and satisfying, there is no reason
why I shouldn't be here for a long time, love."

"You'd tell me if anything changed, wouldn't
you?" He took his mother's small hands into his
own.

"Yes, love, I would." She picked up her appoint-
ment book. "Well, now that you're back, I think we
should plan a festive evening for all our friends and
neighbors, don't you?"

"Ah, Mum, you know I don't like splashy dos. And
besides, it seems we should be putting our funds to
better use."

"Nonsense. We can certainly afford to have a party
now and then. It looks right, you know. Time you
were reacquainted with certain people. And . . .
there are several young ladies who wish to be

formally introduced to you, my handsome son." She smiled and reached up to lightly run the backs of her fingers over his smooth cheek.

"Aye! I'm sure of that one!" Shane stood up quickly, escape on his mind.

"Now, Shane, it's time you began to think of one or two of the suitable young ladies in the valley. I should like to live long enough to be a grandmother, you know. And it wouldn't hurt to consider one of them, especially when adjoining land might be part of the dowry." She sent a coy look in his direction.

"Dowry! I didn't think people thought about dowries anymore. Anyway, I have no desire to recoup our failing fortune by getting myself tied to some spoiled, willful young fluff who'll have me in tow for the rest of my days! If it happens naturally someday, and I rather doubt it will, well, then, it happens. But in the meantime I am doing my bloody damnedest to avoid that unhappy lot as best I can!"

"Shane Daniel Merritt! You will control your tongue, please."

"Sorry, Mum, but please don't concern yourself with my matrimonial state. I'll have my hands full enough trying to sort out the entanglements with Colin and Flame Tree." He bent down and kissed his mother warmly. "And now, I think I'll go to bed. I'm suddenly weary to the bone." He kissed her again.

Vanessa leaned into his kiss. "Good night, son. It's good to have you back." She watched her son with intense love in her eyes as he left the study.

Vanessa had no intention of relenting in her determination to steer Shane in the direction she wanted him to go in matters of the heart. She had caught the electricity that had sparked between her son and Nina Cole at the dinner table. For the moment, she suspected that they were unaware of it themselves. But there was no mistaking it, and it would be only a matter of time before they realized it as well. She'd felt it herself so many years before with Daniel Merritt.

The attraction between the highborn Vanessa Windsor and Daniel Merritt, a jackaroo in her father's employ, had grown so strong so quickly that at last they could not keep away from each other. Although it was quite unplanned, and too soon to be proper, she'd discovered she was carrying his child. In the face of vehement family opposition, and against the laws of the Church of England, they'd run away to be married, worked shares on a sheep station, and produced Shane. It was the hardest and yet the happiest time of her life. They worked side by side, long and hard, to rise above poverty. Her family disinherited her and never forgave her for what they thought was a smear over their social standing in Sydney. She would not let history repeat itself through Shane, and she would not weaken Flame Tree's strength, nor lose it to anyone. Flame Tree belonged to Shane, it was his birthright. Colin was another matter.

She walked to her writing desk and set about making plans for a lavish welcome home party.

Chapter 9

Feeling more comfortable a little more than a week later, Nina discovered what a glorious place Flame Tree was when she took a leisurely exploration of the house and immediate grounds.

The house sprawled in two directions from a central core, and was built of sandstone blocks quarried on the spot at the time of construction. Made of a unique form of corrugated sheet iron hand-formed by an ironmonger in Bathurst, the roof's dark-red scalloped edges stood out in striking contrast against the warm gold of the sandstone walls.

All about the grounds were lush green giant tree ferns, and rhododendron bushes with blossoms of rose and amethyst splashing among dark, waxy leaves. Stands of thick cedars and turpentines lined the outer edges of the expansive back garden, while coolabah and other gum trees provided perches and cover for bellbirds and mimicking lyrebirds. Flanking the entrance and lining the long, circular drive to the front veranda were wide-spreading flame trees.

According to Maude, who had known Vanessa and Daniel since they were first married, as soon as they'd taken possession of the land, the Merritts had planted a single flame tree at the site upon which the corner of their new house was to stand. The tree signified their love—stemming from one base and spreading in grand profusion in all directions. And it was still there, twisted by time and prevailing winds, but aflame overhead with the reddest of blossoms.

Vanessa Windsor Merritt was a daunting woman, of that there was little doubt, but Nina admired her directness, her strength, her determination and commitment to the things she believed in. It mattered not whether Nina agreed with her. Nina understood the most important things to Vanessa Merritt were Shane, Colin, and Flame Tree, and not necessarily in that order. She loved Maude's story, and wished she could have the chance to know the Mum better. But that was a wish that would not have the time to come true.

Nina's most trusted friends were Maude and Anthia, and without them she knew she'd still feel a bit lost. She was even growing accustomed to Derrick and his teasing, and she was genuinely fond of him. Whenever she was among them she was reminded of what it was like when she was a little girl, at home with mother and father.

From the sewing room Maude had unearthed some khaki fabric last used to make trousers for Derrick. With it she fashioned a long skirt and jacket for Nina, replacing her green traveling suit, which had been deemed unsalvageable after the journey from Sydney. She sewed some white blouses from cotton pillowslip fabric, and two long petticoats from thin sheeting. More skirts were constructed from remnants of green and brown light wool. With those and the painstakingly cleaned cream cotton frock she'd worn to dinner the first night, Nina appeared neatly dressed whenever she was in the company of Vanessa Merritt.

Shane had been to dinner only twice during the week since. He spent a great deal of time with the flocks and herders at the out station. Nina had become painfully aware of how she looked for him in the dining room every evening, and felt quite disappointed when it was clear he wasn't coming. A place was always set for him, as if he might walk into the room at any moment. Nina could feel the Mum's hope that he would come, too, and she was less talkative when he didn't. Sometimes the dinner hour would pass in complete silence, especially if Colin was absent as well.

After breakfast on one of her exploration mornings, the air was still cool and fragrant with damp earth as Nina walked along the privet hedges and tree ferns. She'd made a decision the night before. If all she had here were a few months, she was going to see all there was to see, and learn as much as she could.

With the climbing sun warming her skin and the moist air beginning to fill with the fragrance of eucalyptus, Nina felt a sense of her own body and private thoughts as never before. She decided to be a bit braver this morning and go beyond the back hedge. The Mum had dismissed her until luncheon. A walkabout, Maude urged, might be good for her.

Beyond the garden was a green, sloping meadow that seemed to go on straight to the mountains, and the mountains themselves seemed almost touchable to Nina from where she stood. As she'd heard Derrick describe one evening, the air was so clear in this part of New South Wales that distances could easily be misjudged by an untrained eye.

Everything smelled good this morning, fresh and clean and brand new. Feeling newly alive herself, Nina walked briskly in her scuffed brown boots. The full khaki skirt swished against her legs, inhibiting the length of her stride. Skirts were so confining. She wished she could go about in daks, boys' trousers, as Anthia sometimes did when she worked in the vegetable garden. But she knew the Mum would be violently opposed to such bold behavior in a lady.

She headed toward a stand of giant tree ferns that could be seen in the far distance. There should be more than enough time to reach them, sit under their cool canopy for a while, and then get back in time to freshen up for luncheon. She reminded herself that she must ask permission to take a book from Flame Tree's extensive library. She missed those quiet times spent immersed in a long novel. The ferns would be a perfect place in which to disappear for a reading session.

She walked quickly, feeling the air warming as the sun climbed higher in the cloudless azure sky. When she reached the edge of the green canopy she was breathing harder and feeling her leg muscles quiver a bit. Beyond the outermost ferns she heard what sounded like an animal munching on grass, and feet moving in the mulch under the trees. She stopped, frozen where she stood.

All of Derrick's stories came back to her, and she didn't know if she should sneak away quietly or simply bolt and run. It didn't matter, for she found herself unable to move. She tried to recall what Shane had said about Derrick's exaggerating, but was not convinced as the munching grew louder and nearer. The animal was big, she could tell that as the movement through the trees grew broader with long, swishing sounds.

Exaggerated stories or not, Nina decided against finding out what the animal was, and turning around swiftly, bolted and ran away from the canopy. In the run she twisted her ankle, caught her foot on an exposed root, and fell flat on her face in the soft grass. Frantic, she kicked her foot out of the root and tried to push herself up off the ground. Suddenly she was gripped on the shoulders by strong animal claws and flipped over. She shrieked and kicked at whatever had hold of her.

"Whoa! Here now, my girl!"

Nina flinched and stopped kicking. When she opened her clamped eyes, she was staring up into Shane's grinning face. He backed away from her. They stared wordlessly at each other for a long moment, and then he broke into laughter that seemed to mock in echo all around them.

"Well, what . . . is so . . . bloody funny?" Nina spat at him once she caught her breath.

She was still sitting on the ground, legs out in front of her, petticoat up to her knees, exposing high-tied boots over white stockings. Her hands were thrust behind to prop her up, and her hair tumbled all about her face and shoulders. She had to squint to see into his face, which was framed by the glare of the sun behind him.

"Ah, 'bloody,' is it, now? You're learning quickly, my girl!" He stopped laughing long enough to reach over and pick some long blades of grass out of her hair. "Well, for one thing, you've got wet grass all over your face and hair, and I daresay that's not the only place. And for another, that was one of the least graceful exits I've ever witnessed! You put the spooks into Shadow, that's for sure. Could barely swallow his last chaw of grass!"

At the sound of his name, a huge black stallion loped out of the trees, ears pricked high, stirrups swaying from the saddle as he walked. He stopped when he saw Shane, seemed to give the once-over to Nina, and then, as if he knew the rumpled heap of human posed no threat to him, lowered his massive head to graze.

Nina stood up gingerly and brushed the grass from her skirt. "You scared me to death! Did you know I was here?"

"Saw you coming when you broke the crest of the hill."

"Then why didn't you say anything?"

"Didn't think you'd hear me."

"I could have broken my ankle, you know."

"Caw, I surely wouldn't want you to break your ankle, my girl. You'd be more baggage than you were on the trip." His blue eyes sparkled with amusement.

Exasperated, Nina fussed ineffectively with her

clothes. She grew more frustrated with this man each time she saw him. How could she have ever thought he was handsome? It must have been because she was truly in need of money and a place to stay, and he offered the opportunity for both. That's what had made him look so good to her. Her mind must have been clouded, there could be no other reason.

She turned and walked back toward the trees. Shane came up behind her and gave her what felt like a swat on her behind.

"Hey!" She whirled to face him. "What do you think you're doing?"

"There was grass all over your bum. I was just trying to help, that's all. Give it a rest, lass."

She stomped away into the trees, brushing off the back of her skirt as she went.

"You'd better wait just a shake before you go in there," Shane called from behind her.

"Why? So one of Derrick's giant spiders can finish spinning her web, all the better to trap me?"

She continued into the tree cover, tripped over something very large, and fell flat on her face again. The large thing was furry, and it immediately jumped up and onto her back, setting her screaming.

Shane sauntered under the canopy, shoved his hat to the back of his head, and hunkered down beside her.

"No . . ." he drawled, "so Mate can finish burying the wombat bone he found. You're lying on top of one of his favorite burial grounds."

Mate stood with his paws on the back of her shoulders, panting heavily, his tongue hanging out.

Droplets from his mouth landed on the side of her cheek.

"Blech!" she muttered, and tried in vain to throw the dog off her back. Mate was not to be moved by Nina. He waited for a command from Shane.

"All right, Mate, let her up. She didn't mean it."

Mate stepped off Nina's shoulders and stood waiting until she rolled over and removed herself from his burial ground. She sat up slowly and inched her body away from the pile of debris she could not bring herself to look at. Mate waited as patiently as was caninely possible for him, then set about recovering his treasures and kicking dirt over the spot with his hind paws. That task accomplished, he turned around and sat down on the pile facing her, an expectant look on his face.

Shane looked squarely at her. "Well?"

She spat dirt out of her mouth and pushed a lock of hair off her forehead with the back of her hand.

"Well . . . what?"

"I think you owe Mate an apology."

"Wh—? Apology! You're not serious."

"Aye, that I am, and I think it's fairly obvious that so is Mate." Shane and Mate looked at each other, then back at Nina. "We're waiting."

Nina looked incredulously at both of them. "Apologize? To a dog? Look at me! I've practically broken my ankle, I—I tripped over this animal, I'm covered with dirt and who knows what other despicable substance, and . . . I'm expected to apologize to . . . to the very one who did it to me in the first place? I think not!"

"Caw, stop your grizzling. Mate meant you no

114

harm. You did, after all, trespass. He's just being himself. I think that should be allowed, don't you?"

Nina thought about that bit of reasoning for a moment, then had to agree. Mate was probably the only creature at Flame Tree who was allowed to be caught in the act of being himself. She realized she must look a sight, and she relaxed enough to let a smile play at the corners of her mouth.

"Oh, all right." She held out her right hand toward Mate, who sat anxiously awaiting a word, eagerness sparking out of his eyes. "I'm sorry, Mate," she said with all sincerity.

Mate lifted his right paw for her to grasp. Then, sensing that everything was all right, he jumped toward her, knocked her flat on her back with his two front paws on her shoulders, and began to lick her face.

"Ahhh! Does he have to be so forgiving about it? There's no need to kiss and make up, really."

"Here now, Mate!" Shane threw both arms around the big dog's thick neck and hauled him off her.

She lay still, staring up into the canopy overhead, then broke into laughter. "His eyes are very disconcerting, you know. Hard to tell what he's thinking."

Shane laughed out loud. He watched her lying there for a moment, listened to her genuine laugh, and was touched in his lonely places. Suddenly he was consumed with the urge to trace the lace of her chemise that was visible through her blouse just over the top of her breasts, and touch the mane of copper hair that spilled all around her head on the grass. The thought of his hand lifting the thick locks and letting the strands sift through his fingers like liquid gold flashed through his mind. He saw his other hand unfastening her shirt and . . . good Lord, what was he thinking?

Nina moved to sit up then, breaking his reverie. "I must look like something Mate would drag in. Why is it that practically every time I'm to see your mother, something utterly devastating happens to me?" She brushed her skirt, then lifted some of the coils of her hair in an attempt to repin them.

"You look . . ." *totally inviting*, he finished the sentence in his mind, but spoke outwardly, "a little the worse for wear, that's truth. Here."

He produced a blue bandanna from his back pocket. Leaning over, he gently wiped at the dirt on her cheek, then moved to the smudge along the side of her throat. His finger slid over the sensitive cord in her neck, and she felt a shiver run down her shoulder.

Her shirt had opened below the vee of her neckline and a tiny blue ribbon from the top of her chemise peeked out. Above it, in the moistness of the creamy white skin above her full breasts, lay several small blades of grass. Shane searched her eyes for a sign that she wanted him to stop. Seeing none, he slowly trailed the bandanna lower along her skin to carefully wipe away the grass.

The touch of Shane's hand moving down below her throat sent a spate of tiny shock waves over her skin. His touch was gentle, warm, and she did not protest, although a nagging voice in the back of her mind told her she should. Her eyes fell to his mouth. More than anything at this very moment, she wanted to feel his lips closing over hers.

116

Shane abruptly stopped brushing away the grass, and placed the bandanna in her hand. He stood up, gazing at her for a long moment.

"I . . . I'll wait for you outside the trees. You can fix up and then I'll give you a ride back to the house." He looked up toward the sun. "You'll be able to get in through the kitchen and clean up before the Mum sees you." He stepped away, then turned and walked out into the clearing.

Nina sat still for a moment. Had she misread his eyes, or was there a look of longing in them? Whatever it was, she felt it deeply, and knew instinctively her own gaze at him must have held the same look.

She stood up quickly, straightening her skirt, and wiped the dirt off her hands with the bandanna and stuffed it into her pocket. Then she refastened her shirt and repinned her hair as best she could. Mate sat and watched her all the while, curiosity shining out of his even more curious eyes.

Nina looked down at him. "Well, don't ask me. You know him better than I do."

Mate cocked his head one way and then the other as she spoke to him, as if catching every nuance in her voice and understanding her words. Then he scampered out of the trees.

Nina stood there for a moment. All right, she thought to herself, admit it: you wanted Shane to kiss you just now. You've never known a real kiss, but you sense Shane could show you. Forget that . . . you know what the Mum said. He knows a lot of sophisticated women, and after all, there are those Merritt bloodlines to consider, you know.

She was all at once furious at him and at herself, furious at both of them for bringing her into this predicament. She was beginning to like living at Flame Tree, but she had to remember that she would be forced to leave in a few months. But she was even more furious at herself because if she weren't careful, she could fall in love with Shane, and where would that get her?

"Bloody hell!" She stomped out of the trees.

"What?" Shane whirled around holding the reins from Shadow's bridle.

"Nothing. Nothing at all!"

"Here, then, let me give you a leg up." He made a cupping motion with his hands next to the stirrup.

"What? You really think I'm going to get up on the back of this horse?" Her mouth dropped open.

"Well now, my girl, how else did you expect I was going to give you a ride? On me bloody back? Mind, you'd better get a move on. Sun's climbing. Gone eleven already."

Nina moved toward Shadow with great trepidation. She lifted her right foot and put it in Shane's hand. Her skirts tangled all around her ankle.

"If you try to get up there with that foot, you're going to be riding backward," he chuckled. "But, say, that could be an interesting ride for me, now couldn't it, my girl?"

Nina's face burned. "Well, how should I know? I've never been on a horse before."

Her skirts got all tangled again, and she caught her heel in the hem and felt it give.

"I can see we're going to have to outfit you in some

118

daks if you're going to do this often," he chuckled again.

"I doubt I'll have the chance to do this often," she muttered.

He circled her waist with his large hands and lifted her up easily to sit sidesaddle, then adjusted her skirts and swung up smoothly behind her. As he settled into the saddle, the curve of her hip along his thighs disturbed him.

He reminded himself of what the Mum had told him: he mustn't let Nina develop feelings for him. She would have to leave in a few months. He convinced himself that it was best for her, too. But what about what he was feeling for her?

The warmth of her body rocking against his thighs with every step Shadow took became increasingly more unsettling. His arms around her slim middle where he held the reins felt as if they belonged there. The warm scent of her skin filled every breath he took, and made him a little light-headed. It was all a new feeling for him. Every other time he'd been with a woman he had felt only pure lust, physical desire. This was becoming desire on fire, adding emotion to the physical.

Aside from the pain that was meandering up and down her spine as she rocked back and forth with Shadow's gait, Nina felt as if she belonged right where she was—on the back of a magnificent black stallion, with Shane's arms around her. She could not fathom why. He had certainly done nothing to endear himself to her, that was for certain. Most of the time he seemed to be doing everything in his power to make her appear foolish. What's more, she was convinced his dog was an accomplice.

Maybe it was like the things some of her friends used to talk about. Being near a certain kind of man was supposed to make a woman feel all fluttery inside. She'd never truly believed them, until now. No man had ever made her feel like this. But then, she'd never known a man who was anything like Shane. Most of the males she knew were still boys. And some of her aunt's friends, the older men, wore their hair slicked down with pomade and smelled of cigar smoke. They looked at her with eyes that made her feel uncomfortable in her own skin. But the more unsettled she felt being close to Shane, the more aware she was of her own femininity.

Shane was completely masculine, with a boyish quality that was most appealing. His hair blew free in the wind and he smelled of sun, and rain, and earth. He looked at her with sky-blue eyes that reflected the wildness of his homeland and the sensitivity to nature, and penetrated her skin to cause jets of fire to surge through her veins.

Shadow jumped across a burrow hole, and when he landed, Nina's shoulder pressed into Shane's chest. She felt the grip of his arms more tightly across her breasts, then felt them release, and felt herself grow weak. They rode in silence all the way back to the house, as if whatever words they exchanged would make the moments less significant.

From the window of the upstairs sitting room, Vanessa saw Shane ride in with Nina on Shadow. She frowned. When Shane helped the girl down from the horse she noticed that he lingered for a moment with his hands at her waist.

Vanessa went back to a small writing desk and looked at the party plans. She scratched out the date set for three weeks hence. She simply had no choice; propriety would have to be sacrificed. Time was of the essence. She moved the party up to one week from Saturday. It was more than time Shane was reintroduced to the more refined and wealthy young ladies of Hunter Valley.

Chapter 10

"No, no, my dear," Vanessa clucked when Nina emerged from the dressing room in the Parramatta Emporium, modeling an emerald-green taffeta gown. The neckline trailed off her shoulders to plunge to a perfect vee between her softly rounded breasts. The bodice molded around her ribs and ended in a point below her waist where the soft folds of the skirt cascaded over her hips.

"It's breathtaking," exclaimed the shop assistant, "as if it were designed only for you."

"It's the most beautiful dress I've ever seen," Nina breathed. She twirled, catching all sides of her image in the mirror, and reveling in the soft rustle of taffeta around her ankles. "I feel like a princess."

Vanessa came up behind Nina, and caught her gaze in the mirror. "It simply will not do," she said briskly.

Nina Cole was stunning in that dress, and everyone in the shop had cast a more than approving eye in her direction. But Vanessa was not about to allow her to wear it to the party. She knew the impact it would have on Shane, and she had to prevent that from happening. She wanted him to be attracted to one of the young girls from the valley, and Nina Cole in that dress would outshine them all, and would be difficult for him to ignore.

"Oh, but . . ." Nina began.

"Nina, when I said we could shop for a dress for you, I expected that I would select and purchase it for you. I think the pale green print on the far rack is much more appropriate for a young woman in my employ. Try it on, please."

Nina's face registered deep disappointment, matched almost in kind by the shop assistant. But it was the place of neither woman to protest. Nina was in Vanessa Merritt's employ, as she'd been reminded on this and numerous other occasions, and Vanessa Merritt was purchasing the dress. Nina stepped out of the dressing room wearing the high-necked print dress.

"Perfect," Vanessa pronounced.

"I look twelve," Nina said in a low voice.

"We'll take it," Vanessa said.

"Yes, Madam," replied the shop assistant.

Nina sat on a high wooden stool in the kitchen talking to Maude.

"It was a beautiful jewel green, so lovely it almost made me cry. I wish I'd had my own money, but I haven't earned enough yet. And besides, I haven't figured out exactly how to translate dollars into pounds. I always think I have more than I really have."

124

Maude looked up from the pastry board and wiped her flour-covered hands on her apron. "Well, I'm sure you'll be just as pretty in the green print. You'd look pretty in anything. Give it a fair go, lass."

"I know. I must sound like a spoiled brat to you. It's just that I'm beginning to understand what makes me look like a schoolgirl, and what makes me feel like a woman." She nibbled on one of the jam cakes Maude had prepared for tea. "And you know something? I think the Mum knows it, too. She's too stylish a lady herself not to know."

Maude sent her a look of agreement, but remained silent.

"Oh, Maude—I wish I could do something about this. If I simply appeared at the party in that wonderful dress it would be too late for the Mum to prevent it. I have nothing to lose anyway, have I? At least Shane would have the chance to make up his own mind without . . ."

Realizing she'd almost said something she shouldn't, she took a large bite of cake and avoided eye contact with Maude.

"If you don't stop stuffing jam cakes into your mouth, you won't look good in anything. Never saw such a slip of a girl with an appetite like you've got." Maude bustled about the kitchen preparing the tray of tea and cakes. "It's going on for four. You'd best get changed for tea."

Nina went to her room, changed into an appropriate dark skirt and white blouse, and coiled her hair neatly to the top of her head. Walking along the upstairs hallway, she noticed the door ajar to a spare bedroom. She peeked around to see if anyone was there. Anthia was busily washing the window glass and humming to herself.

"Hello, Anthia. What are you up to?"

"G'dye, Miss Nina. Just tidying some rooms for overnight guests to the party. The Mum wants everything just right."

"This is a very nice room."

"It was the Mum's mum's room. They were going to redo it, but she died before they got started."

Nina walked around, inspecting the appointments on the bureau, admiring the crocheted spread and wooden bedposts. On the bed lay a large paper-wrapped package open at one end, revealing a bolt of lustrous fabric. Nina touched it lightly, then started out of the room. She stopped still at the door, then whirled around to Anthia.

"What's that fabric for?" she asked with an excited breathy voice.

"What fabric?"

"There on the bed. It felt like satin."

"Oh, that. That was for sheets and pillowslips for this room. The Mum's mum was a very elegant lady. She loved satin . . . but like I said, she died, and—"

"Does that mean it won't be put to use?" Nina grew even more excited.

"Nay. The Mum has instructed me to throw it away."

Nina went to the bed and pulled the bolt of fabric out of its wrapper. She unrolled it and draped it across her body, switching this way and that while peering into the oval mirror in the corner. The exquisite royal-blue satin held a sheen that reflected light every way it was turned.

"Oh . . . it's so beautiful. It would make a wonderful dress."

"Aye, that it would."

Nina was suddenly filling with ideas and a rapidly growing self-determination. What *did* she have to lose? she asked herself. The Mum insisted she leave Flame Tree anyway. Just once in her life Nina wanted to attend an elegant party dressed as richly as the other women. She didn't want to upset the Mum, but, oh, it would be so lovely to feel beautiful, and to know that other people regarded her so. If she gathered the courage to do it now, at the very least she'd know she'd seized the opportunity to shine. Perhaps then Shane would look at her with new eyes.

"Anthia, if it's going to be discarded . . . do you think your mother might fashion this into a dress for me?"

"Ah, nay, Miss Nina, you can't use that. It wouldn't do. The Mum would never allow it."

"Anthia, I will take full responsibility, and if Maude would do it, oh, I know it would be the loveliest dress at the party."

Before Anthia could utter another word, Nina carefully folded the fabric and placed it back in its wrapper and spirited it away to her room. Then she ran to get to tea on time.

That evening at dinner, Vanessa Merritt watched Shane and Nina Cole carefully. She caught the exchange of glances between them on several occasions, saw his direct and positive appraisal of

127

her, and saw Nina's mouth turn up in a shy smile as she pulled her gaze away from him.

Vanessa was displeased at the pace of what she saw growing between them. She would have to move quickly to stop it. Much as she would miss her oldest son's presence in the house, she would be forced to require him to stay at the out station until the night of the party. She'd have enough sound reasons to make him agree with her. The separation would dilute the attraction between them, she would depend on that.

Colin observed his mother watching Shane and Nina. He knew how acute her mind was, and what it was capable of producing. All she can ever see is Shane, he thought. It was always Shane. But now he sensed something more in his mother. She did not like the presence of Nina Cole at Flame Tree. Not a whit. If he was seeing clearly, he believed she might be jealous. Jealous! Colin would never have thought his imperious mother could be jealous of anyone, but as he watched her now, he believed he was correct.

Perhaps she sensed that Nina was someone she couldn't manipulate as she might a weaker girl. Colin's mind flashed. So, Nina Cole was the real reason behind the party the Mum was giving. The Mum was distressed, worried that Shane might take up with the unsuitable Nina. Colin knew his mother well. She was about to march out the parade of eligible women in the valley, and then orchestrate a match for Shane.

Colin felt his own streak of jealousy. The Mum had never regarded him important enough for her to go to such lengths. Nina Cole's presence at Flame

Tree had affected them all. His mind was becoming clearer about the reasons why, and began to work more creatively than ever before on new plans. He smiled wryly.

"You know, big brother," Colin began with an air of authority, "I've been thinking about the results of your last visit to America."

Vanessa and Shane turned toward him, obviously surprised at his sudden interest in the family business. Colin caught the meaning in their looks, but continued smoothly.

"I think your personal connection with the importers was a successful move. You know how it is, seeing the Australian, the stockman who actually grows the wool. No doubt they've not seen your like before, kind of a cleaned-up American cowboy." He smiled and drank from his wineglass.

"Quite right, Colin," Shane bolstered his brother's interest, "but I hate the gab that goes with it. Puts me out of sorts, having to convince them that our wool is the finest they can buy. I know it is, and I'm giving them a fair price, but they haggle and argue for lower. Don't know why they can't just accept what I say and make the deal. I end up having to up the price and then spend the time letting them work on me to lower it to what I want in the first place. Waste of time."

Colin smiled and glanced at Nina. "Americans always want to be convinced they've gone one up on you. It's their lot."

Nina moved uncomfortably. Colin was probably going to launch into one of his condescending speeches aimed at her, and she'd be forced into the ladylike role of silently accepting it.

Shane caught Nina's discomfort, and tried to ease it. "Aye, well, you've had more experience with Americans of a different sort than I have."

"At least with men, anyway," Colin said directly.

Vanessa cleared her throat. "What's your point, Colin? You've chosen an inappropriate time to discuss family business, and I think you should bring the subject to a close."

Colin ignored her direct reference to the fact that she disapproved of his speaking in front of Nina. "The point is that a smoother approach is needed now. Shane's set them up, but all he really wants to do is produce wool. Am I right, big brother?"

"Spot on." Shane looked at his mother, but her concentration was fixed on Colin.

"It's time, then, for the next move. We need someone else to step in, give them a go at the price haggle, and end up with more to cover export expenses and turn a tidy profit."

"And where are *we* going to find that slick someone?" Shane asked with an edge in his voice.

Colin drained his wineglass. "It doesn't surprise me, big brother, that you wouldn't think of it. Of course I am referring to myself. I am the only one who can perform the act that's needed." He watched their faces.

"You?" Shane did not conceal his surprise.

"Try to be a little less disdainful, big brother," Colin said evenly. "Why not me? I am part of the family, in case you've forgotten. I'm the logical one. I'm sure as an outsider you can see that, can't you, Nina?"

130

Nina stirred nervously at being brought into a personal family discussion. "Me? Oh, I would have no opinion about that . . ."

"I doubt that," Colin fixed his gaze on her, and made a purposeful statement directly to her. "I believe you observe and have opinions about everything, and I hope to discuss all of them with you . . . soon."

"I . . . of course, Colin," Nina answered politely. What was he trying to do? This entire exchange greatly unsettled her. At first she'd felt she shouldn't be present at a private family discussion, but she'd been unable to take discreet leave of the dining room. Now Colin had drawn her directly into the middle of their conversation.

Vanessa was shaken by Colin's speech. He'd never shown even a spark of interest in the family business. While his working participation in Flame Tree's business was what she'd always longed for, she couldn't help but be suspicious of his motives. Why now, why so sudden?

Colin surprised Vanessa, but now her mind moved to a more intriguing idea: she wondered if he might be interested in Nina for himself. She pondered it. If indeed he were, his pursuit of Nina could work to her advantage. If Shane were to believe his younger brother was interested in the girl, she knew he wouldn't interfere, and he'd be more open to pursuing the others she had in mind for him.

Collecting her thoughts quickly, Vanessa said, "A good idea. Nina might be quite helpful to you concerning the manner in which Americans think. Mightn't you, my dear?"

Nina was speechless at Vanessa Merritt's kind tone. Why this sudden turn?

Shane broke in. "Now, I don't think Nina should be expected to know about the American wool import business . . ."

"Why not?" Colin stood up. "We're not asking her to know about wool, just about how Americans think. But it doesn't bear discussion right now—perhaps another time." He leaned down and gave his mother an uncustomary kiss on the cheek. "With your permission, Mother, I should like to retire for the evening." Without waiting for her answer, he walked around the table to Nina. He picked up her hand and kissed the back of it, lingering over it for a moment. "I'll be looking forward to our talk. Let's make it very soon." He walked to the door, turned around toward the astonished and speechless faces. "Shane . . . good evening all." Then he was gone.

Later, out on the veranda, Nina sat on a wicker settee, thinking over the dinner conversation. She pulled a light cream shawl around her shoulders against the cool evening breeze. She was confused about Colin's change of heart, his sudden interest in the family business, and in her. But she was even more surprised that Vanessa Merritt appeared to support his latter interest in particular. She wondered if Shane had noticed that, too. She wished she could know what he thought about everything, and especially what he thought about her.

A rustling sound at the far end of the veranda disturbed her thoughts. She looked up, straining her eyes through the darkness for a glimpse of what or who might be there. Clouds that covered the moon momentarily moved slowly away, revealing Shane's tall, lean form darkly silhouetted against the white post and railing. And then another cloud passed over the moon, and he was enveloped by the same darkness that surrounded her.

He was bathed in silver moonlight for so brief a moment she thought she'd imagined an ethereal vision. She peered intently, as if willing his return to her sight. When the cloud passed again, she saw him leaning against a post, gazing toward the distant mountains, apparently lost in thought.

Nina watched him silently, heard him sigh, and felt she was intruding upon a private moment. She rose, thinking she'd steal away unnoticed. The wicker creaked as she stood, and Shane turned in the direction of the sound.

"Who's there? Colin?"

Nina stepped out of the darkness toward him. "No, it's just me. I didn't mean to disturb you."

Shane's pulse quickened. Nina's form in the cream dress was outlined by a trace of moonlight. On the strengthening breeze, wisteria leaves danced in shadows across her face.

"No, you didn't," he lied. She did disturb him. She disturbed him deeply.

"I'll just say good night," she whispered, taking a step down from the veranda.

"Nay, don't go."

He reached out and took her arm. Nina shivered at his touch. Her shawl slipped from her shoulders. Shane moved closer, lifted it, and pulled it around her. Her hair, loose over one shoulder, caught inside the shawl. He brushed the backs of his fingers along her neck and lifted the locks carefully, sending electric pulses down her spine. She shivered again.

"It is rather cool tonight," he observed, "and damp. Here, take my coat."

He removed the blue jacket he'd worn to dinner and placed it around her shoulders. Instantly Nina was enveloped by his warmth and the aroma it carried from his body.

"Care to walk a bit before bed?"

"That would be lovely," she whispered, her heart beating so hard against the wall of her chest, she was afraid he might hear.

He took her arm and they walked along the damp grass toward the garden. An electric silence crackled between them. Shane spoke at last, easing the tension.

"Don't let Colin's badgering upset you. It's the way he is."

"Oh, Colin's all right. I understand him. He doesn't upset me nearly as much as he did at first."

"Oh?" Shane wondered what she meant by understanding Colin. Had they spent enough time together for her to know him well?

"He's just having difficulty fitting in, that's all."

"He doesn't try, never did. And I can't figure why."

"Can't you?" Nina ventured. She might be overstepping the bounds of privacy, but it was too late to stop now.

Shane opened the garden gate and ushered her through. Moonlight and the moist night air turned it into a fantasy forest of shadowy trees, low, fluttering ferns, and fragrant blossoms. Side by side, Shane and Nina strolled along the stone paths.

"Should I be able to figure him out?" Shane asked.

Nina hesitated a moment. Perhaps she should keep her observations to herself. But then she decided to speak honestly.

"Yes, I think so. I believe you're a great part of the reason he behaves the way he does."

"Me? Why?"

"He's grown up in your shadow. Surely you're aware of that."

Shane was silent. Aye, he knew that, but it wasn't of his own doing. He'd always wanted them to be closer. He'd tried to encourage his brother's involvement with the work and responsibilities at Flame Tree. Colin's resistance and lack of interest eventually curbed his enthusiasm to bring him along.

"I think he may be starting to assert himself now for his rightful place beside you . . . and with your mother," Nina continued.

"Aye, it seemed as much tonight. More than usual. Since you've been here, I've noticed a change in him."

"It's only natural that he's grown into a man," she said.

Colin? A man? Shane thought perhaps he hadn't noticed that Colin was no longer the little boy he and the Mum always considered him to be. He was a man, with a man's needs and desires. Shane thought hard: a man, aye, but was his little brother the man taking more than a passing interest in Nina? As first he'd seemed so set against her presence, but tonight . . . Nay, he couldn't be. He'd never dallied with a serious woman, just those giddy fluffs in the valley or in Parramatta. Nina was as different from them as was humanly possible, not the kind he was ever gone for at all. Could it be Colin had at last grown up and begun to know how to recognize a real woman when he saw one?

Shane realized he'd just admitted something to himself for the first time: Nina Cole was a real woman, and she stirred his masculine blood like no other before her.

Instinctively, almost possessively, he slid his arm around her waist and drew her closer to him. "Are you warm now, my girl?"

Nina's heart pounded harder as her pulse raced. "Aye, that I am," she whispered.

They stopped beside a small pool and sat down on a stone bench. Nina leaned forward to catch her reflection and Shane followed, golden hair next to copper in the moon-silvered still water. Moved by their closeness reflected in the pool, Shane turned toward her, caught her chin lightly with a bent finger, and tilted her head toward him.

Nina shivered under his touch, and her eyelashes fluttered up as she gazed into his eyes. But he wasn't looking into hers. He was fixed upon her moist lips, and was lowering his own toward them. For a moment his mouth hovered in the mist of a breath away from hers. And then he kissed her, lightly once, lightly again, and then captured her mouth completely in his own. His arms went around her, crushing her breasts against his chest. His tongue gently pressed against her teeth until she opened them and allowed him entrance. She melted against him in complete surrender.

When at last he released her lips, he could feel her

body trembling against him. She stood up slowly, but didn't reproach him for so bold an act. Would she let him go on? Caw, how he wanted to go on, wanted more. He stood and wrapped his arms around her slender form.

Nina buried her face against his chest. She could hear his heart beating in rhythm to her own. His soft cotton shirt caressed her cheek. She breathed in the scent of him, savored the feel of his length against her, and her senses reeled when his hand came up to rest on the back of her neck. If he moved again, she felt she might shatter in his arms.

For a long moment they stood in silence, pressed against each other. Shane fought to hold his desire in check, struggled against the wildness in his heart and in his loins. He breathed in the perfume from her hair with every breath. His hands spread across her back and small shoulders beneath his coat, sending a clear picture to his mind of her exquisite form.

He had to stop this, he cautioned himself, had to stop now before he was powerless to stop.

"Nina," he whispered into her hair.

She stirred against him, then stepped back within the circle of his arms, her hands, pale in the moonlight, rested against his chest.

"I must take you back to the house before . . ." His voice trailed off. He released her reluctantly and sensed the same reluctance in her.

Nina felt a chill the moment Shane's arms dropped away from her. She'd felt suspended above herself, watching from some loftier plane as Shane Merritt and Nina Cole kissed and held each other within a moonlit fantasy.

And then the fantasy faded and they left the garden. At the kitchen door she lifted his coat from her shoulders and handed it to him. Their fingers touched as he took it from her. She looked into his eyes expectantly. Why didn't he say anything? Why couldn't she say anything?

He gave her an imaginary tip of his hat, then backed away into the shadows and was gone. Nina stood staring into the velvet darkness until the night chill penetrated her to the core and sent her inside.

Chapter 11

Maude was positive she would be banished to the Back of Beyond once the Mum knew she'd had a hand in it, but she agreed to make the dress Nina desired, and she and Nina spent many furtive hours measuring, pinning, cutting, and sewing. When they were finished, the dress was every bit as beautiful as the one at the Parramatta Emporium, but on Nina it was even more stunning than that one.

Every night before retiring, Nina tried it on and appraised herself in the mirror. She alternated between excitement at the prospect of wearing it and trepidation at the thought of how the Mum would react. As the evening of the party drew closer, she was in a constant state of indecision about whether to wear it or not, and something told her she would be uncertain until the moment she appeared.

She dreamed of the night in the garden when Shane had kissed her, and fantasized about him kissing her again the moment he saw her in that dress. He hadn't been to dinner since then, and the next four days had passed with agonizing slowness as she anticipated his arrival.

Colin had been absent as well, and Nina wondered what he was up to. The Mum spoke of him once during one of their afternoon teas. She hinted that perhaps he hadn't been serious about becoming more involved with Flame Tree, that perhaps he had something more exciting in mind with which to impress Nina. Nina had felt uncomfortable with the exchange, and had not responded with anything but a small smile.

This morning the Mum dismissed Nina for the day. She planned to immerse herself in last-minute arrangements for the party. Nina knew exactly what she wanted to do with her time. She would find her way to the out station and learn just what kind of work Shane did. Her desire to know everything about him was constantly on her mind.

She borrowed a pair of khaki daks and a wool jacket from Anthia, donned a white blouse, pulled on her own brown boots, and slipped out of the house for a walkabout.

Her eyes scanned the horizon as she walked. An hour into her trek she began fully to understand just how vast was the Merritt land. It was much farther than she'd imagined to where the stock, and most likely Shane, would be, and walking would never get her there and back before dark. Out of breath, her legs shaking, she sat down on the hillside to think. There must be a way to manage the distance, but how? Her heart sank.

The sound of hoofbeats from behind broke into her pondering. She turned around, pulse racing with

140

the hope that it was Shane. The rider came into view, and her spirits dropped when she recognized Colin. While he dismounted and walked toward her, she steeled herself for his barrage of caustic remarks.

"And what cultural pursuits are you up to today, Lady Cole?" His voice carried only a trace of that sneering tone she disliked immensely.

"Nothing special. Just a walkabout."

"Ah, I see you're getting the hang of Australian language. How astute of you." He strode back and forth in front of her, tapping a short leather whip against his expensive leather boot. "You don't seem to be getting very far. Perhaps you should turn back and take up more gainful activity—perhaps, oh, needlepoint, or some such frivol. You could always study literature or take up painting . . . ah, but I suppose you'd lack the powers of concentration for such an endeavor." He stopped in front of her, a taunting smile curling one corner of his mouth.

Nina wondered if he'd been nice to her that last evening when they were all together at dinner just as a show for his mother and Shane. She couldn't be certain of his real reasons for it, but he'd certainly not behaved like the Colin she'd come to know.

She looked up at him with unhappy eyes. "Colin, why is it that you dislike me so? What have I done to provoke your constant belittling of me?"

Colin's face registered amazement at so bold a question from her, and he was taken aback momentarily. He turned away from her and stared down at his boots, a change of mood overtaking him.

"It's not that I dislike you. You just represent something—"

"Something that you don't want to be, is that it? Those damnable Merritt bloodlines might have the chill taken off by someone of lesser breeding, shall we say?"

"Possibly . . ."

Nina was growing hot with repressed anger and frustration. What did it matter now if she said something that might insult Colin Merritt? She decided to throw caution to the winds and plunge on.

"What's expected of *you*, Colin? What's expected of *your* Merritt bloodlines, *your* duty to continue the mighty empire?"

Colin was silent. He dropped down beside her and stared out over the rolling green Merritt lands stretching to the horizon and beyond.

"You want to know what's expected of me, what's always been expected of me by the mighty matriarch of the Merritt clan? Nothing. Absolutely bloody nothing. Never. Where once I was a child to be indulged, now I'm just the younger son to be tolerated. So, I haven't really cared about anything or anyone, most especially those Merritt bloodlines you talk about."

Nina instantly regretted that she'd pressed him. "I'm sorry, Colin, I had no right to ask that. But I know how you feel. I felt so loved by my parents, but once they were gone I was just someone to be tolerated by my aunt. So we're rather alike, you and me. Except that I do care about things. But why is it you've treated me as if I were less than nothing?"

He picked up a stick and scratched nondescript lines in the earth. Then he looked up at her. "Because you . . . you're doing what I wish I had the guts to do, striking out on your own, trying something new. And it galls me that a fluff can do it and I can't."

"Well, there's more to me than fluff, as you say." She stretched out her legs over the soft grass. "But what about the things you were saying the other evening at dinner? Why can't you do what you want to do, Colin? Whatever it is, can't you just go do it?"

"Nay."

"Why not?"

"Because of Mother. As a Merritt, I'm doomed to staying at Flame Tree and being a Merritt, with all that implies, for the rest of my life. Mother's whole life was Father. When he died she was determined to let nothing else about Flame Tree die. I'm no use to her, but she can't have me getting away, either. Nothing I do pleases her. The more I displease her with my gambling on fossickers and empty lodes, the more she pays it all off for me. And I do it all over again. It's a way of keeping me attached. I hate it. I'll never please her, and . . . I'll never please myself. But I love her. Aye, I love her. And all I want is for her to love me . . . as she loves Shane."

Nina felt compassion for Colin's confusion, but there was nothing she could say to him. A long silence lay between them. Nina finally broke into it as if thinking out loud.

"I may have made a big mistake striking out on my own, as you say, coming to Australia, but I wanted adventure, so I did it. And I wanted to make a difference in someone's life for once. But that won't happen after all because I won't be here for very long."

"You want to leave Flame Tree?"

143

"I didn't say that . . ."

"Then why leave? Mother's a bit over the top at times, I'll grant you that, but surely you can manage . . ."When Nina didn't respond, he stared long and hard at her. And then his face broke into a revelation. "You've got it for my big brother, haven't you? And Mother won't hear of it."

Nina moved uncomfortably. She remembered her promise to the Mum not to speak of their first private conversation. "Let's just say that Flame Tree, and probably all of Australia, for all I know, will not remember so much as a footprint I left in the dust." She sighed.

Colin's mood lifted. "Well, Lady Cole, you shouldn't leave Flame Tree without at least having seen all of it. If there's one thing I don't muck up, it's wandering over the bush. I can show you every last bottle brush tree and woollybutt on the place. What say? Give it a go with me? It would allow me to square it off with you."

She looked up at him, suddenly hopeful. She sensed he'd surprised himself as much as he'd surprised her with his offer. "Would you take me to the out station? Show me the sheep and the jackaroos?"

"Not on foot, I won't. There is a mare back at the barn would be good for you. Would you straddle a horse?"

"Would I? Let's go!"

Nina found riding astride a horse exhilarating in spite of the pain running up her inner thighs and

144

down the end of her spine. She supposed her unladylike behavior would cause another frown from the Mum and was glad she couldn't see her now. She was experiencing a bold new excitement, and the land was even more glorious to behold from high on the back of the mare.

Colin was an excellent guide. He seemed actually enthusiastic in telling her about Flame Tree, and how Daniel Merritt had built it up from a small flock of the finest Saxon merinos he could afford on borrowed money. There was a swell of pride evident in his voice when he talked about how Flame Tree was the first station in the valley to open wool export to America.

"Colin, you love this place, and you know it," Nina whispered to him.

"Aye, well . . . Shane is the one groomed for it. He's to the bush born, and I'm to the manner born. Mother wants him to be lord of it all, which I don't think he wants to be. She wants me to be just like him and Father, and I can't be. No one can will out here and be satisfied."

"What would make you satisfied, Colin?"

He frowned. "Gold, I guess. I know there's gold here. No one believes me, but I bloody well know it."

"Some try for years without luck," she cautioned.

"I know. I've read in the papers about Australians who've gone to California to strike it rich, and lost everything instead. Now it's Americans who've been leaving everything behind and coming to Australia. Four years ago there was a big strike north of here, along the MacQuarie River. I just know if we keep chipping away at these hills we'll find more wealth than we have ever dreamed."

"Too much has been known to destroy people."

"Not me. I could make something of myself. I could prove to Mother I'm worth something on my own."

Nina knew how much it meant to accomplish something on one's own. She didn't try to persuade Colin that perhaps what he'd said at dinner about taking a larger part in Flame Tree's business was more important than anything he'd been saying before or since. He could prove something more to his mother, and to himself, right here at Flame Tree than he could anywhere else.

They climbed a rise and stopped at the crest. Below, stretching as far as the eye could see and beyond, lay the valley floor, dotted with white tufts. As they moved closer, Nina saw that the tufts were actually sheep grazing on lush green grassland. She smiled at the picture-book scene. A narrow semidry river cut across the valley like a white snake, broken by a wide watering hole cut near a clump of dark green trees at which several of the stock drank.

Nina sucked in her breath at the vastness of the land and the size of the flock, and felt suddenly reduced to a mere speck on the landscape of this incredible Australia. Colin could tell by the look on her face that she'd never imagined such expanse or numbers.

Farther down the valley, settled at the base of a table rock, was a board-built cabin with a wisp of blue-white smoke curling above the chimney. Several horses were hitched along a rail, and near a grove of trees three dogs stretched out in the shade.

146

Colin smiled with satisfaction, and broke the silence. "Looks like we're just in time for the afternoon meal. What a stroke of luck for us. Shall we go down and invite ourselves in, then?"

"Maybe we shouldn't do that." Nina was suddenly reluctant. A feeling that she was throwing herself at Shane overwhelmed her. Worse, she didn't want to chance his being angry with her for invading his male territory.

"Don't be faint of innards now, Lady Cole," Colin said, as if reading her mind. "This is no time to retreat. Advance, always advance!"

Nina gave him a half-hearted smile. His taunting carried no venom, and she took his words almost as encouragement. She shot out her right hand toward him.

"You're spot on about that, mate!" She smiled at him warmly when he shook her hand. "Shall we advance, then?"

Shane sat at the long wood table inside the cabin with seven stockmen who'd been working Flame Tree station since they were barely out of adolescence. Four jackaroo apprentices joined them, and their stiff ribbing of each other and good-natured jokes were things he'd always enjoyed.

Over the last few days, however, his thoughts had been heavy with conversations he'd had with the Mum, and with the information about her health that Derrick had given him on their trip from Sydney. Colin's speech about taking some responsibility at Flame Tree at once made him happy and worried. And always the memory of kissing Nina in the moonlit garden permeated the daylight hours and haunted his dreams. The men had tried to tease him out of his preoccupied, rather detached state, but to no avail.

The coffee was unusually strong at this meal. He grimaced at the first bitter taste of it. Perhaps he should consider a ride back to the house for dinner tonight. He'd wanted to put in several appearances before this bloody soirée the Mum was throwing on Saturday, but he'd been too busy. He wished he could avoid the party altogether. He hated those things. The Mum would hover around him, making sure he met each of the valley's most eligible young women, and giving him a list of their desirable attributes, most notably the situation of their fathers' land. The whole thing promised to be disagreeable at best.

Nina Cole's face swept into his mind again. He guessed he still felt guilty about bringing her to Flame Tree. He probably shouldn't have acted so hastily in hiring her, but he had. And he probably should have given her more details about the Mum and Flame Tree, but he hadn't. No matter how much she thought she concealed it, he knew the Mum felt Nina was not of the right stock for him. Was it possible the reason he could not keep from thinking about her was because the Mum had all but pronounced her off limits?

It was more than that now, and he knew it. He'd begun to realize it during the times he was away from the house, and especially when he rode over the rangeland and had plenty of time to think. He thought about her often, he had to admit, thought about her eyes, her hair, the taste of her lips, the curve of her hip against his leg.

The glow around Nina's mane of copper hair lit up in his thoughts again. He tried to shake his mind of the vision, but it wouldn't go away. Her aquamarine eyes flashed, glittering with defiance at his merciless chiding. Underneath that sweet, innocent exterior breathed a woman of fire and energy. He could sense it every time he was within a few feet of her. Nay. His feelings for her had nothing to do with the Mum.

He frowned. In a few weeks Nina would be gone, and things would be the same as they were before his trip to America. Or would they?

A bang outside the cabin startled all at the table. The door swung open, and a clamor of silverware and tin cups heralded the entrance of Colin, who stood grinning widely in the doorway.

"Look to, mates, and mind your p's and q's. You've a guest!"

With that announcement he ushered the reluctant Nina inside. She walked shyly into the room, a limp and bedraggled creature in daks, mud all over her face, and grass clinging to her mass of wet, tumbling hair.

Their entrance stunned the men at the table. Colin at the out station was shock enough, but Colin with a girl in tow was a landslide surprise. A chuckle came from one end of the table and seemed to infect the others in rapid succession.

"Bit of a setback at the billabong," Colin laughed, pulling Nina farther into the cabin and closing the door. "But she's none the worse for the bath!"

Nina's eyes caught Shane's from the far end of the long wood table. Vaguely she saw Derrick and the others, but Shane's face was sharp and clear, and she could not read his thoughts.

She wished she could disappear, wished she hadn't thought about coming here in the first place, wished she hadn't let Colin bring her into the cabin. But more than anything she wished she'd been a better rider so at least she could have avoided the ungainly spill off the horse and into the watering hole, and made the entrance clean and neat.

Mate crawled out from his usual place at Shane's feet under the table, his large paws making scraping sounds on the wood floor. He ran to greet Nina, standing up on his back feet and leaning against her, happily licking her face. His enthusiastic welcome sent her backward against Colin, whose arms came up along her ribs. She felt the sting of tears behind her eyes, but willed them back. The last thing she wanted to do was cry in front of everyone, especially Shane.

"Gentlemen," Colin announced, straightening her up carefully, "may I present Miss Nina Cole, late of New York City, and nearby billabongs. Lady Cole, your fellow members of the Flame Tree flock."

Chapter 12

The men stood up at once to a loud scraping of chairs and stools on the wood floor. Some tipped their hats, others made exaggerated bows. Derrick stood at the back of the cabin near an iron coal stove watching the scene, a smile twitching his lower lip.

Nina was embarrassed, and speechless at first. Then, gathering as much dignity as she could muster, she curtsied, holding the sides of the loose trousers out with both hands.

"Pleased to make your acquaintances, I'm sure," she said in mock formal tone. Her eyes locked in a steady glittering gaze with Shane's.

It was a good show, but she knew she could not keep up the performance for long. She turned and quickly left the cabin, spurred on by the swell of teasing laughter. She ran into a eucalyptus grove behind the cabin, dropped to the ground, and leaned against a tree. She drew up her knees and buried her face in her arms. A moment later she heard the muffled sound of someone approaching. Before she could move, a wet nose pressed down into her hair and loud sniffing echoed in her ear. She turned her head and peeked over her arm. Mate stood there with a curiously expectant look on his face. To Nina it almost seemed as if he might be trying to console her.

"Oh, Mate." She threw her arms around his furry neck. "It's not your fault this time, don't worry."

He cocked his head when she let go of him. He panted with what she could only deem joyfulness, and looked at her with a kind of adoration from his soft, intelligent eyes.

Nina laughed. "If only Shane looked at me the way you do." She hugged him again and buried her face in his luxurious fur.

"Come out, my girl. I know you're in there!"

Shane's voice startled her. "Go away! I'll come out when I'm good and ready." Mate scrambled away from her and scampered out of the trees. "Traitor!" Nina called after him.

"Come on out, Nina. Don't let that mob of ockers get to you. They meant no harm."

It's not them I'm worried about, she thought to herself.

"All right, then, if you won't come out, I'll come in." He stomped into the underbrush. "You're a sight," he laughed. When she glared at him, he put up both hands in defense. "All right, all right, I'm sorry." Try as he might, he could not keep the laughter out of his voice. "What are you doing here? And with Colin, no less? I thought you two could never spend a civilized minute together, let alone a half-day's ride to the out station."

She stared up at him with wide, glistening eyes,

152

and lifted her mud-caked hair off her face. With the back of her hand she wiped the tears away, leaving muddy trails across her cheeks.

"Colin offered to show me around the station, and I took him up on it."

He hunkered down close to her. "Did you know he would bring you here?" he asked quietly.

She gazed at him for a moment, then lowered her eyes and nodded her head. "I asked him to. I wanted to see what . . . what a sheep station was like."

"I see." He stood up. "Well, then, you should come in and clean up, and we'll show you more."

"No, I can't go in there again looking like this."

"All right, stay here. I'll get a dilly bag and some soap and clean clothes for you. I know a place where you can wash up with some privacy. Would you like that?"

"I'd like that a lot," she agreed.

He was gone only a few minutes, returning with a hempen bag slung over his shoulder. He summoned her out of the trees, and they walked behind the cabin and down a long, rocky slope toward more stands of fragrant eucalyptus and flowering shrubs. Nina turned around several times watching the cabin disappear from view.

"Don't worry. Where we're going you'll not be seen."

The wind whistled around them as they descended the hill and picked their way over rocks and stones. When they reached the bottom Nina noticed that all was still and calm on the grassy floor, and the air was warm and misty. The growth of vines and creepers was thicker, and giant tree ferns grew over the path they walked. All around, the sweet song of bell-birds filled the air, but each sight of them was fleeting.

The foliage grew even thicker. Nina perspired as she fought her way through it, pulling stray twigs from her hair and dodging small branches to protect her eyes.

Soon into the thickest of it she heard the sound of rushing water, too light to be a river and too full to be a stream. When they came out into the sunshine once again, there in front of her, plunging down a moss-covered rocky embankment, was a narrow, silken strand of blue-white waterfall. Halfway down the bank it struck a wide stone ledge which effused the water into a splay of natural shower. Beneath that ledge was another of smooth rock, and below that a wide moss- and fern-rimmed pool. The sun shone through the ferns and vines, creating golden lacy patterns moving over the rippling water, and made blue green shadows in the lush foliage around the pool. A perfect private bath. Nirvana.

Nina was happily stunned. "Is it cold?" she whispered, but didn't really care if it was or not.

"Not very. It comes from a warm spring up above." He pointed above their heads.

Shane opened the bag and produced a large sheet of huck-weave toweling, a cake of soap, a light wool blanket, a drinking cup, a clean pair of trousers, and a vest and blue shirt from the smallest man at the station, and a pair of white cotton socks. He placed all but the blanket, cup, and socks at the edge of the bank, then walked away from the pool to a shaded spot. Spreading out the blanket, he sat down with the

154

bag at the edge of it. Mate ran up to flop down next to him.

"Throw me your boots as soon as you get them off," Shane called to her. "I'll see what I can do about cleaning them up a bit."

She tugged off the wet, mud-caked boots and threw them to him, then stripped off her filthy clothes down to her chemise and drawers and stepped into the pool.

The water was refreshingly warm and no more than two feet deep. Once she was seated on a smooth rock and could see Shane's back to her, she stripped off her undergarments and rinsed them in the clear water. Slipping out of the pool, she hung them on some giant fern branches, then slipped back into the silken water. The feeling was heavenly as the water swirled gently around her, circling her throat and moving in soft caresses over her breasts.

She dipped her head back into the water, letting her hair float around her in a sun-bathed golden crown. The soap lathered well and felt good on her skin. She was surprised to discover how finely milled it was, not the harsh lye soap she might have expected from a shepherd's supply.

Keeping her body under the water and stretching her legs out behind her, she pushed herself with her hands toward the ledge where the waterfall came down. She brought herself up under the shower to sit on the ledge in half-sun. The most glorious feeling of freedom she'd experienced since letting herself out the window of the New York apartment washed over her. The water spilled down on her body, tinglingly delicious, like tiny massaging gentle fingers. But her

155

hair—her hair had turned into a tangled wet mass of burnished copper.

Sounds of heavy splashing in the pool broke into the rhythmic flow of the waterfall. Nina snapped her head around and looked over her shoulder just as Mate was springing out of the water and up onto her perch. The mossy slipperiness of the ledge prevented secure footing for him, and he slid and grunted his way across it to fall into her lap, whereupon they both fell back into the pool. Mate bobbed to the surface and came up on all fours, sneezing and sniffing and shaking his head to clear his eyes and ears. Nina came up in front of him, spluttering and trying to yell at him through a mouthful of water.

Shane stood on the bank, feet apart, hands on his slim hips, his head thrown back, his husky laughter resounding around the pool. Mate bounded by Nina, splashing more water into her face, and scrambled up onto the bank. He stood next to Shane, then shook his body from nose to tail, covering the laughing figure with dog-fragrant water.

Nina rubbed her eyes and opened them just in time to catch that event. She started to laugh quietly, then, unable to stop herself, broke into peals of silvery laughter.

"'Tis amusing to you, is it, my girl?" Shane called out, his wide grin showing a line of shiny, even white teeth.

Nina saw him slowly move his body between her and her undergarments spread out on the trees. He picked up the towel with slow, deliberate movement.

"Shall we see how amusing it continues to be while you soak awhile? Think how you'll look," he

156

curled the fingers of one hand, "all done up like a prune, shivering in the moonlight."

"You wouldn't dare!"

"Now, wouldn't I?"

"That's the meanest thing I've ever heard of!"

"Hardly, my girl. There are meaner things!"

"And I'm sure you've thought of them all!"

His response was another hearty laugh.

"Well, you've enjoyed a great many jokes on me from the moment we met, haven't you? I deserve to enjoy one at your expense now and again." She shivered, and a lock of hair fell over her face. "Besides, this wasn't my fault. Can't you discipline Mate?"

"One doesn't discipline Mate. One arrives at a settlement with him." Shane sat down silently on the pool bank. He took the towel and began to dry Mate's thick fur with it.

"Shane, please . . . I'm starting to get cold. I'll need that towel." She raised one hand and lifted the front of her hair out of her eyes. "And my hair . . ."

Shane stopped toweling Mate's fur. He didn't move for a long moment. Nina thought he might be waiting for her to give in and beg him to let her out of the pool, or else he expected her to give in and just walk out naked as the day she was born. She clenched her chattering teeth. He'd have to wait until doomsday for that, as far as she was concerned. Then he stood up, the blanket held out in his hands.

"All right, my girl, since you've not got the mettle to survive a tepid pool, I suppose I should do the gentlemanly thing . . ."

"Gentlemanly! Hah! Why start now?" she shot

157

back, and was instantly sorry.

"Well, if that's the way you feel about it . . ." He sat back down. Mate looked first at Shane, then at Nina, then back at Shane.

"All right, I'm sorry, I'm sorry. Honest. Please, Shane . . ." She held up her arms toward the blanket.

He watched her for a moment. The sun played across the water, making her appear to be floating in a pool of diamonds. She was so inviting with her arms pale golden in the sun against the blue-green water, her hair a tumbled mass of gold glints falling around her face and shoulders, the tendrils disappearing beneath the water to—he could only imagine—rest over her nipples. He felt a strong urge to throw himself into the pool and sweep her up into his arms and cover her body with a shower of kisses.

Instead, he sucked in his breath and walked toward her, holding the blanket up over his face. He heard her quick splashing footsteps as she walked out of the pool, up the bank, and into the blanket. He let her take it out of his hands.

"Thank you. That was certainly 'gentlemanly' of you," she said, wrapping the blanket around her.

"My pleasure, madam."

She rubbed herself briskly with the blanket ends, then pulled it tightly around her body and sat down on a wide rock in the sun. Holding out the length of her hair, she tried to pick through the tangles with her fingers.

"What am I going to do with this? I shall have to sneak into the house through the kitchen in hopes that Maude can do something with it. I can't let the

Mum see this. Look at it! It tangles as fast as I untangle it."

Shane sauntered over to her. "If you would let me do yet one more gentlemanly thing, I believe I can help you out of this muck you think you're in."

"How?" She looked up at him with wide, gleaming eyes.

"Will you trust me, and not put up a fight?"

"I don't know. Why should I trust you?"

As he came near her, she felt a warm twinge at the bottom of her stomach, and a shiver ran up her spine to the back of her neck.

"Because I know how to take care of that. Come with me . . . and no protests."

She stood up dutifully and, rewrapping the blanket around her body like a sarong, padded barefoot behind him around the pool. Shane picked up the dilly bag as he went, and Mate took the lead, head held high, sniffing the wind. Halfway around the pool they came to the remnants of an old landslide, piles of large pink and gray and brown rocks edging the water.

"Sit," he commanded her, pointing toward a flat rock with several others piled behind it.

She sat, and so did Mate. From out of the bag he took the cup, a small covered tin, a large bone comb, and the soap. He sat down by the rocks behind her, then took the damp towel and placed it at the edge of the rocks and motioned her to lay her head back onto it.

With the cup he dipped water from the pool several times, pouring it over her head and letting it run down through the strands and curls. Then he took

159

the soap, made a thick, rich lather with his hands, and covered every inch of her head and hair with it, soaping the strands and massaging her scalp. She relaxed against the rocks and against his hands, and closed her eyes. The warmth of the sun and the gentle massaging of his hands were a hypnotic combination.

When he finished soaping, he took the cup and dipped and rinsed every trace of it out of her hair. Then he squeezed the thick strands to press out the excess water, and gently pushed her up by the shoulders.

He picked up the towel and pressed it over her hair. The sun warmed both of them. As he watched his hands in her hair and saw the long locks touching the creamy white skin of her back and shoulders, it was all he could do to keep himself from drawing her onto his lap and fulfilling the desire he felt pulling heavy in his loins. He shook his head to release the vision.

He took the little tin, opened it, and took out a dollop of opaque cream. Rubbing it first between his palms until it became transparent, he ran his hands carefully through and down her hair to the ends, covering each strand with a thin veil of cream. Then he took out the comb and gently began at the top of her head and worked down, painstakingly picking apart the tangles until they fell in silken strands down her back. He performed the ritual in silence, a magic moment in time that neither of them wished to break.

Nina felt cared for more than she had since she was a child. The rough stockman who was an enigma in

160

the house at Flame Tree, a shepherd in the bush, and one who enjoyed a good laugh and went about, it seemed, creating events for that laughter, was washing and combing her hair with a tenderness that touched her deeply.

"There," he said quietly, handing her the comb. "You may want to do something more, but I think you'll find it easier now." He turned away. "I'll get your clothes."

"Wait, Shane." She took a deep breath as he turned around. The corners of his sky-blue eyes fanned upward at the corners, reflecting a clear, quartzlike sparkle. "Thank you, this was the nicest thing anyone's done for me in a long while." He smiled and nodded thoughtfully. "What was that cream you used? It makes my hair feel silky." She lifted the long locks and let them fall around her shoulders.

The sight of Nina sitting on rocks in the sun like a water nymph, her hair moving in the light, sending off golden copper sparks, caused a tightening around Shane's chest. He could not take his eyes off her. She looked up at him with questioning eyes.

"The cream . . . aye, it's wool grease." At the frown that formed between her eyebrows, he added, "It's clean, don't worry. It's good for a lot of things. Rub some on your skin." He tore his gaze away from her and turned toward where her clothes lay. "We'd best start back. They're liable to start a search party."

She smiled at him and he felt his heart race a little. He retrieved her underthings and folded them inside the clean clothes, handed them to her, then walked away from the rocks so she could dress in private.

When she joined him she wore the brown trousers.

They fit her full around her hips, and snug to her ankles, hugging her boot tops. Her own scarf was threaded through the belt loops and pulled to a knot at the waist, two long tails resting over her thigh. A fleece-lined brown leather vest covered the light blue shirt that was open at the neck, and she had turned up the long sleeves to just below her elbows. Her hair, still damp from the washing, was swept over the top of her forehead and one side, and hung in waves down her back and over one shoulder.

Shane sucked in his breath. She looked more inviting to him than ever. He had to stop this kind of thinking. It would come to no good.

"Well, my girl," he said instead, "looks like boys' clothes suit you right down to the ground!"

Her response was to throw the wet towel at him.

After she'd dressed, Nina thought, but couldn't be certain, that she caught a look from Shane, a frankly appraising look, one that told her he liked what he saw. She warmed under it for a moment, and then his face changed and he made the comment about boys' clothes suiting her. He was probably baiting her again, but she refused to bite.

Right now she was feeling better outside, and inside, than she'd felt in her memory.

Chapter 13

"Well, it's about time you got back," Derrick said as Shane and Nina walked into the cabin. "Had the billy on for tea 'most an hour. Everything all right?"

"No worries," Shane replied, and spread the towel and blanket over a rack near the stove.

"Well, looky here, missy. You sure look a mite different than you did when you first stepped a boot in here a bit ago!"

"Thank you, Derrick. I think I'll take that as a compliment."

"'Tis meant to be. Here, lass, have a cuppa, 'twill make you feel good."

"Thank you, although I don't think it could make me feel better than I do right now." She sent a sidelong glance in Shane's direction, but he didn't see it.

Derrick quirked an eyebrow at her, then at Shane, then nodded his head knowingly and went back to the stove.

Shane turned abruptly and headed for the door.

"I'd better get out and check on the jackaroos," he said lamely.

"Aye, I suspect you have to," Derrick replied without facing him. Then he turned around and raised a warning finger. "And get 'em back here for evo meal on time for a change. Brought some flyswisher stew and the taste goes bad if it cooks too long."

"Must be everything cooks too long around here, then!" Shane ran out the door just as a wooden spoon was flung in his direction.

"You really care for him, don't you?" Nina asked the older man through sips of strong tea.

"Like a son, aye. Ah, afore I forget, Colin said to tell you it looked like you were in good hands, so he headed back to have dinner with the Mum. Yer welcome to share with us, if you can stand that bunch of rowdies we got here."

Nina worried about Colin's leaving her there, but surely someone would ride back to the house with her. They wouldn't let her go alone in the dark. She smiled. "I think I can handle it . . . now. Sorry about before. It's just that, well, I seem to have this knack for grand entrances and it's rather disconcerting at times."

Derrick eyed her with a crackling wink, and set about getting flour and milk for damper bread. "It's a surefire way to get noticed, that's spot on!"

"It's not exactly the kind of noticing I wanted," Nina responded absently, setting down the mug. "Is there anything I can help you with?"

"You can set the plates out for supper, if you want."

"I do. But first, I think I'll go gather up some of those wildflowers I saw along the path. I think they'd be nice on the table, don't you?"

"Well, now, lass, you don't know what you're working with here. This bunch is not apt to be too mindful of flowers on the table. Wouldn't s'prise me if they et 'em."

"I'll try anyway. Back in a few minutes." She started out the door, then turned back, and tried to sound nonchalant. "Derrick, I'm not sure I'll know how to get back to the house without Colin. Is anyone else going back?"

"I was thinkin' of it. We could use some supplies here. Don't worry yourself none, lass. You won't have to go alone."

Nina smiled, then walked out, a happy, lilting hum in her voice.

By the time Shane returned for supper, he'd somehow got himself in a foul mood. The jackaroos had given him a hard time with their endless ribbing about the sheila he'd gone off with into the woods. He knew instinctively Nina would still be at the cabin. He'd seen Colin riding away, leaving her there to fend for herself. His little brother never did seem to think of anybody but himself.

Shane wasn't sure he could accept it if the men got out of hand at the table with their remarks. He couldn't very well make a scene and reprimand them. They'd never let him forget that, either. And what if Nina misunderstood his defense of her if he was forced to do it?

He strode into the cabin and could hardly believe what he saw. Derrick and Nina were working side by side over supper, chattering like two old cooks. The table had a long colorful cloth covering it. Where in bloody hell had Derrick been hiding that thing? Their usual tin plates and cups lined both sides, with cutlery at each place, instead of thrown into the middle of the table, as it usually was. And in the center sat an old coffeepot, its hinged lid open, with a huge spray of yellow and white wildflowers bursting out of the top of it.

The cabin smelled homey with stew cooking and bread baking and a fruit cobbler sitting on the sideboard. Derrick was certainly producing some interesting things this evo. Even the pot of breakfast syrup was set out for the bread.

"What's all this? Derrick, you old curmudgeon, you've been keeping a lot from us, haven't you?"

"Now Shane, don't start with me. The lass here just wanted to help, and I let her, is all."

"So, I see." Shane grinned widely at his old friend. "Any amber left in the spring house?"

Derrick nodded. "Better ration it out. Not much left, and it's got to do till I get back for supplies."

Shane went out back and returned with a covered tin pail of beer. He took out two tin coffee mugs and splashed the liquid into them. Thick, foamy heads spilled out over the tops and down the sides. He held one out toward Derrick.

Nina grabbed it from him before Derrick had the chance. "Thanks. That looks like just what I need." She downed a big swig. When she lowered the cup, her eyes watered, and a white foam moustache perched over her upper lip.

Derrick and Shane were surprised at her easy taste

166

of amber, and they laughed lightly.

"What?" she asked innocently.

Shane's eyes went heavenward, and he laughed more heartily. "Promise me you'll go just as you are to the Mum's big do next week. You'll make a rather showy entrance!"

"I usually do," she laughed, wiping away the moustache with the back of her hand, and handing the mug to Derrick.

Derrick issued a low whistle when the jackaroos came into the cabin for supper. They'd washed up and changed their shirts, and some had even gone so far as to change their pants. A couple of them had even slicked down their hair with wool grease. Nina thought it might have been appropriate if they'd washed it first, but no matter. It was the thought that was most important.

Nina thoroughly enjoyed herself, surprised at how relaxed she was among their company, even when the conversation centered around her. She liked the openness among them, and was amused by the obvious way they were trying to remember all their mothers had taught them about their behavior in front of women. They labored over speaking correctly and keeping their language less peppery than it usually was.

"Well, it seems a female presence must have a sweetening effect on this usually acid-tongued lot," Shane opined.

"I'm not so sure it'll last very long," Derrick said.

Nina took note of something that seemed rather curious to her. Considering the amount of hard work these men did in the outdoors, and the crude way they

167

lived, they all had very smooth, almost soft hands with clean nails. She mentioned it to Derrick as they washed dishes, observing that his hands looked the same.

"It's the oil in the wool. If you was to throw sheep around often enough you'd never need none of that fancy woman's stuff." As soon as the words fell off his lips, the older man reddened visibly. "Sorry, missy, I didn't mean nothin' by that."

"I know, Derrick. It's all right."

Shane sat by the low fireplace, repairing a leather apron and listening to the exchange between Nina and Derrick. His mood had changed drastically over supper. As he sat next to the unlit fireplace, with Mate curled up asleep at his feet, he was aware of how—what was it?—contented . . . aye, contented he was feeling tonight. He half expected Nina to come sit in the chair by him, a basket of sewing in her lap.

"Derrick, are you ready to leave?" Nina folded a towel and placed it on a bench. "It's a bit of a ride back to the house, so I guess we should be going."

She said it with a half-glance in Shane's direction, hoping he might say he would go with her, but he didn't. He sat silently, intent on his work.

Derrick shot his own look toward Shane. His young friend was concentrating a little too heavily on that old leather apron. Unless he missed his guess, he figured Shane was avoiding the opportunity to be alone with Nina. Now what could he be afraid of? A comely little lass like Nina, she'd be no bother. Derrick smiled to himself. Aye, she was a bother, all right—she bothered Shane something terrible, and that was what he was afraid of! Derrick was in a quandary. Should he simply do his duty and escort the young lass back to the house? Or . . .

"Ow! Blast!" Derrick swore loudly.

Nina spun around, and Shane jumped up, dropping the apron. Derrick hopped around on one foot, both hands grasping the raised ankle of the other. Mate lifted his sleepy head, then lay back down, disinterested in the activity.

"What happened?" Concern was genuine in Shane's voice as he hurried to the older man's aid.

Derrick leaned heavily on Shane's outstretched arm and motioned to the chair by the fireplace. Nina took his other arm and the two eased him into the chair. Derrick groaned loudly, holding his ankle.

"Bloody floor!" He pulled at his boot to remove it.

Shane leaned down to help him. "I still don't know what happened. What about the floor?"

"Caught my boot heel in it, that's what. Twisted my bloody ankle." He groaned. "It's prob'ly broke." He rubbed the ankle through his sock.

"Here, let me look at it." Shane knelt down and reached to feel the extent of the injury.

"Don't touch it!" Derrick yelled. "Hurts like bloody hell, and won't be helped by you probin' around on it."

"All right, all right." Shane grabbed a low wood stool from the other side of the fireplace and set it down in front of Derrick's feet. "Here, raise your foot. It'll keep the swelling down."

Derrick obliged, lifting his leg with great effort to rest it on the stool.

"Well, now, I feel just awful," he moaned. "Here I was about to escort the lass back to the house and I go

169

and do a clumsy thing like this." He raised his eyes to Nina, a wan look on his face. "Looks like you'll have to go it alone, missy. But don't you worry, now—it's not dark enough yet for the most ferocious animals to be out. They tend to wait till it's pitch. But if you hurry, you won't have to be out in the dark-dark that long, maybe only thirty minutes or so, just as the barking spiders come out." He looked with apologetic eyes toward Shane, then back at Nina. "Well, it's the sorriest lot, I am."

Nina's face blanched at the mention of ferocious animals and, God forbid, barking spiders, but she softened in sympathy for Derrick's pain and speech of apology.

"Now, don't you worry about me. I'll be just fine. It's not that far, and it's still light. You just rest. Should I tell Maude to come?"

"No! No, no," Derrick replied quickly. "She'll only worry, and Lord knows she has enough to worry about there. You'd best get started right away." He sent a weak look toward Shane.

"Aye, you just rest . . . mate," Shane gave his old friend a doubtful look. "I'll make sure Nina gets back to the house in one piece. Keep that leg up."

Shane grabbed his hat off a peg by the door, and took Nina by the arm. "We're on our way now," he told Derrick. "Mate will keep you company. You'll be all right?" There was a pronounced half-laugh in his voice.

Derrick grimaced in pain. "Aye. I'll just sit a spell. She'll be all right." He waved them away.

Outside the closed door, Shane stopped and turned toward Nina with a thoughtful look. "You wait here

I'll just get a hat for you. The air gets damp when the sun goes down this time of year."

He waited a moment more, then hit the door hard with an open palm and pushed it wide open. Derrick was mid-stride on his way toward the back door. He lurched to a stop when the door burst open.

"Feeling better already, I see," Shane growled with a caught-you-redhanded tone in his voice. He shut the door quickly behind him.

Derrick looked stricken. "I . . . I just thought a . . . a pint of amber might ease the pain, y'know."

"No doubt." Shane stepped farther into the room.

"What're you here for? Yer not lettin' the miss go home by herself, now, are ya?" The older man's voice held genuine concern.

"Well, I ought to let her start out that way. You'd sure go after her. Would serve you right. Let her see what a big faker you are."

"Aw, now, mate, you wouldn't . . ."

Laughing, Shane lifted a narrow-brimmed hat from a long rack at the back of the room. "No, you old codger. I'll keep your secret . . . this time. But I won't save your lying bum the next! See you tomorrow."

Derrick picked up a tin mug to heave in his direction, but Shane was out the door faster than he could raise it over his head. Derrick grinned. His little ruse had worked like a charm, and Shane and Nina were off on a moonlit ride together. He reached down and scratched Mate behind the ear, then headed out to the springhouse, whistling a merry ditty, a light hop in his step.

Chapter 14

Shane threw his prized American western saddle on Shadow, then saddled the mare for Nina. He helped her up and they set off in the direction of the main house. The sun was going down in a blazing red-orange finale to the day, the jagged horizon cutting into it like great dark teeth.

Nina looked around nervously. Shane rode silently, deep in thought, but when he noticed Nina's skittish glances off shrubs and shadows, he felt he should say something to her.

"Don't look so worried. There aren't any ferocious animals between here and home. That was just Derrick . . ."

"Oh, of course," Nina's laugh was forced, "I should have known. Barking spiders, indeed."

"Well, there are those. Not so apt to be any around here, though."

"Really, Shane, Derrick's not here to join in your silly tactics to scare the foreigner. There's no need to . . ."

"This isn't a scare tactic," he cut in. He knew this would happen—now she'd never believe the truth, thanks to Derrick. "They are big spiders with treacherous stings. I've heard they've been known to sting a chicken and then drag it right out of the barnyard back to the nest. I've never seen it myself, but I've certainly heard the stories."

"That does it! I admit that I've probably been the most gullible female you've ever met, but spiders carrying off chickens? Really, Shane, give me a little credit . . ."

"Fine. Don't believe me. Just don't say I didn't warn you, that's all." He shifted in the saddle, and the leather creaked under his long legs. "I suppose I should tell you about the snakes and lizards while I'm at it. No sense in leaving gaps in your elementary education."

"Why don't we leave that discussion for a more opportune time? I'd want it to be daylight so I could be sure to see the purple stripes and yellow plaid clearly," she scoffed. Actually, she didn't want to discuss snakes and lizards at all, especially in the dark.

"Very funny. Now who's exaggerating? I do think you ought to see the blue-tongued lizard sometime," he said quietly.

"Oh, so do I," she said in a breathless, mocking tone. "I can't imagine staying one day in Australia without having seen a blue-tongued lizard. Do they stick it out and wave it in the breeze so you can really get a good look at it?" she asked in mock awe and curiosity.

Suddenly Shane reined Shadow in and waited

until Nina's horse was abreast of his.

"We'd better switch horses, here," he said, dismounting.

"Why?"

"You ride Shadow. This is a difficult trail along the ravine, and he's much more familiar with it at night than your horse. She's young, and we haven't had her long. I can handle her better than you can."

"Oh, and now I can't handle a horse, is that what you're saying?" she sniffed.

"As a matter of fact I am. You're a . . . a tenderfoot, and it's Shadow that'll handle you. He knows how to pick out the trail in the dark. Now, stop being so stubborn and get down here."

He stood by her horse and held up his arms to her. In the slowly rising moonlight she could see his face, dark on one side and just barely visible on the other. But she could clearly see his eyes blazing, and she knew she'd better comply.

She lifted her right leg out of the stirrup and brought it up over the mare's neck, then kicked her left foot out of its stirrup. Turning toward Shane, she slid off the horse to the ground, his hands gripping under her arms to assist her. He held her up inches off the ground for a moment, then set her down slowly.

Suddenly he felt no desire to release her. The moonlight cast a pale creamy silver glow over her face, lighting the tendrils of hair that fell around it. The picture of her in the pool that afternoon came rushing into his mind and he felt his knees go liquid just a little. She didn't move, didn't struggle to get away from him, just stared up into his face.

Shane's first thought was to lower his head and

slowly consume her lips with his own. He wanted to taste them again, possess their sweetness, even if only for a moment. No, he shouldn't do that. If he kissed her now, he knew he wouldn't be able to stop himself there. He'd want everything from her, want to possess her completely. She was vulnerable, and he'd placed her in a difficult situation when he'd brought her here. She was going to leave Flame Tree soon, he had to keep reminding himself of that. It was just getting so bloody difficult for him to keep his wits about him whenever he was with her.

Nina couldn't move. At first, suspended off the ground in Shane's hands and then set carefully down, she felt totally out of control of her own body. He still held her, gazed down at her with that glittering light in his eyes, and even though she could control it now, she still felt no desire to move.

Nina was afraid to move, afraid to breathe. Why didn't he say something or do something? If something didn't happen soon, she knew she'd crumble from the sheer tension of this moment. He kept staring at her mouth, and she stared at his. Shamefully, she wanted him to kiss her as he had in the garden. She'd thought about that kiss often. Well, she just couldn't stand here like this. He'd think she wanted him to kiss her, and that would never do. He'd probably think it was just a ploy to trap him somehow. Aunt Sadie had told her men always thought like that.

But, she admitted to herself, she'd be afraid to kiss him again anyway. Some of her friends had told her that with just one kiss from some men, a girl could fall completely in love, and then promptly be left by the cad after he'd stolen her virtue. But this time it would be she who would be leaving. Confusion reigned inside every part of her. She felt her legs weakening, and she swayed in Shane's arms.

Shane felt the slight movement of her body toward his. That was all he could take. He sucked in his breath and crushed her to his chest, covering her lips with an all-consuming kiss. To his utter delight, she responded to him, tentatively at first, then kissing him with sweet passion. He pushed his tongue against her teeth and urged them apart. Falteringly they opened, and he slipped his tongue inside the moistness of her mouth, flicking and curling it over every curve and hollow. She moaned softly, and her response set him afire.

He slid his hands up the middle of her back, under her thick mane of hair, to cup the back of her neck and head. Grinding his lips against her mouth with even fiercer thrusts of his tongue, he held her head in his hands. He could not get enough of her, could not taste enough of her.

Nina lost her breath, and a low moan escaped the back of her throat. Crushed against him, she balanced on the tips of her toes. He had control over her with his hands and arms and lips, and she was giving him that control. Her hands moved under his arms and up his back, her nails digging into his shoulders through his cotton shirt. The strength in his muscles quivered under her hands and stirred her to new power in herself. Every inch of her skin was alive with prickling jets of fire.

He molded her body against his lean length, his hard thigh pressing against that private part of her that had never felt such closeness to a man. She clung to him hungrily, and felt the hard heat of his desire burn against her thigh. That was a shock. She hadn't known it could happen so quickly, so insistently, nor could she have guessed what her own response would be. The warm moistness quickly spreading throughout her stomach and below was as unfamiliar as everything else she'd experienced since her arrival at Flame Tree.

Suddenly she was frightened. She pulled away from him, turning out of his grasp. She stepped back until her shoulder touched the mare's side. The horse moved away from the nudge, and Nina lost her balance. Shane reached out and caught her. Wrapping his arms around her, he held her against him, stroking her hair.

Holding her this way filled him with a desire so intense he thought he might burst into a million fragments if it was not fulfilled. The need in his loins was outwardly evident, but the ache within was almost too much to bear. Her luscious body pressed against his, his burning exploration of her sweet mouth, and the memory of her in the sun-sparkling pool with light illuminating her incredible hair and luminous eyes, were almost more than he could take. It would all be too much for *any* man to take, he assured himself. Now he was overcome with the desire to absorb every part of her, and to know every intimate detail of her.

But it was more than physical desire, he knew now. Standing in the moonlight, holding her . . . it was much more than that. He wanted this woman in a way he had never wanted any other woman before.

178

He wanted her beauty, her courage, her intelligence, her compassion, and her humor in his life. Not just for now, not for three or four months, but for as long as he was privileged to walk this earth. He wanted her with him at Flame Tree, out on the rangeland, and in the manor house, if that was forced on him. He could endure anything with her at his side.

"Nina, Nina," he murmured into her hair.

The sound of his husky voice cut through to her conscious mind. She pulled away from him slowly, letting the circle of his arms keep her balanced, and looked up at him, tilting her head back to see his eyes. The moon cast a shadow over his face, and while she could not see his eyes clearly, she could feel their penetrating gaze.

He looked down at her. Her face and hair were bathed in a silver wash of moonlight. He wanted to tell her how beautiful she was, how utterly breathtaking, but the words were lost inside him.

Nina gently pushed away from him, and bent to pick up the hat which had fallen off when Shane took her in his arms.

"I . . . I think we should be going. It's getting late, and it will be difficult for me to get into the house."

He wondered if he should say he was sorry for kissing her like that. Hell, no! He wasn't sorry. He'd only be sorry if she hated him for it. Right now, he didn't think she hated him.

"Don't worry about that. I can get you in without anyone seeing you."

Reluctantly he picked up his hat, then led her to Shadow's side and gave her a leg up. He mounted the other horse and rode up behind her, letting Shadow take the lead. The big black stallion instinctively knew the trail back to the barn. They rode slowly in silence.

Nina's thoughts careened around her mind. She had been thrilled to be in Shane's arms, kissing him as deeply and passionately as he had kissed her. She no longer wondered if he noticed her. He had definitely noticed her. This was real . . . wasn't it? He couldn't have been teasing her this time.

One thing she did know for sure—in the deepest regions of her being, she didn't want to leave Flame Tree, or Australia. It was all too wonder-filled, too beautiful in a raw, unspoiled way, and as sensuous in feeling as the man whose arms she could still feel burning around her.

With a sudden jolt, Shadow picked his front feet up off the ground, pranced frantically, and whickered nervously. His movement almost unseated Nina, but she managed to hold onto the reins and pommel through fistfuls of his long mane to keep her balance. She gripped his sides with her knees.

"What's the matter with him?" she shrieked over her shoulder.

Shane tried to ride up alongside her, but the mare caught the scent of fear from Shadow and set up a struggle against the bit in her mouth and the rider on her back. Shane had his hands full trying to control her as well as get close to Shadow to calm him.

The stallion backed up, pumping his front hooves and snorting as his back legs buckled under him. Then he heaved up with a surge of his mighty strength. The mare slipped in back of him and Shadow's rump came up hard under her mouth, ramming the bit into soft tissue. She cried out in pain and bucked hard, catching Shane off-guard and throwing him off her back. He dropped and rolled away from the frantically pounding hooves, then tried to get up, but lost his balance and fell over the edge of the ravine.

Chapter 15

"Shane!" Nina screamed. She pulled back hard on the great stallion's reins, yelling, "Shadow, whoa, whoa, boy!"

She patted the sweating neck, calling soothing words, and tried to turn him around. At last he stopped twisting and backing, his heaving and blowing calmed, and he settled down. The mare had taken off down the trail and was long out of sight.

Frantically Nina looked around in the darkness. "Shane! Where are you?"

A cloud crept over the moon like long, dark fingers. When it passed, the night was bright, but not enough to diffuse odd-shaped forms into less menacing shadows. Nina started to slide down from Shadow's back, but her foot caught in a length of rope tied to the saddle. She kicked free, dismounted, and tied the reins to a low tree. Patting the stallion's hot neck and speaking quietly to gentle him helped to calm her own racing nerves, and with great trepidation she stepped out onto the trail.

"Shane?" she called in a tremulous voice. God, where was he? If he was playing some kind of game now, she vowed she would make him regret it. But what if this wasn't a game? What if he was seriously hurt . . . or worse?

"Shane?" she called again, a little louder. "If you're trying to trick me now, it isn't funny. Please don't do this." She walked farther down the trail. "Shane? Please . . ."

Dingoes yipped and howled in the far distance, a lonely, plaintive cry. Fighting against fear that threatened to consume her, she struggled to keep her head clear and her nerves calm. But there was nothing she could do about the erratic pounding of her heart.

"Shane!" she screamed it.

"Stop yelling!" came a loud hoarse whisper from somewhere—she could not tell where.

"Shane? Where in bloody hell are you?" Now she was more angry than frightened. "You scared me half to death!"

"I said stop yelling!" he whispered again. "Take just three steps forward—no more."

She complied with his command. "Now what?" She whispered it this time.

"Look down and to your right."

She did, but had to peer over a ledge. She sucked in her breath between her teeth. He was hanging in the ravine, clutching two roots that jutted out from the side. In the moonlight she could see that one leg was draped over a lower branch and the other foot was braced against a root. Below that was nothing but inky blackness.

184

"Oh, my God! Are you hurt?" She took another step toward the edge.

"Don't! Don't come any closer," he warned. "No, I'm not hurt."

Nina was relieved to hear that. "Well, then, why don't you just climb up out of there?" she whispered.

"I don't think I can put much weight on these roots. They might not hold me and I could slip farther down."

"Are you near the bottom?"

"In a manner of speaking, one could say I was."

"Is it far down, very deep?"

"No, not very. Why are you asking me all these bloody questions? I've got to get out of here!"

"I'm just trying to help!" she whispered. "If it's not very far down, why don't you just jump down to the bottom, and climb up on larger branches?"

"Because I don't bloody want to!" he snapped in a loud whisper.

"Well, that's pretty stubborn, if you ask me," she whispered back, her voice straining.

"I didn't ask you!" he shouted at the top of his whisper. "Are you going to help me, or just stand there asking a lot of fool questions?"

"How can I help you if you won't let me come any closer? And why are we whispering?"

"There you go again, answering a question with a question! Do something to get me out of here!" His voice, even in a whisper, was growing more and more agitated with what sounded to Nina to be near panic, and it triggered her own fear all over again.

"All right. What do you want me to do?" She started to move closer, but the edge gave way sending

185

a shower of sand and rocks down onto his head.

"Will you bloody watch what you're doing?" His voice was becoming more agitated.

"I can't! It's pretty dark out here, in case you've been too busy to notice. Why are you so mad? I was worried you'd been hurt ... or worse. I'm only trying to help you."

"Well, then, do it!"

"How? It really looks as if it would all work out much better if you'd just drop down and come up another way."

"Nay!"

"Why in bloody hell not?" she whispered at the top of her voice.

"Because ... because there are snakes down in that hole ... that's why!" He made a shuddering sound.

Nina was silent for a moment, then found her voice again. "How can you tell that? It's so dark down there."

"I lit a match and ... I saw them."

"Oh, God! Ugh, I hate snakes. Are they poisonous?"

"How in bloody hell do I know? I hope you'll pardon me, but I didn't want to get close enough to find out. Now will you just do something to get me out of here?"

"Well, it would certainly help me if you'd be more specific so I could assist you," Nina said spitefully. "Are you ... are you afraid of snakes?"

Silence.

"Shane?" Still no answer. "Shane, are ... are you still there?"

"Of course I'm still here. Where in bloody hell did

you think I was going to go?"

"There's no reason to be insulting." She took a deep breath in effort to calm herself. "Are you?"

"Am I what?"

"Afraid of snakes?"

There was no answer for a moment, then, "Aye, I'm afraid of snakes! There! Are you satisfied now? It's true. The great strong stockman, Shane Merritt, is afraid of snakes. Now . . . do something to get me out of here. They're becoming interested in this conversation!"

Nina covered her mouth with her hand. She was deathly afraid of snakes herself, and if Shane was also afraid of them . . . she shuddered.

Shane swallowed hard. He had to think calmly and rationally, for now he could feel the thin roots he was holding onto pull away just a little from the embankment.

"I'll get Shadow," she whispered, remembering the rope that had caught her foot. She crept over to where the big stallion stood, gathered up his reins, and led him slowly toward the edge of the ravine.

"Not too close! Are you trying to kill me?"

"The idea has been forming rather recently," she muttered. She tied Shadow to a sturdy tree, then quickly released the rope from the saddle. With one end of it she moved carefully toward the edge of the ravine and whispered, "We can use this rope, I think." She dropped one end down to him and went back to Shadow.

"Aye, that's good. Tie the other end very tightly around the saddle horn. Not his neck! You got that?

187

Don't try to kill the horse, too!"

She shot him a glare he couldn't see and removed the rope from around Shadow's neck where she'd started to place it, and looped it over the saddle horn, tying several square knots.

"Done!" she called in their now familiar whisper.

Carefully Shane let go of a root he'd been clinging to, and tried to wrap the end of the rope around his waist, feeling one of the branches his foot was braced against give way slightly under his weight. He was perspiring now, and his hands were moist.

"Damn!" he muttered under his breath.

"What's the matter?"

"Can't seem to get the rope around my waist and tie it securely. Can't make a knot."

"Oh, well, that's easy. You just take the left end and cross it . . ."

"I know how to tie a knot!" he spat up toward her. "I'm quite sure you'll find this hard to believe, but I don't have two ends to work with, nor do I have two hands! I have to hang on with at least one!"

She said nothing, but pulled the rope out of his hands and wrapped it twice around her waist, then carefully dropped to the ground and laid out flat on her stomach. Lowering the rest of the length of rope toward him, slowly and carefully she inched herself over the edge and down, her arms stretching until her hands reached the rope around his waist.

"What do you think you're doing?" he whispered

"I'm helping you. And you can just thank your lucky stars Mate isn't here right now."

She slipped her arms to his waist and felt for the end of the rope. Her hair fell forward, covering her

188

face and falling over his head, and he sensed the moist warmth of her breasts rising from the open neck of her shirt.

"I can't see," he whispered, and then a fleeting thought lightened the moment. If this wasn't such a ridiculous predicament to be in, the idea of her hanging over him like this might be an intriguing one.

"Neither can I. Where's the end of the rope?"

"I think it's around my waist."

"No, it isn't. Light another match."

"How do you expect me to do that with your hair in my face, and this embankment giving way every time I let go?"

"All right. Let me try to do it. Where are they?"

"Breast pocket."

With slow and careful maneuvering, Nina managed to retrieve the matches from his breast pocket and get one lit. The brief glow illuminated their spot, and she could see an oval space in which the snakes lay, their shiny bodies entwined in dark oily knots a few feet below him.

Nina's breath hissed between her teeth. "There *are* snakes down there! Oh, God!"

The flame went out, and Shane blew her hair out of his mouth.

"Did you think I was joking about that, for God's sake? Did you find the rope?"

"I wasn't sure if you were or not. Yes, I have the rope. Here, hold this."

She placed a length of rope around his arm, then proceeded to coil another length of it around his waist and knot it twice.

"I'm going to back out of here now," she whispered.

"Do it very carefully, please, then take Shadow and make him back up. Whatever you do, don't let any slack in the rope. Understand?"

"Yes. Will you be able to get hold of the rope when he starts to pull?"

"Aye, go ahead."

She drew herself away, her hair slipping over his head and into the dirt as she moved. Slowly she stood up and went to Shadow. She spoke softly to the stallion very close to his face.

"Listen, Shadow, I'm counting on you, you understand? We can't lose him. I don't know if I'm doing any of this right, so it's up to you. Are we all set?"

Shadow's ears twitched forward and back.

"Good, we understand each other."

"What are you doing up there, discussing strategy?" Shane called in a husky whisper.

"How did he know?" Nina whispered to Shadow. Over her shoulder she called to Shane, "We're ready!"

For luck, she crossed her fingers, then took up the reins.

"Back, Shadow, back." She pulled on the reins under his mouth, and he started back. "It's a miracle!" she whispered, pleased with her accomplishment.

Shadow backed away, and the rope tightened. She heard Shane groan as he began the ascent, heard the roots and stones crashing down the ravine.

Shadow snorted with nervousness having to step

backward in the dark. He stopped and took a step forward. The rope slackened.

"Nay! Nay!" Shane called out in a hoarse whisper. "Make him go back, back!"

"Can I help it if he didn't want to just then? He's been around Mate too long. Got a mind of his own."

She turned back to Shadow and commanded him back again. He went quickly and she kept him moving, never looking behind her. She just wanted to get Shane out of that snake-infested ravine. Soon she could hear him groaning behind her, heard the sound of his body scraping along the dirt.

"Whoa! Whoa!" he shouted, spitting dust out of his mouth.

Nina pulled Shadow to a halt and turned around. Shane was facedown in the dirt, both hands clutching partway up the rope. She thanked fortune he was out of there.

He lifted his head as if it weighed heavily. "Were you planning on dragging me all the way to the house?" he whispered loudly.

"What? Is that the thanks we get for saving your life?" she whispered back. Then, suddenly realizing they were away from the edge of the ravine and the pit of snakes, she shouted at him, "And what in bloody hell have we been whispering for?"

"I didn't want to wake the blighters!" he shouted back. "Now will you please untie me?"

"With pleasure!" she shouted, yanking hard on the ropes.

"Thank you!" he returned with equal force.

"Don't mention it!" she yelled near his ear.

"I'm not sure how you did this," he muttered as he

picked at the knots around his waist, "but I feel as if I've been knitted into something." Freeing himself at last, he walked toward Shadow, wrapping the rope around his arm as he moved.

Nina pushed a heavy lock of hair up off her forehead, then brushed dirt and twigs off her clothes. Tears began to form at the backs of her eyes. For the several tense minutes she'd thought Shane might be badly hurt or even dead, she'd panicked and felt lost. When she'd found him unhurt but in a potentially dangerous position, she was very frightened. Unbelievable as it seemed now, she realized she'd slithered over the edge of that ravine herself. How did she manage that, considering her own fear of snakes? And all this wretch could do was continue his relentless complaints and criticism. Recognizing now the potential hazards they both had faced, she began to shake.

"You really have no sense of how to be grateful, have you?" She swallowed back the tears.

"Grateful for what? For falling into a snake pit and having you almost help to push me the rest of the way down? Or did you have something else in mind?"

"Why are you making it sound like I did that on purpose? It was Shadow who started it all . . ."

"Shadow . . ." He set the coiled rope on the ground and bent to check the stallion's forelegs. "Wonder what riled him?"

"Is he hurt?" Nina ran to crouch down next to Shane, concerned about the animal.

"Doesn't seem to be." Shadow stood patiently as Shane moved around to check the rear fetlocks and joints. "Might have been one of those snakes. It was

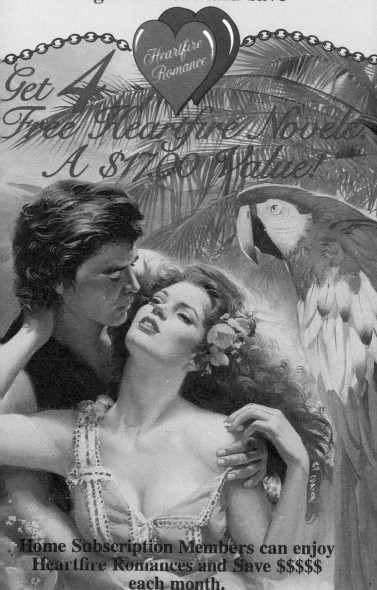

ENJOY ALL THE PASSION AND ROMANCE OF...

Heartfire

ROMANCES from ZEBRA

After you have read HEART-FIRE ROMANCES, we're sure you'll agree that HEARTFIRE sets new standards of excellence for historical romantic fiction. Each Zebra HEARTFIRE novel is the ultimate blend of intimate romance and grand adventure and each takes place in the kinds of historical settings you want most...the American Revolution, the Old West, Civil War and more.

SUBSCRIBERS $AVE, $AVE, $AVE!!!

As a HEARTFIRE Home Sub scriber, you'll save with you HEARTFIRE Subscription You'll receive 4 brand new Heart fire Romances to preview Free fo 10 days each month. If yo decide to keep them you'll pa only $3.50 each; a total of $14.0 and you'll save $3.00 each mont off the cover price.

Plus, we'll send you these novel as soon as they are publishe each month. There is never an shipping, handling or other hic den charges; home delivery i always FREE! And there is n obligation to buy even a singl book. You may return any of th books within 10 days for fu credit and you can cancel you subscription at any time. N questions asked.

TO GET YOUR
4 FREE BOOKS
MAIL THE COUPON BELOW.

Heartfire Romance

FREE BOOK CERTIFICATE

GET 4 FREE BOOKS

Yes! I want to subscribe to Zebra's HEARTFIRE HOME SUBSCRIPTION SERVICE. Please send me my 4 FREE books. Then each month I'll receive the four newest Heartfire Romances as soon as they are published to preview Free for ten days. If I decide to keep them I'll pay the special discounted price of just $3.50 each; a total of $14.00. This is a savings of $3.00 off the regular publishers price. There are no shipping, handling or other hidden charges. There is no minimum number of books to buy and I may cancel this subscription at any time. In any case the 4 FREE Books are mine to keep regardless.

NAME

ADDRESS

CITY _____ STATE _____ ZIP

TELEPHONE

SIGNATURE

(If under 18 parent or guardian must sign)
Terms and prices subject to change.
Orders subject to acceptance.

HF 109

GET 4 FREE BOOKS

HEARTFIRE HOME SUBSCRIPTION
SERVICE
P.O. BOX 5214
120 BRIGHTON ROAD
CLIFTON, NEW JERSEY 07015

AFFIX
STAMP
HERE

probably sunning itself and fell asleep and didn't know the sun had gone down. Shadow must have sensed it, or it woke up and crawled in front of him." He patted the big black rump. "He seems to be all right. I'll give him a thorough check in the barn."

"Are you saying this great big horse is afraid of snakes, too?" Nina was suddenly struck by the idea that all three of them had been helpless against a band of marauding snakes. A dingo howled in the distance, and she shuddered.

"Well . . . I wouldn't go so far as to say Shadow's *afraid* of snakes, exactly, but . . . they do slither about now, don't they? I suppose in the dark he merely felt its presence." Nina stood stock-still, staring silently, during his explanation. Exasperated, he retorted, "Why don't you bloody ask *him* how he feels about snakes? I can't answer for him!"

"I'd rather not discuss it any further, if you don't mind."

The moonlight brightened as a cloud moved away, and Nina could see more clearly that Shane's face and clothes were streaked with dirt and littered with leaves and twigs. The tension drained from her body, and she was filled with an overpowering urge to laugh out loud. It started with a low chuckle in the back of her throat, and then it burst out of her in full-scale laughter.

Shane stood with both hands on his hips, legs wide apart. "Just what do you find so amusing?"

"You, of course. For once, I can laugh at you!" And she broke into a new gale of laughter.

"And why am I to be ridiculed?" he asked calmly.

She walked toward him, still laughing. "Because,

mate, you're covered with dirt, right up to your hair!
Now it's my turn to help you get cleaned up!"

She began to brush him off as hard as she could
with the flat of her hand. She pulled at the twigs on
his head, bringing clumps of hair along with them in
strong tugs, and then brushing down hard on his
backside.

"Here, stop that!" He grabbed her wrists and held
her back from him, a half-smile playing about his
full mouth. "You'll add more bruises than I'm sure I
already have."

She kept laughing. Now that they were both safe
and no one, not even Shadow, was hurt, she couldn't
keep from laughing. It made her weak and sent the
tears flowing out of her eyes in steady streams. She
kept pointing at him and laughing, her arms
hanging liquid from her shoulders.

"So you think this is funny, do you?"

"Y-yes . . ."

"You really think this is funny?"

"Yes!" She barely got it out over the laughing.

"You probably think all this is just too bloody
funny for words, don't you?"

She couldn't speak, could only laugh harder.

"Well, my girl, let's see how funny you think *this*
is!"

He lunged toward her, scooped her up in his
muscular arms, and flopped her like a sack of flour,
stomach down, over Shadow's back.

"Hey!" she shrieked, and the laughing ceased.

He swung up into the saddle behind her sagging
form and urged Shadow around and down the trail at
a light trot. She flung her arm back at him, but her

small fist had little impact on his hard thigh.

"Shane . . . Merritt! You . . . let . . . me . . . down . . . this . . . instant!" The words bounced out of her with every step of Shadow's gait.

"Not on your sweet little bum, my girl." He patted her bottom. "And a nice little bum it is, too."

"How dare you!" she said with outrage.

He laughed loudly. "Oh, I dare very easily, my girl!"

"This . . . hurts." Her breath came out with each bounce.

"Aye, that it does, my girl."

"Stop . . . calling me . . . that!"

"Calling you what, my girl?" He began to sing.

Nina was spitting mad now, but she knew he could not be reasoned with at the moment, and would not let her up, no matter how much she yelled and protested the indignity of it.

"Shane . . . please. I feel . . . sick."

"Got the collywobbles, have you? Well now, you know how to rectify that, don't you, my girl?"

"H-how?"

"Throw up, of course."

"Oh, you . . . are the most . . . exasperating . . . ow!"

Shadow jumped across a rut and Nina thought her insides would be irreparably wrenched. No amount of begging and pleading would get Shane to release her. He just kept singing with the most annoying voice she'd ever heard. Even the dingoes were howling in loud harmony, she was convinced of it. There was only one last threat she could think of that would have any effect on him whatsoever.

195

"I'll tell the Mum!"

He stopped singing, then broke into a spate of wild laughter.

"Oh, now you've really put the fear of God into me, my girl!"

She groaned loudly. Shane stopped laughing. Maybe he should think about the Mum. If she happened to be looking out the window when they rode into the yard and saw them like this . . . he reined Shadow in.

"All right, I guess you've been punished enough for ridiculing me." He dismounted, then grasped her around the waist and slid her unceremoniously backward off Shadow.

"Hearing that singing was punishment above and beyond!" she flung at him.

"Oh?"

He grabbed her again and started to throw her over Shadow's back. She spun around and pummeled his chest with her tight little fists. He caught her wrists and threw them around his neck, then dropped his hands to her waist quickly and hoisted her up into the saddle before she knew what had happened.

"I can't be the only woman who's ever thought you were the most exasperating man she'd ever met!" She was breathless, and Shane thrilled to fire in her eyes.

He stroked his chin for a moment. "Hm, let me think over the legions . . . I believe you are the only one at that . . ." he leaned into her ear ". . . my girl."

"Ooo!"

"Most women think I'm utterly delightful, dashing, charming, you might say."

"*I* wouldn't say that," she replied through

clenched teeth. "But what I *would* say . . ."

"Aye, I've swept a few of them off their feet in my time," he went on, as if she hadn't spoken.

"Not the way you have me!" she shot over her shoulder, then instantly wished she could have bitten her tongue to retract the words. "I mean . . . well, things just happen to me when you're around."

She was digging herself into a deeper hole, she knew that. It was best just to keep quiet. She steeled her eyes forward and clamped her mouth shut. The rooftop of the manor could be seen faintly in the moonlight on the horizon.

"Not the way I'd like them to," Shane whispered, barely audible.

Nina twisted slightly in the saddle. "What did you say?"

He cleared his throat. "Nothing that bears repeating," he answered quietly, "yet."

They rode in silence, their bodies fitting together like the bowls of spoons, rocking gently with Shadow's steady easy gait. Nina relaxed against Shane in spite of herself, given the way his close presence unsettled her so. If the ride never ended, she wouldn't be sorry.

Shadow's hooves made muffled sounds in the dust as he instinctively headed for the open door of the barn.

Chapter 16

Inside the barn Shane slid down to the floor and helped Nina out of the saddle. They looked at each other for a moment. Nina was afraid to speak. She wasn't sure if she would end up laughing or crying, so she kept silent. Finally, she turned to leave the barn.

"If you'll wait until I finish taking care of Shadow, I'll help you get into the house so no one sees you," he offered.

She nodded wearily, grateful for the assistance. He took the saddle and blanket off Shadow, then looked the stallion over, carefully feeling around joints and legs, picking up each fetlock and examining the bottom of the hooves. Satisfied the horse was not bruised nor cut, he let him into the stall and replenished water, grain, and hay. Then he took Nina's arm and steered her toward the back of the house.

"Your window's open," he whispered, looking up.

"Yes." She eyed him skeptically.

"That makes it easier."

"Makes what easier?"

"Climbing up and getting in."

She stopped in her tracks. "Climbing up . . . ? Are you crazy?"

"Occasionally, I'd say. Often, others might say." He guided her forward.

When they reached the corner of the house he pointed to a stone bench nestled in among the ferns and vines.

"Get up on that."

When she stared at him incredulously, he lifted her up onto it, then got up behind her. He felt above her head in the vines growing up the side of the house, and his hand clamped over an iron rung the width of his palm.

"There." He took her hand and raised it to grasp the rung.

"What is that?"

"A handle of sorts."

He leaned down, picked up her foot, and pushed the toe of her boot onto a large rock in back of the bench, then gave her a hoist up.

"Reach up with your other hand," he commanded.

She did so and found another rung. He hoisted her again and she sensed the way in which the climb was to commence.

"Do these things go all the way up?" she puffed.

"Aye, they do."

"Why?"

He chuckled quietly. "The room you're in used to be my room. When the ironmonger came to repair the roof once, Colin and I bribed him into putting in these rungs. We thought it was great fun to sneak out after the Mum and Pop were asleep. Used to sneak down to the pens and play with the lambs." He chuckled again in fond remembrance.

Nina thought of a hundred questions she wanted to ask him about his parents, his childhood, and Colin, but it hardly seemed the time to bring up the subject. And she was becoming profoundly aware of how close behind her he was climbing.

"Ow!" She stopped and placed the ball of her thumb in her mouth.

"Ooof," Shane expelled a breath as his shoulder came up hard under her backside. "Would you please warn me when you plan to stop so quickly? What happened?" he whispered.

"You didn't tell me there were thorns in all these vines. I've been stabbed."

"There aren't thorns in all these vines. Only in some of them." He pushed on her backside and she started to climb again.

"I'm sure it was a lark for you and Colin to sneak out of the house like this, but I feel we're sneaking into the house, as if we've done something we shouldn't have, and we're afraid we'll be caught," she whispered, ". . . and well, we haven't, have we?" She guessed she was asking herself the question more than she was asking Shane.

"Don't think of us as sneaking," he whispered dramatically, "think of us as . . . Romeo and Juliet."

"What?" she sighed at this latest bit of his own brand of reasoning.

"Romeo and Juliet. There's your balcony above us."

"What would you know about Romeo and Juliet?" She looked up and took another labored step.

"You'd be surprised what I know about Romeo and Juliet."

"No doubt. You've probably been seducing girls since you were fourteen years old. Ow!" She sucked on a finger pricked by another thorn.

"Serves you right," he laughed. "Romeo and Juliet were just trying to be together. What's so wrong about that?"

"*They* were doing it to make peace in their families." And what we're doing would only cause a war in yours, she added silently.

"Maybe. Juliet would probably be alive today if she'd just acted like a child and played in the vines and trees instead of getting involved in adult games."

Nina thought about commenting on his remark about Juliet being alive, but passed it by. She took another step. If he hadn't been urging her along with his shoulder, she wasn't sure she could keep going. The height was dizzying and, in the dark, rather frightening.

"Families have a way of imposing things on their children sometimes without knowing the harm they're doing," she said, pulling herself up another rung.

"Sometimes it's better if people think of themselves first instead of trying to right all the family wrongs. Things have a way of working out for the best," he murmured.

Nina was growing warm with the exertion of the climb. She uttered a low groan. "Yes, well, some of us feel we have to do the right thing . . . always."

"How much fun is that?"

"Not much, most of the . . . ow! I'm going to be a mess by the time I get to the window!" She took another labored step, then mused, "I think Juliet stayed in the balcony and Romeo climbed up from below."

"They were children. They didn't know much."

When at last she reached the top, Nina turned at the window and took hold of the ledge. "Well, thank you for seeing me home. It was a lovely evening," she mocked.

"Wait a minute. The least you could do is ask me to come in out of the . . . vines." He gestured around.

"Sorry, it wouldn't be right." She lowered her eyes, feigning extreme shyness.

"That's too bad, Lady Juliet . . ." He pushed by her and crawled through the window and into her bedroom.

She crawled in after him. "What do you think you're doing?"

"Climbing through the window into your bedroom."

"Yes, so you have."

He looked around. A smile played at the corners of his mouth. She could see it in the shaft of moonlight that streaked through the window, and a twinge caught at the bottom of her stomach. He lit an oil lamp near the bed.

"This room is certainly different from when I lived in it."

He looked around in the flickering light and saw a large blue vase holding a profusion of wildflowers, and smiled remembering the ones on the supper table at the cabin. There were books in small stacks on the floor by the fireplace and on the bedside table.

"How was it before?" she whispered.

"Cold. You've made it warm."

He noticed her nightgown lying across the bed in a soft, cloudy white mass. The brush she used to run through her hair lay on the dresser, its bristles pointing up. He imagined her brushing her hair and felt an overwhelming urge to do that for her. He felt as if he'd stepped into her most private retreat, and the intimacy of it sent a surge of warmth traveling along his nerves.

"Now that I've seen your bedroom, I want you to see mine."

When her face blanched, he took her hand and pulled her to the other side of the room, opened the door slowly, and peered into the hallway, up one end and down the other. She started to protest, but he put a cautioning finger over her lips. He pulled her along, a finger laid against his lips over a silent *shh*. Drawing her down the back stairway to the outer wing of the house, he lead her down another hallway to a wide wood door.

Nina's heart pounded in her chest, and the closer they got to Shane's bedroom door, the wilder it raced. Every step brought more thunderous clamor, but she did not stop, did not protest, did not resist, even though a voice from the back of her mind nagged her to do so.

Silently he pressed the latch and pushed the door open. It made no audible sound, not even the merest hint of a creak. The only light was a wide shaft of moonlight that came through lacy curtains under the dark drapes at the window.

Shane stepped to a high oak dresser and lit an oil lamp. The flame moved in slow shadows through the ruby glass shade, and cast a deep rosy glow in a semicircle in the room. He went to the opposite corner and lit a smaller chamber lamp on a candlestand. Its glow through the frosted etched-glass chimney shone down in a pool of soft, creamy light, and sent a pillar of barely moving light up the corner of the room to flare onto the ceiling in a golden circle.

He stood in the center of the room on a deep red Oriental carpet, and smiled while she looked around, genuine surprise on her face. The room was exquisitely appointed, with deep red upholstered chairs. An oak wardrobe which matched the dresser stood at one end, its three top finials barely grazing the ceiling.

Dominating the room was a high, wide four-poster bed with a ceiling-high heavy woven canopy of ecru cord, edged with thick fringe, that dipped down in deep scallops on all four sides. The bedskirt was a dark red-brown, almost as rich in color as the wood-paneled walls, and at one side was a two-stair bedstep. A thick quilt seemed to float over the expanse of bed like a fleecy cloud, over which lay a coverlet fashioned of ecru cotton appliqued with a woven cord that matched the canopy. Four large, thick pillows that matched the coverlet were plumped up against the headboard. Above those was a gilt-framed painting of two people, barely visible in the low light from where she stood, but the woman in the painting appeared to be nude.

Nina's breath caught in her throat, and for a moment her heart seemed to stop. The room, the bed, all of it was fit for a king. She looked at Shane, who stood watching her, an enigmatic smile on his handsome face. The lampglow reflected out of his eyes with quartz-blue brilliance. The whole picture, herself in the middle of it, set up a fluttering in her chest and stomach that was almost uncontrollable. Involuntarily her hands came up and crossed themselves low over her stomach.

"This . . . this is your bedroom?" she breathed, huskily.

"Whenever I'm here."

"It's positively luxurious," she whispered, awestruck.

When at last she could tear herself away from the spot to which she'd seemed rooted, she tentatively started to walk around the room. Passing the bookcases, she ran her fingers along several leather-bound books lined in precise rows. She noted with the quirk of one eyebrow several volumes with titles etched in gold leaf under the main title "The Works of William Shakespeare." She smiled, intrigued to learn that Shane was interested in literature, and even in Shakespeare's classic plays.

"I love his sonnets as well," he cut into her thoughts, and she had the unsettling feeling that he was reading her mind again.

She did not respond, but continued her walk around the room, stepping on the carpet and wood flooring lightly, as if trying to avoid crushing a flower or blade of grass along a pathway.

"I've never seen a bedroom quite like this one."

He stepped toward her, his gaze multifaceted in the light. Her pulse quickened.

"And I'll wager you've never met a man quite like this one, either," he whispered, and stepped so near to her that the heat from their bodies mingled between them. "Have you, my girl?"

"Oh, many . . ." she began, scoffing, but her voice caught in her throat when he reached for her. His hand was strong and warm, and her own was completely engulfed by it.

"There is one thing you haven't seen yet," he said, drawing her slowly and deliberately toward the bed.

"I . . . I've seen enough for now, I think," Nina breathed, resisting his pull.

"You'll enjoy this," he said, not giving in to her resistance. "I promise."

Chapter 17

Nina pulled back slightly when she saw the direction in which Shane was leading her. "Perhaps I could see it another time. I really should go back to my room now."

"This won't take long, and it's rather unique. It might be a long time before you have a chance to see such a thing again. You may never see one." His voice was calm, soothing.

"What—what is it?"

He drew her closer to the bed. "I think it's best you see it for yourself. Just step up here . . ." He pointed toward the bedstep.

Nina's heart pounded wildly against her chest, and her legs seemed to be filled with water. She stepped timidly up onto the small stair.

"Hm," he pondered, rubbing the point of his chin between his thumb and the knuckle of his index finger. "I don't think you'll really have the best look from this point. Let me help."

He nimbly stepped up behind her and slipped an

arm around her waist. Before she knew what was happening he had leaped up, cradling her in his arms, and flipped her flat on her back in the middle of the bed, his body skimming over hers to land flat next to her. His long length touched every inch of her side from her shoulder to her toes.

"Oh!" she cried out, clamping her eyes shut.

"Shh!" he cautioned, "just look up."

She snapped her eyes open and looked overhead. There, woven with an intricate design into the canopy, was an oval mirror. The corner lamp flickered in the glass, sending down a golden wash that illuminated the two of them side by side on the coverlet, their heads together, surrounded by plump pillows.

"Oh!" Nina stopped breathing. *"Oh-h, my!"*

His face smiled down at her from overhead. She snapped her head around to look at him lying next to her, and when he looked toward her, the smile seemed even wider. Then they both looked back up into the mirror.

She was so taken aback by such an idea as a mirror mounted in a canopy over a bed, it was a long moment before she found her voice again. "How did you ever do . . . what makes it stay . . . ? Does your mother know you have *this?*"

He laughed lightly. "Of course she does! This bed used to be hers! Hers and my father's, that is."

Nina stared open-mouthed into their reflection. "That . . . this . . . belonged to your parents?"

"Aye, it did, my girl. You're surprised, I can tell!" He winked at her, and she felt the heat of a blush rise up over her face.

210

"Where did they find such a thing?"

"My father had a friend in England, and he got it from someplace in America."

"America?"

Shane nodded, a wide smile on his face. "Sorry you left, I suppose, now that you've learned what wonderful things can be found there, eh, my girl?"

"Stop calling me that!" She gave him a good-natured jab in his ribs. Then she remembered where she was—in Shane's bedroom, lying beside him on his massive bed! She sat up with a jolt.

"Here, hold on, now!" he laughed. "You can't make the next boat out tonight, you know!" He sat up and circled her waist with both arms to keep her from leaving.

"Shh! Will you be quiet, please? I've got to get out of here and back to my room before someone sees me and misunderstands." She started to crawl to the edge of the bed.

He placed a hand lightly on her shoulder. "No one's going to see you. I'll make sure you get back to your room all right."

She moved out from under his arm and away from him, intent upon getting off the bed. And then, in the flickering light, she saw the painting on the wall over the pillows. When she focused more closely on it, her eyes widened and she sucked in her breath, covering her mouth with her hand.

"Oh, dear," she said through her fingers.

"What?" He sat up and turned his head in the direction she was looking. "Oh, the painting. Interesting, isn't it?"

"Oh yes, it certainly is interesting . . ." Reluctantly, yet purposefully, she leaned forward for a better look.

She'd been right, the woman in the picture was definitely nude, but upon closer examination she realized that the man in the picture was, too. They were lounging in a field of wildflowers, their legs and lower bodies entwined in a most provocative fashion. One of the man's hands was enmeshed in the woman's flowing golden hair, and the other hand rested over her breast. She was holding a piece of fruit or cake to his lips.

In the background she could faintly see what appeared to be two horses grazing near a grove of trees, and . . . was it? Yes! A shepherd dog lay off to the side, chin resting on his crossed paws, eyes heavy-lidded. Nina quelled an urge to lean closer so she could see if the dog had one brown eye and one blue.

"Interesting," she repeated, her fingers still covering her mouth. "And where did your father find *that*, may I ask? Certainly not in America." She slumped back to sit on the coverlet.

"Nay, he didn't. The Mum commissioned it."

"The . . . your *mother?*"

He nodded. "The Mum. You seem somehow . . . shocked. Women have been known to buy paintings, you know."

"Not the women I know, and not that kind of painting . . ." She turned toward him, her eyes wide, reflecting the flickering lamp flame. "The Mum?"

"Aye, she was a comely thing, full of spirit and spunk." His voice was filled with warmth as he spoke of his mother. "My father loved to talk about her when we worked together. He loved her more than life. He didn't exactly say it, but I knew that when they loved each other in this bed, they were full of passion never felt by another man and woman. I believe she felt that way about him as well."

His voice grew darker. "So much of her warmth and feeling was taken away when he died. It's as if the Mum we knew died with him." He let out a long, slow breath.

Nina was moved by his speech, and a little embarrassed by so personal a subject. The idea of a woman commissioning a painting like the one in front of her, or lying next to a man on a bed looking up into a mirror suspended over them, was a startling one for her.

Up until this moment Shane had spoken little of his parents, and whenever he spoke to Nina about anything it was usually only to tease. This was the most he'd ever truly talked to her. She felt more deeply sensitive to him, and leaned slightly against him to show him she understood.

He slipped his arm around her middle, and the pressure pushed a breath up and out of her lips.

"I believe you have that kind of passion, Nina," he spoke close to her ear.

His voice sent shivers along her neck and shoulders. She tried to pull away, but he held her captive in the circle of his arms. He began a trail of little kisses from the back of her ear down the sensitive cord in her neck, and along her shoulder where her shirt was open.

He moved his lips over the skin of her throat like a wisp of smoke, letting the tip of his tongue work its way lightly up over her chin and flick over her mouth and against her teeth. And then he murmured her name with a groan, covering her mouth with his own with first a light caress, then with a crushing, devouring kiss.

His fingers deftly opened the front of her shirt and pushed it off her shoulders. Nina lost her will against his caresses and desires. She seemed unable, but most of all unwilling, to resist him, and closed her eyes dreamily as his lips moved down her throat, over her shoulders, and down the warm, moist path between her breasts.

He lifted and leaned her back over his thigh with his knee bent under her for support, and let her hair fall over his arm to spill out and onto the coverlet like a pool of liquid flame. The heat of his breath against her skin seared her breasts and sent her quickening pulse racing.

He pulled the ribbon of her chemise until it fell open, then gently pushed it aside to reveal completely both soft globes, their dusky peaks upturned and swelling in the lampglow. Shane leaned back to look at her, and caught his breath at her beauty. Her skin gleamed with a golden sheen in the lamplight. She was utterly beautiful under his eyes and hands, and his desire mounted with unbridled speed as his hooded gaze moved over her body. He slipped his hand up the side of her ribs to gently cup a softly rounded breast, the heat in his fingers fanned by the sound of a low moan emanating from far back in her throat as her head dropped back over his arm.

Lowering his mouth slowly until it was poised barely above her throbbing nipple, he murmured her name over and over. He reached out with the tip of his tongue and flicked it over the sensitive point and felt her flinch under the touch. And then, slowly, he parted his lips and brought the dark rose peak into his mouth, holding its warm softness captive within his lips before circling and teasing it with his tongue.

The feel of his breath hot over her breast sent Nina off on a wave of emotion she'd never felt before, but his mouth closing over her nipple caused flames to course along her raw nerves, down through the pit of her stomach, and into the pulsing vee between her legs. Her eyelashes fluttered, then opened.

"Shane . . ." she whispered.

Above her the oval mirror framed them in a rose-sepia tone in the wash of light from the flickering lamps. She was startled, then paralyzed, by the vision of his lean, muscular back and shoulders over her, his hair shining gold and pale wheat as his head moved over her breast, her own hair splayed out over the coverlet. His long denim-covered legs were bent under her back, and her own legs stretched toward the pillows.

She was caught up in their reflection, drawn into it, floating out of it, then drawn inextricably back into it in a dreamy haze in which it was difficult for them to tell where one's body began and the other's ended. There was a constant moving in and out of the oval-framed painting they made in the mirror with his bed as a canvas.

A rapping sound inside her head echoed through her dreamy state. Was it her heart, her blood rampaging through her veins? Something kept telling her she should not do this, must get up, get away. But the voice was weakened by her mounting emotions and fired passion, and she silenced it.

Shane's hand around her breast grew stronger, squeezed harder, and his teeth closed in gentle nips around her nipple. His lips moved over her skin to kiss her other breast, and she thrilled to the touch, closing her eyes, allowing the sensation of his hands and mouth to take her over completely.

And then he was opening her clothes, pulling them off and kissing her as each piece dropped to the floor. Shyly she reached out to touch his shirt, and together they removed it and his trousers. Nina took in the masculine beauty of him, wanting to kiss him where the lamplight now licked over his chest and dark brown nipples. She touched the spot where his heart pounded, then leaned down and placed her lips tenderly against it.

Shane lifted her face, softly touched her lips, and left a trail of hot kisses along her throat, between her breasts, and over her stomach. Gently he urged her back onto the coverlet, and moved along her body, covering her thighs with warm, soft kisses. Nina moaned with a mixture of wanting him to stop, and wanting him never to stop.

Gently he parted her legs and slipped a finger along her opening. She tensed, and he caressed her softly without insistence. Then he pushed a little more and lowered his lips over the golden patch of curls. His tongue traced the path his finger took. She sucked in her breath. Gently he withdrew his finger and let his tongue curl its way inside her, searching, turning her to liquid fire.

He slipped his hands under her rounded bottom

and pulled her tightly to him, his tongue reaching deeply into her, touching a place so electrifying it startled Nina, and her eyes flew open wide.

Above her in the canopy the mirror reflected the physical sensations shooting along her nerves, heating her blood, sending her to soaring heights she'd never experienced. The pressure building inside her matched the quicker, insistent flicking of his tongue. She writhed under his mouth, against his hands, wanted more, desired all of him. And then the explosion came with blessed relief, and she was enveloped in the exquisite joy and pain of it all. At the peak of her thrill, he kissed her lightly inside her secret lips, and she believed every fiber of her body had shattered into countless shards of glistening glass.

Shane withdrew his lips and leaned above her, watching her face.

"I want you, Nina, want you completely." He lowered his hard length to brush against the thatch at the vee of her thighs. "And . . . I want to give myself to you as completely. Will you take me?"

His eyes blazed with a fire so hot Nina felt her mind branded with his name, his desire. There was nothing left inside her to tell her no, tell her what they were doing was wrong.

"Yes," she whispered, "oh, yes, yes, yes."

Gently he pushed against her until the tip of him was caught in the most intimate of embraces. He slipped along the moist path, holding himself in check as much as possible, a task almost beyond his physical capabilities, until he was stopped against the barrier to her depths. He stopped for an almost imperceptible moment, then pressed insistently against it. At last it gave way, permitting him complete entrance, and he carefully plunged into her, pulled back, plunged again, deeper until the exquisite release he sought spilled out of him in a torrent, filling her with the essence of all of him.

Nina cried softly, moaning under his body, and the sheer pleasure of their loving. She'd fantasized about the romance of having a lover, but never the actual moment of making love for the first time. As she lay there under him, rubbing his back and shoulders, her pulse pounding, Nina could not imagine a fantasy more perfect than this reality.

Shane gathered her close in his arms, and buried his face in her neck, whispering her name over and over. He was spent, nestled inside her lovely, moist softness, drifting away to where he wasn't certain, but it didn't matter. He never wanted to release Nina, never wanted her far out of his reach.

Nina's heart still fluttered wildly in her chest, and her pulse beat erratically, pounding in her ears. Her eyes flew open and she caught their reflection once again in the mirror, their legs and arms entwined, her hair spilled out under his golden head.

Then the pounding became intrusive, and her body went rigid with terror. The pounding was not inside her head—it came from outside the bedroom window!

Chapter 18

Shane bolted upright and jumped off the bed. He ran to the window and pulled aside one of the lace curtains.

"It's Derrick!" he whispered to her.

Nina climbed down off the bed, quickly pulling her shirt around her as she went, and backed herself up against the door. Her heart pounded in her ears. When Shane raised the window she could see Derrick's ashen face in the moonlight.

"Good God, mate, I thought you'd never wake up!"

Shane hastily pulled on his trousers. "What's the matter?"

"Bushfire, back range. Thought we had it, but it's really going now." His breath came in hard, raspy gasps between coughs. "Have to move the stock farther away. Come, now, mate. Need every hand available." He swallowed hard.

"Be right there. Get yourself some water."

Derrick nodded and left the window. Shane

whirled around to face Nina. She stood shaking nervously, attempting to get dressed.

"Don't . . . don't say anything," she whispered. "Just go, quickly!"

His face registered brief pain, and then he was gone, running down the hallway and disappearing around a corner.

Nina peeked around the door to be sure no one was in the hallway, and then hurried toward the other wing and Colin's room.

She rapped on his door. "Colin!" she whispered. "Colin, open the door." She rapped again, then opened the door slightly and called in. "Colin?"

Colin's head raised sleepily from his pillow, his dark hair spilling onto his forehead. "Wha . . . ?"

"Colin, it's Nina."

"What? Well, Lady Cole . . . to what do I owe the honor of your appearance in my boudoir at such an opportune hour?"

She stepped in quickly and shut the door behind her. "Get up. They need you out on the back range."

"Need me?" He sat up and rubbed his eyes. "Don't be absurd. Nobody needs me on the back range, or on the front one, for that matter. You have the wrong brother. What time is it?"

"It's almost morning. Forget the time—get up. There's a bushfire. Derrick says they need everybody. Get up and go with me . . . please?" she pleaded with him, and grabbed his shirt and pants from a nearby chair and pushed them at him.

"Go with . . . are you mad?" He got out of bed and looked for his boots. "You can't go out there. Have you ever seen a bushfire? No, of course you haven't."

He wandered around in the half light provided by the moon through the window. When he turned sideways, Nina discovered he was naked. She gasped and whirled around to face the door, leaving her back to him.

"Colin, I have to go, and you've got to take me. I couldn't find my way out there in the dark. Please?"

"No! You can get hurt! Besides, if it's as big as you say, we'll be able to see it from here." He stepped into his pants. "What good am I going to be? I don't know anything about fighting bushfires," he muttered under his breath. He kept putting on clothes and finally his boots.

"It's about time you learned, then!" Nina spat at him. "You'll learn fast and so will I, because you're taking me with you! Hurry!"

Vanessa Merritt had been awakened by the sound of knocking on a door. She got out of bed and put on a wrapper, opened the door to her bedroom, and looked out into the hall. No one was there. Just as she was about to turn back into her room, she heard the door to Colin's room open. She stepped behind her door and peered through the narrow opening. Colin poked his head out and looked up and down the hallway.

Vanessa frowned. What was he up to? He stepped into the hallway. No doubt he was off to a tryst with some no-account . . . and then the door opened wider and Nina Cole stepped into the hallway and closed it behind her. Colin took her hand and they hurried down the hallway to the back stair.

Vanessa stepped back into her room, closed the door, and leaned against it. A wry smile curved at the corner of her mouth. The not-so-naive American fortune hunter had set her cap for her younger, more impressionable son. And all this time she'd been worried Shane might . . .

She smiled openly, took off her wrapper, and got into bed. What an interesting turn of events. It would be easy for her to break up whatever might develop between Colin and Nina. Yes, things did have a way of working themselves out properly. She lay still for a moment, then turned over and fell back to sleep, a smile still on her lips.

Day's first light had set an eerie dull glow in the far distance as Colin and Nina reached the crest of the hill overlooking the valley. Below them spread a dramatic panorama of life in the harshness of bush country.

Numbers of sheep too vast to count moved rapidly eastward toward paddocks away from the giant shearing shed and stockmen's houses, directed by shepherds and jackaroos and several dogs surrounding them strategically on three sides. Against the horizon their silhouettes appeared to move in waves like the ripple of sheets hanging on a line in a breeze. Horses and riders moved around them in quick stops and starts, while the dogs nipped at the back legs of confused and frightened strays.

Behind them, closing in with unfathomable speed, was a rampaging bushfire fanned by a fierce wind which had picked up velocity in the predawn hours. The orange-red glow of flames was punctuated every now and then by fireballs of exploding gas formed by the heated oil from the eucalyptus trees in its path. Burning dry brush crackled sharply behind the bleating of fearful sheep, the insistent barking of dogs, and the shouts and coded whistles of men on horseback. Full of life and energy of its own, the bushfire gobbled up arid rangeland with an insatiable appetite, and fairly nipped at the heels of the horses in its hot pursuit.

Overhead, burgeoning gray clouds piled on top of one another, higher and higher, into opposing walls of smoke-filled fleece. Thunder rolled in behind them like the sound of hoofbeats from a thousand horses. Lightning streaks of white and blue snapped along the horizon, and like the crack of a whip, spurred animals and men to even greater speed.

Nina held on tightly to her horse's reins, struggling against the gusts of wind which mounted in strength and threatened to take her breath away. It blew so hard against her face she had difficulty keeping her eyes open in a frantic search to see Shane's form in the moving sea of animals, fire, and men below. She turned to Colin, who seemed to be going through the same motions.

"Rain's coming!" she shouted over the roar. "That will help, won't it?"

Colin shook his head, and shouted back. "Won't be any rain. Dry storm. Nothing but wind and dust, and that won't help one bit."

"We've got to get down there! They need help!"

"We can't help! We'd only be in the way!"

"Shane needs us!" She strained her voice to be heard over the roar of rampaging fire and wind.

"He doesn't need us to be in the way!"

The wind suddenly shifted and blew with gale force against them. Nina's hair whipped around her face, and she tore at it to clear her vision. The fire moved quickly toward them, and sent contagious fear running through the flocks. A split occurred in the lead animals and a large number of them broke away in a run toward the hill where Nina and Colin were. The men whistled and shouted and one of the dogs came from the back of the mass of sheep. Low to the ground, he ran flat out toward the front of the split flock, but they had too much of a head start and he was unable to reach their leaders. The shepherds and jackaroos had all they could handle with the rest of the flock to go after the strays.

Nina turned back to Colin. "Come on!" she shouted. "We've got to help or they'll lose those animals!"

Colin shot a hand out and grabbed her arm. "Nay! Some are always lost, can't be helped. Stay here!"

She jerked her arm away from his grasp. Kicking her horse in the sides, she lunged forward and down the hill toward the frantically bleating stray flock. When she was almost abreast of them, they turned and surged head-on toward her. There was no time to stop or turn. They surrounded her mare, crashing into her and into each other. The dog worked relentlessly around them, his job made more difficult by the horse and rider now trapped in the middle of the confused mob.

Nina spun this way and that in the saddle while her horse turned and lashed out with a flurry of hooves and neighs; both searched for a way out. The dog came into the center of the animal mass, barking and nipping, and Nina was almost positive it was Mate. His action opened a way for her to spur the mare out of their stampeding numbers. She did so, then whipped her around to come up behind the fear-crazed flock.

From the far side behind the rear line of shepherds and sheep, Shane rode at full gallop and came up alongside of that part of the flock directed by the lead dogs. The wind whipped around him, sending hot particles of dust and brush to sting his face and eyes. He had seen the flock separate and knew every available man jack of them had his hands full controlling and moving the others to safety.

He headed to the split flock in time to see Mate shoot into the thickest of them. He could always count on Mate to think as quickly, if not more quickly, than he did when it came to instinctively knowing what a fear-crazed animal was about to do. Mate was fearless, and Shane rode in quickly to help him.

And then he saw her. In the lightning flashes and red-hot glow of the fire he saw Nina streak by him astride the piebald mare, the wind whipping her copper hair straight out behind her in molten waves alive with the light from the stormfire behind them.

He reined Shadow to an abrupt halt, staring at the scene as if he'd just seen an apparition. Nina spurred the mare to follow Mate's lead, and then, as if with an instinct of her own, moved in and out until the strays were turned back toward the main flock. She rode as if born to it, as if horse and rider were one.

Shane watched in mesmerized disbelief at the beautifully wild image before him. And then it hit him—Nina was doing the most reckless thing she could do, given her naïveté and inexperience in the ways of fire-whipped animals and, regardless of how it looked, her own lack of riding experience. She could endanger herself, the animals, Mate, and the men. He urged Shadow forward and came up beside her.

"What do you think you're doing here?" he shouted over the thunderous roar of nature.

Nina's heart leapt to her throat. Shane's abrupt entrance shook her as much as the threat of stampeding animals around her and the fire behind.

"Helping you!" she shouted back at him.

"Get out of here!" He grabbed the reins and started to pull her away from the flock.

Nina snatched the reins out of his hand. "You need me, and you know it!"

"Get out of here, I said! I don't need you to muck things up! There's no time to save you and the stock, too!"

Shadow spun around and reared up, his instincts pushing him to escape from the flames licking over the tops of dead gum trees and crawling rapidly through dry brush, fanned more and more by the gusting dry wind. Thunder cracked around them and lightning flashed in long forked tongues, the tips appearing to touch the ground behind them.

Shane spotted Mate maneuvering into the middle of the confused flock. The action of the dog and the two riders only added to their frenzy. Shane whistled in code to the dog, and shouted a command, "Mate! Get out of there!" Mate moved instantly and with great agility out and to the back, successfully turning the strays into the main flock. He complied with the command, but did it his own way.

The wind roared higher and suddenly shifted direction. Clouds began to disperse and move away, causing the eerie light of morning to grow brighter, and illuminating the rush of men and animals to the safety they could now sense.

Shane grabbed the reins on Nina's mare once again and led her at a fast clip along the base of the hill to a low cabin cut into the hillside. He reined them to a halt in front of it, jumped down, then dragged her out of the saddle and roughly pushed her inside the cabin. She fell against a low bunk at the back wall.

"This humpy should keep you out of harm's way," he said hoarsely through a dry throat. "Don't come out, I mean it. You'll cause more problems than you could ever solve," he panted, gasping for a clear breath. "The wind's shifted. That will help. Sod over the cabin will help keep you safe." He bent over and coughed in an effort to clear his lungs, and then pulled himself up straight. "I'll put your horse in the sod lean-to in the back. Don't leave here . . . I'll be back." And then he turned and was gone, closing the door firmly behind him.

Nina slumped against the bunk, her breath coming in ragged heaves. Her face felt hot and stinging, and she could feel fragments of grit scraping her eyes. Now that she was inside a protected area, she began to give way to her senses. Every nerve in her body was burning as hot as the fire that raged outside, but she hadn't been able, up until now, to recognize it as fear—at least, not fear for herself. She pushed herself up to her knees and crawled over the hard dirt floor to the door.

"Shane!" She tried to shout it but her voice had no strength above a whisper.

She slumped back against the door in complete exhaustion. The roar inside her head was as intense as that outside the door.

Chapter 19

When Nina roused from the deep sleep of exhaustion, all was ominously quiet. She rubbed her irritated eyes and forced them open. Overhead, a low ceiling made of logs and baked earth sprouted blades of dried grasses growing downward like thin stalactites. Flies buzzed so loudly it seemed as if the room was alive with them. Nina frowned with disorientation, blinked her eyes hard once, and opened them again. Then she remembered where she was . . . the fire . . . Shane.

"Shane." The strain of speaking pricked the back of her throat with searing pain.

She sat up, rubbed her burning eyes, and looked around. She was lying on the bunk. She frowned again. The last thing she remembered was Shane leaving her lying on the floor in this cabin. She had no recollection of getting up and moving to the bunk.

She tried to focus her vision in the low light. The only window in the structure was boarded over, and the narrow spaces between the boards let in crooked fingers of daylight. The air in the room was close and pungent with smoke and smoldering vegetation, and everywhere, everywhere, there were the flies.

She stood up, but her knees caved in and she dropped down hard on the bunk. A cloud of dust from the mattress ticking went up her nose and made her sneeze. Once her eyes adjusted to the light, she could see that the place was filthy and probably crawling with unspeakable vermin other than flies, maybe even those barking spiders Derrick had warned her about. A shiver ran over her body. She stood up again, determined to get to the door safely and without stepping on anything living. She set her feet down one in front of the other as if expecting to hear the sound of eggs crunching under her boots.

When at last she managed to grasp the door handle, she let out a shaky sigh of relief. She yanked hard on it. The door was stuck shut, but came unstuck with a force strong enough to knock her off balance and propel her backward down onto the dirt floor, the handle still clutched in her hand. Her hair flopped down over her face. She dropped the handle and tried to lift her hair up, spitting dirt out of her mouth and coughing as a cloud of dust settled around her.

Sweeping her disheveled hair off her face and up over the top of her head, she saw a shaft of daylight alive with dancing dust particles coming through the low doorway. A shadow passed across it, and then there appeared a large pair of dark brown, almost black bare feet, naked legs rising above them. The base of a long spear rested against a muscular calf.

Nina was afraid to look above the gnarled knees for fear the rest of the body might be naked as well. Her heart pounded wildly in her chest, and her breath caught in her throat. The feet moved apart, and the legs blocked the doorway.

"Oh, my God!" she breathed through tight lips.

Fear streaked through her body. A naked giant! Of course! Why not? She began to shake wildly, and without warning, a nervous laugh erupted from somewhere deep inside her and shattered the tense silence. With an ungainly push, she got to her feet and frantically brushed at her clothes. Laughing and crying at the same time, she set up a steady stream of babble.

"Why am I not surprised?" she giggled, wiping tears from her face and slapping at her clothes with a vengeance, as if knocking off huge insects. "I should be used to things like this by now. It's all probably nothing but a bad dream, a big, bad dream." She stopped still, cocked her head and muttered under her breath, "Aye, mate, any minute now I'll wake up . . ."

She stomped her feet in the dirt. Her boots sent up little clouds of dark red dust, and her hair tumbled down again. She squared her shoulders, walked to the doorway, and peered around and under the doorframe. Her eyes followed the spear all the way up. An expressionless dark face dropped to look at her. No emotion penetrated the stoic exterior except for a slight flaring of flat, wide nostrils. The man's black woolly hair stood out from his head like a mammoth headdress. A bright red band of cloth was tied around his forehead, the tails from the knot hanging down over his ear. Behind him the red globe of sun was so brilliant that it blinded her to anything she might read in the black pools of his eyes. The spear tip rose high over his head and was tied with a multicolored cord. In the reflection of the climbing sun, Nina imagined the point of it red with blood.

"Let me out of here!" she demanded in a display of false courage. "You can't keep me prisoner, you know. I'm employed by Mrs. Merritt, and she would deal quite harshly with you if any harm were to come to me." Nina knew she sounded insincere. Who was she fooling? Even if she suddenly disappeared off the face of the earth, Mrs. Merritt would hardly notice.

The great dark figure did not move, but seemed untouched by her outburst. He stared over her head with his fathomless black eyes, his gaze fixed upon something far, far away. There was not a twitch of a muscle over his lean body. It was difficult for Nina to determine if he was breathing; the only indication she had that he was alive, and not some concocted hoax by Shane or Derrick, was her slight detection of a quiver of muscle behind one side of his sharp jawline.

She pulled her head back inside the cabin and drew in a deep breath. The air was filled with the heaviness of burnt brush and charred earth. It brought tears of irritation to her eyes, and a dryness to her throat. She coughed, and went back to the door.

"Yes, well, I'll just be going, now. Nice chatting with you," she said in as friendly a manner as possible.

She stepped forward with the idea of moving around him, but he lowered the spear and brought the long point of it to rest against the edge of the door opening. Still his gaze did not waver from its focus over her head.

"Oh!" Nina sucked in her breath and stepped back inside.

Perhaps he truly was someone to be afraid of. Quite suddenly it occurred to her that he could be Aborigine, one of a primitive race of people who inhabited the Australian outback. She'd read they'd been known to have cannibalistic tendencies. Was this man holding her as the main course for his evening meal? Now her fear was screamingly real, yet she held it silent within her.

Her eyes darted here and there around the dim cabin. There was no other door; by the time she could tear the boards off the only window, he'd have her ensnared in what would no doubt be an iron grip. Panic spread through her, and her arms and legs turned to liquid. Her head filled with the incessant sound of the hundreds of flies in the cabin that seemed to crescendo from buzz to thunderous roar. Doomed, that was all there was to it, she was doomed.

But wait, Nina's powers of reason flickered through her panic. She pulled herself up straight into a confident posture, flexed her fingers and toes, took a deep breath, then turned on a dazzling smile. All she had to do was break down his guard and then she would make a run for it. Simple.

She sidled toward the doorway, smiling with her whole face and eyes. "Say, why don't we go find ourselves a nice quiet spot to sit down and talk, and get to know each other?" Stoic silence from the doorway. "What do you say . . . mate? I'm new to the country and could certainly use a wise person such as yourself to show me the countryside." Still no response. "Shall we give it a go, then?"

She smiled an even more dazzling smile, then took a resolute step toward the doorway. The dark figure stepped toward her, completely blocking her exit. Nina was certain her heart had stopped for a split second.

Regaining her courage, she tried again. "I'm sure that it's much more pleasant out there than it is in . . . in this filthy hole." She rubbed her hands together and looked back over her shoulder into the humpy. "In fact, I'm certain of that," she muttered, then turned back toward her captor. "And I could use a breath of fresh air and a drink of water. You wouldn't deny a visitor that much, now, would you?"

The dark head lowered into the door opening and one of the wide feet took a step inside. Suddenly, from behind the intruder, an arm shot out, wrapped around his throat, and yanked him backward, knocking him off his feet. The body of a man flew past the door to land spread-eagled on top of him. The spear fell across the doorway. Nina tripped over it making her hasty exit, and fell flat on her stomach in the dirt. The two men wrestled on the ground, and when she could bring herself to take a closer look, Nina saw who her rescuer was.

"Shane!" she shrieked.

The men rolled over, and then the black man had the advantage. He grabbed a handful of Shane's hair, the shock of its golden wheat color a sharp contrast in the dark hand.

"No, no! Let him up, let him up!" Nina ran around them, frantic to help Shane but not knowing how.

Shane grunted loudly and flipped the dark, muscled man over on his back, pressing him flat into the dirt. But it was not enough to hold him. The strong bare arms broke free of the grip, and he grabbed Shane by the shirt front, threw him up and back, and pinned him flat to the ground.

Nina cried for help in all directions, but there was no one within earshot of her pleas. The two men struggled against each other, evenly matched in strength and agility. Nina circled around them in an act of abject futility. Shane spat dirt out of his mouth as the Aborigine twisted him around facedown and bent his arm back up to his shoulder.

Nina could stand no more. She forgot everything, who she was, what she was up against. Running at them, she threw herself upon the dark, naked back, and grabbing large fistfuls of the thick black hair, pulled hard. Then she sank her teeth into the sinewy shoulder.

"Ow!" came a hard guttural voice. "What in bloody hell . . ."

The panther-like body flung up off Shane, let go of his arm, and lurched back to remove Nina's teeth and hands as if shrugging off an offending insect. He pulled up to his knees, then fell back with Nina still attached to him. She dropped down onto the ground and he fell back on top of her, flattening her, his feet flailing the air.

"Merritt," the deep voice growled, "get me out of this!"

Shane scrambled to his feet, rubbing his eyes, trying to reorient himself. When his vision cleared, he stopped in his tracks, threw back his head, and let out a raucous laugh that echoed around them.

The man quickly rolled away from Nina, and sprang up like a wildcat. She lay on the ground breathing heavily, propped on her elbows, knees bent, hair disheveled, with dirt and pieces of brush clinging to it. The Aborigine clamped a hand over the wound at the top of his shoulder and stared at her in disbelief. Then he spun around and faced Shane, who was convulsed in uncontrollable laughter.

"Stop that bloody braying like a jackass and get this hellcat away from me!" The dark man rubbed his hand over the wound, then brought it out to look at it. His black eyes widened. "Blood! She's bloody broken the skin! If I get an infection . . ."

Still laughing, Shane walked over and examined his shoulder. "Well, old mate, I think you'll live, but," he laughed even harder, "she sure left her brand on you!"

"She belong to you?"

More laughter. "Hardly."

"Well, I think you ought to tame her."

"Tame? My friend, you have no concept of what you're saying. Try to tame the wind—the result would be the same."

Watching this cordial exchange between the two, Nina grew more and more confused and exasperated. She scrambled to her feet and stomped over to them.

"What is going on here?" She cast a hard, narrow gaze at Shane, and sucked in deep breaths of air. "I thought he was killing you, and now you're standing

236

here laughing with this . . . this . . . person." She
eyed the dark man up and down, at last able to notice
with relief that a kangaroo skin wrapped his lower
torso. A thong belt held the skin in place, and a huge
boomerang hung from it.

"Killing me? Gingu? Not a Buckley's chance!
Might thrash me to within an inch of my life, but
never kill me! Eh, mate?"

Shane gave the other man a resounding slap on his
back which sent him forward on one foot, struggling
to keep his balance. He righted himself, then
returned the gesture with a stiff blow to Shane's back,
practically knocking him down.

"Righto, mate!" he responded with a wry, toothy
grin.

Shane coughed. "Been mates since we were tots,"
he said between exaggerated gasps. He grinned at
Nina.

"Aye," Gingu concurred, "we go way back, maybe
too far." He flashed a grin at her.

Nina watched them both with a wary eye. The man
was not as huge as he had appeared in the doorway of
the tiny cabin through her exhaustion and fear. In
fact, Shane was more than a head taller. Her nerves
settled and she felt a little braver.

"I—I'm sorry if I hurt you. It's just that you
startled me."

"Bit of a snip, you are," came Gingu's clipped
reply.

"I'm sorry. I thought you were . . . aren't you an
Aborigine?"

"Aye, that I am, and what of it?" He pushed out his
full bottom lip, reminding Nina of a pout.

"Nothing, nothing at all." She scrutinized him from wiry full-haired head to wide, dark feet with spreading toes.

"Foreigner," he said, his voice full of disdain, then reached to pick up a long hunting boomerang from the dust and loop it through the thong belt.

Nina frowned. "I am that, but in any case you had no right to scare the wits out of me as you did. You didn't identify yourself, you didn't even speak one word to me. What was I to think?" she sniffed.

Shane watched the two squaring off against each other with an amused quirk of an eyebrow. Nina stepped back and forth in the thick dirt like an agitated chookie bothered by a pushy rooster. Gingu stood rubbing his sore shoulder, sulking like a reprimanded little boy, mannerisms incongruous to his sinewy native strength and wild-haired appearance.

"I was protecting someone I thought was Shane's friend, and this is the thanks I get," Gingu complained. "If you've given me rabies . . ."

Shane stepped between them, a hand on each shoulder. "Well, now, me mates, what say we all kiss and make up? Call a truce to it?" He smiled at first one and then the other. They both glared at him for his trouble at peacemaking. He shook both their shoulders. "Come on, now."

"All right," Gingu begrudgingly conceded.

"I guess so," Nina gave in.

"Right, then!" Shane's voice was jubilant. "Now let's see how much damage has been done by the fire."

Gingu went to pick up his spear. "Wasn't a big

one, just an underbrush fire."

Nina listened to Gingu with a curious expression. She leaned toward Shane and whispered, "Are you sure he's Aborigine?"

Gingu picked up the question with ears made sensitive from living closely with the land and its creatures. He walked with long strides toward them, glaring at her with his obsidian eyes.

"Why, because of the way he speaks?"

"Well, yes."

Shane laughed. "That's a product of the Mum's work. She thought if Gingu and I were so determined to be friends, we would have to understand each other. I told her we already understood each other, but to her, that meant Gingu should be educated. She taught him to read and speak our language. It was a clash of wills, but she won that battle! She even tried to put him in boarding school with me."

Gingu spat.

"Not one of her better ideas," Shane went on, bending toward Nina. "He simply left and ran home. Rather often, I might add. But, I guess something of it must have rubbed off on him."

"What did the school do about a . . . a uniform for him?" she had to ask.

"They fitted him with several. He just kept tearing them up and making loin wraps out of them."

Gingu spat again.

Nina smiled at that, then whispered to Shane. "I've heard they eat humans. How could the Mum let him in the house?"

Shane leaned into her ear. "Gingu prefers Orientals. He thinks vegetable eaters have a lighter taste.

Europeans are tougher, salty, he says. I'm not sure what he thinks about Americans."

Nina's mouth dropped open in horror, and then she smiled in disbelief of Shane's words. She went to Gingu, who stood staring out across the still steaming black soil plain, ignoring them.

"I truly am sorry if I hurt you, Gingu. Please accept my apology." She held out a small hand toward him.

Gingu stood stoically addressing nature, understanding it on the deeper level known only to those who've been born to it and have lived intimately with it. A small muscle twitched in his cheek. After a long moment he turned toward her and grasped her hand in his wide dark one, pale palm to pale palm.

"I'm sorry I frightened you, Miss . . . ?"

"Nina."

He nodded with an upward tilt to one corner of his mouth, then raised her hand and kissed the back of it. Raising his woolly head, he smacked his lips at the taste of her hand and broke into a toothy grin. She snatched her hand away from him and wiped the back of it on her trousers.

"Very sweet," Shane chided. "Now could we please get on with it?"

The three walked together toward the charred stretch of land in front of them. Saddened by the loss of range grass to the fire, Nina was suddenly filled with a sense of belonging to the country, a closeness to Shane's life as she'd never before felt. The memory of their lovemaking flooded back, and her face burned with embarrassment. She would never have thought she'd have given in to it. No, she hadn't given in . . . she'd followed the desires of her heart and body, and she'd wanted him as much as he'd seemed to want her. How could she even think of leaving Flame Tree now?

The picture of the two of them reflected in the overhead mirror on Shane's bed flashed through her mind, and she shook her head and shut her eyes. If the Mum ever found out about that, there would be a certain kind of hell to pay . . .

"The Mum!" she blurted out.

Shane halted. "Where?" He looked in the direction of the house as if by some miracle they might see the Mum riding toward them.

"Oh my, what time could it be?" she wailed.

Gingu peered up at the white hot sky, shielding his eyes with a wide, flat hand. "Gone for one at least."

"Oh no. I've missed breakfast and luncheon. She'll wonder about me."

"I'm sure she already does," Shane put in with a low chuckle.

Nina spun around, squinting toward the cabin to see if her horse was there. "I thought if I just appeared at breakfast this morning, she'd never know I came back so late last night." She looked guiltily at Shane for a brief moment. "How am I going to explain being *this* late?"

"You'll think of something, my girl, I'm sure of that."

"Well, you could help me with it."

"Me? Why would I want to do that?" he teased.

"That's right! I don't know why you would. It's not you who'll receive the lecture of reprimand."

"I've had my share of them, my girl."

241

"Don't call me that! Can't you even try a little to help me?"

"Aye," he replied, stroking the square point of his chin. "I can do two things to help you."

"Well, what are they?" she rasped impatiently.

"First, I can get Shadow for you and you can ride him home."

"That's a relief," she sighed. "What's the second?"

"I can give you a valuable tip drawn from my repertoire of valuable tips." He stopped and stroked his chin again thoughtfully.

"Will you hurry, please?"

Shane leaned down toward her and kissed the end of her nose. Looking around them in an air of complicity, he whispered, "No need to climb up the outside rungs when you're trying to sneak into the house. Maude never locks the kitchen door!"

Nina's mouth dropped open in horror. "Oh, you!" she flung at him. Then she turned on her heel and marched off in the direction of the house.

Shane's laughter resounded around her. "Not too fast, my girl," he called after her. "Let Shadow catch up with you!"

Chapter 20

Nina was relieved that nothing was said about her late arrival at the house the day of the fire, but she was positive the Mum knew everything—her trip to the out station, the sneaking into the house, the fact that she'd been in Shane's room, and . . . oh, dear God! Could she know about *that*, too?

Nina had no regrets, at least about anything she'd done. But she did regret the strain between herself and the Mum. She *must* know about all of it. What else could have induced her to act as coldly toward Nina as she had over the last few days? In spite of the Mum's austere demeanor and the distance lying heavy between them, Nina felt a strong respect and even a growing fondness for the Merritt matriarch. Her experience during the fire helped her to understand on a deeper level the intensity with which Vanessa loved Flame Tree, and the tenacity with which she clung to its preservation at any cost.

Shane had been to dinner with them once since the fire, but on at least two other evenings Nina had heard his voice, mingled with the Mum's, coming from her study. She wondered if he might be avoiding her now. When her eyes met his at the dinner table, she'd tried to read the ocean-blue depths, but his glances were guarded, his thoughts concealed.

Colin, however, had been utterly charming, arriving for dinner on time, engaging both Nina and his mother in conversation. He would politely ask Nina how her day had been, and inquire, sometimes with a certain knowing look, how she was getting on at Flame Tree. Nina was warm with him. She understood him, and she genuinely liked him, and they enjoyed an easy friendship.

Vanessa Merritt cast a critical eye toward both of them. On the one hand, Colin's spending time with Nina might take the girl's mind off pursuing Shane, and Vanessa was not convinced that Nina had dropped that notion, no matter how much the two of them avoided close contact. Her intuition where mutual attraction and interest were concerned was much too strong to be denied.

On the other hand, she was concerned that Colin might flatter the American just a little too much, and in response, might discover that she could be won over. Then, too, he could be taken with her himself, and apply strong powers of persuasion to keep her at Flame Tree. This would not do in the Vanessa Merritt scheme of things; it would not do at all.

Further, she had observed Colin acting rather strangely of late, secretive, almost gleefully smug. He was up to something, she knew it as well as she knew the back of her well-manicured hand. Perhaps she was too late. After all, she'd seen them together, coming from his room. Perhaps he'd already fallen for Nina Cole. She would have to watch him more closely and prevent him from making yet another in a long line of foolish mistakes. He was immature and impressionable, much of it her fault, she knew. Yes, Colin would certainly bear watching much more carefully than she had been doing.

Early in the day of the party, Nina walked around the big pantry, dodging several hanging flypaper strips as she went, lifting long sheets of protective netting and opening several carefully wrapped packages of food, peering in at their fragrant contents.

"Oh, it's going to be a sumptuous feast. Goodness, Maude, have you prepared all this yourself?"

"Mercy no, but a goodly bit of it, lass. The Mister's been delivering it from several of the folks in the valley, and old Billy MacTeague brings some of the orders by in his dray. Some's all the way from Sydney, some from Bathurst, and the rest I fill in. All except for the rum. The Mister's in charge of that. Nary a drop has touched my hands, and by good grace, never my lips. Maybe a taste of valley wine now and again, but never the rum." Maude bustled about the kitchen while she talked, lining up things as they were to be served.

Nina walked the length of the sideboards, touching each container, anticipating the taste that would accompany the aroma or its presentation on the best crystal and silver that Anthia was busy cleaning.

The caviars and thin breads all in tight containers lined a sideboard, one end of it cleared to receive the fresh fish this morning. When Nina read over Maude's carefully prepared list, she was awed at the different kinds of seafood to be presented to the evening's guests. Topping the list was John Dory, the finest of Australian fish, followed by large prawns, crab, mussels, and something called "blue swimmers."

But it was the crayfish, big as lobsters, she yearned for most. She could hardly wait to sink her teeth into the sweet claw meat dripping with hot butter. If she was homesick for anything from America, it was seafood. The memory of fresh fish unloaded from the boats and transported up the cobblestone streets to the fish market by the piers in New York came rushing back. She had learned early that even in as wealthy a station as Flame Tree, good seafood was rare. Just to bring it from Sydney via the usual transportation to the valley was taking the chance that it would arrive in inedible condition.

"Now, what can I do with one steak-and-kidney pie?" Maude stood next to the big work table in the center of the kitchen, hands on hips, staring down at a lone pie wrapped in a blue towel. "It's from that Smith woman over at O'Rourke station. Has the eye for the Mister, that's what. Knows he's got a weakness for steak-and-kidney pie." She clucked and re-wrapped the pie.

Nina came out of the pantry empty-handed only because of sheer willpower: she did not want to disturb the arrangement of the various trays of food. She plopped down on a high wood stool near the work table, her eyes falling on the towel-wrapped steak-and-kidney pie.

"Maude . . . do you ever get jealous when another woman pays attention to Derrick? I mean, like the pie. Does it bother you that other women find him attractive?"

"Mercy, no! What would I have to be jealous about? If I do say so myself, I can make a better steak-and-kidney pie than that Smith woman ever thought of. The Mister knows that." She took a damp cloth and wiped a free space on the table to make room for filling the special tarts she'd prepared.

"But isn't more at issue than steak-and-kidney pie?"

"What else is there? As I see it, the best way to keep a man from strayin' is to feed him well—outside and inside the bedroom!" Instantly one plump hand flew up to cover her mouth, and the ruddy cheeks grew ruddier at such a bold remark.

"Maude!" Nina stared in amused disbelief.

Maude dropped her hand and vigorously stirred the molasses filling, avoiding Nina's eyes.

"Well, now, lass, that's nothing to get your knickers all in a twist about. If a man did the same thing for a woman, there'd be a lot more happy people around."

"Does Derrick do that for you?" Nina pressed on timidly.

Maude stirred faster, and her face reddened once again. She looked up and watched Anthia carry a tray of crystal glasses into the dining room, then leaned toward Nina.

"Oh, lass, over twenty years together and the only

thing that's changed is that everything is better. Just my way of thinkin', that's all. If you love each other and you make each other happy behind your bedroom door, well, then, it just follows naturally that everything else will work out, come what may. Anything's endurable, if you love each other like that."

Nina looked down at her hands, turning inward to her own personal thoughts. A picture of Shane formed slowly in her mind, unfolding from the toes of his boots to the top of his windblown hair. She followed the line up his body, over the muscled calves outlined against worn pants, over firm buttocks evident through the time-softened fabric, his narrow waist, broad shoulders through the white moleskin shirt he sometimes wore, golden wisps over his collar, and the wind moving through the rest of his hair. A sudden warmth spread over her palms and a deep longing to touch once again that hair, those shoulders . . .

"Maude, did you ever . . . I mean, is it always wrong if a man and a woman . . . you know, if they're not married?"

Maude's cheeks reddened again, and she watched the dining room door for the entrance of Anthia. She quickly began scooping up spoonfuls of the rich filling and slapping them down in quick rhythm on the open tart shells she'd lined up on the table.

"Well, now, lass, I think that's something your mother should talk to you about."

"I don't have a mother, and when I did, she didn't talk about these things with me. I was too young. And all Aunt Sadie ever said was, 'Don't.' I'm confused about a lot of things."

Maude wiped her brow with the back of her hand and shooed away the flies buzzing around her head. "All right, lass, I'll tell you something I've never told another living soul. And you must promise to keep it to yourself."

Nina nodded.

"Once I knew the Mister and I were going to be married, well, we . . . we did make love." She wiped her hands on her towel, then walked around the table to Nina. "This doesn't mean you should, too. There's them that does and them that doesn't. It's something in your heart feels right or wrong. But be careful. Sometimes the heart has a way of confusin' the head."

Nina silently agreed. And Shane Merritt . . . ah, this is where her heart confused her head the most. Her head knew all the facts, but the fluttering in her heart and in her warm, private depths when she thought of Shane was more unsettling than anything she'd ever experienced. She wasn't supposed to have feelings for him, at least, not the feelings she was having. She wasn't the appropriate woman for him; Vanessa Merritt had decreed it.

Yet that night in his bedroom, Nina wanted Shane, gave herself to him body and soul. Her head protested, her heart beat wildly, and her body was powerless to resist him. It had wantonly and without conscience opened like a spring rose to envelop the first drop of morning dew. She had been shocked to know that could happen.

Once the glow of that night faded, Nina fretted over her wanton behavior. Aunt Sadie's words came flooding back. She'd warned Nina against letting a man have his way. "Why would he bother to hitch up the horse if a woman herself is going to roll the wagon right into his barn anyway?"

Every night since, she'd pictured them together in the mirror. She believed him to be as lost in wild abandon as she'd been, which was why his lack of appearance at the house worried her. What was he thinking of her now? Did he think she was a woman of easy virtue? Her eyes burned. How much more proof did she need than his lack of contact with her? Her heart sank heavily, and her throat ached from holding back the words, the emotion.

Realization thundered over her like that rampaging dry storm . . . she loved him! She loved Shane Merritt, and it was quite possible she could do nothing about it. But why couldn't she? Why couldn't it be like the love stories in books, or in her fantasies? Why couldn't he care for her the way she cared for him? Why couldn't they be together and live happily ever after? Does real life have to have a conclusion, like one of Shakespeare's tragedies? Suddenly she felt sick to her stomach.

"What's the matter, lass? You look a little peaked." Maude placed a plump hand on Nina's forehead. "Are you upset by what I said?"

"Oh no, no, Maude. I was just thinking . . ."

"I know, dear," Maude said with intuitive understanding. "I know, and I fear you'll get your heart broke."

"You know?" Nina looked up into Maude's loving face, her aquamarine eyes glistening darkly with unshed tears. How could Maude know? Did she look as different on the outside as she was feeling on the inside now?

"Aye, lass, from the first moment. You were smitten with Shane, plain as day." ·

"Oh," Nina sighed with relief. "Maude, what am I going to do?" She threw her arms around Maude's waist and clung to her.

Maude embraced her, stroking her hair and rubbing her back. The circle of Nina's arms tightened. At this moment, almost more than at any other time, she needed mothering.

"Well, lass, if you know what you want, go after it. That's all I can say."

"I . . . I can't."

"'Twon't do to be faint of heart."

"I'm not, Maude. You just don't know . . ." She pulled away and looked up into the kindly face.

"Now, of course, I know, dear. I know how it feels to go weak with aching for somebody."

"That's not what I mean, although that *is* what I feel."

The dining room door swung wide open and Vanessa Merritt stepped into the kitchen with a frown of consternation filling her sharp features.

"Maude! Why isn't the rest of the glassware available? Anthia seems to be having difficulty locating it." She spoke as if she hadn't noticed Nina sitting at the table.

Maude turned slowly, unperturbed by her employer's harsh tone. "I had them wrapped and placed in the ice house. I thought it might be nice to have chilled glasses for the first champagne toast of the evening. I do hope that meets with

251

your approval, Mrs. Merritt."

Nina noted that Maude took on a carefully perfected manner and diction whenever Vanessa Merritt's impervious presence threatened to upset the balance of things. Vanessa's frown faded, but her features did not soften.

"Thank you," she said, and turned to go into the dining room. She stopped, a beringed hand resting on the door, and said without turning, "At afternoon tea, Nina, you will dress for the party so that I may inspect your appearance. Please be prompt. My time is limited and valuable." And then she was gone.

With a weary sigh, Maude turned back to Nina. "I must get on with my work, lass."

"Let me help, Maude. I'm useless here otherwise." She suddenly felt very, very tired.

"No, lass, you can't. Go take a rest. Something tells me you'll need your strength for this evening."

"I'll say, just to wear that awful green print dress she's making me put on. I do so wish I had the nerve to wear the one we made."

"Aye, it is beautiful, and you are a vision in it. But the Mum would have your head, and mine, too, I'll wager."

"I know," Nina sighed. "It probably doesn't matter anyway." She pushed through the dining room door with a weary hand and a heavy heart.

Maude watched the small drooped shoulders slide between the doors. Poor child, she thought. Completely in love with Shane, and now forced to sacrifice that love for a duty and obligation that had nothing to do with her. Dutiful daughter that Anthia was, she'd told Maude all that she'd overheard between the Mum and Nina and the conversation with Shane. She took in a deep, anxious breath.

"Then what have you got to lose, lass?" she said toward Nina's back, and instantly hoped she would not live to regret that spoken thought.

The swinging doors into the dining room immediately swung back into the kitchen. Nina held them open with both hands.

"What did you say, Maude?" She was breathless.

"Me?" Maude asked innocently without turning around. "Why, I didn't say nothing, lass, nothing atall."

Nina's face lit as if a wash of sunlight had suddenly come through the roof to shine only on her.

"Of course you didn't, Maude. My mistake." She gave the doors an extra push wide, then spun around and ran up to her room, a new lightness in her step.

Promptly at four, Nina entered Vanessa's study, where tea had been set. The older woman sat regally in a high-backed dark red velvet upholstered chair, the white Persian cat purring contentedly as the perfect hand stroked it. In her other hand she held a slim leatherbound volume. She lowered the book slowly and looked up over gold-rimmed spectacles with a critical eye in Nina's direction.

Nina stood in the doorway, hands tucked primly behind her back. Her hair was swept smoothly back, and done up in a tight chignon at the nape of her neck. The narrow band of white lace which adorned the high neck of the green print dress Vanessa had purchased for her in Parramatta delicately framed her pale face. The bodice loosely skimmed her slim waist, and the long skirt hung in straight folds over her hips to graze her ankles. A matching band of white lace circled the hem, below which peeked white stockings and a pair of low-heeled black leather slippers.

Vanessa motioned with the point of a finger for her to turn around. She did so, slowly and properly, as if carrying an imaginary book on top of her head.

"Yes, yes, that will do just fine, just fine." She indicated a chair that had been set near the tea table. "You may take tea, then retire until our guests arrive. You will make an appearance, greet each guest in a cordial manner, and then discreetly take your leave and spend the rest of the evening in your room. Cakes?" She held out a small silver tray with several small cakes arranged on a white doily.

"No, thank you," Nina said politely, and sipped her tea.

Vanessa handed her the volume she'd been holding and indicated that she was to read from the ribbon-marked pages. Nina took the book and dutifully read each piece. During the readings, Vanessa leaned her head back against the velvet, closed her eyes, and stroked the Persian. In that pose, Nina thought she looked almost frail, vulnerable to the blows life had dealt her, and her heart warmed toward the matriarch for a moment.

The readings finished, Nina stood to make her departure. Vanessa opened her eyes, and the vulnerable visage passed as quickly as it had come, replaced by a cold hardness.

"Shall I leave now?" Nina asked politely.

Vanessa nodded slowly. "Yes, I'm afraid I'm feeling rather weary today. Perhaps it's the concern over the celebration tonight. You may go."

Nina turned to leave the room. At the door she turned back to Vanessa. "I truly am sorry that you don't like me, Mrs. Merritt. I shall miss Flame Tree, and . . ." A knot formed in her throat. ". . . And I shall miss you . . . and your family." Then she quickly left the room.

Vanessa Merritt watched the door close behind Nina. She sighed deeply, leaned back, and closed her eyes again. "Oh, my dear young woman," she said into nothingness, "you can never understand."

Chapter 21

Shane knocked on Colin's door about an hour before the first of the more than one hundred guests were scheduled to arrive. He was dressed for the party, the Mum's party, he told himself, even if she did announce that it was being held in his honor. He didn't want the party, didn't even want to be in the house tonight. He was feeling out of sorts, but even in a foul mood he would not deny the Mum's request.

Colin opened the door, said nothing in greeting to his brother, but left the door ajar and went back to dressing. Shane went in, stretched out on the bed, and lit up a cheroot.

Inside his dressing room, Colin stood in front of a mirror, meticulously tying and retying a black silk cravat at the neck of his white ruffled-front shirt. "To what do I owe this rare visit from my older brother?" he called out with a detached tone.

"Now, now, little brother, try to hold down your exuberance," Shane said lightly.

"That won't take much effort," was Colin's low retort.

He came back into the bedroom, picked up his black tailcoat, and shrugged it on, settling himself into it. He checked his impeccably groomed image in the long oval mirror in the corner. Shane noted that his younger brother had grown into a handsome man, with the softly angled jawline and light coloring of their mother. With a sharp pang, he suddenly wished he knew him as an adult as well as he had known him as a child.

Shane sat up on the edge of the bed and blanked the cheroot in a heavy glass ashtray on the bedside table. "Colin, I'm sorry we seem to have so much distance between us now. Sometimes . . . sometimes I wish we could go back to being children again. Life was so much simpler then."

Turning his back on his brother, Colin returned to the dressing room. Shane got up and followed him, watching as he regarded himself in a small shaving mirror, smoothing the sleek sides of his hair. Shane moved up behind him until both faces were visible in the mirror. The reflection framed their heritage, the delicateness of their mother in Colin's face, and the ruggedness of their father in Shane's.

"What's going on with you, Colin? Are you in some kind of trouble? Talk to me. Maybe I can help."

Colin's eyelids fluttered slightly, but he continued inspecting his hair. "What makes you think I'm in trouble?"

"Just the way you've been acting, and well, something Derrick said."

"Meddling old fool. He doesn't know anything."

"And . . . the Mum told me."

Colin slid away from the mirror and went back into the bedroom. "What did Mother tell you?"

"That you've been gambling money on fossickers and barren gold mines. Colin—"

"Don't give me a big brother lecture, big brother. I don't need it, and I don't need your help. I'm capable of making decisions for myself, and I will not be told what to do, nor condescended to."

"I'm not doing that. I know you can make your own decisions. It's just that, well, maybe you could use some sound guidance."

"From you? Hardly. From our dear mother? Or should I say, *your* dear mother, since you're the only one she's ever been able to see. Forget it. That brand of guidance I don't need. You can both *keep* it. Someday I'll show you both."

Shane's big hands shot out and grabbed Colin by the shoulders and spun him around to face him. "Damnit! Have you forgotten what you said the other night at dinner? Or was that all just a muck of nonsense to get you in the Mum's good graces . . . or Nina's? Will you for bloody once think of someone other than yourself? Flame Tree's in trouble, and the Mum is not well."

"I've never been taught how to think about someone else!" Colin shouted. "No one else ever thought about me, so I wisely learned that I would have to do that myself. Who was there for me when I was in trouble?"

"The Mum for one, you bloody fool," Shane shouted back, "and she's still there for you!"

"With her all-important money!" Colin wrenched

259

out of Shane's grip. His voice calmed. "With her money, Shane, with Father's money, with your money. Money. That's not what I wanted . . . then." He sank down onto the bed and dropped his head in his hands. Slowly Shane walked to the bed and sat down beside him. He draped an arm around his brother's shoulders. Colin's back came up straight, shrugging Shane's arm away. He stared ahead into space.

"But it's what I want now." His voice was cold and hard. "If Flame Tree's in trouble, that's your bloody concern. That's the way the Mum wants it." He got up and walked to the door, then paused with his hand on the latch. "And frankly, big brother, whatever solutions there are will be credited to you anyway. When she dies, it simply means I'll be out of her hair, and there'll be more money for me. Now if you'll excuse me . . ."

Shane sprung from the bed and flew at his brother. He slammed the door shut, whirled him around, and landed a punch on his jaw. Colin fell back, his knees buckling under him, and caught himself from hitting the floor by grabbing the arm of a nearby chair. Shane reached down and with both hands pulled him up by the front of his silk vest and perfectly cut shirt. Standing him on his feet, he peered with steel-edged blue into Colin's stunned face.

"You selfish little son-of-a-bitch!"

Colin's face was throbbing a deep red. "Not a nice thing to call our mother."

Shane shook him so hard his head wobbled. "You've not a bloody shred of compassion in your

260

body, have you? You'd bleed Flame Tree of life to finance your stupid get-rich-quick schemes with nary a thought to our mother and father and their life's work, not to mention all the people who are dependent upon us.'' He flung him down into the chair. ''You disgust me. I don't know you anymore. Maybe I've never known you.''

Shane's chest heaved with anger and the adrenaline coursing through his body. Colin slowly righted himself and with a mask of indifference on his face, pulled a gray silk handkerchief from his breast pocket and dabbed gingerly at the bleeding corner of his mouth.

''See you at your party, big brother, and may we all have a high old time.''

Shane turned and kicked the door hard. Then he snatched it open and let it slam behind him as he stormed past Colin down the hallway toward the back stairs.

Colin stayed in the hallway a moment, gingerly rearranging his jaw. A half-smile crept over his lips. His latest schemes had better work. He wasn't sure he could keep up the front, especially if he had to endure his brother's wrath. But it would all be worth it to feel, for once, that he was a hero in his mother's heart, as much a hero as Shane and his father had always been to her. And he wanted to feel the hero in his own heart the way he'd idolized his father and brother. He had to carry out his plans in his own way and in his own time. And with the element of surprise, well, the outcome could be good for all.

Colin returned his handkerchief to his pocket, and started down the stairs.

Inside his own room, Shane flopped down on the bed and stared overhead into the mirror. His mother's words from long ago came back to him in faint echo: "Shane, dear, please take your boots off the coverlet. Boots belong on the floor." Instinctively he moved his feet to hang off the edge of the bed.

He watched himself in the mirror. Was this shaking wretch who'd just hit his brother really Shane Merritt? Was he truly Daniel Merritt's exact copy, as the Mum liked to think? How could he be anything like that gentle, loving man? Had he grown to be what the Mum had grown to be, caring only about work and that all-important mission of keeping Flame Tree alive? Was that who he was, what he was? How was it he'd never honestly thought about it before now?

He clamped his eyes shut to block out the vision of the stranger overhead. The unfamiliar sting of tears burned behind his eyelids, but he forced them back, then opened his eyes. Above him, as if suspended in a dream, was a fantasy painting of himself with Nina wrapped in his arms lying on this bed, her pale golden skin gleaming in the lampglow, her mane of flaming hair spread out beneath them.

Had he really kissed Nina so completely? So demandingly, so lustfully? Had he actually touched her sweet, full breasts and held her succulent nipples in his lips? Plunged his desperate need for her into the untouched soul of her? And had she actually responded to him with her own desire? Or was it all a dream?

He could still see her astride a horse in the middle of that raging fire, and he thrilled to her strength and bravery. She'd ridden into danger as if she was as driven as the Mum to save even a small part of Flame Tree. He'd never forget that night.

Nina occupied his deepest thoughts more and more. She was not the naive little girl he'd first thought, but a living, breathing, warm, and beautiful woman, vital and joyful. She'd taken their teasing and pranks, and even Mate's special brand of affection, with good humor. And how he loved her laugh! He realized now how much it had filled him with an indescribable joy.

He'd had plenty of good times with all kinds of women in his past, but Nina was . . . different, not like the others. He enjoyed being with her, that was true, but he knew now that he'd reveled in every moment simply because they were in it together, and it felt good to him.

But the Mum had her own ideas on how to save Flame Tree. Shane was to marry the right woman, the woman whose family owned the right property. It was the only thing to do, the Mum was convinced of it. Shane was to save Flame Tree. She never considered Colin could have a part in it too.

Shane would not let the Mum lose Flame Tree. It would kill her, and if she was as ill as Derrick said she was, he had to do everything in his power to fulfill her wishes, didn't he? The whole thing seemed to lie in his hands, and he felt the immense weight of it.

After the argument with Colin he had calmed himself with thoughts of Nina, yet those thoughts also disturbed him. Nina. And Colin. Was Colin pursuing her? If he was, it would be the first time he'd been interested in a woman of quality, except perhaps for the young Marston girl, when they were both barely dry behind the ears. Laurette Marston had soundly rebuffed Colin, and because of it he'd ignored or insulted nice girls for years afterward.

Shane shook his head. His younger brother had certainly changed for the worse once he discovered women would flock around him if he just flashed his dazzling smile and his obvious wealth. He'd never been selective, much to the Mum's displeasure.

But Nina was different than any of those fluffs, far and away different, and Colin knew it. Maybe the Mum would allow Colin to marry her if it kept him from embarrassing the family further. As long as Shane did his duty, the Mum might allow Colin to go his way.

But what about Nina? Would she marry Colin, especially now, after the two of them . . . in his bed . . . ?

What a sorry excuse for a man he was. Reduced to this, this kind of thinking, wanting a woman so deep down inside him that the pain could not be eased, and thinking about her marrying his brother, while he married someone else. There must be another way. He desired all of Nina, her mind, her soul, her heart, her humor, her warmth, her love, and aye, her inviting, softly curved body. He longed to possess it all. He loved her, loved Nina Cole more completely than he'd ever loved anything in his life, even Flame Tree.

But, there was his duty to Flame Tree, the Mum, and the memory of his father. And perhaps even to Colin. The admission of it was a mortal self-inflicted wound. He would not recover from this one, he knew it instinctively.

How was he to handle it all? Nina *had* to return to America, that was the only answer, and the sooner the better—for all of them. He would see to it while he still had some of his wits about him. He would begin to make the arrangements for her departure first thing in the morning. He took in a long, deep breath and let it out slowly. The answer to his dilemma saddened him.

A light knock came at the door, startling him back into the reality of the evening. With great effort he hauled his long frame off the bed, straightened his trousers, smoothed out his trim black tailcoat, and brushed the velvet collar. He pulled up the neck of his white high-collared shirt, then tore off the black tie and opened the constraining top two studs. The Mum would just have to be disappointed in the way he was dressed—it was as formal as he could manage this night. And he was not about to exchange his favorite boots for the more formal shoe expected.

He opened the door to the radiant vision of his mother in a long black moiré gown with a triple flounce skirt, a rather revealing low-scooped neck, and long sleeves rounding at the shoulders and ending tightly at the wrists. Her only jewelry was the diamond necklace and earrings his father had given her at the close of the first prosperous year at Flame Tree. Her lovely sungold hair, showing only the slightest trace of gray, was piled softly on top of her head and held with small combs, three perfectly coiled curls extending down the nape of her neck. Shane smiled, deep love emanating from his eyes.

"Will you escort me downstairs, my son? Some of our guests have begun to arrive."

He bowed, then lifted his mother's hand, kissed it, and looped it through the crook of his arm. "It will be my greatest honor and pleasure to escort the beautiful queen of Hunter Valley to the grand ballroom so that she may preside over her subjects. Come, Your Majesty."

She beamed up at him, and the two made a striking couple as they walked together to the ballroom.

Chapter 22

Vanessa Merritt was a gracious hostess, offering a warm and special greeting to her guests as if each was the honored one. Her gatherings, though few and far between in recent years, were always major events in the social calendar of the valley, not to be missed by anyone who was fortunate enough to be invited. It had been said that only once did an invited guest fail to make an appearance at one of Vanessa's parties, and that was eighteen years before, when Greta Marston was giving birth to her daughter Laurette. This evening all of the Marstons were in attendance, including Greta and Laurette.

Shane accompanied his mother around the ballroom for the first hour, greeting old and new acquaintances. He carried a heavy hand-sized glass of the finest rum reserved for the male guests, while the ladies delicately sipped the best valley wines from fine stemmed crystal.

Extra servants, hired especially for the occasion, bustled about in black uniforms with white accents of shirt and tie for the men and lace collars for the women. They served the grand array of canapes arranged by Maude, who had proved herself as adept at preparing repasts for the elite as she was at serving up oxtail stew and damper bread for the outback stockmen and jackaroos.

In one corner a small orchestra played. All around the long cream-walled room, groups of lighted candles or crystal oil lamps set up soft glows to touch the wider circles of light from hanging crystal chandeliers that ran its length.

Older men, dressed in the same dark wool suits they'd been using for years, stood around in threes and fours discussing the latest cattle and wool markets, or the possibility of another long drought and its effects on valuable rangeland. The ladies were resplendent in gowns of brilliant velvets, silks, and taffetas, accompanied by glittering jewels brought out only for such occasions. They gathered in their own groups, chatting, the men supposed, about what women in other groups were wearing. It never occurred to them that the women might discuss, among many other things, exactly what they were discussing.

Many a woman carried on when her husband passed away, just as Vanessa Merritt had had to do. She might concede to the leadership of a son, but always in the background she made it her business to know the count as near as possible in mobs of sheep or herds of cattle, in addition to knowing the station's number of stockmen and their families.

After an acceptable amount of time with Vanessa, Shane left her side to step into several male circles and discuss a few bits of business. His eyes scanned the room on more than one occasion as he talked, and increasingly he found himself unable to concentrate on the conversations he'd joined. At last he admitted privately to himself what he was looking for, what he was waiting for, and that was a glimpse of Nina.

He wondered, since the party was well under way, if perhaps she didn't feel well, or was perhaps intimidated by so large a gathering of monied and landed people. The Mum would not have forbidden her to attend, would she? Nina ought to be here to attend the only party that would be given during her time at Flame Tree. He set down his glass on a tray in the hands of a passing servant. He'd just bloody well search her out, that was all there was to it.

Vanessa turned away from a group of friends and instinctively scanned the room for sight of her older son. She skimmed past Colin, who was brashly holding forth with a group of young men, probably bragging about his latest investment venture. She glided regally toward the orchestra and spoke briefly to the conductor, and to the head servant.

Searching the room once more with eyes that had only sharpened with age, Vanessa noted that Nina Cole had not yet put in an appearance. Her gaze fell upon Shane, and she observed that he also seemed to be looking for someone. When he set down his glass and started for the archway leading to the other part of the house, Vanessa nodded sharply to the conductor. A loud drumroll cut into the mingled din of voices chattering and glasses tinkling, and the conductor held his hands high above his head.

"Ladies and gentlemen, may I have your attention,

please?" he boomed over the subsiding party banter. While he spoke, servants passed through the room with tall chilled champagne flutes and several magnums of the sparkling liquid. "Mrs. Daniel Merritt, your gracious hostess, has asked me to make a very special announcement. You've been invited to Flame Tree this evening not only to share a social evening with friends and neighbors, but to welcome back from a long and successful journey to America Mrs. Merritt's oldest son. Please raise your glasses in a welcome toast to Mr. Shane Merritt!"

Those without a glass in hand applauded, others from several places around the room shouted "Here here!" and drank to the toast. Shane made a wave of thanks and greeting around the room. Then he stopped a servant to pick up a full glass, and motioned to the others to refill the glasses for the guests.

"I would like to propose a very special toast of my own." He raised his glass high. "To Vanessa Windsor Merritt, the lifeblood of Flame Tree, keeper of Daniel Merritt's dream, and abiding strength in my brother, Colin, and me."

He smiled lovingly toward his mother, who stood in the center of the crowd, then tipped his glass to drink. Again a chorus of "Here, here, Vanessa!" came from around the gathering, followed by a round of applause.

Shane watched his mother basking in the glow of their attention. Several of them turned back toward him, and he felt their gaze change. Their animated conversation subsided, and he heard a collective intake of breath from several parts of the room. Most of the guests, along with his mother and Colin, were riveted in a gaze toward him, yet past him. He turned instinctively to look over his shoulder.

Nina Cole stood framed in the dark wood archway, a striking vision in deep blue, awash in the golden glow of candlelight. The gown accentuated her softly rounded curves, and created an enhancing contrast to her sun-golden skin. Her hair, falling in long, soft waves of liquid fire, ending in a rounded curl at her waist, framed her beautiful face, which was touched with the merest hint of rouge and lip pomade. Her aquamarine eyes radiated with the mystery of midnight and the newness of morning.

Shane's breath caught in his throat for one heart-stopping moment. Vaguely he heard low whisperings behind him, and then the tentative strains of music coming from somewhere in the far reaches of his mind.

Nina smiled, radiating confidence. For possibly the first time in his life, Shane was struck speechless and motionless. All sorts of commands careened through his mind. "Acknowledge her presence, then leave." "Nay, escort her around the room. Introduce her to the neighbors." "Nay, don't do that, someone might steal her away." And then, at last, "Don't just stand there, you fool, go to her side before she disappears into the mist that brought her here!" He shook his head to clear it.

Nina had been standing at the archway long enough to hear and be touched by Shane's toast to his mother. The light in her eyes focused only on him, as if not another single person were within miles of the two of them. She'd had time to take in his entire

271

figure, and the burning twinges she'd felt from the first moment she'd encountered him spread through her stomach and below. No matter how seldom or often she saw him now, that burning only grew more intense.

He was the handsomest man she'd ever seen. As she stood listening in the background, she was filled with an admiration and appreciation for his lean body sculpted by work. Even now her hands, her skin, her very center remembered vividly the feel and smell of him. Standing so close to him now, yet so far away, made her blood pound in her ears so loudly it shut out the sounds of the celebrating guests.

The expansiveness of life in this amazing Australia had expanded her own senses, long dulled by the restrictions in her life and in the lives and conventions of her mother and aunt before her. A stunning revelation at least; perhaps a new and heavier burden at most.

Her heart fluttered as the black coat strained across Shane's shoulders when he lifted his glass in a toast to his mother. His hair curled provocatively over the black velvet collar, and she knew its texture would be indistinguishable from the velvet. She blushed as the image crossed her mind of his muscular form hidden under the long back of his coat.

When he turned around to face her, she felt her knees turn to water for just a moment, but then she took in a deep, strength-giving breath which culminated in a dazzling smile. She glided into the room toward him, never taking her gaze from the obvious appreciation in his quartz-blue eyes. Her skirts moved sensuously over her hips as she swayed in slight side-to-side rhythm toward him. He stepped toward her.

And then Colin stepped out of the crowd and reached her side quickly. He slipped her hand through his arm before she had a chance to protest, kissed her lightly on the cheek, and led her past Shane to the center of the room. Several people closed in around them, whispering, "Who is she? Where did she come from?"

As she was guided into the crowd, Nina's eyes caught the hard, disapproving glare of Vanessa Merritt. She cautioned herself to remain steady, keep her strength. Fervently she wished the Mum would understand that all she wanted to do was to show herself at her best, show them she was already a vital part of Flame Tree. She might not possess land or wealth, but she could work hard side-by-side with them if she was allowed that privilege.

Shane watched Nina's glorious vision float past him on Colin's arm. His eyes trailed down her hair from its goldflame halo to the curve that swung against her slim waist as she walked. The light played among the soft folds of the deep blue skirt and seemed to caress the hidden shapes that were her hips and bottom. He imagined a silk petticoat slipping in and out between and around her slim legs, and the vision of it triggered a shot of fire to course along his veins and settle low with a throbbing ache.

He tried to tear his gaze away from her retreating figure, but when she stopped and turned toward him, his eyes were riveted to her pale golden throat down to the low neckline. The bodice of the dress was cut to mold perfectly the curve of her breasts, their

273

roundness softly pushing up and full above it. She was achingly beautiful to him.

An urge swept over him. He saw himself pushing through the crowd to reach her side, sweeping her up in his arms, and flying away on the back of Shadow to their private bathing pool. In this dreamlike state he rained kisses on every inch of skin on her luscious body, making love with her over and over until they fell exhausted into a deep, satisfying sleep.

Watching his brother escort Nina around the room with the polish and expertise of a true gentleman, Shane frowned slightly. He heard Colin introduce her as Miss Nina Cole, recently arrived from America expressly to serve as companion to his dear mother.

Shane scanned the room for sight of his mother, finally locating her beyond the orchestra, near the entrance to the dining room. He was fairly accurate in reading her thoughts and moods most of the time. But now his perceptions had to have been befuddled by Nina's entrance, for he could not fathom what his mother was thinking, could not read beyond the glassy exterior her thoughts about what appeared to be happening between her son Colin and Nina.

And then a most disturbing thought insistently pushed its way into his mind. What if Colin asked Nina to marry him tonight? What if, God forbid, she said yes and ended up staying at Flame Tree as his sister-in-law? The idea of Colin, or any man, for that matter, touching her intimately, kissing her sweet mouth, being touched by her, was abhorrent to him. He was suddenly filled with a burning rage. Jealousy! What else could it be? He was standing there in the middle of a crowd of neighbors and friends, consumed by a burning jealousy.

How ironic it was to discover that he wanted this woman, actually wanted her to be his, and to be faced now either with sending her away, or living in the eternal hell of having her married to his brother. The pain touched him everywhere like the pricks from a thousand thorns.

It was too much all at once, even for a man of his strength and endurance. He reached out to take another drink from the tray of a passing servant, but was stopped when his arm was caught and held by Laurette Marston. She radiated a smile up at him fit to compete with every glass prism in the brilliant chandeliers.

Chapter 23

Nina's entrance was a triumphal one, and she charmed the guests with her graciousness and stunning beauty. As Colin introduced her, the men were quite taken with her, and the women openly admiring or envious. Colin chuckled in amusement. At last, a party at which he could actually enjoy himself!

The orchestra began to play dance music, and Colin led Nina to the center of the floor. He swept her into his arms in a grand gesture, which let her skirt and hair float out behind her as if lifted by a loving breeze.

"Colin," she whispered when he clasped her forcefully to him, "you're calling too much attention to us, not to mention that you're cutting off my breathing and probably my circulation." Her heart was slamming wildly against the inside of her chest, and her hands had gone numb from the sheer tension of her entrance.

"That's the idea, Lady Cole," he laughed, whirling her around through a number of dancing couples who eyed them with unmasked interest. "And I beg to differ. I think I'm doing quite a bit for your circulation."

She cleared her throat and laughed a little. "Perhaps, but maybe you should tone it down just a little."

Colin leaned back and peered searchingly into her eyes. "I don't think that's what you'd like at all. I do believe, Miss Formerly Shy Waif, that you are enjoying immensely the attention you are so blatantly attracting." He whirled her around with a great flourish.

"That's nonsense, Colin, I couldn't think like that."

"Perhaps not before you came to Flame Tree, but you certainly can now. And it is delicious! All the young kittens have their baby fur standing on end right up their unworked backs. I do love it! They'll be buzzing for weeks!" He spun her around, leaned back, and mocked the women's comments in a haughty high voice, "My dear, where on *earth* did you ever find such an *exquisite dress*? Why, it looks as if it were made *expressly* for you." He laughed. "And you blush demurely and say, 'I . . . I can't say.'

"Did you hear that, girls?" Colin continued his mocking. "She has a secret couturier. We must, we simply *must* discover this genius. We must have a gown exactly like it!" He leaned close to her ear and whispered hoarsely, "Never mind that in most cases it wouldn't slip over their very ample hips and thighs."

"Colin, you are impossible." But she had to laugh. He was being utterly charming in an impish manner, and she was beginning to relax in his arms, and enjoy his company.

"Perhaps I am, but I noticed you knocked the jaded eyes out of the stubborn head of my dear, smug older brother." He guided her with long strides around the perimeter of dancing couples.

She gave in and let her guard down completely with Colin, blurting, "Oh, Colin, do you really think he was impressed?"

Colin tipped his head back and laughed out loud. "Impressed? You can't be serious." He scrutinized her face. "Oh Lord, you are serious, aren't you? You must know how incredibly alluring you are this evening. Why, Mother is already scheming how she can reverse the impact of your entrance."

Nina fretted inwardly so much that she hardly heard what Colin was saying. Her eyes darted everywhere seeking a glimpse of Shane. She hadn't seen him since Colin had crossed in front of him and swept her into the middle of things.

"Where is Shane?" she whispered. Then something in Colin's words penetrated her thoughts. "Your mother! Oh Colin, your mother. She will send me packing sooner than she said . . ." She clamped her mouth shut, knowing she'd said too much.

"Sooner than she said she would. Yes, I know about that."

She stared up at him with panic in her eyes. "You do?"

"Of course. Not only is that typical of Mother, but Anthia told me about it. She doesn't want you to

279

leave. You're her idol. She wants to be just like you when she grows up."

The music stopped, and Nina and Colin stepped back as the politely applauding crowd dispersed. A waiter announced the serving of buffet dinner, and several people began to filter from the ballroom toward the dining room. As their numbers thinned, Nina spotted Shane across the room engaged in what appeared to be a serious conversation with a young raven-haired woman in a striking ruby-colored dress. She drew in a quick breath through her nostrils. Colin caught it and followed her gaze.

"Ah yes, my dear brother in a typical pose."

"Who is she?" Nina asked, dying to know, yet dreading to know.

"That's the lovely Miss Laurette Marston."

Colin's eyes narrowed. He'd thought about Laurette Marston for years. His pain at her rebuff went deep. It still hurt sometimes when he thought about it. She was an outrageous flirt, as all of his friends concurred, and usually she gave each of the valley suitors equal favor, bestowing nothing special on any one in particular. But at this moment she seemed to be giving a lot more to Shane than Colin had ever seen her display. An ancient jealousy burned anew in his chest.

"Does she live in the valley?" Nina pressed him, never taking her eyes off the striking pair directly across the room.

"I beg your pardon?" Colin asked absently, keeping his eyes on Shane and Laurette.

"Nothing." Nina looked up at him, then back at Shane and the young woman.

Laurette was watching Nina and Colin, coquettishly flirting with Shane when she was certain they were watching, touching him, sipping wine, and smiling beguilingly up at him over the glass with innocent, round eyes.

Nina's confidence flagged slightly, and she felt the flush of embarrassment creep over her. "Colin, I have to get out of here. I never should have done this, never. I've made your mother eternally angry with me. I knew what the rules were and ignored them. I've got to get out of here as soon as possible." She turned and started to run toward the nearest door, but Colin's hand shot out and gripped her elbow. He spun her around.

"Not yet, Lady Cole," he said firmly, an enigmatic smile on his face. "Come, my dear, it's time you were formally introduced to Miss Marston."

"Colin, no!" Nina shot in a whisper.

"Nina, yes!" he shot back.

Several young men had gathered around Shane and Laurette. As Nina and Colin neared the group, she could hear them laughing and chatting, clearly enchanted by the young woman.

Colin pulled up into his cockiest posture. "Well, good evening again, big brother, Miss Marston." He nodded first toward Shane and then to Laurette, deliberately avoiding a proper first acknowledgment of the lady.

"Nina, Colin." Shane greeted them with as much indifference as he could muster, given his current state of mind. He accepted a glass of rum from one of the servants and tossed it back in one swallow, letting its warmth slip along his ragged nerves.

281

Colin assumed his most gracious manner. "Nina, my dear, may I present several of our neighbors? I believe you haven't had the opportunity to meet many of them yet. Miss Laurette Marston, Miss Nina Cole." He gave a slight bow toward Laurette, then back to Nina.

"How do you do, Miss Marston? It is a pleasure to meet you." Nina forced the pleasantry, aware that the skin on her bare arms was alive with the magnetic force from Shane, who stood so near she could hear him breathing.

"A mutual pleasure, I'm sure, Miss Cole. I regret we haven't had the occasion to meet sooner."

She slid a glittering sidelong glance toward Colin, who failed to see it, since he was watching Nina and smiling at her as if he were her staunchest supporter and benefactor, which in a way he had truly become. Nina caught the look. Obviously Laurette was unused to being ignored by any man.

Colin placed a protective arm around Nina's waist and turned her away from Laurette. "Nina, if I don't introduce you to this mob of drooling lizards, they'll have my head on a platter later." He pointed toward each as he said their names. "Will O'Rourke, Martin Aylesworth, Liam Downing, and this wide-eyed bloke is Angus MacDonald."

Nina smiled a hello to each. They all began speaking at once, asking to take her in for the buffet now, asking to take her riding tomorrow, asking for permission to call on her.

Nina basked in her first rush of honest admiration in so open a manner. How different they were from the chaperoned callers Aunt Sadie had allowed only now and again, as stiff and stilted in conversation as she had been with them. The only other kind of appreciation of a sort was that from rawboned sailors down at the piers in New York, whose comments had been direct and hardly flattering to an innocent young girl.

Vanessa Merritt had quietly stepped up behind their group. She saw that Laurette was visibly upset at Colin's obvious act of ignoring her, but not so much so that she didn't catch the sparks flying between Shane and Nina. Laurette was certainly going to put a damper on that right now.

"Shane, would you be a dear and escort me into supper now?" She batted her long eyelashes at him, and cast another glance at Colin, who this time was well aware of the scene. She looped her arm through Shane's and began to lead him away from the group.

Vanessa spoke directly to her son. "Why, Shane," she smiled lovingly, "I'm so pleased that you and Laurette have become reacquainted. I have an idea, my dear," she turned a radiant smile on Laurette, "I shall invite your family to dinner one evening very soon. Wouldn't that be lovely, Shane?"

Shane's eyes went heavenward, but he smiled at his mother. She'd set her sights on Laurette as an appropriate partner for him, and had already begun the campaign to win him over to the idea.

"How very gracious of you, Mrs. Merritt," Laurette responded with genuine sincerity. "Indeed, that would be lovely, and I'm certain we'd be honored to accept."

"It's settled, then. I'll speak to your mother this evening."

"Colin, will you and Nina join us for supper?" Shane asked quietly.

Vanessa turned toward Nina and Colin before he could answer. "I'm certain everyone will understand if you retire early, Nina. After all, you hardly know anyone, and it can be a bit overwhelming, I know, to be among so many strangers. Good evening." She turned and strolled into the dining room amid a group of well-wishers.

Nina's eyes flew to Shane's face, and she flushed. She'd just been publicly dismissed by the Mum, and it stung. Colin caught her arm.

"I think I'll just steal Nina away from this overeager bunch, and we'll take supper alone on the veranda. It's a lovely romantic evening, and I wouldn't want her to miss it."

Nina looked at him with eyes full of protest, but Colin pressed her close to him. "Shall we, my dear?" he asked strongly, and Nina let him steer her away.

Shane watched them leave and felt Laurette's body stiffen against him.

"What's going on with them?" she asked, a slight tremor in her voice.

"I'm not certain, exactly." Shane frowned. "I've never seen Colin quite so . . . attentive to a woman before."

"Nor have I," Laurette sniffed.

"Well, now, Laurette, I'm not such a bad sort. Let's enjoy supper together . . . unless you'd rather go off with your mob of admirers." He grinned and inclined his head toward the young men hovering around them.

"Nay, I'll go with you," she said glumly.

"I think I'll take that as a compliment, no matter how unenthusiastically given." He watched as the last glimpse of Nina's form in the circle of Colin's arm disappeared through a glass-paned double door that led to the veranda. "I'm feeling a bit fragile myself this evening. Perhaps being miserable together will do us both a lot of good."

He covered the hand that rested on his arm with his own, and led Laurette to the dining room.

Chapter 24

"Delicious, simply delicious!" Colin stretched out on a white wicker chaise longue at one end of the moonlit veranda, smoking a cheroot and feeling rather pleased with recent events.

"Not to my tastes." Nina sat in a high-backed white wicker chair at the other end of the veranda. She broke a leaf from the wisteria that twined its way in and out of the trellis and proceeded to slowly tear it apart along its veins.

"But my dear, how can you say that? Your entrance was superb! You were magnificent! It was too right, Lady Cole, too right!"

"Colin, I'm not Lady Cole. And I'm not magnificent. I'm miserable."

He leaned up on one elbow and peered across to her. "Perhaps you've never felt the pangs of jealousy before," he said quietly.

Nina was silent. Colin was right: her cheeks burned with it. Jealousy. It had come out of her like a newly opened underground spring.

Colin continued to laugh quietly. "And, oh, my dear, you had those other blokes fairly eating out of your hand like hungry lambs. Just delicious! I don't know when I've had a better time at a party, and I owe it all to you." He sat up on the chaise. "Come now, Lady Cole, wipe away the glum. You've just completed a major triumph."

"Colin, be reasonable. Can't you see the nasty outcome to all of this?"

Colin rose from the chaise and stood like a teacher addressing a class. "Well now, let's add it all up. First, you managed to knock the eyes out of big brother. He'll never forget your entrance, you can be certain of that. Second, you made a lot of friends among the other society darlings in the room. They wanted to be jealous of you and sit in their bitchy little groups clawing you to pieces, but you managed to smooth their ruffled fur. Third, every man in the room was struck speechless and fell in love with you on the spot. And you did it all with a dazzling smile, a friendly greeting, and a bonzer dress. My dear, what more could you want?"

Nina sighed wearily. She'd silently been adding up her own evening's tally. In spite of his self-centered displays, she knew Colin liked her and enjoyed being with her. But he preferred to act the expected Colin when in the presence of others. She knew him better than that now, and had learned to trust him.

"I think I'd want to start the evening all over again, wearing that green print dress. I think that's what I could want," she said sadly.

"And double our fun! Ah, Lady Cole, I bow to your wisdom." Colin marched to stand in front of her, and made a sweeping bow of worship.

"Colin, would you please be serious?"

"Couldn't be more serious. You've made my life worth living!"

"Mine isn't. Colin, I'm confused. I thought Shane cared for me, but it seems he cares for another. I wish I could know what his real feelings are for me, once and for all."

"He's always been like that. Less apt for the trap to close, safety in multiples and all that, you know." Colin's tone had become noticeably serious, and had taken on concern for Nina's feelings. "You've truly gone for him, haven't you?"

"Well, it's of no use. I believe he deliberately keeps a distance between us. I thought if he saw me as part of Flame Tree, more than just the Mum's companion, things might . . . Ah, well, after tonight, the Mum will dismiss me summarily." She broke another leaf from the vine and began methodically tearing it along the veins.

"Mother's not that bad. She can be reasoned with."

"Colin, please understand, I have no malice in my heart for your mother. Flame Tree means everything to her, and she will do anything to keep it intact, including marrying her son off to the most appropriate woman. I understand that. She may be in ill health, but her emotional and mental stamina is as strong as I'm sure it's always been. I admire her for that. And I've grown to respect her in spite of her aversion to my presence."

Colin stood silent, taking in her words. He wasn't surprised at what Nina told him. He'd always known how his mother was.

"Then why leave? I believe you've been a fine companion for Mother. I don't ever recall her having any close chums."

"You don't understand. She doesn't even like me. She's not oblivious to my feelings for Shane. Women sense that sort of thing in other women. But I simply don't fit into her master plan. I'm not wealthy, I have no property she can annex to Flame Tree. Flame Tree's in financial trouble, Colin. I can't believe you don't know that. I truly think before she dies the Mum wants to be certain of Flame Tree's survival. She wants Shane to marry someone appropriate, someone like . . . Laurette Marston." She tore the leaf to shreds, then picked another off the vine.

"I've become a threat to her, somehow. She's wanted me gone since the first day I arrived. She suggested I wait an appropriate time, and then announce that I was homesick and would have to return to America as soon as possible. She said it could be easily arranged when the wool was ready to take to Sydney for shipment." Again she methodically tore the leaf down each vein.

Colin had been pacing the veranda as she spoke. He stopped at the wide stairs and spun around toward her. "That doesn't give us much time."

"Time for what?"

"Shearing has started, boat leaves in about a month. Not a lot of time."

"Too much time, if you ask me. What am I going to do for a month? Stay in my room being miserable? Oh no. The Mum wants me out, and after the way I've defied her wishes, I can certainly understand that. I've made a mess of things, haven't I? I thought

290

if Shane showed the Mum that I meant something to him, she could see I'd be good for him. But he hasn't, and anyway, I'm simply not appropriate. Even without Shane I cannot stay at Flame Tree. Aunt Sadie always said 'Be careful what you wish for, you might get it.' Well, I wished for adventure in my life. And now my heart is breaking." The leaf fell to the floor, and she plucked another.

"Stop talking and let me think, will you?"

"Think about what?"

"Shh." Colin commenced pacing again.

Nina slumped against the chairback. Conflicting sensations and thoughts tumbled about in her mind. In many ways Colin was right, it had been a delicious evening. She'd actually felt beautiful for the first time in her life. And she was certain Shane thought so, too. He looked as if he'd been about to speak to her, or do something, just before Colin had rushed to her side. Perhaps it was wishful thinking, but she'd almost thought he'd walk to her side himself, take her around the waist, and float over the dance floor with her in his arms. Who knows how that might have ended?

"I think I have it!" Colin stopped abruptly.

"Have what?" Nina responded wearily.

"A plan to make this come out right for everybody." He rubbed his hands together with self-satisfied vigor.

That was not what she needed. She could not allow him to get her into any deeper trouble. "Ah, Colin, thanks anyway. I have to face this myself, and I know nothing is going to come out all right unless I leave."

"How can you exist like that? Things can always

work to one's advantage. You just have to keep trying other new schemes. Eventually one will work. I know this idea will work for you, and for me."

She plucked another leaf. "Colin, please, I don't mean to be cruel, but look at the trouble you're always into, are still into now. And, well, Flame Tree has problems because of some of the schemes you've cooked up that haven't worked out."

"I know, I know. I'm ready to admit I've given my share of woes to Mother and Flame Tree. But look here, I honestly think this time I've got a foolproof plan to put everything aright, get Flame Tree back on course, make Mother proud of me, for once, and you—you, Lady Cole—can become lady of the manor!"

"Colin, I don't think . . ."

"You don't think my plan can work, I know," he interrupted, "but you haven't even heard what it is yet."

"I know I haven't. I don't mean to be unfair, but so many of your other plans have been disastrous, Colin, that I don't think I need to hear one in which I'm to be involved. I'm feeling bad enough as it is. No, the best thing for me to do is simply face it, take my medicine, and as soon as possible, get on that disgusting ship and return to America. Getting miserably seasick again is just the punishment I deserve. I should have simply minded my own business and done the work I was hired for, and not let my emotions get the better of me."

"Don't be a ninny. You were doomed from the start, you said so yourself. Shane didn't know Mother didn't want a companion, and Mother didn't know he'd taken it upon himself to hire one. You didn't bargain for falling in love with him, and he didn't know he'd get caught at last. You're not to blame. If anyone's to blame it's my pigheaded big brother. He dropped you into the middle of the soup. It's Shane who deserves to cook in it now. Serve him right if he had to marry . . ."

"Colin, don't use old feelings to win new conflicts." Nina picked yet another leaf from the wisteria and set about methodically tearing at it.

"Stop that!" Colin grabbed the leaf from her hands. "You've been more hell on the shrubbery this evening than any drought!" He knelt down in front of her and took her hands in his. "Your problem, as I see it, is that you're afraid to do exactly what it is you really want to do. I believe what you really want is to brazen this out. You want the challenge, you know you do. Come on, admit it! Now's your chance. Do as I say, and I promise you, you will be living at Flame Tree as Mrs. Shane Merritt!"

Nina's blood heated and her heart pounded faster. Perhaps Colin did, for once in his life, have a plan that would work. Wait—no, she had to be wise, keep her head. Colin's plans had never succeeded before. How could she be sure whatever he was scheming now had the possibility of success? She could not take the chance. She would just have to take a reprimand from Vanessa Merritt, and as soon as possible, leave Flame Tree.

She stood up and walked to the veranda stairs. "Colin, I appreciate what you think you're doing for me, but I think I simply have to face it and leave with what little dignity I have left."

"Doing for you? What makes you think I'm doing this just for you? Listen to this one, Lady Cole, I've a lot at stake here myself, and when I get through with this plan I shall be in Mother's good favor for the rest of my life. And if you get what you want along the way, all the better. She'll forgive even that when I'm finished. I know this well."

Nina had to admit that even without knowing his plan, Colin had just made the first bit of sense to her since they'd come out on the veranda. Whatever he was planning was, as usual, for himself.

"You're forgetting something else, Colin. Shane hasn't said he wants me to stay. It's simply no use. Forget whatever wild scheme you're concocting. It won't work. At least, not for me."

Colin went to her and placed his hands on her shoulders. He turned her around and pushed her back toward the chair.

"For heaven's sake, of course Shane wants you here. Even I know that. He's gone for you, too—just too stubborn to admit it. I know the look. He's never had it before, so I know it's real this time. My plan will clear that all up for him, too."

Nina plopped down in the chair. "What makes you so sure he cares anything at all about me?"

"Does he tease you?"

"Yes."

"Does he take the teasing much farther than good taste would dictate?"

"I certainly think so."

"Does he take teasing from you?"

"Well, I don't overdo it, you know."

"Does he put you in, shall we say, rather uncompromising positions sometimes?"

"That's none of your business!"

"Oho, but that clinches it!"

"Clinches what? Colin, will you start making sense?"

"I am making sense. I'm making perfect sense. I knew it! Shane is gone on you, too, and he's running scared. Now I *know* my plan will work." He rubbed his hands again, and laughed a satisfied laugh.

"All right," Nina said wearily, "what is this plan that I am about to become embroiled in?" Fervently she hoped she wouldn't end up cooking her own goose in the process.

Colin pulled her to her feet, and put his arms around her gently. "Stick with me, Lady Cole, and I'll soon turn you into Sister-in-Law Merritt."

She dropped her head onto his chest and gave in, letting him be her brother and the master of her fate. Colin rubbed her back and stroked her hair, soothing her. A satisfied smile broke over his face.

Shane left Laurette amid a group of admirers, stealing the moment for a breath of fresh air. He stepped out onto the veranda and breathed deeply. The night was soft and moonlit, reminding him of the night he'd strolled with Nina in the garden. Nina . . . she was breathtaking tonight. Everyone exclaimed over her, and Shane felt enormously proud, even if he hadn't the right to feel that way.

He thought about Colin, thought about their sibling scrape before the party. They'd both get over it sooner or later. But what was Colin doing with

Nina? When she'd stood in the archway, it was as if she was waiting for someone. And then Colin was at her side in an instant. He'd swept her around the ballroom, basking in the admiration she received. He'd been very attentive to her, and Nina responded as if it was the most natural thing in the world to be on Colin's arm.

Shane frowned. There couldn't be anything serious going on between Colin and Nina. Colin couldn't concentrate long enough to . . . The Mum wouldn't permit Nina to be a part of Colin's life for the same reasons she was against Nina becoming a part of his life. Perhaps it was time for him to sort out his muddled thinking and present it to the Mum, and Colin . . . and Nina.

He started down the veranda to a side entrance to the ballroom. And then he stopped abruptly, his pulse racing. Nina and Colin stood in the moonlight, locked in a close embrace.

Chapter 25

"Why?" Nina sat at a dusty worn wood table in the middle of a cabin far from anywhere she'd ever ridden on the Flame Tree land. "Please tell me why I was fool enough to let you talk me into this feather-brained idea."

"Because you know this will work." Colin walked around the cabin. "Caw, I haven't been here since I was a wee one."

"Neither has anyone else, I'll wager," Nina muttered, reluctantly forcing herself to look around. She decided to try to ignore the thick, filmy spiderwebs that draped like curtains in corners and from beams. "Colin, I can't stay here."

"Of course you can. It will all be worth it in the end."

"Why do I feel the end is near?"

"Buck up, woman, this won't take too long. You'll never have to step a wobbly foot on that ship, believe me."

"Be reasonable, Colin, I can't be out here alone. I

hardly know where I am, for one thing, and for another, there are probably wild animals and bushrangers lurking about. I think I'd rather face the Mum than any of those." She stood up and made for the door.

"Nina, Nina—come here." He sat her down in a straight-backed chair. "This is the cabin my parents lived in before the main house was built. Mother was alone here plenty of times while Father was off. She survived because she knew he'd be back, believed in what they were building together. And you're doing the same thing, then, aren't you? Of course you are."

"But what makes you think Shane will do as your father did? I mean, your parents came here together. Together, Colin, not separately, with one sneaking in here without the other's knowledge. That's not what you might call building something together, now, is it? Even in your addle-brained state you must be able to see that."

"You know, Lady Cole, I'm finding it rather difficult to help you out of your dilemma. You seem to have no faith in this plan or in yourself. I'm not sure you're going to make a success out of this if you don't try harder."

She jumped to her feet, hands planted on her hips, and stood very close to him, peering up into his face with blazing eyes. "I didn't cook up this plan, if you will remember! I hardly know any of the details. I'm finding it rather difficult, Lord Merritt, to have faith in much of anything these days, especially an idea you've concocted and dragged me into!"

Colin broadened his stance and planted his hands firmly on his hips as well. "Dragged you? You seemed pretty interested in it last night when I told you Shane was most likely in love with you, and your staying out here alone would bring him galloping to your side to protect you!"

Nina's eyes widened. "What do you mean 'Most likely'? You told me you knew he was . . . whatever you said . . . *gone* on me, that's it, you said you knew he was gone on me. And I, the fool, I believed you, and here I am in no-man's-land in a cabin that's probably home to everything but humans, and now you have the gall to tell me Shane is 'most likely' in love with me? Where was my head? I didn't have even one glass of wine and I was taken in by your schemes. Please, please, I beg you, take me to that ship, push me on, make me get roaring seasick! It's the least you could do for a . . . a . . . what is it Derrick called you once? A twit! That's it! I'm a twit, an even bigger twit for letting you talk me into this!"

Smoothly Colin picked up his hat from the table and strode to the door. "When you've had a chance to think about this, you'll see I'm right," he said with maddening calm. "I'll be back in a day or so with more provisions and news of how the plan is proceeding. Just bolt the door at night. You'll be fine, believe me. With any luck you won't have to be here longer than a few days."

He walked out the door leaving Nina fuming, her mouth open at the audacity of his departure. Suddenly Colin threw open the door again, and peered around it.

"Derrick called me a twit, did he? Imagine that!" And then he was gone.

Nina sat down hard in the chair. She breathed

299

deeply, continuing to fume at becoming a willing participant in Colin's latest scheme. She propped her elbows on the table and dropped her chin in her hands.

Colin's powers of persuasion had been strong enough to make her think he might possibly be right. Stronger than that was her own desire to make it all work out. She was afraid to believe Colin in this venture, but she was afraid not to believe him, too. After a long string of losing propositions, perhaps he was due for a success.

She lifted her head and looked around. "Might as well get familiar with the place. It's going to be home for a while. But not forever . . . I hope."

Maude had told her that after shearing time was over, the fleece would be sorted and classed, and the bales made ready for overland transfer to Sydney. There they would be loaded on ships bound for England and America.

"And I may be among the bales." She quirked an eyebrow. "Or . . . maybe I'll be going back to Flame Tree." At this moment, she couldn't decide which was the lesser of two evils.

She walked outside the cabin and stood on its small front veranda. Even small cabins in this country had verandas. She smiled. That was kind of nice.

A mob of kangaroos loped by in the distance. How peculiar to have become accustomed to their numbers passing now. She remembered how astonished she'd been the first time she'd seen one the day she'd ridden on the wagon with Shane and Derrick. Since then they'd become a sight as often as sparrows or mice in New York, and she realized she'd begun to take them for granted almost as much. She watched them now, bounding across the black soil plain as if they owned it, until they disappeared.

"I'll be serving tea tomorrow at four," she called after them. "And probably every day after that," she said into the wind. "Feel free to drop in . . . anytime . . . day or night."

Sighing, she walked back inside. Confronted with the sheer filthiness of the cabin, she felt her wistful mood disappear. She supposed she'd better find a way of cleaning it, and preparing a place to sleep. Colin had gathered as much as he could think of in the way of food and necessities, and she'd managed during the few minutes she'd had in her own room to dress in shirt and daks and bring a few other clothes and some toiletries.

Quite easily the thin boards covering the windows came down when she used a hard stick as a pry. She pushed on the outside shutters and they opened with a resisting creak. The air was dry and still warm, with a touch of crispness on sporadic quick breezes.

"It's May. That means autumn here. Can winter be far behind? And when it comes, will I still be here? Or will winter always live in my heart as it does right now?"

She thought about how different this was from May in New York. The maple trees in Madison Square Park were past budding, probably already leafing out, and the baseball teams that played there would be suiting up again. She'd thought of New York and Aunt Sadie occasionally, but not once had she felt homesick.

Even the upside-down weather here had not

distressed Nina. It was unquestioningly different from what she'd been used to, but with each passing day she was becoming a part of the land, the country. And more and more Australia and her wonders had become an intrinsic part of her. But the flies . . . she was convinced they flew in flocks in Australia, and like them or not, they were a part of it as well.

"Ah, well, get on with it, then." She went back to surveying her cleaning chores.

The open back window over the cooking area revealed a lean-to covered with a tarpaulin held down with ropes. She could distinguish sharp bulges and odd shapes through it.

"Hmm. Furniture? That would be nice," she mused.

She left her cleaning chores in favor of her inquisitiveness, and went out back. The rope knots securing the tarpaulin were sealed tight with water and time, and she could not unlace them. She took a knife from the provisions Colin had packed, and worked with it like a saw to cut through the jute thickness. With great effort she got through two lengths of rope, releasing the taut pressure on the covering. She lifted one edge of the tarpaulin and exposed some of its cache. A musty, damp smell of age assaulted her nostrils, and she stepped back quickly.

"I suppose there're indescribable creatures under there, too," she said loudly, for the benefit of whatever might be lurking under the tarp. She self-consciously looked around, as if expecting someone might have heard her. "Well, I'll just have to find out and take care of them," she called.

Near the lean-to she found a stack of kindling wood standing against the back of the cabin. She took a small piece of it and gingerly whacked it over the tarpaulin. Nothing scurried out, nothing moved. She whacked it again, this time a little more forcefully, and when again nothing appeared, she walked around the mound, hitting the tarpaulin repeatedly until she felt positive nothing lived inside.

Overhead several brilliantly plumed parrots flew out of the ghost gums with a flurry of beating wings. Nina felt a shiver run up her back and spread over her neck.

"At least those are harmless and didn't come from under here," she muttered.

Carefully lifting the tarpaulin and rolling it back over half of the mound revealed two straight-back chairs similar to the two inside the cabin, a small table with a shelf under it such as might be used at bedside, a wood crate with two heavy glass oil lamps, another crate containing tin dishes and utensils, and several odd-shaped items that Nina suspected might be tools.

Standing on end with chairs and other things stacked against it was a long wood platform with short, thick, square legs, the frame of which was woven in intricate fashion of rope tied in intervals with rather fancy knots.

"A rope bed, I'm sure of it! And if it is, how do I get it out?"

She eyed the pile like an artist looking at a still life. One by one she took down the stack of chairs leaning against the bed and set each piece in the afternoon sun. They were stained from dampness and the wood felt soft, but she thought they might clean up and be functional after they dried out. She took a piece of gum branch and hooked it into the top row of latticework on the bed and pulled. The branch slipped, sending down a shower of dirt from under the tarpaulin. Nina's hair, though pulled back and plaited in a long braid, was attracting more dirt and flies than ever before. It was most annoying, but she was determined to get the bed down, so she would just have to suffer them.

After several tries, the branch stuck fast to a strategic spot on the bed. Pulling hard, she felt it give away from its wedged position.

"I suppose it could be holding up the pile of other things behind it. Oh, oh, too late now to worry about that!"

Her last hard yank had pulled the bed free and it was falling toward her in jerking, stopping, jerking motions. She backed up quickly to get out of its path. It fell in front of her, bringing several other objects with it, including the tarpaulin, which fell over Nina like a dark canopy. She dropped to the ground with the awful thing covering her.

"Bloody hell!" she cursed into the musty darkness.

Spitting, kicking, and sputtering, she wriggled out from under one end. Nothing very heavy had fallen on her and she wasn't hurt, but she was scared out of her wits. Scrambling to her feet, she brushed her clothes frantically in case any insects had clung to them, and twisted her head around in every direction, looking for someone or something that might have accosted her.

She let out a breath of relief. "There's nothing, you

silly twit. It's just spooky. Makes you afraid of your own shadow, my girl." Now don't you start calling yourself that, she admonished herself.

Perspiring from the exertion, she attracted flies faster than ever before. She was fairly certain they were coming out from under the tarpaulin. Perhaps they'd all been sleeping in there and she had disturbed them when she'd hit on the covering. Adjusting to their annoying presence had not been an easy task, but right now they were more than she could bear. She swiped at them with doubled fists.

She uncovered the bed and inspected it more closely. It was in surprisingly good shape, dirty from years undercover, but still sound. She ran inside for the broom she'd seen in a corner. Briskly she swept off the bed. She smiled. It would do nicely, once the quilts and pillow that Colin had packed were arranged over it.

"Well, at least I won't have to sleep on the floor."

She stood with her hands on her hips, and a satisfied smile crossed her mouth.

"This must be what it feels like to be nesting. Or am I squatting? I've no right to be here, after all." Except that Colin had ensconced her here. "No worries. Best to make up the bed and think about an evening meal."

She looked toward the far horizon. Once it started, the sun would go down rapidly, and she wanted to be as fully acquainted with her temporary home as she possibly could before that happened.

The wattle-and-daub construction of the cabin looked sound, or at least as if it might keep out rain and deter the wind. She couldn't tell about the roof.

"Hope it doesn't rain tonight."

There was a light-colored stone chimney up the outside, and an open fireplace inside. She knew enough to get into the fireplace and look up the chimney while it was still daylight to see if anything blocked it. A little light filtered down from the top, and she could see some blockage of vines and other debris. She hoped there would be enough of a draft to pull the smoke up and out. A cup of tea in a little while was going to taste marvelous.

A few busy hours later, Nina sat on the veranda of her new home, a cup of tea held snugly between her hands. The bed was inside and made up (her back was just beginning to ache from the struggle of moving it), and the smoke had cleared out, after a fashion. It had taken a hot fire to push the debris up and out of the chimney, but go it did, with a great *whoosh.* She had to run out to see that some of it hadn't settled on the roof or on dry brush nearby. Luck and a slight wind had taken care of that, and she'd managed to get to the little burning clumps on the ground and stomp out any smoldering that might have proven dangerous.

Inside, the little cabin glowed with the lantern she'd brought with her.

"I must remember to tell Colin when next he comes that we'll need more lamp oil and new wicking for those other lamps. Well, now, doesn't that sound as if I've laid claim to this place?"

She'd swept and brushed, and hauled water from the little creek that flowed behind the cabin to wash things until she was reasonably sure that, for the first night at least, she would not be disturbed by spiders and other indescribable creatures. Nothing could be done about the flies except to use the netting she'd brought to drape over the bed and the extra piece of it she'd attached to her hat.

She was tired, bone tired, emotionally tired, mentally tired. The uncertainty of everything weighed heavily on her. She leaned her head back against the wall and gazed first out over the plain, then overhead. The sky was vast, went on to the Back of Beyond and more, and was filled with the light of countless stars.

"Is Shane looking up at those stars right now?" she asked into the night. Perhaps, but is he alone? She left that unspoken.

She was certainly alone, but for some strange reason she no longer felt afraid. Even though she could see nothing for miles, not another cabin, not another human being, she did not feel afraid. The mournful howl of dingoes in the far distance picked up as the night grew darker.

And then she knew why she was not afraid. She was free.

Yet freedom had its own restrictions. She could not go where she pleased, see whom she pleased. She was a prisoner here in an unlocked cell, and at the end of her time she would once again be free to go. But not to go free, if it was to be back to New York and the old confinements.

Right then, on that lonely veranda on an empty plain somewhere in New South Wales, Nina pronounced a resolution. "No matter the outcome here, I will not return to my former life. I'm not the same

307

girl Nina Cole was then. I'm the woman Nina Cole is now."

Nina's life had become her own, and it was up to her to take care of it. She had proved, was continuing to prove to herself that she had something inside she'd never recognized before, something no one else had recognized in her. Her own essence and fire were just that, her own, and they would take her wherever she had to go, provide her with what she needed for whatever she had to do.

And right now she wished upon every star in the vast Australian sky that whatever came to her would include Shane Merritt.

Chapter 26

Shane dropped onto his bunk at the out station's main cabin, bone weary from work. It had been a successful roundup and the sheep huddled together bleating in holding paddocks, awaiting their turns in the woolshed. It was grueling work, requiring long hours both on horseback and off, but the shearing was well under way.

The time was both exciting and sad. Shane loved the excitement generated by the crew of shearers who worked their way through the valley until they'd been at every station. They were a robust bunch of rough, hard-working blokes, long-armed from years of bending over and shearing sheep. But they brought with them an air of reckless adventure coupled with seasoned living in the outback and bush. Up to their armpits in dip and fleece, they worked a fast pace from dawn till dusk, shearing, sorting, classing, baling. Shane was always a bit sad when they left. But then the cycle started all over again of breeding, feeding, moving, caring for the animals, never knowing what the year would bring in rainfall or drought. Always the expected and the unexpected, but he loved that, too. He was born to this, and had never wanted any other life.

The aroma of strong coffee assaulted his nostrils. Good old Derrick. He always kept the oversized beat-up black pot going on the back burner during shearing time. It might have been simmering there from the night before, but a man could always count on it being available. No telling what it might taste like. A man could count on that, too.

Wearily Shane crawled out of the bunk, and poured a tin mug full of the thick brown brew. His first taste was always a small one, as if preparing his tongue for the onslaught. Keeping in true Derrick tradition, the coffee was strong enough to stand a spoon in, if it didn't eat directly through the metal.

"You're back," Derrick observed as he came from behind the cookstove, his arms full of firewood. "Wind's picked up."

"Aye," Shane responded dully, and sat down at the table.

"What's eatin' you, mate? Look as if you've been drug to Bourne and back." He dropped the load of wood next to the fireplace with a loud clamor.

"Just tired, I guess."

"Well, now, mate, as I see it, there's tired, and there's tired."

Shane lifted his head and eyed his old friend wearily. "Please, Derrick, I don't have the energy to figure out your philosophy today."

"There's the tired a bloke gets when he's put in the

good day, and that's a good tired," Derrick continued, ignoring the remark, and set about his busy work in the cabin. Derrick was never idle, always busy at something.

"Then there's the tired a bloke gets of the hard life, the poor life, the struggle for a day's wage that wouldn't buy a billy o' stew. Then there's the tired a bloke gets tryin' to figure out a woman, and that's the tiredest of all, 'cause you can't figure 'em, no use to tryin' it. You just figure you got it right and they change everything. Just as bad tryin' t'figure yourself out when there's a woman in it. Now, I'm not one to meddle, and since you've got no worries in the day's wage, the way I see it, you've got the look about you of tryin' to figure a woman, or figure yourself. Makes a bloke tired in the head so's he's more tired in the body. That's the way I see it, 'course I ain't of them that asks in where I ain't wanted."

Shane suffered Derrick's dissertation without interrupting, then looked up at him with a wry smile. "Are you through now?"

"What?"

"Are you through scrutinizing me like an inquisitive parrot?"

"All I'm sayin' is, you look more tired than usual for you at shearin'. You enjoy shearin' time, usually, so I was just wonderin' if maybe you had your mind on somethin' else. 'Course, I wouldn't want to ask in where I ain't wanted."

"Give it a rest, mate. You're right, as usual. I am feeling more tired, or I have something else on my mind, or something."

Derrick poured himself a cup of the coffee, took a

swig, and spat the mouthful into the fireplace with a grimace. He strode over to Shane with the pot and refilled his cup.

"Nina Cole wouldn't have anything to do with what's botherin' you, now, would she, mate?" He returned the coffeepot to the back of the stove.

Shane took another sip of coffee, frowned and shook his head. "How do you drink this stuff?"

"I don't. Would she?"

"What?"

"Nina Cole. Is she what's botherin' you?"

"Of course not! Why would you think that?" Shane stood up and looked out the window over the far rangeland.

"Well, how would I know why I think that? Can't be 'cause you've been actin' peculiar for most a coupla weeks now, and that just happens to be as long as she's been gone, now, could it?"

"Do you ever ask a simple question?"

"That is a simple question."

"Then why's it got so many words?"

"'Cause it takes that many words to get through to you. Why can't you give a simple answer?"

"Because."

"Too simple."

"All right, all right, I can't give a simple answer."

"Why not?"

"Because there's nothing simple about it."

"Could be simple if you wasn't so bloody stubborn."

Shane turned around slowly and set the cup of offensive coffee down on the table. "Now, what does that mean?"

"As I see it, you got the Mum's worries about the homestead, your brother's worries about whatever he worries about (though as I see it, he's got no worries of his own), and the Mum's worries about how you marry and when you marry, so you got everybody's worries includin' what you think are Miss Nina Cole's worries, so you don't take care of your own worries. 'Course, that's only how I see it."

Shane rubbed the sides of his ears as if they were tired. "What's that got to do with my being stubborn? And in case you forgot, Nina Cole has disappeared, and since I brought her here, I think I ought to worry just a wee bit, don't you?"

"If you wasn't so stubborn, you'd have whisked that fair bit o' sheila off and married her!"

Shane flopped back down on the bunk. "Something comes to mind here, Derrick. The lady would have had to consent to such an arrangement."

"And just how could the lady consent when you didn't ask her?"

"She wouldn't want me to ask her."

"How do you know that? Did you ask her?"

"Of course I didn't ask her!" Shane was shouting now.

"Why not?"

"Because. Will you please get on with it?"

"All right. Makes no never mind to me, but if you was to ask me, I'd say she wanted to stay at Flame Tree."

"Well, I'm not asking you."

"Why, because you're afraid I got it all figured out right about Nina, and now it's too late?"

"You know nothing about the girl."

"Girl, hah! What about that dress she wore to your party?"

"You weren't even there."

"Was too. Stayed in the kitchen with Maudie."

"All right, now get this, will you? Nina didn't know what she was getting herself into when she came here. I made a mistake. The Mum saw it and I didn't. It's too hard a place for a girl like Nina, not born to it. Something is always happening to her. Colin's a handsome boy, shoots off his mouth about money and big plans, and, well, it looked like it might have turned the girl's head. Bound to happen. In another few weeks I'd be able to help her get back to America before something too awful happens, and I can't find her."

Derrick was silent, tapping his fingers. He always did that when something didn't settle quite right with him.

"In case you haven't noticed, Nina's not a girl anymore, she's a woman. And Colin's no boy, only acts like one. And you're stubborn enough to marry that Marston girl so's the Mum can feel Flame Tree won't be lost, what with the Marston land that will come with the weddin'. Then you'll pay off Colin's debts and let him marry Nina, or else you'll send her back to America. All neat and tidy, ain't it?"

Shane sat up quickly and hit his head on the overhead bunk. "Marry Laurette Marston!" he shouted, as if that was the only part of Derrick's pronouncement he'd heard. "Who said anything about Laurette Marston? You've gone daft." He rubbed his head and winced at the tenderness.

"Well, that's what the talk is. That's what the party

was about, findin' the right one for you, and you know it. No secret about that. I saw the Mum good as you did. Happy as a chook with a bag of corn when you took the Marston girl to supper."

"I admit that's what the Mum wanted and I indulged her, but I agreed to nothing else except the party."

"Well, mark my words, as I see it, t'won't be long afore you're married to that one, and everything will be all neat and tidy."

Shane got up and grabbed his hat. "I don't want to hear how you see things any longer. I'm going out to the far range and look for strays. By the time I get back, maybe you'll be gone from this notion, and we can have a sane conversation." He snatched the door open and was gone with a slam.

Derrick smiled. He supposed he would never understand why young folks always had to have life spelled out to them when it was plain as the noses on their faces.

Chapter 27

Colin was faithful at returning to the cabin every two days with extra provisions, books, and news for Nina. The cozy little place was beginning to feel like home to her in a strange way. It was lonely without people around every day, but it was satisfying to have time alone to read and think. She was stimulated by the physical labor of providing for herself, and had grown comfortable with the place and the land around it.

But it was now almost four days since Colin had visited, and Nina began to feel a little fretful about it. Early in the morning she took a walkabout after her tea and biscuits, heading northwesterly, toward the outback. Winter was advancing, according to the Australian calendar, but still it did not hold the damp chill that was the portent of a New York winter. She took self-satisfied pride in having become acclimated and knowing how to dress for whatever the elements would deliver.

The cabin soon disappeared behind her and she

walked on, scanning the countryside for any glimpse of a man on horseback or in a carriage. Outstretched arms of ghostly dead gum trees, reaching for something unknown in the sky, loomed on the horizon as the landscape grew sparser and drier. Here and there a wallaby hopped, or she found a lizard sunning itself on a rock. The only other living things moving were more of her beloved kangas, and several emus running swiftly in front of her, inquisitive looks in their widely spaced eyes as they passed on their way to somewhere . . . the outback, or Back of Beyond. Only they knew.

Nina cautioned herself not to roam too far from the cabin. If Colin arrived and she wasn't there, he'd worry or leave, and she wouldn't hear the news from Flame Tree. Not that he'd had that much to tell. All he talked about was how close he was to making a strike in one of his latest ventures. Sometimes he off-handedly mentioned that shearing time was progressing well, or encouraged her to have patience.

Always she asked him the same questions. How long would the shearing go on? How long did he think she could have patience? His answers were always indirect. Shearing was over when it was over, and she must keep her patience for as long as she needed it. Neither one of them spoke of Vanessa Merritt.

A foreboding swept over her that she was becoming lost. She turned around to head back, but somehow nothing on the landscape looked familiar. Panic struck.

"Now, just stay calm," she told herself. "What direction did you take?"

The sun climbed higher, and she seemed to be walking into nowhere, into nothing she'd known before.

She remembered the stream behind the cabin. "Find the stream, follow it," she instructed herself. She ran up a small rise. "There it is!"

Miraculously, a half-dry stream appeared cut into a gully below her. She followed it until she was tired and growing fearful. She sat down next to the stream bed, which had grown drier and drier until at last nothing was left but a narrow band of cracked earth. She looked up it, down it, beyond it.

"Face it, you're lost, and lost here is seriously lost."

She dropped her head to her knees. No matter how comfortable she'd grown here, she did not know all the nuances of this country as the natives did. A feeling of desolation swept over her.

Suddenly a clawlike hand came from nowhere and clamped onto her shoulder, jolting her deepest fear to leap into her throat. She let out a scream that echoed into the nothingness around her. The claw released at once, and she scrambled away from it, trying to regain her footing. Her breath came in ragged gasps, and her heart pounded, making her dizzy. She managed to stand up, still backing away, then froze.

Gingu's lean black form stood in the stream bed, a yellow-toothed grin lighting his wide face. Nina clutched at her chest and panted in relief.

"Gingu! Thank God!" She tried to catch her breath and coughed. "The least you could have done is warned me of your approach, spoken, something . . . anything."

Gingu shrugged. "You were doing all the talking.

If I'd said anything you would have run, then I'd have had to run after you, then you'd have been more scared."

Nina stared at him. His reasoning was simple and true. There was no way for her to respond. Her thumping heart began to subside to more natural rhythm.

"You . . . you're probably wondering why I'm way out here." She didn't know if she should tell him, or exactly what she should do.

"Nay." It was a flat answer, without emotion.

"No?"

"Nay. You're staying in the cabin."

"You know about that?"

"Of course."

"Of course you do." Gingu seemed to know everything just by sheer intuition. "Um, well, you see, Gingu, I have this small dilemma now."

"You're lost."

She nodded glumly. Everything, he knew everything. "Would you mind showing me the way back?" Of course he would know where the cabin was.

Silently he turned and started up the stream bank. Nina wasn't sure if that meant he would show her the way back, or if he was leaving.

"Gingu?"

"Come." He motioned her to follow, and she did so eagerly.

They walked for a long time in silence. Nina followed the dark form. His long strides reached out with wide, flat feet born of a shoelessness inherent to his race. His instincts were strong and sure, and Nina did not question his knowledge or his honesty.

They walked over twists and rises and gullies in the landscape until at last the roof of the cabin could be seen. Nina decided he'd either taken her back a different way, or else she'd been so preoccupied with her thoughts on her walkabout, that she hadn't seen the terrain as she traversed it. When they reached the cabin, she invited him in for a cup of tea.

"A cuppa?" he asked with his now familiar grin. "Too civilized, but I've been known to drink it now and again. Thick, please."

"Thick?" Nina frowned the question, then lifted her forehead. "Oh, you mean strong. I can do that."

He watched her stoke up the fire in the old iron cookstove, and she thought she detected a glint of amusement in the black eyes. Gingu did not show emotion, not that she'd ever seen, except for the wide grin, and the anger he'd expressed the day she'd sunk her teeth into his shoulder. She made the tea "thick," as he'd requested, and presented it in tin mugs. They drank in silence until she could stand no more of it.

"I've been waiting for Colin these past few days. He's not usually so late. I wonder what's keeping him."

Gingu swallowed the tea and made a face of distaste for it. "The wedding, I should guess."

Nina coughed over the tea. "W-wedding? What wedding?"

"Flame Tree."

"There was a wedding at Flame Tree?" Her voice went weak.

"Aye," he nodded, and forced another gulp of tea.

"Who? Whose wedding was it?" Her eyes were big and shining moistly, and she held the cup in a grip so tight her knuckles whitened.

Gingu shrugged.

"Think, Gingu, think. What did you hear? Were you there?"

"Me. Nay. One of those snooty girls, I guess. I forget her name."

Nina blanched. The only name that came to mind at the mention of the word "snooty" was Laurette Marston. She was afraid to ask, but she had to, and she hoped Gingu would remember.

"Uh, Gingu, could the name be Laurette Marston?" She watched his face for any trace of recognition.

Gingu placed his cup carefully on the table. He stared into space, obviously thinking about the name. He was taking too long. Nina was frantic with the need to know. If he'd been wearing a shirt, she'd have reached across the table and grabbed it by the collar to shake the answer out of him. As it was, grabbing him by the flesh would not be possible. She didn't dare lay a hand on him again.

Slowly Gingu began to nod. "Aye, that sounds right."

"Oh!" Nina was stricken, and slumped back in her chair.

Gingu stood, then strode soundlessly to the door. "I will leave now. Need anything?"

Wanly, she looked up at him, then shook her head slowly.

He opened the door. "I will come back another day."

She nodded. "Thank you, Gingu. As long as I am here, you are welcome anytime."

Gingu left as silently as he had come to her rescue. Nina sat still as death at the table, her hand still gripping the cup. A wedding at Flame Tree. Shane had married Laurette Marston. No wonder Colin hadn't been to see her. He knew how upset she'd be, and he hadn't the courage to tell her about it. Another of his schemes gone sour. Yes, he would have a difficult time of it explaining that to her.

It was over. Everything was over. Suddenly she felt weary to the core. The waiting, the wondering, were over. She stood up.

"Be reasonable, Nina," she admonished herself, "you took a chance, wanted adventure, got it all. You didn't even consider you'd not be wanted where you went, never bargained you'd fall in love with the man who brought you here. But it's over now. Or . . . it never was."

Now what? She was out here, wherever that was, alone, unprepared as to what to do next. Eventually Colin would show up. Even he wouldn't let her sit in the bush and starve. He'd be repentant, and she'd let him, but then she'd make him take her to Sydney. It was the least he could do after this.

Suddenly she realized she hadn't begun to cry. She'd been sitting there, numbly gripping the tin cup, as if to let go of it would mean letting go of a flood of emotion. The sun had gone down outside the cabin and inside her heart, but she hadn't cried. What would be the use of it, anyway?

Woodenly she rose and lit one of the glass oil lamps. She could think better in the light. Yet, once the flame glowed, no new thoughts entered her mind. The only thing she heard was the echo of her own voice saying it's over, it never was.

A loud knock at the door gave her a start. That would be Colin, arrived at last to tell her the news. She didn't want to see him, didn't want to hear the words. She sat still. The knock came again. At last she stood up. The sooner she faced it, the sooner it would be out in the open.

She pulled the door open quickly. "Colin, I was wondering when you were going to get here . . ."

But it wasn't Colin.

Shane stood in the doorway. He snatched off his hat and twisted it round and round in both hands. "Nina—!"

She stared at him. An appearance from Shane was something she didn't expect, and she could say nothing.

Shane kept turning his hat nervously. So here she was. Here, and waiting for Colin. What a scoundrel his brother truly was, making her stay hidden here alone while he had other things on his mind. But he blamed himself more for the sorry mess she was in. And now it was up to him to help her through this.

"Nina, I'm sorry. I didn't know you were here. I saw the light and had to check things out. Nobody ever comes here, and I, well, I was concerned, that's all. Are you all right?" he asked carefully.

Her eyes blazed. She'd humiliated herself at the party, then run away, agreeing to some scheme of Colin's, got lost in the wilderness, was found by an Aborigine who told her the only man she'd ever loved had been married to someone else only a few days ago, and now, here stood that very man, asking if she was all right. What a question! Suddenly it seemed like the biggest joke of all time. She turned her back on him and went to the table. A laugh began to bubble out of her quietly.

"Am I all right?" she laughed. "Am I all right? What else could I be?" She kept laughing.

Shane came into the cabin and closed the door behind him. "Nina, I'm sorry."

She laughed louder. "Sorry? You're sorry? Why, Shane Merritt, whatever for?"

Shane frowned. More than anything he wanted to console her, make up for the wedding, make up for everything she'd suffered. "I'm sorry things didn't turn out quite the way you wanted them."

She turned around to face him, her eyes wide and dark blue-green, glassed over with unshed tears. "And what way was that, Shane? I'm not even sure I know."

How ironic it was, to stand here in front of him, and in light of recent events, still be unable to say what was in her heart. But maybe that was right . . . things left unsaid could be forgotten more easily later.

Shane could not answer her question. He, of all people, had no answers.

He looked around the humpy in effort to avoid those piercing eyes. How homelike and inviting the place felt to him. He wished he could sit by the fire with her and tell her what the last few days had been like, the work, his thoughts, his dreams. But the fireplace was cold, as stone cold as her eyes.

"Did you do all this?" It was almost a whisper of awe, and his arm swept around the coziness of the small cabin.

She nodded.

"By yourself?" Instantly he wished he could retract the question. Colin must have helped her. To his surprise, she answered with something other than what he'd expected.

"Yes, I did it by myself. I hope you don't mind. I know this was your parents' first home, I know I don't belong here, and I hope you don't think I'm violating a sacred place, or something. I didn't know this was where Colin would bring me. He had an idea that . . . obviously things didn't work out as he'd planned."

"They seldom do."

He had to disagree with her about one thing: she did indeed belong in the cabin, she looked so at home in it. It felt right that she was here. Shane knew he'd have tried to recreate with her what the Mum and their father had shared together in this cabin if he'd had the chance, if he'd taken the chance. He watched her, a longing aching in every muscle to take her into his arms and stroke her lovely hair.

He moved to the fireplace an sucked in a deep breath. "Does this work all right? I can make a fire. And I have some lamb and fresh yabbies from the river in my bag. I'm not a bad cook, I could make supper—I mean, if that's all right with you."

Supper! The nerve of the man! Nina fumed inwardly. Hurt was now being replaced by anger. How could she have fallen in love with a man who was so insensitive that before the memory of his own wedding had grown dim, he was in a cabin with her, calmly discussing supper as if he had nowhere to go?

"Supper? Thank you, no." She turned around. She

:ouldn't face him. "Shouldn't you be . . . *home?*"

"Home? Nay, no one's expecting me. So, is it upper then?"

She did not answer.

Shane was undaunted by her silent rebuff, and enewed with strength and conviction. Without waiting for an answer, he built a fire and lit it, then vent out to Shadow and took the meat and crayfish rom a hempen bag slung across the saddle. He unsaddled Shadow and tied him at the back of the abin. Instinct took him to the same place he'd tied he horse he'd ridden as a child, when his father had rought him out to show him the cabin where Flame Tree essentially began, where he, himself, began. He oved this cabin and was sorry he'd been too busy to isit it for so many years. And right now it seemed so ight that he was in it with Nina.

He would make her last days in Australia wonder-ul. He'd show her things she'd missed, cook for her, augh with her again, make her happy, make her orget Colin's hurt. Then he'd get her to Sydney and n the ship to America. He'd see that she was safely board, and leave her with at least a sense that omeone had cared about her through her difficulty, nd that Australia was exactly what he'd told her bout when they first met—a wonderful, exciting, ruly perfect place to be on earth.

He shooed some flies away from his face. Maybe he'd have to overlook the flies to see the perfection learly. And maybe, just maybe, she'd consider taying. Wait! What was he thinking?

Quickly he went back into the cabin. He threw the ag down on the table, then took Nina's arm and led her out to the veranda. "You just sit here and watch the stars come out. I'll make supper. I promise not to poison you. Believe me, I can cook. I'll call you when it's ready."

She let him lead her, then sat dully on the veranda. He left the door open, and she could hear him inside, rattling dishes and pots and humming to himself. Humming to himself, as if nothing save the moment was on his mind. She felt numb in her head and numb in her heart.

Soon the smell of roasting lamb wafted out of the cabin and floated in front of her, its enticing fingers tickling her nose. It was a wonderful aroma, she had to admit that. How ironic. She had dreamed of this, dreamed of his being with her, sharing a meal, sharing conversation, sharing life. And here he was as if no other earth-shattering event had happened in either of their lives. Here he was, cooking in the cabin that belonged to his parents. And humming.

Was this another of his jokes? Now what should she do? Conceal the hurt, play the game, see just how far this man would go?

Nina sat pondering. There was only one thing to do: she would just ask him outright. They had to talk about it. Something this important could not be left unsaid between them.

Chapter 28

The moon had already risen when Shane stepped out onto the veranda. He could not see Nina's face, but the sight of her with the moonlight casting a pale silvery glow over her hair made him catch his breath. He cleared his throat.

"Dinner is served, my girl . . . lady."

When she looked up at him, he smiled broadly and bowed to her. A white towel was wrapped around his waist and tucked into his leather belt, an absurd short apron over brown twill pants tucked into the ever-present worn brown leather boots. His leather vest over a pale blue shirt seemed richly lit with the glow of lamplight behind him in the cabin. The moon was clouding over, but still it reflected from his blue-quartz eyes with a magnetic light.

Nina stared at him with a hard blue-green gaze turning at once to a velvety softness at the vision of him bending toward her with his irresistible looks. The warmth in his eyes began to melt the iciness with which she'd surrounded herself since his arrival. She rose slowly and their eyes locked. Then she remembered how angry she was with him and pulled her gaze away.

He led her inside the cabin. If he was playing a joke, it was the most beautiful one she'd ever seen. The room was softly aglow with undulating light from the glass lamps. He'd moved the table closer to the fireplace, and the dark glow from the fire warmed the colors in the quilt he'd spread over it. A candle flickered at one end. In the center he'd placed the pot of late autumn wildflowers she'd picked, and set out the tin dishes and cutlery she'd unearthed from the lean-to. A bottle of wine was waiting to be poured into two sturdy glasses.

At the other end was a platter containing roasted lamb surrounded by heaps of crayfish. Another plate held boiled vegetables, and a basket of bread sat near the fireplace. She smiled in spite of her anger. The repast was fit for royalty.

"You really had quite a bit to choose from here," he said lightly. He talked amiably as he seated her at one end of the table, then poured some wine into the glasses. "The wine was a surprise. I'm glad you had some here."

"Colin brought it."

He winced, then sat down at the other end of the table and proceeded to slice the lamb. He heaped a plate and passed it to her, then filled one for himself.

If things had been different, Nina would have swooned in his presence. She had to admit he was right, he was a pretty fair cook. The supper was delicious and cooked perfectly. She watched him eat. He enjoyed it, she could see that. He was savoring every mouthful, and talking about the shearing and how quickly and smoothly it had gone.

At first she listened with detachment, and then with interested attention, visualizing the shearers, strong long arms working with incredible speed and care to remove the fleece in one intact piece. She longed to be a part of it as Shane described it, stand waist-high in piles of fleece, watch the sheep leave the woolshed with confused looks on their faces only to end up in the paddock shivering in their wrinkled nakedness. She knew sheep were stupid, but still she felt sorry for what she perceived to be their embarrassment at the indignity of it all.

And here was Shane, sitting across the soft glow of a firelit table, sharing wine and supper with her, his rich baritone voice falling over her like the cloak of a thick quilt, wrapping her in its warmth and security. She felt embraced by his voice, lost in the azure of his eyes, drawn to his lean, hard body, mesmerized by the firelight dancing over the shock of wheat-hued hair that persisted in dropping onto his forehead.

Maybe it was the wine, maybe it was the glow in the cabin, but she felt herself melting more in his presence, felt her bones go liquid, felt that longing ache of desire below her stomach. She knew she could not leap up and run away, for her spine would not support her, her legs would not unfold to push her upright. And she had no desire to run away, anyway. She had turned to liquid flame and was powerless to quell the fire.

Shane ate with a flourish. Maybe it was the wine and the food, but he'd never felt more comfortable than he did at this moment, in the cabin of his parents, in the presence of this beautiful, desirable woman.

The firelight played on Nina's long, loose copper hair, picking up and illuminating the light the sun had already painted there. Her eyes sparked with golden jets which leaped across the table and pierced his heart and mind. He had a sudden desire to stand up, walk over to her, pull her to her feet, envelop her in his arms, and kiss her with every last ounce of love and desire he was feeling at this very moment.

He steeled himself. She'd been hurt by the whole Merritt clan, and he couldn't take advantage of her in this most recent hurt. He ached for her, and wished so much that he could make her feel better, help her through it, show her that what had happened with Colin was for the best in the long run. He'd been his own fool six ways to Sunday and gone, and he'd pay for it the rest of his life. But that wasn't important in the face of her hurt.

He smiled warmly from across the table.

Nina thought if Shane smiled at her like that again she'd dissolve. He was cutting her to ribbons. He must have felt guilty about her, about everything, and this kindness was his way of assuaging that guilt. How far could he take this? How much of this could she take?

A light knock came at the door. Shane's brow folded in a fleeting frown. It was probably Colin, and if it was, he'd finish the job on him he'd started the night of the party. He rose and walked to the door, pulling it open with great force. The dark form of Gingu was quickly illumined by the cabin's light.

"Gingu, mate, good to see you." Shane let out a

tense breath and grabbed his friend's hand to draw him into the cabin.

Gingu held back. "Nay, mate. Just wanted to be sure the woman was all right. Going to be cold tonight."

"She's fine, Gingu." They both looked around and smiled at her.

"Good. She was upset about the wedding."

Shane pushed Gingu outside and shut the door behind them. He didn't want Nina to have to hear any more about it. No sense in having her hurt further.

"I know, Gingu," Shane whispered, "my brother continues to prove himself a cad. But it's done. No way to reverse things."

Gingu looked confused. "What did the brother do now?"

It was Shane's turn to appear confused. "Why, the wedding, of course."

"Aye, the wedding." Gingu was thoughtful. "Is that bad?"

"Of course it's bad. Don't you see? He must have promised Nina so much, and he knew he could never fulfill that promise."

Gingu stood stoically silent. "I try, but I never understand everything, mate. Tell me once more."

Shane looked over his shoulder to be sure the cabin door was closed. "I haven't time to go into all of it now. Colin married Laurette Marston. I think he may have promised Nina he'd marry her."

Gingu stared at him with mounting confusion. He cocked an inquisitive eyebrow. "Little brother was going to marry Nina?"

"Aye, I think so."

"But he married somebody else?"

"Aye."

"Nina didn't know?"

"Nay."

"Now I really don't understand."

"Why not?"

Gingu rubbed his chin and shook his head. "Colin was going to marry Nina, but he married another. Nina would have married Colin, when she really wants you. I'm glad I'm Parkengee, and we don't have this kind of problem." He turned and melted away into the darkness.

"I know," Shane said and turned to go into the cabin. Then his hand froze on the latch, and he spun around. "Gingu!" he shouted a loud whisper. *"What* did you say?"

From near the edge of a grove of trees, Gingu turned around and grinned in the moonlight. Then he was gone.

Shane stood frozen on the veranda. A sharp wind curled around the cabin and struck him in the face. "She really wants you," Gingu's voice echoed in his head. Is that what he said? No, he must have heard him wrong. After all, he'd admitted he was confused. Still, Gingu could know in that uncanny instinct of his something he himself had not recognized.

He was letting his imagination get the better of him. There was no time now to pursue this and try to figure it out. He had enough to think about. Nina was hurt, and she was leaving soon, and even though he knew it was for the best, he didn't want her to go. The Mum seemed to be feeling stronger, and she hadn't spoken about Nina much, except to tell him she'd left Flame Tree. That, and the onslaught of shearers, and Colin's surprise wedding had been more than he'd wanted to think about all at once. Where had the simplicity of life gotten to, and when had all this bloody confusion taken over?

He opened the door and went into the cabin. Nina had cleaned off the table while he'd been outside with Gingu. She was pouring water into a chipped teapot, calmly making tea.

"What did Gingu want?" She set the teapot down, then seated herself at the side of the table closest to the fire.

"Oh, he was just checking to see if you were all right. I guess since you branded him that day he thinks you own him." Shane laughed and avoided meeting her eyes.

"He doesn't really think that, does he? I mean, it's not a custom of his people, is it?"

"Nay, I was teasing. He was just being a friend."

Nina nodded and stared into the fire. "I guess friends do that, don't they?" she asked in a faraway voice.

"Do what?"

"Oh, watch out for each other, stay available through hurts and disappointments."

"I suppose so," Shane said quietly, wondering if she was referring to him, and hoping he was making that up to her now by being with her and showing her that he was more than a friend.

The two sat silently, both staring into the fire, both seeing in the reaching flames a dream of completeness as yet unfulfilled. Shane took a long swallow of

335

tea. It flowed down and seemed to move along his veins and nerves, softly warming him inside as the fire did on the outside. "Comfortable" was the word that best described his feelings. This was comfortable, sitting here with Nina by the fire in a cozy cabin. He looked over at her. She sat hunched over, the cup held in the circle of her hands, watching the flames move up in their quest for the air outside the chimney.

The firelight played along her hair and set aglow the light wisps all over it. He was struck once again by the way that light seemed to shape itself into a halo over her head as it had the first morning on the wharf in Sydney, except that this time it moved down the length of her hair in a pale silvery glow that made him think of a veil. Her skin seemed almost translucent with a deeper golden blush to it from days in the sun and the light from the fire.

He remembered the night of the bush fire, when he saw her silhouetted against the raging flames and smoke, and how like a fiery angel she'd appeared out of the destructive rampage. He'd been struck motionless then, and he was struck motionless now, mesmerized by the beauty of the woman she'd grown into, and caught in the trance caused by the vision.

Nina stared beyond the fire into a vast unknown far away. She thought about a place Derrick had mentioned once, the Never-Never, that's what he called it. It lay somewhere beyond the outback, and somewhere beyond the reaches of her heart. The moments now with Shane were bittersweet. It felt so right to her, so comfortable to be sitting here with him, and so wrong to be having to leave.

Shane broke the silence first. "Ah, there's something we should talk about, my girl." She turned her gaze on him. He couldn't read it, but he almost turned too weak to go on. He swallowed hard. "Gingu said something before he left . . ."

Another knock came at the door. Shane started to get up. "Caw, does everyone know where this place is?"

"Let me answer it this time." Nina rose quickly. "I'm sure it's Colin, and I'd like to speak to him alone, if you don't mind."

Shane had a few choice words he hadn't finished saying to Colin as well, but he understood Nina's need to say what was on her mind. He nodded. "Just call me if you need me."

She opened the door and Colin stood framed by it, a smile spread across his thin lips. He was dressed in an evening suit, hardly appropriate for a cold night ride into the bush. Nina stepped quickly out onto the veranda and closed the door behind her.

"Well, it's about bloody time you got here!" she whispered.

"Now, wait a minute," Colin said, his smile fading. "When you hear the news, you'll forgive me for being so late."

"I've already heard the news, and I don't see how you can expect me to forgive you for it."

Colin looked puzzled. "How did you hear about it?"

"Gingu told me."

"Of course. Gingu's the biggest link in the bush telegraph. Why are you so angry? Because I didn't tell you first? I couldn't, you know."

"Why couldn't you?"

"And when would I have time for that? Things happened so quickly, I hardly had time to make the arrangements myself."

"Arrangements? *You* made the arrangements?"

"Of course. Well, Laurette did a good deal of it herself, but I had to put the plan into action. You knew I had a plan. It was a lovely wedding, and Mother couldn't be happier."

"Well, of course she's happy. Laurette is most appropriate to be the wife of a Merritt son."

"That she is, what with all that lovely land that comes with her. And surprise, surprise, there's an equally lovely little gold mine in the northeast corner of it, not a prolific one yet, mind you, but it could certainly be worked enough to provide a comfortable income for years and years." He buffed his fingernails against his lapel and blew on them with a smug look on his face.

Nina dropped her hands to her sides in a gesture of despair. "Well, that makes everything just perfect, doesn't it? Fairy tale wedding, land and gold to save Flame Tree, the Merritt heir married to the absolutely perfect wife. How neat and tidy."

Colin's face broke into a wide grin. "Come on, Lady Cole, buck up and be happy for me. Now the way is clear for you to get on with your life."

Nina looked at him incredulously. "Colin, you're not making any sense. I thought you understood that getting on with my life meant including Shane."

"Aye. And?"

"And, and, well how can that happen now? For God's sake, he's married to Laurette!"

"He's married to—what are you saying? You're saying you think Shane married Laurette?"

Nina stamped her foot in the dry earth, sending out little clouds of dust. "Will you *stop this?*" she shouted in a whisper. "You've just told me about the wedding, Gingu told me about the wedding, *Shane* told me about the wedding. How much more proof do I need?"

Colin threw his head back and laughed out loud. When he finally looked down at Nina, he could see in her face that she was serious and she was in pain. He grabbed her shoulders and peered hard into her eyes.

"You haven't been listening to a thing I've been saying, have you? Now I understand why you're so angry. I'm about to change all that for you, Lady Cole, so listen carefully. Shane's not the one married to Laurette Marston, I am."

Nina jolted as if suddenly hit in the middle of her back. The breath went out of her and her knees went to water. "You?" she breathed. "You're married to Laurette?"

"Isn't it delicious?"

"But I thought . . . I mean, at the party . . . Shane . . ."

"Just listen. Laurette and her family came to dinner one evening. Remember Mother inviting her? The Mum was going on about Shane, all that rubbish. I couldn't take it anymore, so I went outside for a smoke. Well, the next thing I knew, Laurette was kissing me. Me! All right, I admit I flirted with her outrageously at dinner. Even stroked her knee under the table, if you can imagine that."

Nina stared beyond him into the growing darkness. "You . . . you married Laurette?"

"Aye, Lady Cole, haven't you been listening? We just started talking, and the next day I rode over to see her and we talked some more. And we both admitted we've been pigheaded and prideful since we were tads, and . . . well, we discovered that we love each other. Here I had this grand plan to lure Laurette away from Shane, but I never got a chance to put it into action. We just . . ."

"Colin!" Nina threw her arms around his neck. "I'm so happy for you!"

He hugged her back. "Think of it. I, Colin Merritt, found a way to make it all happen! Call me the Purveyor of Dreams Come True, but I've done it, haven't I? I've found the way to save Flame Tree, put myself in favor with Mother for the first time in my life, and get the gold mine I always wanted. Didn't I tell you I knew it would all happen?"

"Aye," she whispered, "you told me."

"Oh ye of little faith, you didn't believe me, did you? Can't blame you, no one ever has. But they will from now on, won't they? They'll see I'm a force to reckon with. Flame Tree will be back to its old glory and more, and Colin Merritt is the reason why." He picked her up in his arms and swung her around, ecstatically happy and obviously pleased with himself. "Well, I suppose I should be charitable and say my big brother did a bit himself. And truth to tell, I couldn't have done it without Laurette. Can you believe it? She actually loves me!"

Nina smiled with him. Colin was boasting, and with good reason. "Of course I can believe she loves you, you twit! You're right, you *are* a force to be reckoned with. I'm sure the Mum is very pleased."

"Now's your chance, then, isn't it?"

"Chance for what?"

Colin sighed and his eyes went heavenward. He shook her shoulders again. "The chance you've been wanting. Have I left you out here too long alone and your mind's gone daft? Your chance with Shane, of course. No more obstacles now, the door is wide open. I *know* big brother's gone for you. I'll just find him and straighten this whole thing out. Leave it to me." He turned to go to his horse.

"No!"

"Why not? I've just discovered how good I am at solving everyone's problems, what's one more?"

"Colin, he's here, but I don't want you to talk to him."

"Here? He's here? You mean, in the cabin?"

"Yes, in the cabin."

"Well, then, what's all this bleating about? You're here, he's here, nothing stands in your way, couldn't be cozier, another problem solved. Caw, I'm good!"

"Colin, stop it. Just because he's here doesn't mean a thing. Besides, I'll be leaving for home soon."

"Home, hogwash. This is your home, and you know it as well as I do. And he needs you here with him. You'll just have to *do* something to get him to admit it. He's a stubborn lot. You'll have to be clever."

"I can't do that."

"Why not?"

"It's not right. And besides, I don't really know what it is you think you know. No," she shook her head, "it's just not right for me to trick him."

341

"Oh, I see. Not ladylike, is that what you mean, Lady Cole? Or are you still faint-hearted?" He pushed up the end of his nose with a forefinger. "Forget all that uppity tucker. It won't work out here. I'm a prime example of that. Now, I've cleared a path for you. Get yourself into action, Lady Cole, before you find yourself rocking on the boat to New York!" He swung up onto his horse.

"But what about the Mum?" Her voice was shaky.

"All in due time, Lady Cole, all in due time. Leave her to me." He tipped his hat and rode away, leaving Nina standing in the waning moonlight.

The wind blew harder, and the air became sharper, more stinging. Thin, dark fingers of clouds crept slowly across the moon, and a distinct dampness began to settle over the darkness. She turned toward the cabin. Inside, soft lamplight turned the windows a cozy red-orange, inviting her into the warmth. She shivered, and walked to the door.

Chapter 29

Hunkering down in front of the fireplace, Shane used a green eucalyptus stick to poke at the gray and white ashes under the crackling fire. Nina had been gone for what seemed to him like hours, but then, he knew she and Colin would have a lot to talk about. How his little brother was going to squirm out of this predicament, he could not imagine. He wanted to rip Colin to shreds for the way he hurt Nina, but he knew it was best they work it out between themselves.

He moved to a low stool at the edge of the hearth and smacked the stick against the top log and watched a few sparks fly up the chimney. How ironic that it was Colin who'd contributed to saving Flame Tree from dissolution and made the Mum happier than she'd ever been with him. Just like a cat, he thought. Drop Colin from the top of a dead ghost gum and he'll land on his feet, just like a cat.

He shook his head and a smile spread lazily across his lips. His little brother had surprised him, and he was proud of him, and glad he and Laurette had both grown up and recognized how they felt about each other. Their marriage certainly took the Mum's pressure off him for a while, that was, until she came up with another idea. He hoped he could stay one step ahead of her.

He watched the flames flare and recede, crackle and whisper. How he longed to see the light of sparkle and flame again in Nina. His eyes swung to the door when he heard it open, and he stood up as she stepped in. Quickly she moved in front of the fire, hugging herself and rubbing her upper arms. She shivered audibly. He reached behind her to get her shawl, which was draped over a chair. He wrapped it around her, letting his hands linger on her shoulders.

She shivered again, not so much from the cold this time as from the touch of his hands along the sides of her neck. His nearness was never more disturbing to her as it was at this moment. The heat in his fingers held more power than the leaping flames in the fireplace in front of her. Once again she felt herself melting toward him.

"Nina, I apologize for the behavior of the Merritt family. And I especially apologize for my brother's behavior. What he did was unforgivable. When I was finally able to leave the shearing shed for one evening, I went home. You weren't there, and the Mum said you'd left. I believed, I mean, I thought you'd gone to Sydney so you could leave for home."

Outside the rain began, big, cold drops hitting the roof and knocking against the windows. He took a step nearer to her.

"Colin's all right," Nina whispered. "I'm not

344

angry with him. I hope he and Laurette will be very happy."

"No worries about that. He's finally got what he's always wanted, in every way. I just wish he hadn't had to hurt you to get it."

Nina turned toward him. "Hurt me? He didn't hurt me. It's all just been a misunderstanding, that's all. He thought . . . well, actually, I hoped . . . I mean, well, he thought that you and I might . . ."

Shane's eyes blazed. He placed his hands on her shoulders. "You and I . . . might what?"

A loud knock sounded at the door.

"This place is as busy as the Sydney Custom-house," he muttered. "Now what?"

He pulled the door open with great force. Derrick stood with water dripping off his dark hat and from the end of his nose. The wind whistled around the corner of the veranda.

"Sorry to bother ya', mate. Just wanted t'let ya' know we're back for the last mob, and will muster 'em out at first light." Derrick spoke in chopped, rapid tones, his eyes flicking first to Shane, then to Nina, and back again. A small grin played about his mouth. "Bit heavy, it is, to be out in it now. We're in the cabin up the line, so if you was to want out with the musterin', we'll be there."

"Thanks, mate, I'll be there before you're off."

Derrick nodded and tipped his dripping hat. "G'devo to you both, then."

"Wait, Derrick . . . how'd you know we were here?"

"Gingu told me." He turned and disappeared into the dark rain.

Shane nodded. He closed the door and turned back to Nina. "Now, where were we?"

"I'm not sure," she whispered.

"Maybe I can help, my girl," he said gently. Might as well say everything now, he thought. It would be good for both of them. "I've been a real jackass."

She looked up at him, startled at this new approach.

"After we . . . were together," he went on, "I began to think about how things might change for us. But then, I realized it was Colin you were in love with, and I . . ."

"In love with Colin?" she interrupted, her face blanching in complete surprise. "Where did you get the idea that I was in love with Colin?"

"Well, I thought once that you were . . . and then at the party when you and he disappeared, and then he . . . *aren't* you?"

"In love with Colin? In a pig's eye! How could you think that when we . . . when I . . . after you and I made love? Did you think I was like those . . . those fluffs, as you call them, at the MacQuarie? Shane Merritt, if you're trying to throw me off the track, it won't work this time."

"Off the . . . what are you babbling about, my girl?"

"I'm not babbling, and don't call me that." She threw off her shawl and started to pace the room. "I've been taken in by your jokes, I admit that, but this time it won't work. Oh, no. I've become a lot smarter since I moved to Flame Tree. Clever, you're very clever, that's for certain, but this time you can't outwit me."

346

Her pacing had him turning his head from side to side, following her as she talked on.

"Oh, I know what you think," she continued. "You're so worried about your own hide getting shorn, you throw gates in front of all your imaginary pens."

Shane scratched his head, bewilderment spread across his face. "How I wish I knew what we were talking about."

"I know you now, aye, that I do," she laughed lightly. "All right, all right." One hand cut high through the air. "I'll lay it all out for you, clear as bush sky. You think it's you I'm in love with, that's what. Oh, yes you do, that's it, don't try to worm out of this. You think I'm in love with you, trying to trap you or something. You were so scared, you were just going to let me sail off to America, and you'd be free as a lyrebird in the thickets, wouldn't you?"

Shane ran a hand through his hair, more confused than ever. "Nina." He tried to stop her from talking, but she pushed him away.

"Wait, wait, I'm not finished. This time I'm not going to let you get the best of me, no sir. I want to straighten everything out." She faced him holding one finger in the air. "I'm not in love with Colin, never have been. He's a good friend."

Shane took her arm. "Will you please stop babbling for one bloody minute so I can think?"

She pulled her arm away. "Not until I finish. The man I love will love me, and want a home with me, and . . ."

"Aye! And I'm that man!" Shane shouted, clamping his hand over her mouth.

Nina stared up at him wide-eyed.

"Well, don't just stand there, babble something," he chided, dropping his hand.

"Wh-what did you say?"

"I'm a man of few words. If you didn't hear it, well, I try never to repeat myself." His eyes twinkled. He walked to the fire and picked up the stick and poked around in the ashes.

She turned around slowly, eyes burning into his back. "Shane, please, no jokes now," she whispered.

He stood up, turned and walked toward her without a word, gathered her into his arms and closed his warm lips over hers. Holding her and kissing her until his longing was fired to the exploding point, he felt her surrender in the circle of his arms. He drew away from her. Her face remained tilted up to his, her eyes closed, lips parted.

"You know," he said quietly, "you've been wrong about everything since the first night I met you, wrong about Australia and wrong about me."

"And you've been wrong about me as well." She opened her eyes and the spark of a blaze glistened in their blue-green depths.

His grip tightened around her waist. "Truth to tell, I knew you were gone for me that first night in the hotel." He used the most smug voice he could manage without breaking out in laughter. "But I didn't want you to think I knew how you felt, thought it might embarrass your fragile sensibilities."

Her mouth dropped open and jets of fire flew out of her eyes. She struggled against him, but he held her tighter. When she started to speak, he kissed her deeply.

"Aye," he went on calmly, one eyebrow quirking up in enjoyment of his own amusing command of the moment. "I knew it all along. That's why I stayed away from the homestead so much. Couldn't have you go getting all willy-willy. Good thing you couldn't keep your secret, and you let me know."

Nina's breath came in short gasps. "Let you know? Oh, you truly are the most *conceited* person I've ever met!"

"Nod's as good a wink to a blind horse, my girl," he grinned, holding her firmly against him.

"And I think you've got the ends of the horse mixed up where you're concerned, my boy!" She tried to wrest away from him.

Clearly enjoying this repartee, he laughed heartily. "Funny, is it? You think *everything* is funny. Everything's a joke to you isn't it?"

"Not this time," he said hoarsely. "Not a Buckley's chance."

"You are so . . . bloody exasperating, Shane Merritt!"

"You even talk like us now! Bloody, indeed!" he laughed.

"You just barge into the middle of everything," she went on, ignoring his remark, "as if you have all the answers, never giving anyone else the chance to say anything."

"Here, my girl, and stop babbling." He lowered his mouth close to hers.

Nina paused for only a second, then threw her arms around his neck and kissed him with everything she'd been holding inside. His hands slid up her back, under her hair, and clasped behind her head. He ground his lips into hers, then urged her teeth apart to thrust his warm tongue into the sweet moistness of her mouth. Her hands moved up the back of his neck to entwine in his hair and pull his head down even closer to hers.

Carefully he tore his lips away from hers, eliciting a low moan of protest from the back of her throat.

"I love you, Nina," he whispered hoarsely, "probably since that first morning on the wharf in Sydney."

She smiled up at him. "I give up. You're right, I have loved you from the very beginning."

He bent down and scooped her up into his arms and carried her to the bed. Slowly he lowered her onto the thick quilts, then leaned close to her face, holding his mouth just above hers. His lips hovered over hers like mist over the neck of a newly opened champagne bottle. Then he claimed her lips, pulling their soft fullness inside the hungry warmth of his own.

Tenderly he removed her clothes, following his hands with kisses over her skin until she felt as if every pore was on fire. The last to come off were her stockings. He slipped them down, kissing the insides of her thighs as he moved. As each stocking was slipped off, he picked up her foot and kissed the top of it, then held it up and kissed each instep. The touch of his lips sent waves of heat over her body with reaching fingers until she was aflame with desire.

Outside, the wind howled and rain pelted the roof, walls, and windows; and the eucalyptus tapped loudly. He stood up and removed his clothes. As he shrugged out of his shirt, she leaned up on one elbow and kissed the naked flank nearest her. Her action startled and thrilled him, and he knew instinctively if he were to look at the place where her lips had been, he would find the perfect imprint of them branded into his flesh.

He turned toward her. His naked body gleamed golden in the firelight, and he looked to her to be an exotic god.

He lay down on the bed next to her and gathered her into his arms, kissing her deeply and sensually and lingeringly. His hand slipped up her ribs to find and cup her breast, squeezing gently around its fullness and flicking over the nipple with his thumb. Her back arched, pressing her breast more tightly into the palm of his hand. He pulled his lips from her mouth and moved them down to capture the rosy point. She moaned, and he leaned to slide his lips across her satin skin to circle the other nipple with his tongue.

Arching higher, she let her head fell back. He slid his hands down to her slim hips and trailed his lips over her stomach to just above the vee between her legs. He slid his hands under her buttocks and cupped their firm roundness, lifting them slightly. His eyes traveled up to her lovely face. Her breathing was rapid and her eyes were closed in ecstasy. His gaze traveled back down her body, catching the firelight dancing in golden shadows over her skin, setting aglow the red-gold curls lying just below his lips.

Nina felt the mist from Shane's lips as he trailed them along her body. Every fiber in her was crying out with desire and longing for him to envelop her, take her completely. When his mist warmed the insides of her thighs, she strained up to him, desiring him to do the next ultimate thing, whatever it took to quell the surging heat of her desire.

Slowly his lips descended over the exquisite golden curled vee between her legs. His tongue probed the warm moistness of her soft folds, and her mind drifted back to the night in his bedroom under the canopy mirror over his bed. Now, on the thick quilts in a cozy cabin, his body slipped along hers, and he hovered above her, supported by his hands and arms on either side of her. She felt the sleek hardness of his desire pressing into her thigh, and instinctively moved her legs apart to admit him. His azure eyes reflected the undulating flames from the fire, and held the gaze from the swirling aquamarine depths of her own.

Shyly she pushed against him, and tenderly he slipped inside her. Her response was a small thrust. She slipped her arms around his neck, entwined her fingers in the thickness of his hair, opened her mouth, and pulled him hard down to her. She pushed her tongue into his mouth, hesitantly at first, and then firmly explored inside it, flicking over his back teeth. She thrust up with her buttocks. His hands slipped down to cup them, and he pushed himself into her so far he thought he would be lost in the sheer beauty of their loving.

She pulled her mouth away from his and cried out a little, then moaned in the pleasure of their bodies melding together in the heat and fulfilling need of their mutual desire. He leaned up and slipped out of her, but she wrapped her legs around the back of his thighs and pulled him back inside her. Again and again he slipped out of her, and again and again she pulled him back, until he could hold back no more and released the mounting passion inside him in a high-crested wave that engulfed them both.

Her inner muscles gripped and held him as he spent himself inside her. One by one the waves crashed over him, smashing against the shores of his being, until at last the tide of his desire ebbed and flowed away. As the last wave swept him down, he leaned over and circled first one engorged nipple and then the other, suckling, nibbling, pulling, while he slid up and down with wet sleekness inside her.

She raised her head, buried her face in his hair, still gripped in her fingers, and let him carry her to the heights he'd reached, suspending her there until the last of the small explosions subsided.

She could feel his heart pounding in rhythm with her own as they lay locked in each other's arms, breathing deeply, their bodies glistening with the dew of love in the glow of firelight. Reaching behind and pulling a quilt up over them, he slid to one side of her and pulled her close to rest her head in the hollow along his shoulder.

"I never knew," he said sleepily.

"I did," she responded dreamily.

He smiled, and they fell into the deep sleep of lovers.

Chapter 30

Shane awoke to the aroma of fresh coffee. He rolled over, at first not remembering where he was, and then recalling completely. His eyes still clamped shut, he felt along the bed for the warm, luscious body he so vividly remembered from the night before.

"Where are you, my girl?" he asked sleepily.

Droplets of cold water fell onto his face and he sat bolt upright.

"Open your eyes, mate," she laughed. "I'm right here!"

"What are you doing?" He rubbed his eyes and wiped his face.

"Waking you up. You've a job to do."

"What job? It's not even morning yet. Caw, listen to that wind."

"At least it stopped raining. You seem to have been robbed of your memory since last night." She held out a tin mug. "Here, have a cup of coffee, that should bring it back."

"Oh, my memory is very sharp regarding last

night." He grinned up at her and accepted the mug.

She was wearing his blue shirt, the tails of it bobbing provocatively against the back of her thighs when she walked.

Her eyes dropped to below his chest and she smiled, then went back to the cookstove. When he looked down, he was embarrassed to discover he was lying there naked as a shorn sheep and just as wrinkled. He grabbed a quilt and threw it over himself, spilling a few drops of coffee as he did so.

He took a long swallow of the coffee, and coughed and choked on it. "Aargh! Who taught you to make coffee, Derrick?"

"Righto, mate," she laughed, "and speaking of Derrick, you'd better get out of that bed before he comes to get you."

"Bloody hell," he cursed, "I forgot about the muster." He flew out of the bed, groping for his clothes, and dressed quickly.

"Good thing I didn't," she said confidently. "Breakfast is ready."

"Breakfast?"

"Of course. It wouldn't be good for us to go out on a muster without breakfast."

"Back in a minute," he said, heading out the back door to the privy.

She sat down at the table, her hands circled around a cup of coffee, and looked over at the bed. The shape of his form was still imprinted in the bedding. Closing her eyes, she recalled the night of ecstasy spent in Shane's arms. They'd made beautiful love together. It felt right, natural, as if they'd always been like that together and would always be like that.

And it had seemed so right and natural for her to rise and make breakfast for the two of them. Yes . . . aye, it was right. She'd known it would be.

Shane burst through the back door. "Us? Just what did you mean by 'us'?"

She drank her coffee calmly and set the cup down. "Us means you and me, of course."

"Oh no," he sputtered, dropping down at the table. There is no 'us' where the muster's concerned. We've a lot of work to do, and it takes a special kind of cooperation, with people who work well together." He took a biscuit and smeared a dollop of jam on it, and took a hungry bite.

"Hm," she responded coolly, "what about last night? Wouldn't you say that was a kind of muster that worked well because of the special cooperation of two people? Ham?" She held out a plate with several slices of cured pork.

His face reddened. He took the plate of ham out of her hands and dropped two slabs on his plate. Studiously he cut them, chewed them carefully. She ate a biscuit and jam, then poured more coffee.

She rose. "I'm going to get dressed while you finish your coffee."

She placed her mug on the sideboard. He was up as quickly and moved behind her, his arms circling her waist, his face buried in her hair.

"Nina," he whispered, pressing close to the full length of her body, "you are so beautiful, and I want you so very much."

She turned in his arms, slipped hers up to encircle his neck, and kissed him deeply.

"I've never been happier, Shane. I want you, too,

357

and oh, how I love you . . . my boy!" She kissed him again.

He opened the shirt and slid his hands inside it over the taut, smooth skin of her back, around her ribs, and up to cup her breasts. Tenderly he kissed each nipple. The feel of her enflamed him immediately, he was consumed by a hunger for her that demanded fulfillment.

He dropped his trousers and stepped out of them. Nina's eyes fell and she sucked in her breath at the magnificence of him. Tentatively she reached out to touch him, gently placing a finger on the tip. He moved against her finger and she pulled back, smiled, then touched him again.

Shane closed his eyes. Her touch ignited him with an intense flame. Shyly at first, she ran her finger along the length of him, then boldly she clasped him with both hands, stroking the velvety-soft skin. He moaned in pleasure. If he didn't pull away from her now, he would explode right where he stood, and he wanted more of her. But more, he wanted to give her as much pleasure now as she gave him.

Hotly his mouth claimed hers. He dropped his arms and clasped the rounded softness under her hips, and then lifted her. Instinctively she opened her legs and grasped him around the waist, crossing her ankles behind him. He plunged his hard head into the fiery depths of her, and they both cried out in the sheer ecstasy of it.

She buried her face in his neck. His breath came rapidly, and his heart pounded to the rhythm of every stroke. With strong but gentle hands, he lifted her hips and bottom and guided them forward and back till it was she who stroked him as he held her impaled against him.

Shane waited with a strength he never knew he possessed. He felt her liquid heat envelop him from deep inside where she held him captive. When she reached her peak, he released his own pent-up passion and the very essence of him filled her and mingled with her own.

They clung to each other, locked in the complete embrace of their love, pulses racing, panting for breath, skin moist with the immediacy of the two of them together.

Slowly he walked to the bed. He sat down, still holding her wrapped around him. She reached around and pulled up the quilt, drawing it around them like a cocoon, and they rocked inside their own warmth, silently holding each other, and feeling, just feeling, for a long time.

When they could bear to separate, he set her gently down on the bed and stood up, reluctant to move away from her.

"I've got to leave, my girl," he whispered, holding her face and kissing her deeply. "Every fiber in me wants to slip inside that quilt and hold you forever, but . . ."

"I know, my love." She wrapped the quilt closer around her and smiled up at him. "I know."

He dressed, then went out to saddle Shadow. When he came back into the cabin, she was dressed in daks, undershirt, moleskin shirt, and boots.

"I'm ready," she announced.

"Nina, you can't . . ."

"Oh, but I can, and I'm going to. If I'm going to be

359

around here very much I'm going to learn how to muster, and whatever else."

"You don't have a horse."

"Down in the back shed. How'd you think I got out here with Colin, in a bullock dray? I'm going Shane, so you can forget about trying to stop me. You can't." She picked up a hat and oilskin wrap and stood waiting.

He let out a long sigh of futility. There was no use in arguing with her.

"Then let's go, sun's on the way. Derrick'll be fretting already."

Chapter 31

When Shane and Nina reached the line cabin, Derrick and the others were mounted, ready for the muster. Upon seeing Nina, those among the most experienced shepherds did nothing to conceal their annoyance at her presence. But the jackaroos clearly thought it a lark and were going to enjoy watching this woman once again amidst a mob of bleating, scampering sheep. After he ran at both Nina and Shane in an exuberant greeting, Mate was raring to go, as were the other dogs.

The jackaroos remarked about how cold it was, but to Nina it was more damp than cold. She was used to the penetrating cold of a New York winter, and out here so close to the equator the winters were much more temperate than she'd experienced. It was brisk but energizing, and she was exhilarated by the prospect of riding out to muster.

Shane went into the cabin to get a duster for her. She put it on, and the long split tails brushed along her boots as she sat astride her horse. She pulled the dark brown hat a little tighter over her forehead, and pushed a few stray tendrils of hair up under it, She slipped on a pair of his gloves, much too big, but they would keep her hands warm.

Mud was everywhere there had been dry earth before the rain, but the reduction of flies was a blessed relief. The horses picked their way laboriously over formerly dry stream beds that had turned into mud slicks overnight, sometimes sinking deep above the fetlocks in the brown muck.

Splitting up and spreading out, the shepherds and jackaroos went their own ways, and by mid-afternoon had rounded up and brought together over two hundred animals. Nina marveled at the size of the flock, but Shane told her this was the smallest to be brought to the paddocks for shearing. These were the last of those which had strayed away from the other flocks.

The muster had also roused a mob of kangaroos almost as big as the flock. Other groups of the big red kangas had run by them, and several small flocks of emus. At the top of a table rock, Nina had sat astride her horse, watching the flurry of animals, birds, and men below running as if in a maze to find the prize at the exit.

Toward the end of the long day, Derrick rode with Nina and Shane toward the cabins. They followed a narrow river bed, once dry from a long drought, and now turned to thick mud from the rain. Mate ran far ahead of them. When he'd been out of sight for a few minutes, they heard his frantic barking.

"Leave it to Mate," Derrick laughed, "always manages to find a couple extra."

Mate's bark changed, was muffled, and then broke out into an alarming cry. Shane kicked Shadow out on a run in the direction of his voice, with Derrick and Nina close behind. He reached a watering hole and was off Shadow before the great stallion had come to a full stop. A huge boomer kangaroo had Mate down in the water, and with the use of a powerful hind leg and strong front paws, was pushing the frantically struggling dog under the water with the intent to drown him.

Nina screamed at the horror of the scene. Derrick was off his horse and on a full run behind Shane. The big kangaroo seemed to be the only one in the vicinity of the hole. It was possible there had been more, but Mate's bark had probably scared them off.

Shane and Derrick jumped into the watering hole in the midst of the splashing and roiling of mud. Shane threw his arms around Mate's thick body, while one hand reached under for his chin to pull it up. The kangaroo leaned back on his tail and kicked out with the strength in his hind feet of a hundred-fifty-pound man, flailing at Shane while still keeping the gasping, fighting Mate under water.

Then Derrick was out of the water like the force of a geyser, dodging the flailing feet and landing a punch on the side of the kangaroo's thrashing head. The impact of the connection was less than it could have been because Derrick lost his balance and fell into the water.

Nina felt helpless as a baby. The scene before her was something out of a nightmare in which the dreamer is powerless. And then from behind her came a piercing shout. She whirled around in time to

363

see Gingu release his hunting boomerang, snapped like a ball of ammunition from a slingshot. The cold whistle of it cut through the air and sent a shiver running through her. Aimed with precision, Gingu's throw landed the boomerang on target—the head of the struggling kangaroo.

In less than a heartbeat a black blur raced past her, long hunting knife up and gleaming in the sun. A moment later she saw the flash of the blade over his head, then swiftly and surely it plunged into the neck of the kangaroo. Blood mixed with muddy water as the great animal fell, front paws swatting the air.

Fear paralyzed Nina. Amid the shouts, animal grunting, and roiling water and mud, she could not find Shane, determine if Derrick was all right, nor catch any glimpse of Mate at all. And then Gingu's blade flashed again, bloodied and lethal, and she saw it plunge once more into the great fighting roo. The animal rolled like a capsizing ship, and Shane's head bobbed above the water behind it. Nina let out a cry of relief.

Shane held the kangaroo's head under the water, and at last the powerful back feet pushed with less and less intensity until they went limp and disappeared in the murkiness.

Frantically Shane searched for Derrick. He spotted Nina. Relieved, he whirled around, wiping water and mud from his eyes until he found Derrick. The older man's face was contorted with the exertion of hauling Mate's limp form out of the mud. Shane struggled to get to him, threw his arms around Mate's hind quarters, and lifted him out of the choking mud and up onto the riverbank. They laid him over a smooth boulder with his head lower than his feet. Nina ran to where they were working over him, and took the great mud-matted head into her arms.

"Keep his head down and his mouth open, and don't cover his nose!" Shane ordered, his face full of love and concern for his dog.

Tears flowing down her face, Nina followed the orders as if in a trance, forcing her fingers into Mate's mouth and letting his long tongue hang down. Derrick pumped the soaked hind legs in a running motion, while Shane felt along the ribs for breaks. Finding none there or along the spine, he rapped the dog on the back with an open hand, then pushed up under his lungs in a methodical rhythm.

"Come on, Mate," Nina whispered, "let this one be your ultimate trick."

Water began to dribble slowly from Mate's mouth as the two men pumped his strong body. And suddenly Nina felt the jaws resist her hands. A cough came from low in his throat and a weak kick pressed against Derrick's hands.

"Come on, Mate, old boy," Shane coaxed, "come on, boy, not time to leave us yet."

Mate coughed harder, gagged, and choked.

"Let go of his mouth now," Shane told Nina. "He's going to start fighting, I think . . . I hope."

And fight the great dog did. He coughed and vomited, then struggled to right himself. Derrick and Shane lifted him and stood him on his feet. He wobbled and fell, and looked up with frightened yet grateful eyes as they lifted him again. He hobbled away from them, coughing and sneezing, and panting.

At last Mate turned around and wobbled back toward them. There was a collective sigh and a cheer from all three as he got to the center of their group. He looked up wanly at each one, his eyes cloudy and caked with mud, as they petted his head, scratched behind his ears, and rubbed his thick wet coat. Then he shook himself hard, covering his rescuers head to toe with muddy splashes.

Nina burst out in a tear-filled laugh as she wiped mud from her eyes and hair.

"Hooroo, Mate!" Derrick laughed, scrambling to get away from the shaking animal. "This is the thanks we get for saving your miserable life!"

Covered with mud, his hair dripping water, Gingu walked over to them sheathing his knife, a satisfied grin lighting his face. Picking up his boomerang, he wiped it on his thick hide wrap and tucked it into his thong belt. Shane jumped up and pumped his friend's hand.

"Thanks, mate, I doubt we'd have saved him without you."

Gingu's grin widened. "We needed some extra meat for the corroboree tonight anyway," he said proudly, referring to his people's ceremonial dance.

"You're going to eat that kangaroo?" Nina was genuinely shocked.

Gingu nodded as if to say it was the most natural thing in the world to do.

"But, how can you? I mean, they're such wonderful animals."

"Wonderful?" Derrick spat. "That big one almost killed Mate, and I've seen 'em kill other dogs. They'll kill a man, too, they're that powerful. Eat all the

366

grassland, too. Caw, during a drought it's a fight to keep enough for sheep or cattle, without competing with those bloody roos. Overrun with 'em at times. Nothin' wonderful about the blighters atall."

Nina could not respond to Derrick's outburst. She'd marveled at the speed and agility of the odd-looking creatures, and she'd grown to love seeing them pass so near. But Derrick knew them differently, saw the destruction of which they were capable. And Mate had come close to being a victim. She'd been horrified at the sight, and had seen the pain in Shane's eyes as he'd worked over the animal that was as much a friend to him as many people. Still, the idea of killing them—or, God forbid, eating them—was repulsive to her.

"Derrick's right," Shane concurred calmly, "and kangaroo meat is a staple for Gingu's people. We have it occasionally at the out cabins. Much as they are part of this land, they can be a menace, and have to be thinned out now and then."

Nina had no choice but to accept their explanations. They knew best. She brushed herself off and rounded up her horse. The others did the same, and left Gingu by the watering hole, dressing out the kangaroo carcass. The three rode away, following the riverbed to the holding pens outside the shearing paddock. Mate followed closely behind, making his own pace.

They rode awhile in silence, then Derrick broke it with a comment about the time remaining until the shearing was over. The shearers had been working for almost three months, and were shearing their last numbers now. Some of the bales had already been sent to storage houses at the piers in Sydney, awaiting shipment to England and America. Rounding a vast stand of cedars and still following the riverbed, Derrick in the lead peered out intently over his horse's ears.

"Roos," he announced, "ahead in the mud."

Nina could see at least two kangaroos in the stream bed, looking as if they were sleeping. They did not get up and bound away, as they usually did, or least perk up their ears in awareness of the approaching riders.

"Mired, they are," Shane observed, drawing closer to the animals. "I don't think they're dead."

He dismounted and moved in slowly toward the animals. Nina and Derrick dropped down as well, and as they neared the edge, they could see three gray kangaroos—a boomer, a doe, and a joey—barely breathing and collapsed, near total exhaustion. All around them was evidence of a struggle to free themselves from the oozing mud, but their struggles had served only to mire them deeper.

Without a word to each other, Shane and Derrick waded into the mud and dragged the doe out and onto dry land on the opposite side of the stream bed. Then Shane scooped under the joey and lifted him out to lay him beside his mother. Derrick uncovered the feet of the big male, and tried to roll him onto his back. Silently Shane returned to his side and the two of them dragged the kangaroo out, working against the strength of the sucking mud.

Nina crouched down at the stream's edge, her arm draped around Mate's neck. She watched in mesmerized amazement as the two men worked, struck by the fact that they could kill a kanga to save their dog, and in less than an hour work hard to save the lives of three others stranded in mud.

Shane and Derrick pulled the almost lifeless body of the big male up to his feet and placed his forepaws on Derrick's shoulders. The animal's head dropped limply to one side. Staggering under the weight of it, Derrick began a kind of swaying dance with him while Shane pulled the powerful tail out in back of the animal for balance. Derrick nodded that he was under control, and Shane went to assist the doe. He hauled her limp body up to face him in the same manner, and he and Derrick stood near each other, doing a wobbly dance with the roos.

Shaking her gaze, which was glued in awe to the two men dancing with kangaroos, Nina stood up and waded across the mud to where the little joey was lying. Her feet sank in with each step and the mud sucked one of her boots off. She tripped, falling on her face on the bank, managing to drag her other foot out before that boot was lost as well. She landed with a great expulsion of air and a loud "Oooph!" Turning to look over her shoulder, she watched her boot sink slowly till just the top could be seen.

Scrambling over the bank, she crept to where the little joey was sprawled. She got to her knees and picked the little fellow up to stand him on his feet, taking her cue from Shane and Derrick. It didn't work; he toppled over no matter how often she tried. Frantic to save him, she scrambled to her feet and picked up the weighty, flopping bundle. She threw his forepaws over her shoulders and rested the small muddy head at the base of her neck, his back feet and tail hanging straight down against her.

She walked around crooning to the joey, patting him on the back as a mother would burp a baby, and pumping his back feet.

Soon a low grunt came from the big male.

"There's the distress signal," Derrick spoke with some difficulty under the weight.

The big roo opened his large brown eyes and stared straight into the smaller brown ones of Derrick's.

"If I was dancing with you, I'd grunt, too," Shane muttered under the burden of the doe.

"He's a better partner than you'd ever be," Derrick grunted back. "Caw, that did it. He's coming to, he'll live."

"You'd better get him over to those trees," Shane motioned with his head to a stand of cedars. "Soon as he figures out you're not his wife, there'll be bloody hell to pay."

Derrick struggled with the big wobbly kangaroo toward the trees. The animal was grunting more often and breathing harder. Shane followed with the doe, who had begun a similar but quieter grunting. They laid the animals down next to the trees, where they could rest and regain some strength, and to give themselves time to get away from them.

Then Shane remembered the dog. "Mate," he called, "where are you?"

"Over here," Nina answered in a loud whisper.

Shane turned in the direction of her voice and found her sitting beneath a cedar, the joey cradled in her arms like a baby while she rocked him and he stared up at her with wide, liquid brown eyes. Mate, disheveled and mud-caked, sat dutifully at her side, gazing down at the baby kangaroo as if he were the proud father.

"Isn't he adorable?" Nina crooned over the joey as she stroked its crossed front paws.

"Mate? Aye, he's always been a love," Shane said cutely.

"No, the baby, of course."

"Adorable, simply adorable," Derrick cut in impatiently, "but his parents won't think you're adorable if they wake up and find you cuddling him. They'll provide you with the same hospitality their cousin showed Mate back there. Now, put him with his mother and let's get out of here!"

Nina's eyes flew to Shane's face, a pleading in them he would have found hard to resist in another situation.

"Derrick's right, you're asking for trouble. They're frightened, and their reaction is likely to be extreme."

Reluctantly Nina got up and carried the joey to where its mother lay. She set him down near the doe's stomach and watched as he weakly attempted to crawl to her pouch. The doe was alert enough to move to afford him entrance, and the gray fur and red-brown mud on the joey soon mingled with that of his mother.

"G'dye, mates," Shane tapped two fingers to his forehead in a salute to the roo family. "No need to thank us. And don't get up, we were just leaving."

The three turned to cross back to where their horses waited. Slogging quickly across the mud, Shane bent down and tugged on a boot top that showed just above the mud.

"Yours?" he asked, turning to Nina, who was

hobbling through the muck, trying to hold her sock on with one hand. "You ought to try to take better care of your things."

She grabbed it from him and turned on a smile that melted his insides. The time has come, mate, he told himself, for you to decide what to do about Miss Nina Cole, and it's best not to wait too long.

Chapter 32

"Do you think Vanessa and Daniel ever did this?" Nina peered at Shane over a glass of wine.

"I have no doubts," Shane replied, lifting a soft cloth of warm soapy water and gently moving it over her shoulder, watching rivulets flowing down over her breasts.

She slipped lower in the big metal tub, entwining her legs around his in the warm, fragrant water. A roaring blaze from the fireplace warmed the cabin, and lamps and candles glowed around them. They touched each other intimately beneath the water.

The muster, the kangaroos, the mud, all were hours behind them, and they reveled in the soft, long moments of evening.

Nina's eyes closed dreamily. "If I become any happier, I'll burst from the sheer fullness of it."

"Aye, times like this are what make all the rest of it worthwhile, my girl."

She smiled. "I don't ever want to leave here."

"Nor do I, but you know we must, and very soon."

Later, they lay locked in each other's arms after long, slow lovemaking. Shane nuzzled her ear and spoke in a voice full of emotion.

"I feel reborn with you, Nina, my girl. And I will feel this forever, because of you."

Nina nestled closer in the warmth of his body, protected, secure, loved. Time had no boundaries. She drifted to sleep against him, holding fast to her dream.

"I'm not so certain I should go back to the homestead," Nina said to Shane as she packed the few clothes she had at the cabin into her traveling bag.

"Aye, you should," he answered seriously. "It's time. The Mum's not feeling well lately, and she seemed a bit sad when I was there this week. I think seeing you again would cheer her up."

"Oh, Shane, how can you say that? She didn't want me here in the first place, and I disappointed her profoundly, and angered her at the party. Then I left without saying a word to her. Why would she want to see me? I do believe I owe her an apology, and so perhaps I should go back to do that. How I wish we could be friends."

He closed the traveling bag for her, then stood up straight. "Actually, I think she owes you an apology."

"For what?" Nina was honestly surprised to hear him say that.

"The Mum was in a mood to confess after the wedding, and one of the things she told me about was the conversation she had with you your first evening at Flame Tree."

"Oh." Nina looked down at the floor.

"Aye. That must have terrified you. She must have seemed like a tyrannical matriarch, which she's not, truly. She's tough, and has her own sense of what is right and wrong—for Flame Tree and for the Merritt sons, that is."

Nina nodded. "I know. I can only respect her for it. I admire that she knew so well what she wanted, and that she had precise plans on how to go about getting it."

"Then you don't hate her?"

"Of course not. I think she's an incredible woman, and I wish I could be just like her."

"You are, my girl—at least, you have many of her finer, softer attributes."

"Thank you, I'll take that as a compliment."

"It was meant to be one."

"Are you anything like Daniel Merritt?"

"The Mum thinks so, but I'm not certain of it. He was a real gentleman, and a gentle man. His sense of fairness was strong, and his compassion knew no boundaries. He was unselfish—a giving man, and a good father."

"And do you think you are none of those things?"

"I know I'm some of those things, but not all."

"And will you . . . do you think you'll be a good father?" Nina colored at the audacity of her question, at first, but then felt strong about it, believing she and Shane had transcended all barriers between them.

"Aye, I think so. But I will discipline with love and teaching."

Nina smiled. "That's because you're part Daniel Merritt and part Vanessa Windsor, and it seems as if you possess the strongest assets of both."

"You're a poetic baggage, aren't you? I think the Mum's missed your reading to her."

"She should bring Anthia along to it. That girl is crying for some of that kind of attention. She's very intelligent, you know, just needs guidance and nurturing."

Shane nodded. "Time we left."

Nina sighed. "I shall miss this old place, what did you call it? A humpy? Aye, I shall miss this old humpy. It's been a splendid home."

They walked out and he latched the door behind them. Nina stood on the veranda for a moment, breathing in the crisp, clear air. A flock of chattering galahs flew over, their colorful plumage waving like a banner against the sky. In the distance a small mob of kangaroos could be seen bounding against the horizon.

"The roos," she whispered. "Do you think mine is among them?"

Shane laughed. "I think they must all be yours by now, my girl. Come."

As they rode away from the little cabin in the bush, Nina felt a twinge of sadness settle into her heart.

Returning to Flame Tree was a different experience from what Nina had expected. The Mum was reserved, more so than usual, but not altogether unfriendly. She accepted Nina's apologies and offered one of her own. Maude and Anthia were excited to have her back, and Anthia begged for stories of her stay in the bush. Colin was more charming than ever, and even Laurette was friendly.

But something else was different. She was different now, and nothing would ever be the same again. She'd learned that dreams can come true if you took a few risks to help them along.

One evening, a week after her return to Flame Tree, the family gathered for the evening meal. Vanessa Merritt sat in her usual place at the head of the long table in the dining room, with the chair at her right hand reserved for Shane, whether he was present or not.

The chair at her left was for her younger son. Colin sat there this evening in a black dinner suit, sporting a new, heavy gold ring encrusted with diamonds. Laurette was seated at his left, a pale green conservative dress with a high neck complementing her dark coloring. Nina smiled to herself. The Mum had willed out where dressing a Merritt wife was concerned.

Nina wore a stunning deep blue dress with a lace yoke of ecru cotton, and short, full sleeves. Maude had been so certain that she would return, she'd made it for her soon after she'd disappeared. Now Nina sat next to Shane's chair, but he'd been present for dinner only twice since she'd been back. Supervising and working at the paddocks, finishing the shearing, sorting, grading, and baling had taken up much of his time. Being together during those dinners had seemed natural and life-giving, as if these times would go on forever. She missed him when he wasn't there, but understood his absence.

". . . Laurette's ring should be ready soon, as well," Colin was saying when Nina became aware of the conversation going on around her. "Our wedding rings were rather plain, but now that the mine is producing more since I took over, we felt it was time to buy rings much more appropriate. Stunning, don't you think?" He was holding out his hand, fingers down, so all could admire it.

"A bit over the top," Vanessa remarked dryly. Her expression softened as Colin's face dropped, and she added, "But really quite suitable for you, my son."

Maude was serving the first course when Shane burst into the dining room. When he appeared, Nina's heart stopped beating for a split second, then started again, rapidly, loudly. She was positive all could see the red flush that crept up her throat and spread over her face. Would he always affect her like that? Without hesitation, her heart told her yes.

"G'devo, all," Shane said with a lilt in his voice that suggested he was satisfied about something.

"Tell us, big brother," Colin said, leading the conversation.

"Tell you what?" Shane replied with an enigmatic smile, taking the chair beside Nina.

"Your secret?"

"Secret? I have no secret, little brother. What's for dinner, Maude? I feel like a dingo gone without mutton for a month!"

Laurette grimaced at the uncouth remark. Nina smiled in amusement. The man certainly knew how to turn a phrase.

Throughout dinner Colin connived to find out what secret Shane was harboring, for he certainly looked as if he was doing just that. Laurette talked about a party they'd been to at O'Rourke station, her voice animated and sincere when she said she wished Shane and Nina had been there. Shane bantered in his light-hearted way, flirting with his mother as he'd always done. Vanessa stayed calm and ruled over the proceedings in her regal way, the Persian cat as always curled at her feet. Nina enjoyed the entire scene, smiling, joining in the polite conversation, pleased to be part of the group, feeling a strong sense of family.

When dinner was over, Nina made her way to the parlor, where Vanessa had summoned her for some before-bedtime reading of a new work. She was about to enter the room when Shane stopped her in the hallway.

"Nina, I have something very important to tell you."

He stood tall above her, and looking down on her, was struck once again by the halo that veiled her hair as a result of the lampglow emanating from the parlor. His heart thumped against his chest, and his palms grew moist. She looked up at him with trust and love shining from her eyes.

He drew in a deep breath. This was going to be the hardest thing he ever had to tell her.

"The last of our wool has been loaded. The ship for America sails day after tomorrow." He reached into his breast pocket and pulled out a packet. "These are your passage documents. You are to be at Sydney docks at six evo that day. Derrick has arranged to take you tomorrow so you will arrive in plenty of time. I'm sorry I couldn't give you more notice, but I had no choice."

"Shane . . . wha . . . what's wrong? What did I do? I thought . . ."

He spun around and walked so quickly down the hallway, Nina felt he was almost running away from her. And then he was gone.

Her knees buckled, and she fell against the wall outside the parlor door, too numb to speak or to cry. Then she pulled up, ready to go after him. Vanessa came to the doorway, and reached out to catch Nina's arm.

"Come in, my dear," she said quietly, and drew Nina into the room.

Nina slumped into the wing chair and stared into nothingness. Vanessa sat silent, waiting for the expected flood of tears, or outburst of words. There was neither. When she did speak, it was over a hard knot in her throat.

"I don't understand," she said dully, her forehead resting against her bent fingers.

"It is his way, my dear." Vanessa put out her hand, intending to stroke Nina's hair and soothe her, but she pulled back. "As it was his father's way."

"But why? Tomorrow . . . I'm to leave Flame Tree tomorrow." Nina raised her head and looked at Vanessa with luminous, pain-filled eyes. "I had come to love it so, and to love you, Mrs. Merritt. You've taught me so much, Flame Tree has taught me so much. I thought I would stay here forever. I thought Shane wanted me to stay forever. I just don't understand."

Vanessa stood up wearily. "He has made his decision, and it is for the best. You must pack now.

Derrick will want an early start."

She had once again been dismissed by Vanessa, but it seemed to Nina that there was a different feeling behind it, almost caring. She rose to leave, heart heavy. Vanessa came close to her.

"You will come to understand, my dear," she said knowingly, "you will come to understand." She embraced Nina for the first time, patted her cheek, then slowly left the room.

Nina climbed the stairs to her room as if walking through a nightmare. She would be leaving Flame Tree the next morning, and it was breaking her heart.

Anthia was given the privilege of traveling to Sydney with Derrick and Nina, something she had never been allowed to do until this morning. She was excited, and commented on everything she saw. Derrick seemed nervous and jumpy, and Anthia's presence helped to ease the heavy silence that fell between Nina and him, and afforded welcome relief from the tension.

Once again the crush at the Sydney Customhouse was maddening and confusing, but Nina walked through it in a trance. Her passage documents indicated she would be sailing on the *Ada Pearl*, the second voyage of a ship commissioned expressly for the Australian trade with America.

Nina boarded, looking over her shoulder for any sign of Shane, praying that he had changed his mind and would prevent her from leaving. A steward led her to a cabin. He took her bag inside, and she followed him silently. With a quick smile, he retreated. She sank down on the bed and flung her arm up over her forehead, and lay there thinking.

At least this cabin was going to be more comfortable than the one she'd come over in. Two portholes let in the sun, and the rich maple walls reflected the light warmly.

She thought she smelled flowers, and wearily turned her head toward the scent. A huge splashy bouquet in purple, rose, and white, punctuated with waxy green leaves, dominated a bureau. Next to it was a silver bucket, a towel-wrapped bottle of champagne, set at a rakish angle. A card was propped against the bucket. She got up and reached over to pick it up. "Best wishes to the bride and groom. Captain John Sinclair," was the greeting in fluid script.

She whirled around. Now she could see that this bed was wider than the one in the first cabin she'd sailed in. The whole room was bigger, and clearly fit to accommodate two people.

"Bloody hell, they've put me in the wrong cabin," she sputtered aloud. "The bridal suite, and isn't *that* ironic?"

She was about to go and find a steward when a loud knock came at the door. No doubt that man had recognized his error and come to rectify it. She opened the door quickly.

Mate sat there panting. Immediately he jumped up, sending her back to plop down on the bed.

"Mate! Wha . . . ?"

The great furry dog sat at her feet, a big white satin bow tied around his neck, an excited expression on his face.

Then the familiar rich baritone voice that thrilled her resounded from the hallway. "Well, little baggage, have you settled into this old barn yet? I see Mate's afforded you his usual welcome."

Shane stepped into the cabin, a spray of white flowers in one hand and a bottle of champagne in the other. Nina stared blankly at him, her heart pounding wildly in her chest, her head spinning.

Shane rushed on. "That's it? That's the way you greet your new husband, or least your husband-to-be? Well, I can tell you, my girl, I don't find it agreeable."

"Shane, what on earth . . . ?"

"Nay, on sea!"

Nina's eyes brimmed. "Is this another joke? Shane, if it is, it's the most despicable . . ."

"I know, but I wanted to give you the happiest surprise of your life. Am I forgiven? This is about to be your honeymoon, in case you didn't recognize it."

Nina stood up on wobbly legs, a smile playing at the corners of her mouth. "But we're not married."

"The Captain will be glad to oblige us once we're at sea. What do you say?"

"I don't know what to say. Oh, what about Mate? Can he spend three months on a ship?"

Colin's head poked around the door. "He can't— no canine loo. He's going with me. And as for what you should say, say 'aye' as soon as my twit of a big brother asks you properly to marry him, Lady Cole. Then you'll be Lady Merritt of Flame Tree!" He lifted his eyes. "And Colin Merritt makes yet another dream come true. Get on with it! I'm late for the haberdasher's now!"

He pushed his big brother to his knees and took away the flowers and champagne. Shane took her hand and, love shining from his eyes, looked up at her full in the face.

"Will you marry me, my precious girl?"

She stood looking down at him, returning the love in his eyes. The nightmare had turned back into a fantasy dream come true.

"Aye, oh Shane, yes!" she whispered breathlessly.

Shane stood up quickly, took her in his arms, and crushed her with a deep kiss. Colin let out a relieved sigh, grabbed Mate by his bow, and escorted him out of the cabin.

"Come on, old boy, we are not the kind of witnesses they need right now," he laughed. He turned back toward the cabin, hand on the door latch. "When I solve a problem, I really solve a problem, don't I, Lady Merritt? Caw, I'm good!" He shut the door behind him and was gone.

Shane released her lips and leaned back to gaze into her glistening aquamarine eyes. His hands slid up to her coiled hair and released the pins. She leaned back, letting it fall. Waning sunlight through the portholes effected a shimmering veil over her long tresses, and he drew in his breath hard.

"I love you, Nina," he whispered.

"Who?" she asked in a deliberately innocent tone.

"I love you, my girl!" he shouted this time, his head thrown back and his face to the ceiling as if telling it to the world.

She clasped her arms around his neck tightly and kissed him deeply.

"Never stop calling me that!"